CW00642857

DAVID EBSWORTH is the pen name of writer, Da
and Regional Secretary for Britain's Transport
was born in Liverpool (UK) but has lived for the
North Wales, with his wife, Ann. Following
write seriously in 2009.

For more information about the author an
www.davidebsworth.com.

Also by David Ebsworth

The Jacobites' Apprentice
A story of the 1745 Rebellion. Critically reviewed by
the Historical Novel Society, who deemed it
"worthy of a place on every historical fiction bookshelf."

The Assassin's Mark
A political thriller set towards the end of the Spanish Civil War.
"The characters are so incredibly vivid – there are characters you adore,
others that annoy you and all of these are so expertly devised that
you simply cannot help but miss them all when you finish the book,
and you will finish it; this is not a novel you will be able to put down."
– Rachel Malone, Historical Novel Society

THE KRAALS OF ULUNDI

A NOVEL OF THE ZULU WAR

DAVID EBSWORTH

Best wishes from David

SilverWood

Published in 2014 by the author
using SilverWood Books Empowered Publishing®

SilverWood Books
30 Queen Charlotte Street, Bristol, BS1 4HJ
www.silverwoodbooks.co.uk

ISBN 978-1-78132-211-6 (paperback)
ISBN 978-1-78132-212-3 (ebook)

British Library Cataloguing in Publication Data
A CIP catalogue record for this book is available from the British Library

Set in Bembo by SilverWood Books
Printed on responsibly sourced paper

Dedicated to the indomitable spirit of the Zulu people,
the memory of those on each side who died in the Anglo-Zulu War 1879,
and the David Rattray Foundation

In memoriam to Robert Gardner, 1949-2013

List of Characters

To avoid spoiling the story, further information about asterisked characters is contained in the Historical Notes at the end.

Historical Characters
Alderton, Assistant Commissary Thomas: 1834-1879
Bassano, Napoléon Hugues Maret, 2nd Duc de: 1803-1898
Behrens, Nathaniel (American showman): 1848-1913
Bellairs, Colonel William: 1828-1913
Biddlecombe, Detective Constable John James: 1840-1882 *
Bland-Hunt, Lieutenant-Colonel Robert William: Royal Marines
Brander, Captain William Maxwell: 1852-1927
Buller, Colonel Redvers Henry: 1839-1908
Carey, Annie Isabella: 1852-1922. Plus her children, Edith Isabella: 1872-1901, and Pelham Adolphus: 1878-1913 *
Carey, Lieutenant/Captain Jahleel Brenton: 1847-1883 *
Cetshwayo (tet-sway-o) kaMpande, King: 1826-1884 *
Chelmsford, Second Baron, Lord (Frederic Augustus Thesiger): 1827-1905
Cornelius Vijn: b. 1856 *
Crookenden, Captain Henry Humphreys (Royal Artillery): b. 1844
Davies, Colonel Henry Fanshawe (Grenadier Guards): 1837-1914
Deléage, Paul: 1850-1888
Drummond, The Honourable William Henry: 1845-1879
Dunn, John Robert (IsiZulu name, Jantoni): 1834-1895 *
Eugénie de Montijo, Empress of the French (María Eugenia de Palafox-Portocarrero de Guzmán y Kirkpatrick): 1826-1920 *
Farini, The Great (William Leonard Hunt): 1838-1929 *
Glyn, Colonel Richard Thomas (24th Foot): 1831-1900
Grandier, Ernest (Weatherley's Border Horse)
Grenfell, Major Francis: 1841-1925
Griffin, Stephen "Bill": 1823-1903
Grubb, Corporal Jimmy (Bettington's Horse)
Hackett, Major Robert (90th Foot): 1839-1893 *
Harrison, Colonel Richard (Royal Engineers): 1837-1931
Heseltine, Captain Gerald Altham (Royal Marines): b.1842
Langazana, Queen: approx.1778-1884

Le Tocq, Trooper Nicolas (Bettington's Horse)
Lomas, J (Royal Engineers and Orderly to the Prince Imperial)
Longcast, Henry William (1850-1909)
Luckhurst, Captain Alfred Henry (S.S. *Clyde*): b.1844
Mkhosana kaSangqana Zungu: 1830-1914
Mnyamana kaNgqengelele Buthelezi: approx.1809-1892
Molyneux, Captain William: 1854-1916
Napoléon, Prince Imperial, Eugène Louis Jean Joseph: 1856-1879
Ntshingwayo kaMahole Khoza: (shing-way-o) 1809-1883 *
O'Reilly, Surgeon-Major James
Sceberras, Lieutenant-Colonel Attilio (98th Foot): 1827-1884
Scotchburn, Miss Octavia: 1828-1885 *
Wells, Sister Janet: 1854-1911
Collectively: Hlabanatunga, Langalabelele and Xabanga/Tshabanga (warriors
    of the amaZulu involved in the killing of the Prince Imperial)
And, collectively: Colonels Harness, Courtney and Whitehead; Majors
    Anstruther and Pleydell-Bouverie (the officers of Carey's Court Martial)

Historical Characters with Fictionalised Roles
Klaas – a Zulu Christian convert, also known as Barnabas, and used by
    Cetshwayo as one of his messengers to Lord Chelmsford, the British
    Commander, during the king's various attempts to negotiate a peace. He
    appears again as possibly one of the guards sent by Cetshwayo to oversee
    the release of the French captive, Ernest Grandier. *
Shaba (Tshabanga kaNdabuko) – also Xabanga/Zabanga: the Zulu who struck
    the fatal blow that killed French Prince Imperial Louis Napoleon *

Fictional Characters
Amahle: Shaba's sister
Cornscope, Simeon: An associate of William McTeague
Jupe, Pastor Jago: An associate of William McTeague
Mandla kaSibusiso: A Zulu *induna*
Maria Mestiza: McTeague's wife
McTeague, William (IsiZulu name, kaMtigwe)
Mnukwa: A Zulu *induna*
Mutwa: An *isangoma*
Ndabuko kaMahanana: Shaba's father
Sibusiso, Zama's grandfather
Twinge, Theophilus: An associate of William McTeague
Umdeni: Shaba's friend
Zama kaMandla: Daughter of Mandla kaSibusiso

Preface

This is a work of historical fiction: fiction in a historical setting. In this case the Anglo-Zulu War of 1879.

The subject is enormously popular and has a huge following. It has its experts and I respect them immensely. I would not dare to tread on their expertise. I am a writer of fiction, not a historian. All the same, as a writer I believe that my setting should be as accurate as possible – up to the point at which the inventive mind, the teller of tall tales, takes over from historical knowledge. Having said that, I also believe that it is only fair to explain the main areas in which I have strayed away from the archives, and hence the historical notes I have included at the end of this book.

Hopefully, the overall result will excite those who enjoy a 'good read' and give a wider understanding about this astonishing period of history to readers who, from the paucity of other historical fiction on the remaining six months of the conflict, could be forgiven for believing that it began with the disaster of Isandlwana – which took place on 22nd January 1879 and is depicted in the Burt Lancaster and Peter O'Toole movie, Zulu Dawn – and ended with the defence and Victoria Crosses of Rorke's Drift (KwaJimu), fought on 22nd – 23rd January 1879 and immortalised in the Michael Caine blockbuster, Zulu. Finally, I hope to avoid the outright enmity of those who would know very well – without this clumsy explanation – the many times when I may have strayed dangerously from 'the facts'. Any actual errors, of course, are all my own.

When my story opens, the Zulus themselves had become a powerful military state only in the first quarter of the Nineteenth Century under the leadership of King Shaka. Before Shaka, they were simply one of the many clans among the Ngoni people who had been part of the Bantu migrations down the east coast of Africa for over a thousand years. And this particular clan was established in the early 1700s by a man called Zulu, son of an Ngoni chieftain, Ntombela. The word *iZulu* literally means 'sky' or 'heaven', so that the clan name, *AmaZulu*, implied both that they were the People of the Man called Zulu, and also the People of Heaven.

By the late 1870s, the British had ambitions to create a federated dominion of South Africa. But there were two major obstacles – the independent states of the Dutch Boer settlers and the Kingdom of Zululand. A pretext was needed to begin dismantling these obstacles and, as a start, the British High Commissioner, Sir Henry Bartle-Frere, seized upon the excuse of a relatively minor border incident to present an ultimatum to the Zulu king, Cetshwayo, requiring him to disband his armies – an ultimatum that could clearly never have been met. And thus, without any authority from the Crown, the British army already in Cape Colony under Lord Chelmsford, launched an invasion of Zululand. The Anglo-Zulu War had begun.

This novel picks up the conflict's story at the end of March 1879, and it does so very often from a Zulu perspective – as a result of which there is a great deal of 'language' to cope with. So the glossary which follows may help, at least a little. Even here, however, there may be some confusion from my decision occasionally to use two spellings for the same word. The most obvious example is the name of the battlefield at Isandlwana. I have used that form whenever anybody is referring to the site in English. But where somebody is thinking or speaking in the Zulu language, I have used the IsiZulu spelling eSandlwana, or sometimes (and more authentically) the image that the word conjures in that tongue. IsiZulu is an exceptionally descriptive language. As it happens, the small rocky mountain near which the British were so badly defeated on 22nd January 1879 resembles, in form, a small house or grain hut, and 'eSandlwana' is the IsiZulu word for that thing. Hence the reason that I sometimes refer to the engagement, from a Zulu viewpoint, as the Battle of the Little House, or similar. The mountain has other descriptive names too, depending on the angle from which it is viewed – the Frog, or the Second Stomach (the reticulum of a ruminant) – and the local Zulus also know the place as the Mountain of Murmurs.

Apart from this, I have followed the protocol that the names of people, their titles, or the names of places are non-italicised, while other IsiZulu words appear in italics.

Lastly, the dates at the start of each chapter are, of course, given in the form with which we are most familiar, even where the chapters themselves tell the story from a Zulu perspective. But these are largely to give the reader some sense of chronology.

David Ebsworth
December 2013

Glossary

IsiZulu spellings, rough meanings and a few pronunciations
in the English alphabetical order.

AbaQulusi — (abor-kloosi) A northern tribe/clan, allied to the Zulu
amabutho — (amah-boo-tour) Zulu regiments, sing. *ibutho*
AmaFulentshi — (amah-foo-lern-sheer) The French, sing. iFulentshi
AmaNgisi — (amah-ing-ee-see) The English
AmaSwazi — (amah-swore-see) The Swazi people who hold the territory north
    of Zululand. In their own tongue they are the bakaMswati, and their
    language siSwati
AmaZulu — (amah-zoo-loo) The collective name by which the Zulus knew
    themselves, meaning "the people of heaven"
Baba — Father
bhoma — A fence or palisade of interwoven thorn bush
buchu — (boo-too) A shrub of the *genus* Agasthoma
cosi — (coe-see) So be it!
cosi, cosi, yaphela — (ya-pay-lah) And so, and so, it ended
eHlobane — (eh-thlo-bar-nay, with the *thl* like Welsh *Ll*) A mountain,
    meaning "beautiful place"
Emahlabathini — (ay-ma-thla-ba-teeny) A Zulu royal homestead and the plain
    on which it stands
Emakhosini — (eh-mar-core-seen) Meaning "valley of the kings"
Emoyeni — (eh-more-yearn-ee) Meaning "place of wind/spirit"
eNgilandi — (en-gear-lan-dee) England
eSandlwana — (eh-san-zwa-nah) Meaning "little hut/house" but also "second
    stomach of a cow", all of which the Mountain of Isandlwana resembles
eSiklebheni — (eh-see-care-beh-nee) A Zulu royal homestead
giya — (ghee-yah) A dance
Hlakanyana — (thla-kan-yar-nah) A folklore dwarf hero
Hluhluwe — (thloo-thloo-way) A Zulu homestead, meaning "monkey thorn"
iklwa — (ick-wah) The Zulu broad-bladed stabbing spear, commonly known by
    the British as an Assegai (a Dutch word)
iBhunu — Boer
ilobolo — (ee-law-bo-law) Dowry
imizi — (e-me-zee) plural of *umuzi*, a homestead

impi — (em-pee) Army

impisi — (em-pee-see) Hyena, meaning "purifier"

indlovu — (in-dlo-view) Elephant, meaning "the unstoppable one"

induna — Leader or commander, plural *izinduna*

iNgcugce — (ing-coo-say) A Zulu female regiment

iNgobamakhosi — (in-go-bar-mah-core-see) A Zulu regiment, meaning "bender of kings"

ingonyama — Lion, meaning "master of all flesh"

ingxotha — A brass arm ring, awarded by the Zulus as the greatest of honours

iNkatha yeSizwe yaKwaZulu — (in-kar-tah...yeh-seeze-weh...ya-qua-zoo-loo) The Zulu sacred grass coil, plural *iziNkatha*

ikhanda — (e-carn-dah) Royal homestead containing a barracks for a royal regiment, plural *amakhanda*

iNkosi — (en-core-see) Lord

inyamayembulu — Iguana meat

inyanga — (in-young-ah) A diviner, witch doctor capable of smelling out evil. Plural, *izinyanga*

insizwa — (in-see-zoo-wah) Unmarried

inwaba — (in-war-bah) Chameleon, meaning "lazy mover"

iphetifokha — An invented word, that Tshabanga mis-hears for "petty-fogger"

iphiti — (e-pee-tee) Small antelope

isangoma — (e-sun-go-mah) A witch-doctor medium, a spirit-speaker

isanusi — (e-sun-new-see) A herbal healer, medicine man

ishoba — The cow-tail tufts worn as arm and leg decorations

isicoco — The head-ring, sewn into a man's hair to show he is married

isidwaba — (e-see-dwer-bah) Woman's black leather kilt

isigodlo — (e-see-god-low) The various female members of the King's household, and also that section of the royal enclosures in which they were quartered

isihlangu — (e-see-thlan-goo) The larger, more traditional Zulu shield from Shaka's time

isijula — A throwing spear, plural *izijula*

IsiZulu — The Zulu language

Ityotyosi — (itty-otty-ossy) The river near which the Prince Imperial died

iviyo — (e-vee-yor) A company-strength group of warriors within a regiment

iwisa — (e-wee-sah) A hunting club, knobkerrie, meaning "bone breaker"

izinduna — The plural of *induna*, a leader or commander

izikhulu — The Zulu King's senior advisers, his Council of Ministers

amaphoyisa — (ama-pour-yee-sa) Meaning "the police"

iziqu — (e-see-koh... though, actually, this last syllable is really a *tock* sound, made with the tongue) A necklace

Izimu — A folklore trickster, ogre

Jantoni — The Zulus' name for John Robert Dunn

Ji! – (Jee!) The most common of the Zulu war cries

kaffir – Origins disputed but, in the 19th century, a term shared by both British and Dutch to generically denote the ethnic black peoples of southern Africa. In the 20th century, under Apartheid, it became (and remains) a particularly offensive racist insult. It would have been used widely in 1879 but appears in these pages only sparingly.

KaMtigwe – My invented Zulu name for McTeague

kholwa – (Corel-yah) A Christian convert, plural *amakholwa*

Kraal – A Dutch word meaning "cattle enclosure" but adopted generally by the British to mean a Zulu homestead

KwaBulawayo – A former royal homestead

KwaJimu – (qua-jee-moo) The Zulu name for Rorke's Drift, meaning "Jim's place" (it was built by James Rorke)

KwaNodwengu – (qua-no-do-wern-go) A Zulu royal homestead, close to oNdini, and the name by which the Zulus knew the Battle of Ulundi

KwaZulu – The land of the People of Heaven

laager – A Dutch word for a barrier created by a square or circle of wagons

Mama – Mother

mayile – A dance

mbayimbayi – (um-by-um-by-ee) The Zulu nickname for British artillery, allegedly because, when King Shaka had asked for a cannon from the British, they had fobbed him off by promising one *'by and by'*

Mfecane – (um-fair-car-nay) Scattering storm, the name given to the intense South African inter-tribal wars of the early 19th century

Mthonjaneni – (um-torn-jar-nanny) Mountain, meaning "place of little water"

Nguni – (n-goo-nee) The predominant race of East and Southern Africa, part of the wider Bantu group. Also, the cattle that are unique to them

nkawu – (n-car-woo) The vervet monkey

nkonkoni – (n-core-n-core-nee) Wildebeest, meaning "revered champion"

nsangu – The IsiZulu word for *Cannabis Sativa*

oNdini – (on-thee-nee) Cetshwayo's royal capital, known to the British as Ulundi, meaning "the heights"

qaqa – (ka-ka… though, once again, this is another pair of IsiZulu *click* sounds) Ritual disembowelling of dead enemies

Sekhukhuni – (say-koo-koo-nee) One who moves in the dark

sambane – (sum-bar-neh) The ant bear or aardvark

siyakhuleka ekhaya – (see-yah-coo-lurk e-car-yah) Once upon a time

Sobhuza – (so-boo-zar) The name of the headman at the kraal where the Prince Imperial died

ubhoko – (oo-bow-coh) A blocking stick, used in stick-fighting

uDhloko – (oo-dock-oo… the middle syllable is a deep *clock* sound) A Zulu regiment, meaning "the savages" *udibi* – (oo-dee-bee) Zulu boy, serving adult relatives in a regiment

udonga – Gulley, ravine

ugwayi – (oo-go-way-ee) Narcotic snuff

ukuhlomula – (oo-coo-thlo-moo-lah) The practise of honour-stabbing fallen
  enemies

ukujoja – (oo-coo-jaw-jar) Impalement

ukungcweka – A stick-fight

ukusoka – (oo-coo-soccer) Circumcision

Ulundi – see oNdini

umabope – (oo-mah-bow-peh) Climbing plant with red roots, chopped to
  decorate necklaces and chewed before battle.

uMbonambi – (oom-bow-nahm-bee) A Zulu regiment, meaning "evil omen"

umbengo – Ritual vomit

umbhumbluzo – (oom-boom-bloo-zo) The more modern battle shield designed
  by Cetshwayo

umHholandi – Dutchman

umemulo – Puberty

uMgungundlovu – A former Zulu royal homestead, meaning "place of the elephant"

umkhoka – The Buffalo Bean plant

umnyakanya – The basket-work ball, part of a Zulu head-dress

umnumzana – Head of a homestead or clan/family

umquele – The padded Zulu headband

umuthi – (um-oo-tee) magically enhanced medicine, using organic materials,
  to create anything from cures for head colds, poisons for hunting spears,
  curses against one's enemies, to courage and protection from harm in battle

umutsha – A calf-skin loincloth

umuzi – A homestead, village (in Afrikaans, a *kraal*)

uMvelinqangi – The Zulus' Creator, the "One Who Came First"

uMxapho – (um-ka-po) A Zulu regiment, meaning "the mongrels". There's
  no easy way to explain 'x' in IsiZulu. It's a click at the back of the throat

umyeni – Husband

uNokhenke – A Zulu regiment, meaning "the skirmishers"

USuthu! – (oo-soo-too) Zulu war chant, meaning "followers of Cetshwayo"

utshwala – Sorghum beer

zila – Part of the Zulu cleansing rituals needed after slaying an enemy

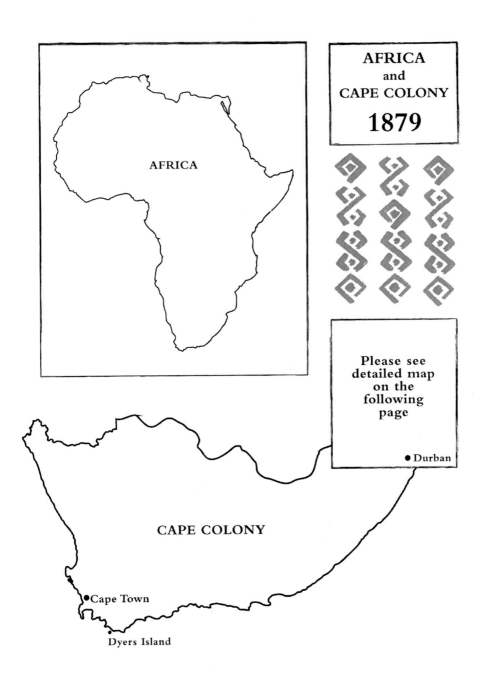

AFRICA

AFRICA
and
CAPE COLONY
1879

Please see
detailed map
on the
following
page

● Durban

CAPE COLONY

●Cape Town

Dyers Island

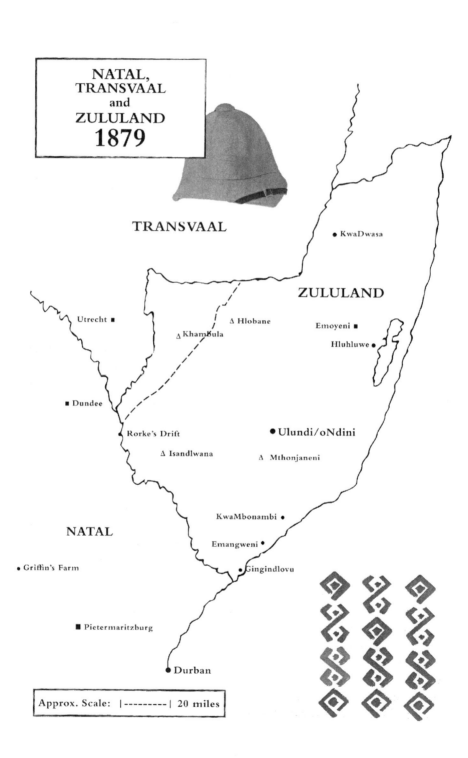

NATAL,
TRANSVAAL
and
ZULULAND
1879

TRANSVAAL

ZULULAND

• KwaDwasa

Utrecht ■

Δ Hlobane

Δ KhamBula

Emoyeni ■

Hluhluwe •

■ Dundee

Rorke's Drift •

• Ulundi/oNdini

Δ Isandlwana

Δ Mthonjaneni

NATAL

KwaMbonambi •

Emangweni •

• Griffin's Farm

Gingindlovu

■ Pietermaritzburg

• Durban

Approx. Scale: |---------| 20 miles

Chapter One

He had washed the blade of his stabbing spear, his prized *iklwa*, many times already. It would be rinsed again today, with the blessings of his ancestor's spirits, their shades, to herd the red soldiers finally from the land of the AmaZulu.

'Yet I do not understand them,' he said, as the regiment slowed to a walk 'Why do they not go home?'

'They are beyond understanding, friend Shaba,' said Umdeni, using the shortened form by which Tshabanga kaNdabuko was more commonly known. 'They come here wearing the same scraps of cloth that they use in their own land. And they cannot go home lacking victory. Otherwise the Fat Queen will eat their souls.'

The soldiers had been here for three moons. Tshabanga knew because he had already fought them. Back when the enemy first invaded. He and his *ibutho*, his regiment. At the hill they called eSandlwana. After the Great King had summoned them for the gathering before the battle. And after, at the muster's end, the King had called forth selected regiments to challenge each other's prowess. So it came to pass that Shaba was chosen to speak and *giya*, to dance, for the Evil Omen, challenging any member of their rivals, the uNokhenke, the Skirmishers, to kill more of the whites than he himself might do. He had even pledged his sister, Amahle, as collateral for his wager. Then he had indeed danced, leaping high in the air, or pounding the ochre dust to clouds of musk in which his own fate, the fate of his family, the fate of the whites he had yet to encounter, the fate of his nation, all would be forged. And finally, after the *giya*, after the cleansing, the Great King had sent them forth, eight regiments that would stampede the red soldiers back across the River of the Buffalo. Back into the land that the whites called Natal.

'You remember the fight?' said Shaba, as the numberless naked feet of the *ibutho* rattled the grass, a noise like the sea dragging shingle down a beach.

'Nothing but the hour when the sun turned black,' said Umdeni.

It was a moment melted into memory. A great magic, only to be expected at a time of such upheaval, such destruction, such a torrent of death. And because he had killed, there had later been the isolation, the cleansing, the cutting of the willow wands, the waiting. To discover which regiment the

1

Great King would consider had played the most glorious part in the battle. For the warriors of that *ibutho* alone would receive the privilege of cutting their willow-wood into beads, the beads fashioned into the great necklace, the *iziqu*, that Shaba, Umdeni and all those others of the Evil Omen regiment – the uMbonambi – now wore, slung across their bodies or wound about their necks since the Great King, Cetshwayo kaMpande, had honoured them with the award. All those who had fought at eSandlwana, in recognition of the fact that, while individual valour might be important, it was the efforts of the collective that drew forth victories.

'I remember I killed,' said Shaba, 'but I do not remember the faces. Only their whiskers. I took many of them.'

'I remember afterwards,' Umdeni turned to him, 'when we had shared our honour cuts upon the slain. When we had opened them so they would not haunt us. How must their red soldier friends have felt, when they came back and found them all? How much shame?'

'And there is this also,' said Shaba. 'That they do not fight as a single army. Why is it so?'

'Because they too are fat,' Umdeni replied. 'Like their queen. They need many cattle to fill their fat bellies. More than they can steal from one place alone.'

It was true. The red soldiers had arrived in KwaZulu – this land that resembled nothing more than the head of a beautiful speckled bull, its face turned up towards the sun where it rises from the ocean – with three separate *impis*, three armies. One in the centre of the neck, that which had been destroyed at eSandlwana. One below the bull's chin, near Shaba's own home, close to the great water. And these, here, that annoyed the beast's ears. A veritable thorn in the Great King's side.

Yesterday this pestilence of soldiers had ventured out from behind their wagon walls to steal even more cattle. At the place they called eHlobane. But there they had stirred up the AbaQulusi Clan, friends and allies of the Great King, part of his royal regiments – the Sharp Points, the Bender of Kings and the Fly Catchers. They were well-named, these Fly Catchers, for they had helped to flick the red soldier flies down from the mountain, swatted and killed them in swarms. The cattle had been recaptured, they said, and the people were happy. Though Shaba knew that, every year, the precious animals became fewer and fewer. The lung fever that the whites had brought with them when he was young. Those without number that the traders from Natal took as payment and profit for their goods every summer.

One day, Shaba would have many cattle of his own. If the Great King allowed his regiment to marry, he would hope to have distinguished himself to such a degree that he would attract a good wife by granting some of the beasts to her family as *ilobolo*, her dowry. He might even receive some as a mark of favour. And why settle for just one wife? He might only have one eye, but this distinguished him, he thought. And he could always claim that he had lost it in battle. He would become the respected head of his homestead. To excel in the craft of his clan. And more. Perhaps his name woven into the tales of his people. So much rested on today. For the red soldiers had fallen back to their camp, where they would be crushed once again.

On the high ground, the ghost shades of their ancestors wrapped around them, a fine damp mist. But when they dropped down towards the Valley of the White Patient Ox, back into the sunshine, they picked up the pace at their *induna*'s command. The rhinoceros run. Short, easy steps that ate the ground.

'You should not have mentioned cattle, Umdeni,' said Shaba. 'For it has made my belly ache again.'

They had been five days upon the road and the livestock they had brought were long gone, the porridge mostly eaten, the sweet cane too.

'Never mind,' said his friend. 'Look, there is a homestead.'

Sure enough, away to their left was a cluster of huts. An empty cattle enclosure. Some old people from a local clan. A small boy with a flock of sheep. A few goats. And Shaba found himself caught against his better instincts in a minor stampede as forty or fifty of the warriors broke away from this left flank to reach the unexpected gift. The old people ran forward to protect their animals but they were too few to save them all, for the beasts scattered and several sheep were quickly slaughtered, carried away. Hoping to do the same, Umdeni had taken a fine ewe by its tail, but the boy and a grizzled old man had the head, tugging in the opposite direction.

'The *USuthus* need to eat, master!' cried Shaba. 'So that we are strong enough to drive away the red soldiers.'

'What use is that,' said the old one, 'if we have all starved in the process?'

The tortured sheep bleated with indignation as the tussle continued.

'Help me,' Umdeni said. But Shaba was unable to set hands upon the sparse fleece. The old master had made him feel guilty, even before the *izinduna*, their commanders, arrived to scold them, beating them with their goads and berating the warriors for their disrespect, for behaving little better than the red soldiers themselves.

Thus, Shaba reached the regiment's resting place, in the middle of the forenoon, on the banks of the White Patient Ox itself, feeling all the remorse of an admonished child again, rather than the pride of a warrior who, like all others in the uMbonambi, had seen thirty-five summers. Yet when he did arrive, the ranks were all astir. There was food, though little more than a mouthful of porridge. But there was news too. News that spread like a bush fire, from

3

those that had fought yesterday and who now waited for them, the news that command of the *impi*, the whole army, had been passed to Ntshingwayo kaMahole Khoza.

'It is a great omen,' said Shaba, forgetting his shame. For it was Ntshingwayo who had led them to victory at the Battle of the Little House, at eSandlwana.

And they were promised another today, as the praise names of Ntshingwayo were recited time and again by each *induna*, along with those of the Great King, while the entire army was marshalled into an enormous circle and the *izinyanga*, the medicine men, moved among them with their cauldrons, spattering the warriors with the holy liquids, *umuthi*, brewed from secret herbs and body parts taken from the enemy.

'Now my belly is hurting too,' said Umdeni.

'You are hungry – but you will eat well when we drive the whites from their camp,' called their own *induna*, Somopho Magwendu.

'He has the ears of a she-lion,' whispered Shaba. Yet the sight in his one remaining eye was as sharp as the *induna*'s hearing and he had caught a movement. Distant. Away on a ridge of the eZunganyene plateau. Horsemen. Not red soldiers. Nor even the black coats from Natal. But those who wore cloth the colour of dried dung, with the wide, foolish hats of Dutchmen. Though not Dutchmen themselves. For the Dutchmen had no real love for the red soldiers either. Apart from a very few, they had left these invaders to fight their own battles.

Shaba rose, pointed his *iklwa* towards the hills.

'White riders,' he called. 'White riders!' And his cry echoed about the surrounding slopes so that, like the swell of the ocean near his home, the ranks of the regiments followed his action, an initial dark ripple that grew to a mighty wave. A wave that began to roll slowly towards the horsemen.

This was how it began at the Battle of the Little House also, he thought, recalling the decision that the regiments should not attack. For the moon was wrong, said the Wise Men. But then they had been discovered. And they had been obliged to attack after all.

The wave, however, did not travel far. For the *izinduna*, it seemed, had clear instructions from their new high commander.

'You will wait!' shouted Somopho Magwendu. 'Today we will not attack until it is the white man's eating time.' The instruction was repeated through the ranks, across the regiments, and the wave came to a temporary halt.

'I wish there had been no further mention of eating,' said Umdeni as they were marshalled into position within the column that would form the left horn of the beast. There was the barest minimum of confusion as the regiments, disciplined and well-drilled, moved to their respective places.

'It will not be long before we take the red soldiers' food,' said Shaba. 'But this time we must be more careful.'

4

Umdeni laughed, crook-toothed and flared nostrils.

'You remember the black beer?' he said.

And Shaba remembered. Stone bottles of the stuff. Though it was more blue than black. That smelled fair but tasted foul. The white men had all been dead. Every last one except the handful that had run away. The men from the uNdi Corps and the married red-shields of the uDhloko regiment had gone ahead to KwaJimu, the post at the river ford which Englishmen called the Drift, where the red soldiers had left some of their men. Yet only their sick men. Shaba laughed. For the uDhloko had not done well. The soldiers may have been sick, but they had fought all night from behind their walls and the warriors could not shift them. And, meanwhile, the rest of the *amabutho* were enjoying the spoils from the eSandlwana camp. The food had been good and there had been *utshwala*, strong ale. Large amounts of strong ale.

'I was very drunk,' said Shaba, 'by the time we found the black stuff.'

He had still been drunk when the men of the uDkloko had joined them again, disgraced, the next day. For the red soldiers were still at KwaJimu.

Shaba was squatting in the flattened grass, regimental shield on the ground beside him, its dark hide – flecked with palest grey – providing a dry resting place for his percussion rifle. The grass was still damp, and the rifle needed great care. It was older than Shaba himself, though still a prized firearm, purchased originally for two cows, though now worth only a sheep. All the same, it was one of the newest among the Evil Omen since most of the modern guns, taken at eSandlwana, had gone to the veteran married regiments. *It is no great thing anyway,* he thought, since he still favoured their more traditional weapons – the *iklwa* stabbing spear, his *izijula* throwing spears, and the *umbhumbluzo* battle shield whose efficient size and pattern they owed directly to the innovations of the Great King Cetshwayo kaMpande himself.

He examined the blade of his *iklwa*, tested it for sharpness. His father – a renowned worker of iron from a long line of iron-shapers – would have approved the care that Shaba had taken with it. *That is my dream too,* he thought. *Apart from the cattle. To excel in the craft of my clan. To have good trade with the charcoal burners. With the ore collectors. They say that the amaChube in the Nkandla Forest are the best smiths. But my own clan is better. I will make our clan famous across all the lands for our iron. And yes, I will marry well also.*

He was so engrossed in his thoughts that he barely noticed the other *amabutho* as they passed in front of his own ranks. And it was Umdeni who flicked at Shaba's *ishoba*, the tufted cow-tail that he wore as a fringe on his left arm. He looked up, noted the dark brown and plain black shields of the Skirmishers forming alongside them. They had seen little of their rivals since the great battle, though this was not unusual given the size of the army. More than twenty thousand, they said. An astonishing number.

'I see you, Tshabanga kaNdabuko,' cried one of the warriors from their newly arrived neighbours. And Shaba recognised his tall frame, thinly scarred features, the wisp of beard on his chin. The same fellow against whom he had been chosen to boast and *giya*.

'I am here, brother,' he replied, with the appropriate gratitude. It was inherently understood that, until somebody saw you, greeted you accordingly, you did not truly exist. A person was only a person because of other people, after all.

'That is good, One-Eye, Warrior of the Evil Omen,' said the other. 'But how many did you kill at the Battle of the Little House?'

There was no reason to lie about such things when surrounded by the comrades of your own regiment.

'I stole the souls of seven red soldiers,' called Shaba.

'Then you owe me your sister,' laughed the warrior, though it was a cold and lonely thing, this laughter. 'For I killed eleven! You will want to keep your honour, I imagine. So I will come for her when we have fought today. You may be an Evil Omen to others, but when I take your sister it shall be you who feels the sorrow.'

The threat was real, tangible. And he was gone, pushed along by an *induna*, leaving Shaba to cope with the chaffing from those around him. A vision of Amahle too, as the uMbonambi themselves were called to arms and ordered to advance.

'That fellow is an idle braggart,' said Umdeni.

'You think so?' replied Shaba. 'I am not so sure. Do we know his name? His clan?'

'No, my friend. Though he has plainly taken the time to learn your own. But if we survive this day, I will make it my business to find out!'

He could sense his sister all around him. Literally. For there was almost nothing that he wore which she had not fashioned for him. The loin cloth with its cow hide belt, the soft calf-skin flap that covered his buttocks, the civet fur tails which hid the plaited grass sheath of his most private parts. The *umquele* headband, its tube of leopard skin padded with the dried cow dung of his father's cattle. Not the head ring of the married regiments, of course. That would come later. But, first, he had to face the battle. And protect Amahle.

They halted at last in sight of the white men's eKhambule camp, a long time later, when the sun was high, the last of the mists vanished from the valleys. Yet would they attack this place? The commanders had originally said not, that the Great King had decreed a prohibition on assaulting such walled positions. There must be no repeat of their repulse at the Drift, at KwaJimu. So the camp should be flanked until the red soldiers had no choice but to come out from their defences and pursue them. Or fight them in the open. Though now there seemed to be uncertainty about this plan, for the new leader, Ntshingwayo, was not a man who feared the frontal attack.

Their five columns were spread across high ground which sloped downwards to a cluster of huts, beyond which a ridge rose away from them into the distance with the soldiers' camp running along its summit. It appeared weak, vulnerable. A hillock to the right like a big sleeping hound with a bristle of rocks around its spine. An enclosure of wagons to the left, being used as a cattle pen. Stolen cattle, of course. A wall of sticks joining the hillock to the wagons on their lower ground. But behind these there seemed to be many more wagons, formed in that which the Dutchmen called a *laager*, though it was difficult to see from this position. The ground fell away on each side of the ridge, sharply to the left, less so on the right.

The medicine men, the *izinyanga*, moved among them once more. Time for the final rituals, and Shaba pulled a thin wooden spoon from his hair. He untangled a bone-tipped bottle and its neck cords from the leather belts that carried his percussion cap and shot pouches, his powder horn. Carefully, he poured some of the finely ground preparation onto the spoon, snorting the dust up each nostril in turn. Then he pressed his lips tight, breathed fast through his nose until he began to feel the battle heat stir within him.

From the camp he heard the bugles, watched the activity as the white men's small tents were taken down, red uniforms gathering behind their flimsy barricades. But the commanders still seemed uncertain. They were arguing. The Great King may have set the strategy but it was the leader here in the field who would set their fate – sometimes even the warriors of the regiments themselves. And it was plain that these thoughts were not Shaba's alone, for among the ranks of the entire *impi*, the war cry of each regiment began to echo in the air.

From the uMbonambi, 'We bring you bad tidings! We bring you your death!'

And a single cry that united them all too.

'We are the boys from eSandlwana,' they sang.

Then the chant of defiance, 'What do you come here for?'

And, as twenty thousand feet hit the ground with the chant's rhythm, raised the sweet scent of the earth to his nose, Shaba knew there would be no clever tactics this day. No more debate among the commanders. The beast was already formed. The Sharp Points at the front tip of this left horn, with his own Evil Omen regiment behind them and the Skirmishers, the rival uNokhenke, on their flank. The solid chest and loins of the centre: the two regional corps of the uNdi and uNodwengu – the Dust Raiser and Black Mamba royal regiments, with the Leopard's Lair, the Men from uDududu, the Lions and the White Tails – and, finally, way over on the far side, the four thousand wild young men from the Bender of Kings *ibutho* forming the right horn.

They had a fearful reputation, these warriors of the iNgobamakhosi, having got themselves embroiled in an argument last year with the Dust Raisers over women – and left sixty of them dead. And Shaba saw that, today too, the right horn was anxious for blood, the first on the move, sent to encircle the northern side of the red soldiers' camp.

On this side, the left horn was also under orders, a steady pace over the broken ground but dropping steadily towards the camp's southern edge. Sometimes they caught a glimpse of the iNgobamakhosi's dark shadow as it moved away from them while, at others, they began to see more of the camp itself, the second enclosure of wagons, a *laager* considerably bigger than the first and, between them, some of their *mbayimbayi* big guns, the black eyes of their barrels following and threatening the Evil Omen even at this distance, so that Shaba felt the red mist of his anger consume the beating of his heart. He did not fear the battle, but he did not relish these preliminaries, the seemingly endless time during which expectation could gnaw so badly at the bravest man's innards.

They paused to regroup on a rise above an *udonga*, one of the many ravines that split the slopes here. Umdeni was at his side once more, adjusting his own unfamiliar belts, shifting an ancient musket with its cow's gut sling to a more comfortable position on his back and moving his spears from throwing hand to shield hand.

'Look,' he said, 'the Bender of Kings has found its battle.'

And so it had. Far off, a party of horsemen had ridden out to attack the iNgobamakhosi. Yet no more than perhaps a hundred. There was a slender line of smoke, then a delay until the rattle of their guns reached Shaba's ears.

'They must not take this bait,' he murmured.

'The Bender of Kings will eat them,' said Umdeni.

'A hundred men do not attack four thousand without a very good reason, my friend.'

And the reason was soon clear. The right horn halted from its westward line of march, broke off from its flanking movement and turned to face the horsemen. The Bender of Kings, enraged by the bullets, surged forward into the smoke although, by the time they reached it, there was nothing to grasp but a wraith of the smoke itself, because the horsemen had mounted, galloped back towards the camp, all except for a party that ran away to the west. Yet those that were left stopped to fire once more. A manoeuvre they repeated again and again.

'It must sting them,' said Umdeni, and Shaba shared the frustration that the regiment must feel at pursuing this elusive and cowardly foe. *Cowardly*, he thought, *but clever*.

There was a brief lull, the line of the *ibutho* forming itself afresh on the far side of the sleeping hound hillock, the remaining horsemen now safely returned to the company of their red soldier friends. A moment of silence, then chanting again from the Bender of Kings, far distant but perfectly clear, the voices rising and falling.

'Come back, Johnnie!' they sang. 'Do not run away. For we would speak with you. We, who are the boys from eSandlwana!'

They jeered. They boasted. They beat their shields. And they shook the earth with their charge.

The smoke from the white men's fusillade spread like a squall blown from the southern coast, the commotion that followed not a rattle this time but the full-throated bellow of a winter storm-beast. Then the pale cloud crept away, thinned and vanished so that Shaba could see that a terrible witchcraft had been worked.

'Whey,' he said, 'they have vanished with the smoke.'

And so it seemed. For where the *ibutho* of four thousand had been, where they had rushed in the fury of their onslaught, now there was simple stillness, a fresh and silent mound sprouted from the ground along the breadth of the regiment's former frontage.

Shaba imagined that his eyes must lie, and even though it soon became clear that most of the iNgobamakhosi had survived, thrown themselves to the ground, he knew that hundreds must have died to form that awful harvest. And it was almost worse when the survivors, still so many in number, began to rise from their cover, shrinking back in the face of renewed and sporadic fire from the red soldiers. The Bender of Kings in reluctant retreat like a whipped dog was a shocking thing to behold. But no time to think about it. There were orders. Determined signals from the commanders away on the heights that overlooked the whole scene, so that Somopho Magwendu was soon among his company of the Evil Omen.

'We move,' he shouted, standing on a rock, pointing ahead down the slope with his own shield, the *isihlangu*, much larger than those carried by the warriors. Somopho was an old veteran, favoured the axe rather than the spear, and wore with pride the red and green headband Lourie feathers of his rank. Yet even veterans like Somopho, Shaba learned, were not invulnerable, despite all the ritual, all the medicine of the *izinyanga*.

A bullet took the older man from behind while his shield was still across his chest so that he seemed to spring off the rock, ran forward, almost as though he would charge his own men, eyes so very wide and fearful, his teeth set in a harsh snarl until he fell at Tshabanga's feet, the entry wound visible on his back, ripped into his flesh.

'Impossible,' said Umdeni, calculating the distance from the camp.

But everything was possible this day – a day already so very different from the glory they had known at eSandlwana and eHlobane.

'We will revenge him,' said Shaba as they were hurried on by the other companies.

He glanced back and to his right, just in time to see the mighty chest and loins of the beast begin their advance. Steady. Solid. Loud. It stirred him. And the battle frenzy blazed upon him once more. He felt the muscles in his legs and heels start to harden, the sinews of his neck to swell. Even his eyes, even the sightless one, seemed to grow and protrude, his ears to ring, his jaw to chew, his teeth to grind. It stayed with him as they loped down, crossing one *udonga* after another, the red soldiers' camp and the battlefield no longer in sight from this low in the valley, where they were soon mired, knee-deep, in mud.

Ahead of them now, the ground rose steeply again towards the southern side of the whites' position, and they stopped in the marshland of the valley floor while the horn's commanders conferred.

Shaba glanced up towards the rim, his ears filled by the confused clamour of the unseen battle raging above them, drowning any sounds except the repeated crash of volleyed rifle fire, a background crackle of individual shots and the steady thudding of their *mbayimbayi* big guns. The smoke that drifted over the edge was no longer white, he noticed, but like eSandlwana it had begun to thread evil black whispers that would eventually silence the whole sky.

'I think that today,' said Umdeni, 'we shall be chosen to lead the attack. I can feel it in my water.'

'That is just your normal problem,' Shaba replied, looking to those around them. 'He still pisses himself before each battle.'

'Pissing myself is like our friendship, brothers,' said Umdeni. 'Everyone can see it, but only I experience the warm feeling it brings.'

The warriors laughed. They were ordered forward, forcing their way out of the sucking morass, climbing, in places so steep that Shaba was forced to scramble on hands and knees, sliding on loose scree or grasping tussocks of grass to haul himself upwards. A long climb with the battle noise stopping for a while, then beginning anew as – he imagined – fresh attacks were launched by the centre regiments. And every effort fuelled his frenzy. *Hold them*, he thought. *Hold them while we scale these heights. And then we shall close around these stealers of land. Around them and over them. We shall devour them.*

Suddenly, the ground became less precipitous, the incline less severe, so that they edged onward until, with caution, they could see the camp above them. Directly to their front was a long and solid wall of wagons, defended by the red soldiers. To the right, everything was chaos. There was another wagon *laager*, perhaps half the size of the one they faced. It must have been the one they could see earlier, full of the stolen cattle, that which was joined to the sleeping hound hillock beyond and forming the eastern corner of the whites' position.

For there the royal uNdi Corps was pressing home its attack until, finally, it was forced to pull back. But from here it was plain that some of the red soldiers, too, were running from the wagons. The commanders of the left horn could see it also. There was a brief discussion. Shaba glanced at Umdeni, smiled.

'Now, we shall see,' he said, but immediately registered the disappointment on the face of his friend, who was looking over Shaba's shoulder to where the men of the Skirmishers, the uNokhenke, were moving to the fore, passing the Evil Omen, boasting that they would win the fight for them. Shaba could not see the warrior who had taunted him earlier about Amahle but he could picture him. He could remember his words. *'So I will come for her when we have fought today.'*

The Skirmishers stormed away up the slope. And though some of the soldiers may have run, the storm that met them was still heavy. Rifles and the *crump, crump* of a *mbayimbayi*. It seemed to take forever but, finally, the uNokhenke had forced their way right to the wagon wall itself. It was a true fight now, between the stabbing spears of the warriors and the bayonets of the white men, with the maddened bellowing of the cattle as background noise, neither side giving way until the war cries of the uNdi Corps, somewhere unseen on the far side of the struggle, were added to those of the Skirmishers. *They must have renewed their attack,* thought Shaba.

And now the war cries were replaced by great shouts of *USuthu!* to show that the red soldiers were dying at last. Dying and falling back so that the Skirmishers were soon scrambling over the wagons, in among the cows, seizing the *laager* for themselves and pouring their own rifle fire into the retreating enemy. Retreating but in good order, either to the bigger wagon enclosure here in front of Shaba, or further uphill, to the wall of rocks around the sleeping hound. Retreating but not without a valour of their own. Shaba watched as a red soldier jumped from the relative safety of this nearest *laager* and ran across the open ground, which sang now with the whine of bullets, to rescue not one of his own but a wounded black warrior, one of those who fought for the Fat English Queen.

'They are a worthy enemy,' said Shaba. 'But still, they should not be here.'

'Then we shall wash our spears with their blood again this day,' said Umdeni, as the uNokhenke consolidated their position away on the right, firing at the large wagon enclosure and also up at the hillock. At the *mbayimbayi* too, which the soldiers were now moving. A good sign, surely, thought Shaba as the uMbonambi themselves were called forward, formed their lines and began a steady bee-swarm advance towards the wagons. But, to their surprise, the red soldiers did not stay within the enclosure. Instead, a group of perhaps two hundred came out into the open, formed their own lines, even though they too were taking fire from the uNokhenke away on their flank. They seemed pitifully few; a tenth of the Evil Omen's force, and still such a distance away that Shaba knew his own rifle could not reach them. So they charged forward, his battle fever, scarlet haze, upon him once more.

The red soldiers disappeared behind the rolling smoke of their guns, throwing their bullets like angry hornets that burned into the warriors on Shaba's left and right. Blood and brain splashed across his face. He was momentarily blinded, tried to stop, to wipe the mess away, but was pushed forward by those behind. They bunched together. He knew that it was foolishness but he could not help it. In the face of volley fire they should spread out, separate. But their instincts forced them to a different response, closing ranks instead.

Shaba found himself clambering over a line of bodies, two and three deep, the original front ranks of the regiment. Mangled, many still alive, imploring, but too badly ripped by the bullets to ever survive.

Another volley. The entire regiment staggered, seemed to stumble, then raged on to scale one more mound of the dead and dying, greater than the first. Tshabanga's own body, his shield, his weapons, glistened with the debris of his fellows. He thought about Umdeni, turned to see him still close, still on his feet, still running. A third volley; followed almost immediately by the screech of incoming slaughter from the *mbayimbayi*, or perhaps the scream of a long pipe. Shaba could not tell. But he saw its effect as it ploughed a devastating line backwards into the centre of the regiment. Arms were sliced away, mangled meat and bone white shards. Heads were torn from torsos, babbling, deep scarlet spindrift. Innards spilled from stomachs, purple, grey and shit stench.

This time, the line of the slaughtered was too high to scale. There was no strength left to them. And he was in the front rank now, near a badly mutilated *induna*, half-buried in the mound but still alive. Shaba pulled at his arm, seeing the bronze ring that marked him as favoured by the Great King.

'Get up!' he screamed. 'Get up and lead your company, old man!' But the *induna* would never get up again and, through his own raging confusion, Shaba saw the red soldiers coming through the smoke towards them, no more bullets but their bayonets levelled for a charge. 'Cowards!' he screamed at them, staring along the hill of the dead. 'This is no way for men to fight battles!' For he knew there was only true honour and courage in being able to gaze directly into your foe's eyes when you killed him.

But at least those who were left of the uMbonambi would turn this into a contest that the white men would remember. He shook his shield at the enemy in frustration, launched the first of his throwing spears, then the second, though both fell short. Another *induna* tried to urge them over the mound of bodies, but there was a safety here behind the barricade of sacrifice, and slowly the uMbonambi line faltered, began to fall back so that few were left to receive the downhill shock of the red soldiers' bayonet charge. But Shaba was there. And Umdeni was at his side.

There was one of the whites on the opposite side of the wall. He was short with many whiskers. Too fat for a warrior. Too winded by his advance. Too rancid in his body smell. Too much fear in his alien, lifeless blue eyes. He feinted at Shaba, pulled back to thrust, and died when the *iklwa*'s blade first sliced his neck open, then drove through his heart. He made that small gasping noise that all men make when the *iklwa* enters them, a sound mimicked by the first syllable of its name, and then the second syllable, the sucking sound as it is pulled free.

'*USuthu!*' cried Shaba. And then, '*Inkomo kababa!*' as they would sing whenever a cow was sacrificed for the great ceremonies. *My father's cow!* But as he turned to let Umdeni cut the fallen white, to share the honour of the kill, he saw his friend taken in the side by a bayonet, stagger back. Shaba leapt to catch him, realised that they were almost alone, the whole regiment edging back down the slope. Still defiant, but falling back. *Will I die here too?* he wondered, taking Umdeni's weight and helping him away, while bullets flaying into the ground about them holed his shield, barely missing the rifle he carried there. He expected to feel the red soldiers' steel with every step, but as he risked a backwards glance he saw that they had stopped on their own side of the carnage mound, using it to pour a murderous fire into the retreating uMbonambi.

At last he found some rocks, laid Umdeni down in their shelter, looked back to the enemy, saw that they were led by an *induna* at their centre, an ivory tobacco pipe clenched between his teeth. So, in his fury, Shaba let go of his desire to kill this man face to face. He took his rifle, placed the butt on the ground and, as steadily as he was able, poured a measure of black powder from the horn down the barrel, rapping the gun on the ground as he had been taught. Bullets still showered through the air around his head but they were less now, for the red soldiers had other problems. They were still taking fire from the cattle enclosure while, away to the left, the third regiment of this horn, the Sharp Points, had moved stealthily further along the ravine and climbed to higher ground so that they too were now able to shoot down at the camp. In response, the *induna* with the tobacco pipe began to arrange his men, that they could defend themselves on each side and take their own turn to withdraw.

From the leather pouch at his side, Shaba took a small patch of cloth, held it over the open end of the barrel and set a lead ball in its centre, pushing them both down with his thumb. Then the metal rod, using it to ram the ball and patch all the way home, in contact with the powder, but not too tight. The red soldiers began to move although the *induna* seemed reluctant to leave their position, still encouraging one squad to keep firing down the hill, as though determined to kill Shaba personally. *Well, I shall not die in this place,* he thought. He looked down to check that Umdeni was still alive, heard him groan, lifted the rifle and pulled the hammer back as far as it would go, set one of the percussion primer caps on its nipple and sighted along the barrel with his good right eye, squeezing the trigger but forgetting – as he always did – to pull the gun tight into his shoulder. It deafened him, flashed bright yellow, and smacked into his chest with all the force of a young buffalo so that he dropped the rifle in his pain, turned to help Umdeni back to his feet and only then looked towards his enemies, the ache in his shoulder and down his side forgotten when he saw the red soldiers' *induna* in the arms of other whites, blood pouring from his forehead.

Shaba felt a glow of pride. Glory. Though he could not be sure that the shot which had surely killed this man was truly his own. But he shouted '*USuthu!*' in any case, his voice cracked and parched, his hunger and thirst suddenly returned to him with a vengeance. And it was indeed a moment for vengeance. For all those who lay heaped upon the grass. For Somopho Magwendu. For Umdeni kaMthinga.

He picked up his friend, and dragged him as carefully as he was able down the steep terrain. *If I followed the instruction,* he thought, *I would leave him behind. They say that those torn apart by the guns can never be healed. But this wound is from a blade. It may not be too deep.* But he knew in his heart that this was illusion, that the hurt was grievous. So he half-carried, half-dragged Umdeni along, not descending fully to the valley floor but edging along the slope, traversing each gully towards the place from which they had first observed the camp, to the rise from which Ntshingwayo still directed the battle.

It took a long time, and he constantly feared that he would be seen by one of the *izinduna*, instructed back to the fight. But there seemed to be many with the same thought and task as himself so that, when he eventually hauled his friend up onto the plateau, he found the grassland littered with wounded warriors. Wounded so badly. Grotesque images to scar the brain forever. As though some great Vulture Spirit had been at work, baring bones, stripping faces of their flesh, devouring eyes, turning chest and belly cavities inside out.

'Are we winning?' whispered Umdeni, the muscles of his face rigid with pain. He had begun to froth at the mouth as though, somehow, the wound was in his lungs. There was a small cut, almost a long scratch above his left hip and then, above it, the deep puncture, still oozing blood. He had been grinding his teeth even when unconscious and when awake, as now, seemed to suffer violent pain in his back, his innards clearly damaged beyond any healing power of the medicine men. The spasms were getting worse and worse.

Shaba looked down at the ridge.

'Yes,' he said. 'The Bender of Kings has reformed. They are sweeping away those cattle stealers.'

But it was a lie.

The iNgobamakhosi had indeed rallied but had died in droves trying to take the hillock and its wall of rocks. And now, on the other side, the last of the

Skirmishers and Sharp Points were being driven from the cattle *laager* and the higher ground beyond. At every point, the *amabutho* were falling back, leaving unfathomable numbers of slain behind them.

'Then it is a good time to die,' said Umdeni.

'Whey,' replied Shaba. 'Something in your water again? There is never a good time to die, fool. And it is certainly not your turn today.'

But he saw the pain seizure again, the torture in Umdeni's yellowing eyes. And below, as the regiments streamed towards Shaba, he saw the horsemen once more, riding out from the large wagon enclosure. The same horsemen who had started the battle would, it seemed, now finish it.

'You are a bad liar, Shaba kaNdabuko,' said Umdeni. 'Slayer of Red Soldiers, Worker of Iron. And my friend. But you cannot be with me anymore. I have a journey to make now.'

Shaba's eye was caught by a curious sight just a short way below them. Two warriors – older married men from the AbaQulusi Clan, he thought – were too badly wounded in the legs to stand. But they sat leaning together, still holding the good rifles that they must have taken from the whites at eHlobane. Each of the gun muzzles was held below the other's chin, both exploding at the same time.

'I could make the journey with you,' said Shaba.

Umdeni focused upon him.

'No,' he said. 'You must go home. Take care of your beautiful sister. Raise cattle. Marry well. Be a maker of sharp iron. And my friend...' A spasm of pain bit into him. 'I am sorry. About your eye.'

He gripped Shaba's fingers, shook them, then threw them aside and averted his gaze.

Shaba touched his friend's head. Just once. Then took his shield, his spear, and left. But he did not stray too far. There was a place where a gulley opened on to the plateau from still higher ground, a cluster of rocks at its head where a single man could conceal himself well and still see all that happened below. So Shaba kaNdabuko watched through tear-misted eyes, all through that long evening as the horse soldiers hacked at his fleeing people, stopping to kill the wounded, often with their own spears. As though shooting them with bullets or cutting them with swords was too good for the fallen, a waste of the whites' resources.

He watched hundreds die. He could hear some of the warriors begging for mercy. *But why should the white men spare them?* he thought. *For we take no prisoners either. It makes no sense to take prisoners. And they are no different from us. Though they have no rituals to follow. So perhaps they will help Umdeni after all.* Yet he thought not. For they might not have ritual, but they had hatred. They had revenge. And he had heard the stories, like everybody else, of the evil things done to the wounded warriors left behind after the fight at the Drift, at KwaJimu. So he was proud that Umdeni kaMthinga did not beg when, finally, they came for him. He had no *iklwa* of his own with which he could be killed, of course. Instead, they picked up an old musket and beat out his brains.

Shaba remembered Umdeni then as he had been in life, the times they had spent together as boys, as *udibi*. The ear-piercing that marked them by age. The *ukungcweka,* the sparring match with sticks between them that had taken his eye. And he would have given the other gladly now also to keep his friend beside him.

'So,' he murmured, 'spears were truly washed well today. Though the spears that were washed are not our own – but those of the red soldiers.'

Chapter Two

Carey was thrown from his bunk as the troop ship struck.

He cursed himself for not rigging his lee-cloth but he had been so damned tired when he finally reached his berth that he had given it no thought. Thirty-six straight hours on duty at Table Bay, after all. Dried out in the Alfred Basin and the *Clyde's* skipper, Captain Luckhurst, insisting that they could not proceed until every inch of the ship's coating had been inspected; Borthwick's patent anti-fouling composition liberally daubed wherever it was needed. Hot work. Filthy work. The new drafts and every available coolie pressed to the task. But worth it, by God, if it meant arriving all the sooner at Durban and delivering the drafts to fill Chelmsford's tragically depleted ranks. Worth every suppressed curse and complaint he heard whispered behind his back; worth every moment of lost sleep if he, Lieutenant Jahleel Carey, could gain the promotion in Zululand that had eluded him during all his service in the West Indies and subsequently.

'Is it normal in the army, then,' his father had sneered, *'to still be a lieutenant at thirty-one?'*

And he had promised Annie that this campaign would be the making of him. Promised himself... well, so many things.

He steadied himself against the side of the bunk as the *Clyde's* freshly cleaned hull began to grind and settle once more, plates screaming, shuddering up through the bulwarks. There was a single storm lantern, barely enough light to see his shipmates. But he could hear them plain enough. Oaths. Curses. A hint of fear. Then boot-nails slipping and drumming down the companion-way.

'All officers on deck, gentlemen!' It sounded like Colour-Sergeant Stephens.

'What the devil's happened, Colour-Sergeant? And what time is it?' cried Carey.

'Just turned four-thirty, sir. And gone aground, it seems. But the Colonel says right away, sir, if you please.'

Carey struggled into his clothes, his undress uniform. Difficult task, given the angle at which the vessel lay, lifted at the bow. Among the confusion he hauled his way out onto the still dark boat deck and eventually located the

Colonel at the starboard rail with the skipper, the first mate, and several other officers from the ship and from the drafts.

The Colonel peered into the heavy fog. 'Put her astern, Captain?' he was saying.

'I think not, Colonel. That's the mistake the *Birkenhead* made. The rocks opened her up like a sardine tin. We've three feet of water in the hold already and the pumps not coping at all.'

Carey saw the look of dismay on the faces of his companions at mention of the *Birkenhead*. But it caused Carey to smile. Involuntarily. How typical of life to treat him this way. To give him yet another chance. Another beginning. And then to pull the rug from beneath his feet. But in all the risks that he had considered before volunteering for Zululand, he had never once contemplated the possibility of being taken by sharks. Then he pulled himself together. The guilt, of course. He felt the eyes of the Lord upon him. Those lost from the wreck of the *Birkenhead* deserved something better than his dark, self-deprecating humour.

'Then shall we not float again at high tide, sir?' said Colonel Davies. He sounded impatient, as though the answer was obvious. He had, after all, begun his service to the Queen as a midshipman in Her Majesty's Royal Navy.

'I take it you never sailed these waters, Colonel? Tidal range is marginal. We're at High Tide now, just about. According to the Almanac, only six feet and three inches above Chart Datum. At Low Tide, the rocks will show but by then the water in the hold will be too deep to carry out any repairs.'

'But this can't be the Birkenhead Rock, surely?' said Davies. 'Are the reefs not charted, Captain?'

'We rounded Danger Point some time ago. If the fog had settled before we entered the bay, I should have set a course further to seaward, bearing south-east to take us around Dyer Island and the Geyser. As it was – and given your need for haste – it was perfectly reasonable to make for the channel. We were caught out, sir. Slowed to eight knots. Doubled the watch. But the helmsman...'

Caught out like many others, thought Carey. The *Windsor Castle* only the previous October, as well as the *Birkenhead*.

'It's rather academic, at the moment, wouldn't you say?' said the Colonel. 'So that's it. We've struck Dyer Island?'

'It appears so, Colonel. And aground both fore and aft.'

Davies turned to his own officers.

'Very well,' he said. 'Assembly to be sounded, gentlemen. Captain Brander to post sentries over the boats and the spirit room. Time to test the mettle of these fellows, I think.'

'Marching order, sir?' said Carey.

'No, Lieutenant, they can assemble in their sea kit for the time being.' The ship lurched once more, shifted astern slightly, so that they all grabbed for the rail or any other hand-hold. 'My God,' the Colonel continued, as the Clyde shook to another stop, 'will she go down so soon?'

'I've ordered the anchors to be laid out, Colonel,' said Luckhurst. 'That will hold her for now. But go down she will, sir. There's no doubt of that!'

The men of the newly formed 'D' Company, 1st Battalion, 24th Regiment of Foot – one of five companies on board destined to replace those so shamefully lost at Isandlwana – were a decent bunch for the most part, Carey had found. There were eighty-seven other ranks in D Company, slightly less than intended, but not a bad haul considering the meagre amount of time that must have been available to the recruiting sergeants as they visited the public houses scattered through the towns and villages of counties bordering the Welsh Marches. As usual, the healthier and more wholesome types were from agricultural stock, sprinkled with the customary collection of more insipid industrial labourers, a few from the criminal fringe. But all enticed to escape their previous circumstance by an offer of the Queen's Shilling. His own responsibility for them was only temporary, but they gave him a sense of pride. And, at least, a captain's duties for the time being. *A decent bunch*, thought Carey. *But always at least one bad apple in any barrel.*

'Permission to speak, sir?' said Private Brock, and Carey shuddered. Brock was a hard-drinking, ungodly man.

Confound the fellow. Another grumble, no doubt.

'What is it, Brock?' Carey noted the satisfaction on the soldier's mouth at the realisation he had made a mark.

'Beggin' pardon, sir. But will we be issued with our proper uniforms, sir? It's bleedin' perishing up 'ere.'

'Watch your lip, Brock,' said Colour-Sergeant Stephens. 'And if you've got any questions, speak to your corporal, or speak to me. But don't be troubling the officer, now. He's got better things to worry about than your kit, lad!'

'And you'll all be warm enough before too long,' said Carey, knowing that the white cotton drill in which the men had assembled would be perfectly adequate for the work that lay ahead. The scarlet serge frock coats and Oxford mixture trousers of their service dress had all been safely stowed in the hold after the last Marching Order Parade on the previous Sunday.

It can stay there too, thought Carey. *At least until we get the men safely ashore.* But he could not help thinking that they looked slightly absurd in their blue stockinette caps. Still, they had fallen in with the greatest order and regularity, here on the raised quarter deck. There had been little need for Reveille at five and, by the time the bugle was heard, most of them had already rolled hammock and blanket and paraded at the stores. They had been excused mess cleaning this morning due to Assembly being called, and had left no room for complaint on Carey's part.

Colour-Sergeant Stephens seemed broadly satisfied too with his own inspection. A button to be fastened here. Belt and pouches straightened there. A rolled greatcoat more securely attached by the rear braces. Foreign service helmets correctly slung from the valise. Mark II Martini-Henry rifles all present and correct.

'Greatcoats, sir?' whispered Stephens.

'I don't think so,' Carey replied. 'You'll spoil them with kindness, Colour-Sergeant.'

'Quite right, sir. It would do my reputation no good at all.'

'But let's get them moving anyway,' said Carey. 'The Colonel's instructions are that all boats should be readied for abandon ship and then, the Good Lord willing, for the men to be fed.'

So they divided the Company into four sections, one to each of the stern lifeboats. The coxswains had already adjusted falls slightly to compensate for the ship's unnatural angle, allowing the cutters to hang horizontally on their davits, and they were now performing their final checks – plugs in place, towlines secured, falls cleared for running, gripes ready to be shipped, oars in place, tiller pointed but clear of the after-block. And, one by one, but almost simultaneously, they reported to the deck officer.

'Lifeboats clear and ready to lower.'

'Then let's get their gear stowed,' replied the deck officer – Mumford by name. 'What d'you say, Lieutenant?'

Carey agreed, and two of the men from each section were detailed to clamber aboard, receiving the valise equipment and rifles from the rest of their fellows and, under the watchful eye of the coxswain, stowing them where they would be safest, along with a breaker of water and a bucket. There was a deal of chatter among the sections about the purpose of this latter item, but they became more quiet when they found out that it was not, in fact, a sanitation facility but, rather, a bailer in the event that the boats should be swamped. *Unlikely though*, thought Carey, for the water had an oily stillness, with almost no swell. He checked his pocket watch. Nearly five-thirty.

'Very well, Colour-Sergeant,' he called. 'The Company to go below. Breakfast. But keep them sharp, won't you? The Colonel's likely to want them under way before long.'

Breakfast was never a lengthy process in any case. *It doesn't take long to eat biscuit and drink tea*, thought Carey. *But I should try to get something as well.* In his own mess, life seemed almost unaffected by the crisis unfolding outside. Food was plentiful and hot, the cooks on board the Clyde not being renowned for their culinary imagination but at least they followed the Aldershot Instruction Manual to the letter. *"Cookery is the art of preparing and softening food by the action of fire, so as to render it fit for digestion."* And there was chocolate as well, steaming and delicious.

'How are you getting along, Carey?' It was William Brander, Captain of 'A' Company.

Already a captain, thought Carey. *And must be five years my junior. It comes from courting a Colonel's daughter, I suppose.*

'Fine, sir,' he replied, as jauntily as he was able. 'Long way from Cornwall and Hampshire though.' He found that he resented Brander whilst, at the same time, seeking some affinity through their respective family links to the south coast.

'It certainly seems a long time since Woolwich,' said Brander. They had embarked there on the first day of March, more than a month earlier. 'By the way, Carey, the Colonel says that we should make sure there's bully beef in each boat. Fresh water in the barricoes too.'

'Already done, sir,' Carey smiled.

'Excellent, Lieutenant.' Carey felt that Brander's approval was condescending, but he had no time to dwell on it since one of the Colonel's orderlies had arrived.

'Excuse me, gentlemen, but the Colonel says prepare to disembark.'

Within five minutes, Carey had collected the Company ledgers, slung them into a canvas haversack, and was back on the quarter deck, his men falling in once more between the vent cowls, while Brander had gone forward to the boat deck where his own company and the sick were assembled.

Just turned six, and the sun coming up fast.

'So where are we, exactly, Mumford?' Carey said to the deck officer as they gazed over the starboard rail. 'Have we hit the Birkenhead Rock after all?'

'No, sir. Not on your life. We're sitting on a reef. That's Dyer's Island over there.' There was land to the south, rocky and indistinct, perhaps a mile away on the starboard beam. 'On the far side, there's Geyser Rock. And the channel between is called Shark Alley.'

The word sent a shiver down Carey's spine and he could hear that the men from the closest section had also caught the reference.

'They reckons,' he heard Brock say, 'that when the *Birkenhead* went down, there was four 'undred what went in the water. Sharks took the bleedin' lot.'

A corporal in the section told him to pipe down and Brock muttered something about wetting his whistle.

'An' there's another thing,' he said. 'What's goin' to 'appen to the porter ration today?'

There would be no pint of porter issued today, Carey was certain. But just then the bugler sounded *Commence Firing!* – the usual signal that the men were allowed to smoke. It was a privilege that Colonel Davies had allowed them periodically, but only when the men were assembled, as they were presently, up on deck. There was a ragged cheer, and those that were able took the opportunity to light their pipes.

For his part, Carey used the moment to enjoy his own stimulants — a private word with the Lord to protect his two remaining children. He took their photographs from his jacket pocket. Edith, now seven. Baby Pelham Adolphus, not yet one year old. But it was little Jahleel that he thought about. The baby boy that, six years ago, had survived only a week. The baby with Carey's own name. Jahleel. It meant 'God Waits.' A moment of guilt, for he believed himself punished by God whenever conceit overtook him. God waits. *Yet, in time,* he thought, *patient service to God will reward me with better things too.*

At *Cease Firing!* dottles were knocked overboard and the men brought back to attention, while Carey recited a prayer.

'Steer the ship of my life, Good Lord,' he intoned, 'to the quiet harbour, where I can be safe from the storms of sin and conflict. Show me the course I should take. Renew me in the gift of discernment, so that I can always see the right direction in which I should go; and give me the strength and courage to choose the right course, even when the sea is rough and the waves are high, knowing that through enduring hardship and danger we shall find comfort and peace.'

'Amen to that,' mumbled several of the men and, at precisely six-twenty, the order was given for the disembarkation to commence.

The single smoke stack of the *Clyde* seemed no more distant than when they had shoved off, an hour before. The blue funnel with the white 'T' of the Temperley Line was still perfectly clear, while landfall to the north remained hazy. Sharp on the nostrils though. *It cannot be greater than a mile,* thought Carey, *but it seems so much more.* They were still following the compass bearing issued to the coxswains, and the four boats remained relatively close together. Brander's small convoy, on the other hand, seemed scattered across the sea to his right, and Carey drew some foolish satisfaction from the sight.

Departure from the *Clyde* had been smooth, the boats each lowered in turn, the falls unhooked, and some simple seamanship lessons for those who were complete lubbers. To remain seated unless instructed to do otherwise. To always move about the boat — if such movement had been agreed — as close to the centre as possible. To grasp some simple handling of the oars, applicable to those allocated the task. The correct way to *Up oars!* To *Let fall!* And the all-important method of the stroke. *Give way together!*

Well, thought Carey, *after an hour's practice they seem to have mastered the art — more or less.* Each oar lifted in approximate unison as high as the gunwale, wrists dropped to feather the blade flat, the blade thrown forward so far as the rowlock would admit, then dropped in the water. Easy-like, the coxswain had insisted. No splashing. None of that hand-over-hand nonsense. A gannet had followed them all the way from the ship and, as Carey watched the bird's gliding grace, caught the yellow at its throat, he was jolted by the bow man's cry.

'Shark!'

And there it was, away to port, perhaps two hundred yards, a large dark fin that sent the rowing rhythm all awry. Pointing and panic.

'Belay there!' shouted the coxswain, then remembered his station, looked quickly at Carey. 'Beggin' pardon, sir,' he said.

'Not at all,' Carey replied. He gave the fellow a reassuring smile, then shouted, 'Back to your oars, men. Pull steady now.' And the coxswain regained control, calling the stroke until they were moving regularly once more.

'The sea's starting to build too, Lieutenant,' he said. And so it was, though the coxswain did not seem overly concerned, launching into an unsought narrative. 'I know a cove who'd been on the *Birkenhead* when she went down, sir.' The story was the stuff of legend now, Carey knew. 1852, and the vessel – in these same waters – had been carrying four hundred and ninety soldiers, twenty-five wives, thirty-one children and a crew of one hundred and thirty-four. The ship sank within thirty minutes, just enough time to get the women and children in the boats while the troops stood to attention on the decks with parade ground precision. They had established something of a protocol, a drill, for behaviour in such forlorn circumstances. The epitome of British *sang froid*.

Barely two hundred souls had survived.

'Your shipmate lived to tell the tale though,' Carey said.

'He reckoned that the sharks were choosy,' said the coxswain. 'Lots of men had stripped off. To help them swim, see? But this cove knew it was important to stay warm. So 'e went in fully clothed. And guess what, sir? Them sharks had so many to pick from, they took all the ones who were already undressed for them. They knew, sir. That the clothes would spoil their feed.'

Carey heard Brock's voice from within the boat.

'I bleedin' knew we should 'ave been issued our proper uniforms. 'Ere, where's my pack? Somebody get me my greatcoat!'

'Sit down, Brock, you bloody fool,' called Carey as the soldier began to clamber over the thwart to reach his kit, causing one of the rowers to catch a crab in the process and the boat to rock. The man reacted by swiping Brock with his fist.

'Oh my good gawd,' said Brock as he fell across the gunwale, tried to steady himself and fell sideways into the sea.

He was floundering badly, the other soldiers laughing. But Carey's eyes were drawn back to the shark. It had never truly left them, circling at a fixed distance, though it was circling no more. Rather, it was coming steadily closer in a series of serpentine gyrations.

'Bow man,' yelled Carey. 'Boat hook if you please!'

The sailor pulled the wooden shaft of the gaff from beneath the thwarts and threw it, two-handed, over the heads of the boat's occupants so that Carey was able to execute a deft catch. It gave him just enough reach to put the hook within Brock's grasp, for the man was drifting astern now and the amateur oarsmen lacked the skill to back-stroke and bring the boat under control.

'Help me!' cried Brock, unable to avert his gaze from the direction of the approaching fin, his arms still threshing the water.

'Then grab the blasted pole,' Carey replied. He was gratified to see that he had finally caught Brock's attention and the soldier did, in fact, seize hold of the handle, one fist gripping the large bronze hook at its end. 'Now, hold tight, man!'

He hauled Brock towards the transom and, with the coxswain's help, began to pull him unceremoniously over the stern. Brock was hardly co-operative, however, his arms flailing again as he released the boat hook and tried to find a purchase on any hand-hold that would release him from the water more quickly. And Carey found himself half-strangled as Brock grabbed the canvas straps of his haversack, twisted them in his hands. The coxswain saw the predicament and, in an effort to help, took his knife from its sheath, sliced through the material, releasing Carey and gripping Brock's arm, finally landing their catch safely back on board. Carey grabbed for the satchel and missed, while a ragged cheer broke out from the section, taken up by the other three boats – the whole Company having apparently watched the drama unfold.

Carey had a final sight of the bag, the precious books that it contained, as it slipped below the surface. He looked once more for the shark, as though it might somehow now come to his rescue, but the beast was gone.

'Surf, sir!' called the bow man, and they left Brock to his own devices while Carey and the coxswain peered towards the shoreline. It had, in the end, come up remarkably fast and there was, indeed, a strong surf running, a heavy white line, spray-shrouded, along the sand as far as the eye could see.

But there was no sign of Brander's boats and Carey looked to the sailors for some guidance.

'Nothing out here,' said the Coxswain, 'so the beach must be steep-to, sir. Best to run the boats straight in, then swing their bows to starboard, half-round, when we're just about to ground. Then the men out on the starboard side only. That way the surf will lift us high and dry. The men can help – but without getting knocked about too much.'

Carey gave orders for the men to take off their boots and roll up trouser legs in preparation while the coxswain made sure that each of the boats should follow a similar strategy to the one he had outlined. Then instructions to the oarsmen, followed by the command, *Way enough!* The oars were brought inboard – not a pretty manoeuvre but adequate. They felt the first kiss of sand beneath the keel. The coxswain swung the bows about and the men on the starboard side jumped over the gunwale into the shallows, heaving against the clinker-built hull until she touched the hard, when the rest of the section clambered ashore to help pull her to the high-water mark. But no further, since the boats would need to return in due course with a minimal crew to assist in the rest of the disembarkation. *God willing*, thought Carey, *that the ship stays on the rocks that long.* Yet she was still there for the present, he saw. And he should have felt pleased. His Company all safely ashore. One man saved from the sharks. But no joy of Carey's was ever quite unalloyed. No enterprise ever quite entire. So, instead of satisfaction, he experienced only further guilt, wondered how he would feel when called to explain his loss of the ledgers.

Brander found him near noon, having come slogging down through the dunes from the south-east.

'Fine piece of work, Carey,' he said, admiring the bivouacs which 'D' Company had rigged with the previously unused boat sail and spars to provide temporary shelter from the sun.

'We had plenty of help, sir,' Carey replied. 'The Surgeon-Major and young Farrer were already here ahead of us. They seem to have been separated from your own flotilla.'

'Yes,' Brander coughed. 'Rather lost track of them, I'm afraid. Still, all's well, eh? Managed to find a farm though. In the bush. We'll send a messenger to Simon's Bay.'

'Ah,' said Carey. 'I may have jumped the gun, sir. There was a Dutch gentleman, Mister Van der Byl, here to meet us. He offered to have a telegram sent. He'll be back soon, I imagine.'

'And what shall it say, Carey? This telegram?'

'I took the liberty of sending it in my own name, sir. But on behalf of the officer commanding our troops on board the *Clyde*. To the Commodore at Simon's Bay, of course.'

'And the message?'

'Short and sweet, sir. Transport *Clyde* ashore off Dyer's Island. Ship making water. Troops landing on beach.'

'Well,' said Brander, 'concise at least. And you've sent the boats back to the ship, I see. Did the same myself. Colonel will be pleased. Wouldn't want to be there too long, I imagine.'

'I sent them off at eleven, sir. And I scribbled a quick report for Colonel Davies. Lie of the land, that sort of thing.'

'Damned efficient, Lieutenant.'

'Not entirely, sir. I'm afraid I managed to lose the Company books. They fell overboard.' Carey forbore to mention the shark incident.

'Lose them, you say? How very careless. Colonel will have something to say on that score, eh? Still, you've the air of an officer accustomed to command, if you don't mind me saying so.'

'I was Garrison Commander at Accra for a while, sir.'

'As a lieutenant? What age?'

'Eighteen, sir.'

Carey watched him make the calculation. Garrison command at the age of eighteen, albeit at a far-flung outpost? Still a lieutenant thirteen years later? Carey would have asked himself the same question. *So what happened in between?*

'Regiment?'

'Third West India, sir.'

Brander snorted, believing he had found his explanation.

'Ah,' he laughed, 'just native levies, then?'

'Jamaicans, sir. Fine soldiers. Their disposition makes them admirably suited to the task. Something in their nature.'

'If you say so, Carey. Ever under fire with them?'

He made an effort to meet Brander's gaze, searching for any sign that there might be further ulterior motive behind the seemingly innocent enquiry. *Does he know?* he wondered, then dismissed the idea.

'Just once or twice, sir,' he said.

Carey had posted sentries at intervals along the dunes and one of them shouted now.

'Horseman coming in!'

It was the Dutchman, Van der Byl. Carey effected the introductions and the farmer confirmed that he had dispatched his most trusted field-hand with the message to Caledon's telegraphic station. Brander, for his part, was interested in a fresh water supply and Van der Byl offered to show them a decent well.

'But it's two miles away,' he said. 'If you gentlemen would care to accompany me, I can supply you both with horses. And a cart too, maybe.'

'Capital idea,' said Brander. 'Well, Carey, what do you think? Why not assemble your men, get them moving to join my lot. In the bay, over there. Then perhaps we might take up Mister Van der Byl's kind offer.'

Carey put the necessary arrangements in place – Surgeon-Major Ward and the limping Lieutenant Farrer having the admirable services of Colour-Sergeant Stephens on which to rely – before setting off at a brisk pace behind Brander and the Dutchman. It was hot now, Carey's extravagant sideburns dripping sweat. He wondered whether he should shave them but decided, illogically he knew, that he would probably grow them into a full beard instead, in the fashion that was prevalent here at the Cape.

'So, Lieutenant,' said Van der Byl when he had finally caught up, 'Captain Brander tells me that you're one of the *Boomvogels*?'

Carey was confused.

'I'm sorry, sir…?'

The Dutchman laughed.

'Special service officer, aren't you?' he said. 'The first lot that arrived, with Chelmsford, we Dutch called them *Aasvogels*. They're the vultures that you see circling in big flocks out here. Just watching for something to die so they can swoop down and pick up all the choice parts of the carrion while it's still fresh. No offence, gentlemen. It was just the way it seemed to us. All those fine officers and gentlemen climbing over each other to get the best administrative posts.'

'I volunteered for service in South Africa, Mister Van der Byl,' said Carey, 'because I believed that God and my country needed me here.'

'No need to be so prickly, man,' said the Dutchman. 'I didn't include you. You've arrived too late to be an *Aasvogel*.'

'And the *Boomvogels*?' asked Brander.

'A different breed altogether,' said Van der Byl. 'They tend to hunt just in pairs. But still in company of other predators. So for those of you who've arrived late, there are only the transport and escort duties left.'

'But still vultures,' said Carey. 'And in company with predators. Is that how you see the British Army's presence here, Mister Van der Byl?'

'I have no personal axe to grind, Lieutenant,' replied the Dutchman, 'but there are those who say that Lord Chelmsford has forced this war on Cetshwayo. An unlawful invasion, gentlemen, not even authorised by your own Government.'

'Hardly that, sir,' said Brander. 'They're still sending out fresh levies like ourselves, d'you see?'

'That's just to help extricate Chelmsford from the mess he's made, isn't it? And revenge for Isandlwana, I suppose.'

'It's a damned strange stance to take, sir, if you'll forgive me,' said Carey. 'Is that a common view among the Dutch? After all, sir, Cetshwayo had forty thousand men under arms. It was clear, was it not, that they posed a threat to the entire Cape – yourself included?'

'You've much to learn about the Zulu, gentlemen. Cetshwayo musters his young men every year. To help build and repair his royal kraals. To bring in his crops. To herd his cattle. He has enough trouble holding on to his throne – given the number of rivals he has – without risking a war with Britain. But Chelmsford, now. And Frere too. They have personal ambitions. To bring together all the separate colonies here in one huge British dominion of South Africa. That's the prize, gentlemen.'

'That's hardly logical, sir,' said Brander, 'if you don't mind me saying. After all, they'd not only have to deal with the Zulu but all the other colonies as well. The Dutch colonies too.'

'Well, you've already annexed the Transvaal, Captain. 'And maybe that's the reason there are so few of us Boers willing to help you. Because they know that we'll be next in the firing line.'

*

'Khambula?' asked Colonel Davies when he came ashore at the encampment. It was three-thirty. Brander and Carey had only recently returned from their sojourn to the hinterland carrying the remarkable news.

'Yes, sir,' said Brander. 'Van der Byl had sent the rider to Caledon with Mister Carey's note. He'd crossed on the road with the messenger coming south. The fellow arrived while we were still at the farm.'

'And three battles, you say?'

'In almost as many days, Colonel. Sounds like we took another beating at this place.' He pointed at his notes, pronounced the word syllable by syllable. 'H-lo-ba-ne. That would have been last Friday. But made up for it in trumps the next day at Khambula.'

'That's Wood for you, gentlemen,' said Davies. 'Fine soldier.' His views about Lord Chelmsford, overall commander of the British forces, remained unspoken, whatever they might have been. 'And this third affair?'

'Up the coast, sir. And just yesterday. North of Durban and much closer to us, so the news came in faster. Can't make head nor tail of the place though. You remember how the blackie pronounced it, Carey?'

'Gin-gin-dlo-vu, sir.'

'Gin, gin, I love you!' laughed Brander, though Davies seemed not entirely to understand the jest. 'Well, yes,' continued the Captain. 'Exactly that. Not much detail though. It seems that Lord Chelmsford was leading a column to relieve Colonel Pearson's garrison.' Pearson had been under siege at Eshowe, they all knew, for three months. 'The darkies attacked the column and our fellows drove them off. Gave them short shrift, it seems. And only a handful of casualties – on our side, at least. Oh, but Lieutenant-Colonel Northey killed, sir.'

'Northey?'

'60th Rifles, sir.'

'Ah!' said Davies. 'Poor fellow. But it seems the tide has finally turned, gentlemen. About time, too. We'd not want to miss the show, of course. It should cheer up the men, don't you think? Though you seem to be doing a pretty fine job of that already. And the Dutchman supplied all this provender?' Van der Byl had given them a bullock wagon as promised, laden with cheese, corn, fresh meat, barrels of clean water.

'Yes, sir,' said Brander. 'He demanded a chit, of course. But at least the men are fed. A nice supplement to their bully beef.'

'Well, it's an admirable spot you've picked too,' said the Colonel. 'Well-protected. Just enough brush and grass to keep the dust down. Terrible country for dust, this. Tea will help, naturally. As usual.' He smiled and they each turned towards the boats, still unloading the second wave of disembarkation from the *Clyde*. The Colonel himself and a couple of horses already safely ashore, of course. More stores, including the ammunition cases – and the inevitable chests of tea. 'As soon as they're finished, we'll get them back out to the ship and bring ashore the rest. Poor Luckhurst as well, of course.'

'Was it bad, sir?' said Carey. 'When you left?'

'Twenty feet of water in the hold, Lieutenant. We made those rafts over there from some of the sheep pens, the hen coops, hatches, ladders – just about anything we could get our hands on. Luckhurst was in a bit of a funk by that stage. Sent some men into the rigging with life buoys. Thought she was going down then and there. We had to put poor Limerick over the side. Which reminds me…' He searched for his servants, Taylor and James, found them still running the Colonel's favourite charger back and forth across the sands. 'Taylor, there!' he bellowed. 'Is he dried off yet?' The servant confirmed that the horse was indeed now dry. 'Good fellow!' shouted the Colonel. 'Then a brush down, warm blankets and his usual feed, if you please. Now, where was I?'

'Captain Luckhurst thought she was sinking, sir?' prompted Carey.

Colonel Davies glanced his way. He was a handsome man, Carey thought. Sandy hair, moustache, aquiline features. And he also recognised that Davies was a competent chap, somehow distinguished from the normal run of his fellow army officers by a long early naval service, initially in the Burmese War, later in the Baltic during the Russian war. Then, after changing services, an equally eminent career in the Grenadier Guards.

'Quite so, Lieutenant,' he said. 'Stroke of luck, really, when some of the Dutchmen from Dyer's Island put off in their own boats, come to have a look at what was going on. Didn't come too close though for a while. We had to shout like fury. Fire our pistols. Get their attention. They came up quickly enough in the end, I suppose, and we got most of the other troops ashore. Hopefully, those last few boats you've sent off will bring back Skipper Luckhurst and the remaining stores.'

But it was five forty-five when Luckhurst finally joined them and, when he did so, the accompanying boats were almost empty. Their only cargo seemed to be the officers' luggage. A fine lace filigree of surf was worrying sand from the shoreline, the waves a continuous barrage of incoming shellfire and, above them, a belt of black-bellied high cloud was rimed by the final remains of the day's sunlight.

'I could not, in all conscience, allow your men back on board I'm afraid, Colonel,' he said, breathless after struggling up the beach. 'She's in a most parlous state, gentlemen. Parlous.'

Colonel Davies looked unimpressed.

'So the men's kit? Their uniforms? Sixty-eight thousand tons of canned meat? We are to leave it all for the sharks, sir?' he said.

'She could go down any second,' said Luckhurst. 'We should count ourselves fortunate, sir. Every man jack on board saved. Three thousand rounds of ammunition. Most of your other supplies. It could have been so very different, Colonel. In a rough sea, I doubt that any would have survived.'

'Yet the ship still swims, Captain Luckhurst. You see, sir? She still swims.'

'And I regret, Colonel,' said Carey, 'that I must report a further loss. 'D' Company's books and accounts went overboard when we were landing, sir. All except the defaulters' book which was in the possession of Colour-Sergeant Stephens.'

'Damned careless of you, Mister Carey,' said Davies. 'But I expect the men all have their own small books?' Carey supposed that they did indeed. 'Then I suggest, Lieutenant, that you impound the blasted things before the rogues discover your loss and begin to make favourable adjustments to their debts. Besides, it will give you the opportunity to create the ledgers afresh. Admirable work for a special services officer, I should think.'

'If you say so, sir,' replied Carey, the word *Boonvogel* echoing in his brain. Was this to be the extent of his quest then? Confined to a series of administrative functions rather than find his grail?

'If you don't mind, sir,' said Brander, 'I would feel it remiss if I failed to mention Mister Carey's excellent work when we first came ashore. Wonderful initiative. And speaking of sharks, the Lieutenant's modesty has made him omit to mention the fact that he personally saved one of the men from certain death. An attack by one of the beasts, sir. Besides all that, it seems that he also has a remarkable talent for map-making.'

'Shark attack, Carey?' said the Colonel. 'Good gracious, I had no idea. And you studied map-making at Staff College?'

'In truth, sir,' he replied, 'it's been something of a specialism since I joined the service. But yes, I qualified first in my class last year.' It had been one of Carey's new beginnings. A decision to supplement his years of field service by securing a place at Camberley for those aspiring to become more senior officers. He experienced a reluctant gratitude towards Brander for his generosity in alluding to the fact.

'Then I shall mention your gallantry in dispatches, Lieutenant. I'll need full reports from you, naturally. Some supporting evidence from yourself, Brander, if you would. And I will make good use of you, Carey, when we move to join the column. Somebody with a skill in cartography would be a welcome bonus in this country.'

'And when,' said Carey, 'do you think we might be able to begin the march inland, sir?'

'With any luck, once your message gets through, they'll send another ship. Tomorrow perhaps. Day after at the latest. I expect we'll need to return to Simon's Bay to re-equip. Then on to Durban. From there, we should be able to reach the column by the end of the month.'

Dear Lord, thought Carey, *please do not allow it to all be over before then.*

He so desperately needed this new beginning. And there had been so many new beginnings already. His marriage to Annie. France. The children. Staff College. Now this. *The Lord might wait,* he mused, *but time and tide wait for no man.*

'See, Colonel,' said Captain Luckhurst. 'Did I not tell you, sir?'

All eyes turned to the south, across the sand, the breaking surf, the intervening stretch of darkening water, to the reef and the stricken hull of the *Clyde*, distant but still plainly visible. They heard the groan, the awful death rattle as she slid backwards off the rocks. A minute, but no longer, and she had slipped, like one of Carey's many dreams, forever into the depths.

Chapter Three

Sunday 6th April 1879

For a brief moment, McTeague believed his life might be at risk as the Zulu King, Cetshwayo, burst from his royal hive on the higher slope beyond the kraal's circular parade ground.

The King looked furious – as well he might, considering the unnecessary reverses so recently inflicted on his armies. A powerful figure, darker skinned than many of those around him, Cetshwayo's legs were slightly bowed, and he possessed a regal corpulence towards which McTeague was working hard but still merely aspired. And McTeague was not fearful of the risk, naturally. He simply recognised that the thing existed. In fact, he considered himself relatively impermeable, prided himself on the fact that he had never faced a situation from which his tongue and his wits could not extricate him. Even when he might have been cashiered from the army, dishonourably discharged, he had managed to talk his way into an amicable parting of the ways, a modest stipend which had shown a tidy profit on the bargain. *Twelve years ago*, he thought. *How the years desert us!* In any case, when all else failed, well, a fellow could always scarper, as Mister Punch might say. Tactical retreat, that sort of thing. He looked around now for a suitable bolt-hole, a line of escape to meet such an eventuality. But there was nothing obvious.

Emahlabathini gave its name both to the whole of the plain, north of the White Umfolozi's middle reaches, and also to this particular kraal – really a military barracks – which stood here, perhaps ten miles from the King's main residence at Ulundi, which the Zulus called oNdini. Like any such stronghold, this one consisted of two extensive circular palisades, Camel Thorn trunks, with the dwelling huts, dozens of them, clustered between the inner and outer rings, interspersed with trees and spreading from the larger royal dwellings. The inner circle formed the central arena and McTeague's possible access to the main exits was blocked by the warriors of Cetshwayo's army arrayed here. He knew that not all of the regiments had returned but, still, there must have been ten thousand men gathered in the arena. They had been noisy, chanting and singing for some time in the dusty heat, and bearing no resemblance whatsoever to a force defeated. But they fell silent at the Great King's dramatic entrance.

Three carved stools had been arranged before the doorway of Cetshwayo's house – a rare honour since none of the King's own subjects was permitted to sit on chairs of any kind in his presence – and a line of his chief advisors, his counsellors, his holy men, his *izinduna*, his commanders, stretched away on each side of the seats.

The seats themselves were occupied by McTeague, by McTeague's wife – Maria Mestiza, resplendent in her khaki shirt and dark skirts, her bush hat, her bandoliers, her twin holsters – and by the Dutchman, Cornelius Vijn.

'Where are my young men?' bellowed Cetshwayo. 'Where?' His voice echoed around the hills, while flocks of birds took to the wing above his head.

McTeague, who had been here long enough to understand every word, saw the distinguished figure of the King's chief councillor, his First Minister, climb to his feet. He was a stocky man, with a considerable beard. A great orator, McTeague thought, having met him many times in his trading deals with the Zulus.

'Many have returned to their homesteads,' said Mnyamana kaNgqengelele Buthelezi. They fear for their crops. Their cattle. Their families.'

'Is that not what you told me after the Battle of the Little House?' yelled Cetshwayo. 'So where is the discipline? And what are you doing, you chieftains and captains of men, if you cannot have your warriors follow a simple instruction? Besides, I am not speaking of those who have gone home. I am speaking of those who will never see another First Fruits.'

'Three thousand are missing from our ranks, Great Lord.'

His demeanour was mournful, theatrically so, like an amateur actor on a Drury Lane stage.

'Three thousand lie dead, First Minister, because my orders are ignored. Did I not forbid an attack on those places where the red soldiers have their walls and wagons to defend them? And now, so many of my young men gone!'

'We had no choice, Lord. The Bender of Kings was attacked by the horse soldiers. They had to react. Two of my own sons lie among the fallen. And did I not, myself, warn of the dangers in attacking the camp at eKhambule?'

'Yet you surrendered command of the *impi* to another when you should have carried out my orders yourself,' said Cetshwayo. 'It was foolishness that caused them to take the white men's bait. They are young. But their commanders should know better. Hold them in check against their youth. Let the commander of the iNgobamakhosi come forward.'

Another Zulu lord stood in his place. He must have been in his mid-forties, McTeague imagined. Long-limbed, moustache, small forked beard, almost bald except for his head ring.

'I see you, Great King.'

'And I see you too, iNkosi of the iNgobamakhosi. What will you say to me about this betrayal?'

Well, thought McTeague, *that was to the point. This could get nasty.*

'I have never betrayed you, Lord,' said the iNkosi. 'And the thing happened as First Minister Mnyamana has said. We could not leave the red soldier horsemen to eat our regiment without defending ourselves.'

'You fell into their trap. And having fallen into it once, you forgot my orders entirely. You drove the horsemen back into their laager. And then? Did you then remember my instructions and continue to surround them, to draw out the whole of their strength?'

'They have so many guns, Lord. Better guns than those of our regiments.'

'We have plenty of guns,' said Cetshwayo.

And McTeague knew he was right. After all, had he not personally supplied the King with many of them? It had been quite a feat. Ten thousand weapons brought in through Portuguese Mozambique by his operations alone. *Couldn't have done it without dear Maria's help, of course!* he thought. Cetshwayo remained suitably grateful. *Might not be so happy, though, if he knew it was me who leaked the fact that he has them to the Natal newspapers.* The headlines had caused quite a stir. Forty thousand-strong standing army of Zulus. A daily threat to the safety of every Colonist in the region, British or Dutch. Many of the warriors young men, unmarried, mischief and mayhem in their hearts. All armed with modern rifles. Well, 'modern' might not have been strictly accurate. But at least a few dozen were decent enough breech-loaders. And most of the warriors were part-timers, of course, who spent their year building and herding for the King. Helping the royal economy, so to speak. *Well, isn't that exactly my own role in life too?* McTeague mused. *Keeping the wheels oiled. Trade must flow.* And no point selling weapons if they were never used. Needed replacing. Updating. Best not to be too fussy about the truth either. It would all be fine in the end. God kept a tally of one's minor misdeeds but, so long as one prayed for His guidance, how could the Almighty not forgive a fellow, come Judgement Day? *So long as one is always honest with God, well...*

'You are with lies!' Cetshwayo was screaming at the iNgobamakhosi commander. 'Lies! You do not deserve to be a chief among the AmaZulu. Why should I not have you killed for your treachery?'

McTeague could almost smell the tensions among the ranks behind him, noticed the Dutchman carelessly turn his head to see the effect of Cetshwayo's taunt on the already agitated warriors, saw Cornelius Vijn turn quickly back again when he understood the threatening posture of the regiments, heard the stamping feet and the rival chants begin once more, tasted the dust that they churned into the air. *A powder keg,* he thought. *Cetshwayo holds them together for the most part. But when he's no longer here, this country will be wide open for the taking.* A thought not so very far removed, he knew, from that of the British Government's representatives in Natal.

The Great King's First Minister, Mnyamana, intervened.

'Hear me, Lord,' he said. 'This is a respected leader. He has shown his mettle already at eSandlwana, at eHlobane, at eKhambule, and now at Gingindlovu.'

'Yes,' said Cetshwayo. 'Another defeat at kwaGingindlovu. For the same reason. The same reason!'

'And our men fought like lions, Lord. But you are right, Great King. Naturally. We need to plan our strategy. And yes, Lord, to follow your orders. I am your First Minister, Great King. If the blame belongs to anybody, it must belong to me. If anybody deserves to die, it must surely be me.'

Cetshwayo thought for a moment. There was a terrible silence. He glanced quickly at his personal guards. Then shook his head.

'Luckily for you, my friend, I need you still. Your counsel remains worthy. But I need to hear the words of these white traders too.'

The King gestured towards the three stools, and McTeague, praying that the Almighty still watched over him, kept his gaze fixed firmly on Cetshwayo's feet as ten thousand voices behind him began baying for the whites to be slain.

It seemed that Cetshwayo was still unsure about whether Maria Mestiza was man or woman. He was particularly fascinated by the shape of her facial features, the sloping forehead of the Miskito Indian, but the broad nose and generous lips that spoke of African blood. McTeague had first encountered her when she was running guns to Marcus Canul's *campesino* rebels, among whom she enjoyed the nickname Maria Cuchilla – Maria the Knife. Then, after his discharge from the army, with his commission sold, they had become business partners, freighting illicit whisky and gin across the border from Honduras into Nicaragua. And when things had become too hot for them, it was Maria who had suggested Africa as their next destination. She insisted that there was royalty in her veins. That in Africa she could become a queen with dominion over her own lands. She had the morals of an alley-cat, a marriage to alcohol, but she was the only creature that McTeague had ever loved.

The royal dwelling in which they sat was not the largest of the Great King's residences but it was still impressive. The Acacia branches which formed the core of its walls towered upwards, bent together to form the roof and the hut's typical beehive shape. They were sealed against the weather by carefully braided grass and reed. The floor was a glass-hard surface of dried and polished dung compound, from which rose the eight carved rock alder columns that helped to support the structure's mass, as well as the internal partitions of Cetshwayo's private chambers. But the whole central section of the hut was open, an elaborate fire pit in the middle and, opposite the low entrance, three wattle panels, like altar screens, McTeague thought. There were narrow shelves on the highest part of the panels, supporting richly carved figures, neither saints nor apostles but, rather, the King's ancestors. Beneath them, hangings of incredible beauty, hand-appliqué, the finest embroidery, beaded accents, each depicting one of the folklore tales so popular among the AmaZulu.

The screens formed a lofty backdrop for one of Cetshwayo's thrones, carved in the local manner from a single piece of mahogany, the legs deceptively delicate, linked by curving struts, asymmetrically related to each other. It appeared almost impossible for the thing to support the King's weight, but there he sat before them, in all his majesty, surrounded by his ministers. In contrast to outside, there were no stools in here, and McTeague was uncomfortable on the floor, despite the thickness of the matting. The Scotsman's cherubic cheeks, darkly oiled hair and moustache, belied his approaching sixtieth birthday, and he felt every one of his years, obsessed now with the prospect of failing health.

'You hear how my young men call for your white blood?' said Cetshwayo.

McTeague heard the Dutchman whimper alongside him, while Maria tensed, stifled some verbal defiance in a rare moment when discretion overcame her valour.

'Great King,' said McTeague, 'I would surrender myself willingly to the spears of your warriors if it would help in any way to change the events of the past week.'

'I think you would betray me,' said Cetshwayo, 'for just twelve pieces of your bible silver.'

Twenty, at least, thought McTeague. *Genesis 37:28. And the price escalated to thirty by the time we reach the New Testament. Matthew 26:15. I must do something about a version of the Good Book in IsiZulu.*

'But why should we betray you, Lord?' he said. 'We owe you all that we have.'

'Dunn owed me everything too.' McTeague heard a catch in the King's voice, risked a surreptitious glance at Cetshwayo's face, shocked to see a tear upon his cheek. 'But where is he now? He has not only abandoned me but trained horse soldiers to fight against me at Gingindlovu.'

Yet it was Dunn, the English hunter and trader, who had supplied the weapons that helped Cetshwayo secure his kingdom in the first place, back in '72; Dunn who had built a veritable empire, seven thousand subjects within Zululand on the strength of it; Dunn who had also abandoned everything he owned before the British invasion, gone over to Chelmsford. Most of his property and possessions had been seized and burned – but not the dwellings at eMoyeni, the Place of Wind and Spirits, that McTeague now shared with Maria Mestiza. *Well*, thought McTeague, *Dunn is no more than an amateur in this little game.*

In the manner so typical of her, Maria now lifted her gaze from the floor and stared directly into the eyes of the King. It was an unforgivable breach of custom, etiquette and Zulu law, one that Cetshwayo would not have tolerated in anybody else. But from Maria Mestiza he accepted many improprieties. Apart from anything else, she was permanently intoxicated, a fact that the

King seemed to accept as a sign that she was an *inyanga*, a mystic and a healer.

'My people,' she said, 'face the same problem as your own, Great King. Our lands stolen by the British, a greedy people with no respect. And they kept us as slaves because of their guns. But we beat them many times, Lord, with only the *machete* and the Cross. Our fists and our faith.'

'Then why are you here, Witch Woman, rather than your own land?' said Cetshwayo. 'Is it not true that the British are still there? And you...' he turned to Cornelius Vijn. 'Are your Dutchmen not also simply dogs that run at the heels of the Fat Queen?'

Vijn spoke the Zulu tongue in a nervous tremolo, quite unsuited to its complexities, its clicking consonants, its sibilant syllables. But he could make himself understood well enough. McTeague guessed that the man was perhaps twenty-two, maybe a bit older. He had first come across the Dutchman four years earlier, when the young fellow arrived in Zululand with his ox cart, seeking a share of the trade.

'My people are too proud to run at anybody's heals, Highness,' said Vijn. 'They have no love of the English. And the difference between the Dutch and the English is that my people are happy to settle here, to live alongside the Zulu, without stealing all their lands. I told the English, last year, that they had nothing to fear from the Zulu. I told John Dunn the same when I met him.'

'And did he agree with you?' said the King.

'Why, yes. He said that he could not understand how the English could have helped you win your throne and now, so suddenly, seek to take it from you once more.'

'Many of my people believe it is because the Fat Queen has too few people of her own to bring in her crops, to herd her cattle, to build her royal palaces,' said Cetshwayo. 'So she means to capture all the men, put them to work in her mines. To marry all our young women to her own white warriors. To carry off all my cattle. It is the reason that the regiments fight so hard. They would rather die than live under the whites.'

'I do not believe, Great King,' offered Vijn, 'that they mean to steal your young men and women.'

'Just our land,' said Cetshwayo.

'And your cattle, Lord,' said McTeague.

'I sent them cattle. Many cattle. And I agreed to send them the young men that they said had done bad things, broken the English laws – even though they had broken none of our own.'

Yes, thought McTeague, *but your warriors turned them back. Refused to surrender either the cattle or the men that the British had demanded.*

One of the King's ministers spoke for the first time.

'The cattle are safe now,' he said. 'We stopped the whites from stealing them at eHlobane. They are all protected. Even the thin cows of the uMholandi...' he pointed his cow-tail switch at Cornelius Vijn, '…are now part of the royal herds.'

Which, of course, explained the Dutchman's presence here, McTeague knew. The lad had struck a couple of decent deals with Cetshwayo and the King had taken something of a shine to him. He liked to have white folk around him as exotic additions to his court. But when Vijn's own cattle had been stolen by renegade Zulus now gone over to the British, Cetshwayo had made sure they were retrieved, mingled with the royal herds for safe-keeping, and Cornelius Vijn received the royal summons that he must come too. Naturally, Vijn himself interpreted the King's kindness and consideration in a modestly different way. He had been a house guest of Cetshwayo's for more than a month already.

'But the cattle will not remain safe,' said Maria Mestiza, 'if the British continue to advance.'

'And what would you advise us, Witch Woman?' said Cetshwayo.

McTeague adjusted his monocle. *This should be interesting*, he thought.

'I am here, Great King,' said Maria Mestiza, 'because it is the land of my ancestors. Before the British slavers carried them away to the lands of swamp and pestilence. And yes, the British are still there. But when we fought them in the open, as your regiments did at eSandlwana and eHlobane, we beat them. Ask him!' She pointed at McTeague, who was able to verify with the intimacy which comes from first-hand experience, that she was correct. *The rout at San Pedro*, he thought. *If only the men had stood, I would have stood with them. Of course I would!* Maria laughed as though she had read his thoughts. 'And do not let him tell you,' she said, 'that he would have stood his ground if only the soldiers had done the same. He was the first to run.' She cackled at him.

'Fine words,' said another of the ministers, rising to his feet. 'But each time we try to bring them to battle, they stay behind their walls where our spears cannot reach them.'

'Then tell your *impi*,' she spat, 'to stay close to the red soldiers. Send out flying companies of your best men to harass their scouts. Fight them with the little war. With *la guerrilla*. And then, when they are most vulnerable, catch their columns when they are strung out along the march. Or crossing our rivers.'

'We did that,' shouted the iNkosi. 'At Ntombe.'

'And did you not slay them?' said Maria Mestiza.

Indeed they did, McTeague remembered. At Ntombe, the Zulus had surprised Captain David Moriarty and his convoy in a badly prepared position, killed him and his eighty-strong command. Only a handful of troops had survived.

'The Witch Woman is correct,' said Cetshwayo. 'And were these not the orders that I issued? That the whites must not be attacked where they have built their walls?'

'But the red soldiers,' said another minister, a desiccated ancient, 'cut off the heads of our dead and loaded the skulls in their wagons. Why do they do that? Are they savages?'

McTeague knew that an entire mythology had sprung up among the AmaZulu about the unsavoury practices of the British. And with good cause.

'It is a despicable thing to do,' said McTeague. 'But it is in the nature of the English. To cut off the heads of their enemies.'

'I remember the pictures in your book, KaMtigwe,' said Cetshwayo. 'Thomas Cromwell. The pirate, Raleigh. And women too. Anna Boleyn. Mary, the Queen of your Scotsmen.'

'Even a king,' said McTeague.

'When did this happen?'

'Oh, Mighty Lord, it was very recent.' Cetshwayo, to whom brutality and cruelty were hardly strangers, was appalled. 'And now,' McTeague continued, 'the Fat Queen demands that her soldiers should bring heads to her. So she may see how well they have fought.'

Cetshwayo had a prized captive, it transpired. But he was not English. McTeague, Maria Mestiza and Cornelius Vijn had been invited by the King to help interrogate the fellow.

He was tall, painfully thin, unkempt, and he wore the faded buff uniform of an irregular cavalryman. They kept him guarded among some of the other possessions that the Zulus had taken from their victories. Only a small sample here at Emahlabathini but still a veritable cornucopia. Fine linen. Greatcoats. Silver spoons. Ladles, knives and forks. Soup tureens. Saddle and harness. Ink-well and blotter. Canned meats and bottled beers. Blankets and folding beds. Campaign desks and writing table. Gilded candlesticks. Swords. Bayonets. And ammunition, naturally – case upon case of .450 calibre Boxer bullets. *Damn'd fellows are getting just too good at supplying themselves*, thought McTeague.

'We can get no sense from him,' said the *induna* who had captured the man at Hlobane. 'I speak some of the white man's tongue, but this one seems to speak it even less than I do!'

'My friend, my Dutchman,' said Cetshwayo, with a nod towards Vijn, 'tells me that there is no common language that all the whites can understand. Is that correct, KaMtigwe?'

'It is indeed correct, Lord,' McTeague replied. 'Shall we try to talk with him?'

'It is a terrible irony,' said Cetshwayo, 'that I have been asking my *izinduna* to make sure they take some white prisoners since that day the red soldiers first invaded. They might help us in our negotiations. Help to show that we are civilised. But my warriors are always too keen to make their honour cuts, to wash their spears. And now, when we finally have one alive, he seems to speak only the language of monkeys.'

With a modicum of trial and error, however, it became apparent that the language in question was actually French. Vijn's grasp of the idiom was better than McTeague's, so the Dutchman functioned as interpreter.

'His name is Grandier,' he said. 'Ernest Grandier. Born in Bordeaux. A cutter of stone.'

It seemed that Grandier had come to the Cape seeking his fortune. He claimed that he had done well. Very well indeed. A man of great wealth. If only the Great King would let him go, he would promise to come back with gold. Plenty of gold. Or cattle, of course. Yes, cattle would be best. And thank God he had now fallen in with decent white folk.

'Well, I think he's a fanciful fellow,' said McTeague. *And it takes one to know one*, he thought.

'If he has such wealth,' said Cetshwayo, 'ask him why he needed to take a silver shilling from the Fat Queen.'

Cornelius Vijn put the question.

'He says that they forced him,' said the Dutchman.

'What unit?' said McTeague, and he understood the Frenchie's reply perfectly well. *Je ne sais pas*. His claim that he did not know. 'Look,' McTeague said to Vijn, 'tell him that he is, indeed, now under our protection. Tell him who I am. Major William McTeague, formerly of...' He struggled a moment to find the IsiZulu words, switched to English. '...of Her Majesty's Third West Indian Regiment.' Cornelius Vijn began the translation. 'Tell him that I am here from Lord Chelmsford. To negotiate with King Cetshwayo. I can help him. But he must be honest.'

Grandier looked uncertainly at the three non-Zulus before him. From the ragged young Dutchman, to the mixed race woman with the bush hat and bandoliers, and the cherubic smile of McTeague himself. But they bore little resemblance, the latter knew, to a diplomatic mission.

'Weatherley's Horse,' Grandier said, his English heavily accented. 'My *commando*, it was in the battle. But too many Zulus. We try to ride back down the mountain. My friend is *blessé*. Wounded. I try to help him. So they take me. The Zulu.' Cornelius Vijn explained his words to the Zulus.

'He is a liar,' said the *induna*. 'I found him hiding in the rocks at the foot of the mountain. On the opposite side from the red soldiers. He had run away.'

'I would suggest, Your Majesty,' McTeague said to Cetshwayo, 'that we play along with the fellow's story. He might be useful to us.'

'Bring him some of the tobacco and the juniper spirit that we found in the white camp,' said the King to one of the *indunas*. 'Show him that we mean him no harm. Now,' he said to McTeague, 'we will ask him about the traitor, Hamu kaMpande,' said Cetshwayo. 'Where is he?'

But Grandier was equally ignorant on this subject too, knew nothing about the current whereabouts of Cetshwayo's brother and rival, now gone over to the British.

'I fear that we may learn very little from him, sire,' said McTeague.

'Tell him to explain why I am being destroyed,' Cetshwayo bellowed. 'At least that! Why?'

The question shocked McTeague and he saw that it shocked Cetshwayo's *izikhulu*, his high councillors, too. In truth, McTeague was still unsure which way the war might swing. Until the last few days, he had been convinced that these AmaZulu, the People of Heaven, could just possibly pull it off. Chelmsford had presided over one disaster after another, only the defence at Rorke's Drift, at KwaJimu, diverting attention from his ineptitude. *Played that up for all it was worth too,* he thought. *After all, they had nowhere else to go, for pity's sake. And how long did they hold the place? A day and a night? Good grief, those poor fools at Eshowe were under siege for two entire months. Lost more men there too, though most of them from fever and dysentery.* The Zulu defeat at Gingindlovu had effectively brought the siege to an end. McTeague had been surprised by the outcome. Surprised and worried. And now Cetshwayo was almost publicly acknowledging defeat. *Time to reconsider my position,* he thought.

'It seems,' he said, when Grandier was unable to answer this final and most difficult of Cetshwayo's questions, 'that you are slandered by name, Great Lord, and slandered by nature.'

It was a play on words – the meaning of Cetshwayo being, after all, 'one who is slandered' – which amused McTeague. It amused the *izikhulu* also. It even seemed to lighten the King's dark mood, at least a little. And Grandier, the Frenchman, drew comfort from the change of atmosphere too, looked about him with an expression of hope in his eyes. Hope turned to positive exuberance when a travelling trunk was dragged from the piles of booty.

'Will I live then?' he said in his broken English, as one of the *izinduna* rummaged among the contents, discarding shirts, socks, a bible, until he found a simple but well-used briar pipe in a leather pouch, a tin of Lambert & Butler's Gold Flake and a bottle of Gilbey's London Gin.

'The Frenchman wants to know if you will permit him to live, Lord,' said McTeague.

'Are you worried about his life, or your own?' replied Cetshwayo. 'My warriors would kill you all without a moment's hesitation.'

Cornelius Vijn made that pathetic whimpering noise again.

'Where are your *cojones*, Dutchie?' snarled Maria Mestiza. 'He won't harm us.'

'But his warriors may do so,' said Vijn.

'That's true, of course!' said McTeague. 'But he'll protect us so long as we're useful to him. Or try to, at least.' He turned to Cetshwayo. 'Great King,' he said. 'Why not show him the big guns? The *mbayimbayi*. Use them

41

to send a message to Chelmsford. He values them highly.'

Cetshwayo thought about it briefly.

'And perhaps it will help with the French also,' the King suggested. 'If I send this man back, perhaps the French will see our good faith, influence the Fat Queen.' McTeague concealed a smile. *I fear that his grasp of international diplomacy may be somewhat lacking*, he thought. 'It is a strange thing, KaMtigwe,' Cetshwayo continued, 'but it was always the French that I feared. Never the English. I used to dream that it was they who would cause my downfall.'

He barked orders at an *induna*, then made his way to the exit of the storage hut, ducked through the low exit, Grandier hauled behind him. The Frenchman still clutched the briar pipe in one hand, bottle in the other, a slug trail of gin spilling in his wake.

'*Qu'est-ce qui se passe?*' he screamed. What's happening?

'Tell him to pipe down,' McTeague spat at the Dutchman. 'For God's sake, he'll have the whole *impi* on us.'

The gathered regiments had jumped to their feet as soon as Cetshwayo appeared again, spears pointed to the sky, ten thousand voices singing the royal salute, rank upon rank of the Zulu women ululating a greeting in his honour.

'Kill the whites! Kill the whites!' chanted the warriors, and Cetshwayo made no move to still them as he led the way down to the upper section of the open enclosure, its inner gateway now guarded by a pair of seven-pounder Rifled Muzzle-Loader field pieces which had once belonged to a two-gun section of 'N' Battery, British Army 5th Artillery Brigade, the bones of their bombardiers still bleaching on the slopes of eSandlwana.

'Tell him that he shall live,' said Cetshwayo, 'so long as he carries my message to Chelmsford.' Scattered about his feet lay the evidence of the Zulu attempts to operate the guns, the leather harnesses with which they had been manoeuvred, a variety of different shells, the percussion caps that they had tried to use in place of the proper friction detonator tubes. Cetshwayo raised his voice, his regal demeanour restored, so that the regiments would hear him. He projected his voice in that way that McTeague so admired among these people, for it rose on the thin end of summer air, danced upon the dun-coloured slopes that set emaHlabithini in this natural amphitheatre. 'Tell the Frenchman he must let Chelmsford know that we have the *mbayimbayi*. It is a great dishonour that Chelmsford should have lost them. But I shall return them as a sign of our good faith. And two hundred head of cattle. Also in good faith. Because too many of our young men have died on both sides. He will tell Chelmsford it is time to make peace. He will tell Chelmsford it is time for him to leave our lands. He will tell Chelmsford that only death awaits him if he does not do so.'

'*USuthu!*' shouted the warriors, and McTeague recognised it as the war cry of Cetshwayo's personal followers, used when they killed in his name, but serving also as a badge of collective pride, of supremacy, of wealth and well-being.

The Dutchman relayed the King's words and hope flared in Grandier's rheumy eyes.

'I will take the message,' he croaked, as Cetshwayo's mahogany throne was carried from the royal dwelling and set firmly between the guns, a blanket-wrapped bundle of rifles, ammunition cases also, laid alongside. The King settled himself squarely upon the seat, signalled for the noise to subside. His high councillors likewise settled around Cetshwayo. He shared some amusing observation with them, issued some whispered instruction to First Minister Mnyamana. The old fellow stood, dutifully.

'*Mayile!*' he shouted. '*Mayile!*'

And the women crowded forward, to form the beginnings of a circle and, with apparently total spontaneity, at the same time started to clap a steady rhythm, half singing a simple refrain to which the rest provided a melodious response.

Good Lord above, forgive this sinner, thought McTeague, *but these are handsome beauties.*

The only concession of the Zulu women to anything resembling western modesty was the piece of dressed ox-hide or cloth that they fastened about their waists. For the rest, to McTeague's eyes, they were admirably naked. Many wore a red top-knot on the back of their heads and he believed that these were the married women, or perhaps those available for marriage. Maybe both, for some of them carried children strapped to their backs. He had a fine collection of wives already, of course. *But always room for a few more*, he thought. *Especially when you see them like this.*

Maria would not be happy. She was never happy when he took new wives. Not jealousy, of course. She thought of herself more as his bodyguard than anything else. More a business partner than a conjugal spouse. But she rejected any notion that he might genuinely love her, happily grasped the fact that his other women were more a product of his lust for them than his affection, and saw yet more additions to his household merely as an irritating encumbrance. She could generally be pacified, however, with the argument that great chiefs measured status by the number of wives that they possessed. And, while the complement of his own harem may now have surpassed a dozen, he was still sadly deficient compared to his rival, John Dunn. *How many does the fellow have now? Forty? Forty-five. I've damn'd well lost count.*

'Tomorrow,' Cetshwayo was saying, 'we shall also send emissaries to the amaBalobedu. To their Rain Queen. We will ask her to send a great flood, like in your bible, KaMtigwe. A flood that will trap the red soldiers in mud. And once they are trapped...'

*

43

McTeague watched the warrior receive his rewards. And few others had received recognition this day. No willow wand necklaces. No regiment of note.

'But this man,' shouted the King, 'is Tshabanga, son of Ndabuko the Iron-Maker. When the rest of you were running away, this one stopped to use his rifle. He used it to kill a mighty *induna* of the red soldiers. A giant among their ranks. So, from this day forward, he shall be entitled to use the honour name, Giant Slayer. Come forward, Tshabanga, Giant Slayer, son of Ndabuko.' The young man moved hesitantly, tall and stick-thin, with just one good eye. The other, the left, was milky, blind. He knelt at Cetshwayo's feet, received a modern Martini-Henry rifle that the King took from the blanket. 'You will use this to kill more of the whites,' he continued, 'and you shall have five cattle from the royal herd as tribute for your deeds.'

The warrior's face glowed with pride as he stretched out his hands to receive the weapon, careful to keep his gaze averted from that of his lord and master. But as he edged backwards, returning to the short line of others waiting to receive the King's favour, he could not resist lifting the rifle towards the sky.

'*USuthu!*' he yelled, and the regiments took up the cry.

'There is this also,' said Cetshwayo, 'that our true friend, KaMtigwe, for the loyal service that he continues to give us, shall be granted another wife from those eligible for marriage. Know, People of Heaven, that he has my blessing and protection. For he has counselled well today.'

He must have been reading my mind, thought McTeague. *Bless him. Need to take it steady this time though.* Wife number thirteen had given him a considerable amount of satisfaction but he had paid something of a price for his pleasure. Chest pains. Excruciating. A distinct shortness of breath. Debilitated for days afterwards.

Maria Mestiza invoked some Miskito curse while the Dutchman gave him a look of such contempt that McTeague was uncertain whether it was driven by envy or pure Calvinism. *Well, I shall atone to God in my usual way,* he thought. *And I shall, naturally, follow the requirements of Exodus 21:10. 'If he takes him another wife, her food, her raiment and her duty of marriage he shall not diminish.' Well, I never have. Diminished any of those things, that is.* He was feeling pleased with himself and thus almost missed the heated exchange that was taking place between Cetshwayo and Chief Ntshingwayo. McTeague caught enough of the words to know that the hero of eSandlwana was complaining bitterly about the King's decision to honour this white interloper, about the fact that it was the *izikhulu*, the Council of Ministers, that had been responsible for the forthcoming change of strategy, not this glass-eye and his Witch Woman. But, unfortunately for Ntshingwayo, the King recalled that he was also responsible for the disaster at eKhambule, and he waved him aside.

'Know this too!' Cetshwayo continued. 'That there shall be no more useless attacks on the white men's camps. In future, if any disobey this order, they shall see me. And I will be the last thing they shall see. In future, if we must fight them, we fight only on ground of our choosing. I hope that their iNkosi, Chelmsford, will see reason now, when we offer to return the *mbayimbayi*. That he will sue for peace. But, meanwhile, we shall sting them like the gnat. We will form new companies of scouts. Brave men like Tshabanga kaNdabuko, Tshabanga the Giant Slayer, taken from each of the regiments and working together. They will be chosen men. A chosen *induna* to lead them too. The bravest of my brave. They will follow the rivers, these swarms. And the hidden valleys. They will be always in the shadow of the whites whenever they try to move. Biting them again and again until, finally, we shall catch them in the open, spread too thinly to build their walls, to *laager* their wagons. On that day, if Chelmsford and his Fat Queen have not sought to make peace, we will destroy them.'

There seemed no end to the dancing, though the sky remained unblemished, not even a hint of precipitation. *Perhaps when they send to the Rain Queen*, McTeague mused, and wondered whether the Lord might accept a prayer from himself to supplement the dancers' efforts. *How would that go?* he wondered. *A prayer from the most devout of His servants to aid the Heathen.* And, throughout, Cetshwayo sat still and attentive, as though he too had sprung entire from the mahogany. He only seemed distracted on the occasions when Ntshingwayo, or one of the other chieftains, ventured to engage the King in heated debate, attempted to persuade him to some alternative viewpoint on the war's conduct.

McTeague took advantage of one such propitious diversion to move closer towards the Dutchman, leaning across Maria Mestiza so that Cornelius Vijn would hear him clearly. At the same time, he clutched the sleeve of Ernest Grandier's tattered uniform shirt.

'Tell him, Dutchie,' said McTeague, 'that when he takes the message to Chelmsford about the guns, he must take another one too.'

Vijn looked quickly towards Cetshwayo, like a nervous child afraid of being caught in another's classroom mischief.

'Can we trust him?' said the Dutchman.

'He speaks no Zulu and barely any English,' hissed McTeague. 'Personally, I would be more concerned about whether we can trust *you*, Dutchie.'

Maria Mestiza caressed the bone handle of her hunting knife.

'The Dutchman knows,' she said, 'that he has more to fear from Maria Cuchilla than from a hundred Zulus. *¿Verdad*, Dutchie?'

'We are all in this together,' said Cornelius Vijn. 'But be quick. What is your message?'

'Tell him,' said McTeague, 'to make sure Chelmsford knows that he has friends in Cetshwayo's camp. That it is Major McTeague who will make sure his guns are returned. McTeague who will deliver Cetshwayo to him, if he wishes.'

The Dutchman looked uncertain but he whispered the message anyway, in rapid French, while the dancers finally completed their ritual and Cetshwayo returned to his hut.

McTeague eased himself to his feet, rubbed at cramped muscles, just as somebody touched his back, caught him by surprise, caused him to straighten too quickly, a spasm of pain in his spine, the monocle falling from his eye.

'What the...' He spun around, found himself confronted by a warrior, pinched face scarred in several places, a thin wisp of beard sprouting from his chin. But his most startling characteristic was the way in which he held McTeague's own gaze. *Like a damn'd European*, he thought.

'I see you, iNkosi,' said the warrior, in broken English.

For a moment, McTeague thought about the message he had passed to Grandier, wondered if they had been overheard. But the Zulu's demeanour seemed to pose no threat.

'I am here, warrior of the Skirmishers,' he replied. He was rewarded with a sly smile. An informed guess, for the fellow was probably in his mid-thirties, unmarried, and his shield was black cow-hide without markings. So almost certainly from the *ibutho* which they called uNokhenke, the Skirmishers. 'You have excellent English,' he continued, spreading the words slowly, like honey over bread.

'I was raised by the Dutch,' said the warrior. 'But now I am indeed numbered among the uNokhenke.' He changed idiom, spoke now in IsiZulu. 'And is it true, iNkosi, that you can choose your new wife from any of the women ready for marriage?'

'The Great King normally takes delight in selecting on my behalf. Naturally, he has never made a poor choice.'

Maria Mestiza spat a Miskito obscenity at McTeague, a wicked jibe at his virility, and the Zulu turned towards her, uncomprehending but averting his eyes, at least, from the Witch Woman.

'I know a woman who is available,' he continued. 'A very beautiful woman. She could bear you sons, iNkosi.'

Sons, thought McTeague. There were already children, of course. Many children. Black children. So much for Maria Mestiza's taunt, then. But no sons. Strange, yet there it was.

'And this woman,' he said, 'you are sure that she is beautiful?'

'Like the most wondrous of our Nguni cattle, Lord. A hide of golden brown. Docile yet intelligent. Fertile and free from disease.'

'Your sister, perhaps?'

'No, iNkosi, not my sister.'

'Cousin then? Or a niece?'

'Not a member of my family, Lord, though part of my household now.'

'How so?' said McTeague. 'And if she is merely a member of your

46

household, how might you prosper from this?'

'The war will not last forever, iNkosi,' said the warrior. 'And when it is over, I think that many things may have changed. They say that gold may soon be more valuable than cattle. And they say that you have much gold, Lord. You will see that this woman is worth much gold. We can agree a price for her, if you wish it. The woman was pledged to me. As collateral. In a wager. A wager placed by that same fellow you saw earlier, swaggering in the light of the honour that our Great King bestowed upon him. Tshabanga the Giant Slayer. He lost the wager, iNkosi.'

Chapter Four

Wednesday 16th April 1879

Nightmare visions of Umdeni's death returned to him every time he slept. The red soldiers. The rise and fall of the musket butt. His friend's blood and brains upon the rocks. The valour with which Umdeni had faced his last moments.

It was Shaba's own fault, he now realised.

He had wished for too much. He had been greedy, like Gingile the Hunter in the story from his childhood. *Kwasuka sukela...* Once upon a time, Gingile had heard the call of Ngede, the Greater Honeyguide, and – as was the custom – followed the little bird when it led him to a great fig tree where it settled on a branch. The bird cocked its head, singing. '*Chitik, chitik, chitik,*' it cried. 'Come now! Here it is.' So Gingile made a fire stick, climbed with it to the hive, used the burning brand to drive out the bees and, when they had left, drew out heavy handfuls of the dripping honeycomb full of grubs. Juicy and white.

Ngede the Honeyguide waited patiently on the branch for its normal reward, since hunters – human or otherwise – always left the little bird an offering. Some of the waxy comb, full of the larval bees. It had always been thus. But on this particular day, Gingile had simply taken all the spoils, laughing at Ngede's protests and returning to his homestead.

Then, weeks later, Gingile had once again heard the call of the Honeyguide, remembered the sweetness of the honey he had gathered, and watched as the bird settled in an umbrella thorn to sing its tune. He made a fire stick once more, gripped it between his teeth so that he could climb into the tree, while Ngede sat and watched him. But there was no buzz of bees this day, so Gingile climbed higher and, as he did so, he came face to face with a leopard sleeping in the branches. Gingile screamed, woke and startled the beast. The leopard swiped at him with her paw, claws slicing across his forehead so that he fell backwards out of the tree.

Gingile had been lucky that the leopard could not be bothered pursuing him, so he managed to drag his broken body back home. He would carry the scars upon his forehead forever more, and would never again follow the Honeyguide. But his children, his children's children, all the way down to Tshabanga kaNdabuko, would hear the tale and learn respect for the little bird.

They would know that, when there is honey to be harvested, you should never be too greedy, you should always leave a little to share with those to whom you owe your fortune, to give them the thanks they deserve.

Well, he thought, *as soon as we have taken this white man back to his friends, and I have received the cattle from the Great King, I will make an offering to the ancestors, take home my new wealth and give one of the beasts to my father.*

He did not understand the whites at the best of times, but he understood this one even less. He belonged to the AmaFulentshi, a tribe that were neighbours to the English and Dutch – great rivals and often at war with each other, though Shaba could discern little difference between any of them.

'They say that they were nearly a great people,' he said to the others around him while they shared porridge as the awakening sun smeared carmine streaks against the last grey clouds of night.

'Creatures like that one?' said the Company's *induna,* Mnukwa.

'Perhaps he is a bad example,' Shaba replied. 'A stunted calf. Like those produced when a bull is kept for too long, and covers his own daughters.'

'And who says they were nearly great?' said another of the warriors, Langalabelele. He spoke with the slow drawl of his district. 'These AmaFulentshi.'

'It was the German preacher, Volker,' said Shaba. 'He came to Hluhluwe, six winters ago. Seeking followers for his iNkosi, Jesucristo. He said that the AmaFulentshi had recently fought a war against his own people. The AmaFulentshi had been beaten very badly. It was the end of them. The preacher, Volker, said that the AmaFulentshi are finished now.' Shaba suddenly regarded their captive in a new light. Some sense of empathy. He pitied him. 'But he told us,' he continued, 'that their King, who was called Napole...' – Shaba pronounced the strange word with great care, '...that he was the nephew of another with the same name who had been King long before. That this other was a great legend. Who always wore an enormous hat. Who had only one arm. But who had led great hordes of warriors in blue coats that swept all before them, conquered many lands.'

'But not the lands of the AmaZulu,' said Mnukwa.

'No,' said Shaba. 'Not these lands.'

'And did this preacher for Jesucristo find many followers at your homestead, Giant Slayer?' asked Langalabelele.

'Not many,' Shaba replied. *Though he found a few,* he thought. And he remembered the one who had become a *kholwa,* changed his name to Joseph, later accused of being a poisoner by some of the old women in the village. They had dragged the fellow out one day when the missionary was visiting. So he could see, they said, the evil of the Jesucristo followers. And they had burned him with fire sticks – like those used by Gingile to frighten the bees –

until Joseph had confessed his crimes. The preacher had offered them cattle in exchange for Joseph's life and it had seemed that the offer would be accepted. But while the missionary was negotiating with Shaba's father, the women had dragged Joseph to the river, thrown him to the crocodiles, calling him 'kaffir', the way the whites did whenever they sneered at the People of Heaven – and all the other folk of these lands.

'They are quite mad,' said Mnukwa, 'these *amakholwa*. The preachers came to my own homestead many times. Trying to tell us that this Jesucristo is the king of all kings. Even the children laughed at them. *How can this be?* they used to say. *When we have our own King – and he has never even heard of this Jesucristo.* So the preachers told us that the demon they call Satan would punish us for all eternity. Because we would not believe in their god.'

'It makes no sense,' said Shaba. 'Why would this Satan, the enemy of their Jesucristo, punish those who had served *him*, instead of their god? Would he not rather reward them?'

'In any case,' said Langalabelele, 'our own lore is full of demons – and heroes who simply drive them away. With trickery. Or with spears. Do these followers of Jesucristo have no heroes?'

They all shrugged.

'I asked the preacher once,' said Shaba, after a pause, 'why our Great King had never heard of this Jesucristo. You know what he said?' They did not know. 'He said,' Shaba continued, 'that Cetshwayo had not yet heard the word of their god. He told me this with great difficulty. Because he did not speak IsiZulu very well. And it occurred to me that this god they worship – who they claim made everything, knows everything – perhaps does not speak IsiZulu either. What sort of god can it be that does not understand the language of the People of Heaven?'

They laughed, and Mnukwa poked the prisoner with the shaft of his spear.

'Get up!' said the *induna*, and the white man stirred, fear filling his eyes as it did every time he woke and recalled his whereabouts. He said something in his own idiom, strange sounds, yet linguistic rhythms almost like Shaba's own. What else had the preacher told him of these AmaFulentshi? That they thought the English hilarious. That their breath smelled foul, like a rancid swamp. That they were a nation of fornicators. That they enjoyed pulling the legs from frogs. What else? And could they truly have conquered many lands. Yet here was another wonder. For when he had been issued with his old percussion rifle – the one he had left upon the battlefield and now replaced with the fine new weapon which the Great King had personally placed in his hands – somebody had told him that it, too, had been fashioned by the AmaFulentshi. He had forgotten that. Until now.

He thought about it as their small party dragged the miserable specimen towards their destination, a halter tied around his neck. They had left most of the Company back in the hills to the south. On the near rim of the ridge that joined the Tamela, the Inyati and the Pondwana peaks. This new Company, this Swarm, fifty strong, one of the many mixed regiment groups with which the Great King was determined to fight his 'little war' – as he himself described it – by which they might draw the red soldiers out into the open. So Shaba's companions were men from his own Evil Omens, and also from the Skirmishers, the Bender of Kings, several others. And from the main Swarm, Mnukwa had chosen just five to guard the white man on this final stage of the journey, to lead him back to his own lines near eKhambule.

They had left emaHlabithini three days ago and made appallingly slow progress. Because of the white man, naturally. They had kicked and cajoled, threatened and bribed, but he had seemed entirely incapable of anything but a snail's pace as they followed the pathways and passes above the White Patient Ox towards the eZunganyene mountains, almost retracing the route they had taken before the last battle.

It was late morning when they saw the horsemen.

'Dutchmen,' said Shaba. They were easy to distinguish for they wore no uniform at all, just the everyday clothes of the iBhunu farmers.

'I thought we had killed all those that rode with the red soldiers at eHlobane,' said Langalabelele. 'I know that we ate their chief.' He made a chopping gesture in front of his lips, blowing on the tips of his fingers as he did so. 'I saw him die.'

The Bender of Kings regiment had been there, of course. The Sharp Points. The Fly Catchers too. But eHlobane was also the home to Cetshwayo's great allies, the AbaQulusi Clan. It was they who had seen the thick of the fighting. And living among the AbaQulusi was the legendary Prince, Mbilini kaMswati, rightful ruler of the neighbouring AmaSwazi. The Prince had been in exile here since the days of King Mpande, and the Fat Queen hated him, it was said. Called him Hyena. For he was very successful at raiding the Dutch farmers. And his ancestral lands across the northern river. Or the *amakholwa* converts to the Jesucristo. It was said also that the Prince was one of the excuses used by the Fat Queen to invade Cetshwayo's Kingdom. Because the Great King had not punished Prince Mbilini for whatever she thought he had done wrong.

The long bulk of eHlobane was before them now, in the distance, a little to their right, flanked by the flattened peaks of Ntendoka and Ityenka. To their left was the Great Gap and, further left again, the black ramparts of eZunganyene. They stood on a low rise, with three scrub-covered fingers stretching, digging deep into an ample valley, rivulets dancing across the knuckles, falling between callous rock to plunge through fern and moss. Beyond the valley, broken ground all the way to that dark escarpment, treeless, vacant of the herds and flocks which would normally have given it life, its homesteads abandoned or burned. Parched and bare. For the waters all flow eastwards here, down towards the reeds and mud swamps where the Black Patient Ox is born, far from the birthplace of its brother river, the White Patient Ox, away in the north-west.

Mnukwa poked the prisoner again.

'Look,' he said. 'There are your friends.'

He pointed towards the horsemen and the white man peered roughly in the required direction but seemed neither to see nor understand. So Mnukwa grasped the fellow's skull, forced it to face correctly. extending his arm and finger so that the man could sight along them. Yet there was still no response beyond a further look of stark apprehension, and the *induna* pushed the prisoner away from him in exasperation.

'Remove the rope,' he shouted.

Shaba lifted the halter from the man's neck, then shoved him in the general direction of the Dutchmen. The fool took only a couple of steps, then turned back to his captors. They had seen such behaviour before, of course. When the children of their homesteads might care for a sickly kid goat which then later found difficulty returning to the flock of its own kind.

'Go!' said Shaba, waving his arms, herding the prisoner northwards.

'Be careful,' said Mnukwa. 'We don't want to attract the iBhunu.'

The Frenchman at last seemed to understand, began to move away from them, and Langalabelele shook his stabbing spear at him for good measure, while Shaba pointed the barrel of his new rifle in the general direction that he should follow. But within minutes the white man had veered away to the east, still unaware of the horsemen, and now running a course roughly parallel to that being followed by his potential rescuers.

'He will never find them,' said Mnukwa.

'Why should we trouble?' said Shaba. 'Leave him here to die.'

'The way he's going,' Mnukwa replied, 'he'll run all the way back to emaHlabithini – and the Great King will have our hides. Come on!'

He led them from their vantage point, down into a gulley that would help them head off the white man. They could no longer see the horses but Shaba was confident that, if necessary, they could outrun them over this rough ground. They had almost overtaken their quarry and now began to beat lightly upon their shields, to make small whooping sounds until, having terrified him sufficiently, they managed to turn him back onto a more helpful track while, from the top of a rise, they watched the fool's clumsy descent of the far side, the horsemen so close now that the Dutchmen finally saw him.

Mnukwa and his men dropped into the grass, vanishing from view. There was a risk that the Frenchman might give away their presence but they doubted that he would be sufficiently coherent to make himself understood. And they were correct. They could hear him, just about, stammering and jabbering like a demented monkey, the leader of the Dutchmen growing visibly more frustrated with the fellow until, finally, he was hauled up behind one of the riders. Their leader took a pair of the far-seeing glasses from a pouch on his saddle, surveyed the surrounding hills for a long time, then ordered his troop to turn for home, towards the Great Gap.

The warriors remained still for a long time until even Shaba's sharp vision could no longer reach them.

'Well,' said Mnukwa, 'there is one thing upon which we may depend. That we have at least seen the last of the AmaFulentshi.'

The second patrol, when they saw it, was very different from the first. Red soldiers on horses were an unusual sight. For red soldiers fought on foot. Shaba had learned this. Horse soldiers wore cloth of black. Or blue. Or shirts the colour of dried dung – like that of the Frenchman, or the Basuto folk that rode for the Fat Queen. So here was an unusual thing. And there was a second thing out of the ordinary. For the warriors they were pursuing were not AmaZulu.

Mnukwa had led his small group back to join the rest of the Swarm on the ridges to the south and then, following the instructions given them by the Great King's First Minister, they had made their way on a circuit of the local homesteads, gathering the latest intelligence about the red soldiers' movements. But there was little to discover. Few left who could tell them anything. For the settlements were mostly deserted here also. The clusters of huts and cattle enclosures around eNgeniseni, Shalala, Kulabatu and ebaQulusini either smoking ruin or populated only by the old, those too feeble to travel.

A great silence had settled upon the Company and Shaba knew that they shared a common fear – that here was the fate that awaited the whole country if they could not quickly bring the Fat Queen's regiments to battle and defeat them. They would be left with nothing but soot-stained wasteland. Everywhere, from the sharp-peaked Barrier of Spears to the Blue Ocean. Fire-blackened, it would become, filled with the chimneys of the whites, belching clouds of poisonous filth to blot out the sky in the same way, it was said, as the homesteads, the townships, the capital of the Fat Queen herself.

So they searched for soldiers that they might kill. To restore their spirits, their manhood. But they had not expected to find any so soon. And in such a strange situation, in pursuit of warriors so evidently belonging to the AmaSwazi. They also were a proud people. Perhaps too proud. For when they went into battle, they still kept the habit of wearing full ceremonial uniform. Cloaks of animal hide. Fringes of cow-tails on arms and legs. Elaborate head-dresses, with ear-flaps of monkey skin, the black and white feathers of *intshe*, the ostrich, and the huge basket-work ball, the *umnyakanya*, woven through with porcupine quill and the long sable plumage of *isakabuli*, the widow-bird.

Larger shields, like the *izihlangu* which the People of Heaven carried to war before the days of the Great King's reforms. These were such warriors, lean and strong, led by a grey-beard with a mantle of zebra pelt. Yet led badly. For the defile through which they ran, the red horse soldiers at their heels, had no escape, simply a vertical wall at its end from which the AmaSwazi would be shot while trying to scale its face.

'This way,' said Mnukwa, leading the Company across a fast-flowing stream, scrambling down the boulders through which the water grumbled and groaned, separating the group so that some would arrive at the defile's head, while a second party moved towards the soldiers' rump, and Mnukwa himself, with Shaba and Langalabelele close behind, kept low among all the cover which the terrain could provide, to bring themselves near the horsemen's flank. Thus, they would be the chest and loins of this small *impi*, whilst the others should act as its horns.

But why, Shaba asked himself, bounding from rock to rock, and maintaining a tight grip on shield and rifle, would the AmaSwazi be so far south? The Swazi had no great love for the People of Heaven and many of them from along the border had been persuaded to fight on the side of the red soldiers, still wearing their full regalia with only the addition of a coloured rag strip around their arm to identify them as servants of the whites. And many of them had died, too, at the eHlobane fight.

He was still at Mnukwa's tail when the *induna* crossed the stream once more, returning to its left bank, into a patch of stunted trees, though not all the warriors in their group followed him. It seemed reasonable that they should spread themselves along this edge of the defile as the red soldiers finally came in sight through the low branches that were sharp with the smell of pine resin. But it was a mistake. For Shaba saw that those who had remained on the opposite side of the rivulet were now virtually stranded on a rock outcrop.

Before him were the soldiers. There were perhaps a dozen of them, mostly dismounted now and formed into a firing line, the rest either still in their saddles or holding the horses a little to the rear. Yet it was a ragged line, the bearded whites laughing and calling to each other like hunters in their harsh tongue as they moved clumsily up the width of the small valley, then pausing at the command of their own *induna*, guns raised and the sky filled with the crash and echo of their volley – aimed, Shaba assumed, at the AmaSwazi. These would be Swazi from the borderlands too, of course, but belonging to those with family ties and other binding loyalties to the Great King, followers of their exiled Prince Mbilini, whose stronghold lay on the farther side of the Trough River, the Phongolo, among its impenetrable gorges and deep pools, at Mbongweni. The Prince had fought at their side at eKhambule, of course. *But why so far south?* he wondered once more, as they broke into the open ground beyond the trees.

The effect on the soldiers was immediate, for three things happened at the same instant. Shaba could not see them from here, but he clearly heard the war cries of the right horn, whose warriors must by now have appeared at the head of the defile.

'Ji! Ji!' they were shouting.

Then the men from Mnukwa's group on the other bank of the stream began to fire down on the white men from the crag to his right. Mnukwa himself took up the shout, 'We are the boys from eSandlwana!' while launching one of his throwing spears towards the enemy line. It was a skilful cast, the blade burying itself in a soldier's chest as the fellow turned his astonished gaze to this new threat, laughing no longer. The hunters now hunted. For, despite the reverses which his people may have suffered in recent weeks, Shaba knew – every warrior in each *ibutho* knew – that the Battle of the Little House had scarred the red soldiers deeply. They were good warriors, certainly, but the story of that fight could spark in them a terror which must be seen to be believed. The terror of surprise attack.

He saw it now. Three of the whites simply threw down their rifles and ran for the horses. And even the horses seemed infected by the fear of their masters, bucking and screaming, two of them breaking loose from the soldier who tried to hold them. *Well*, he thought, as he threw his own first spear, *they are right to be afraid*. He would wash the blade of his *iklwa* again today. In honour of Umdeni. There had been no time for medicine, nor cleansing. No snuff either. But his battle fury needed no stimulant as he ran towards these filthy violators, these destroyers of his lands. With their ugly pink faces. Their red coats. Their leggings and helmets the colour of sickness shit.

'Take prisoners!' shouted Mnukwa, and Shaba remembered Cetshwayo's admonition that red soldiers should be captured wherever possible. True red soldiers, not useless AmaFulentshi.

Easier said than done though, he thought.

The whites were falling back in a group, bullets pecking at the dirt and stones all around them from the crag and the head of the defile. Erratic fire that put fear into Shaba's guts. He remembered eSandlwana, some of their own warriors mown down by the careless bullets of friends. So he ran left, down the gulley in the same direction as the soldiers but just far enough away to stay outside the field of fire.

Mnukwa saw the danger.

'Come back!' he yelled, for Shaba, Langalabelele and the others were being forced by the gulley's sides on a path that was leading them ever closer to the red soldiers, further from their friends, and in numbers now reduced to almost equal those of the enemy.

The whites had closed together into a tight clutch, seemingly determined on a final volley before trying to flee, and gathered just in front of the horses, which still reared and shied at the noise about them. Shaba saw rifles raised to shoulders. He knew that his death was staring at him. He saw no future beyond this moment. No fame. No wealth of cattle. No wife and no dowry.

He imagined that Umdeni stood alongside him.

'Down!' said the spirit.

'Down!' cried Mnukwa.

But Shaba, warned early by his friend's ghost was already throwing himself to the dusty earth as the bullets blew through the air like wind through the high passes. A warrior fell beside him, still living, twitching, sobbing, but the side of his face removed, so that the tongue lolled useless from the open cavern of his jaw, the teeth and bone exposed on its far side. Shaba rolled, looked up to see half the soldiers leaping for their saddles, the other three or four fumbling in waist pouches for ammunition, terror making them clumsy as they pushed forward the weapon's lever action, tried to slide a fresh round into the breech.

Like a miracle, Langalabelele still stood, unscathed.

'USuthu!' he howled, and jumped over Shaba to close with the soldiers before they could fire again. The red-coated *induna*, already mounted, had a revolver in his hand, waved it unsteadily towards Langalabelele. He fired. And missed. Then he fell from the horse, with Langalabelele's second throwing spear stuck through his arm. There was confusion. There were more shots. Shaba was up, following Langalabelele's example, Mnukwa now at *his* tail. More warriors too. The AmaSwazi rushing in on the right, their white cow-tails streaming from arms and legs. Shaba realised that he had bitten his own tongue when he hit the ground, so the iron taste of blood filled his mouth. The taste of his own homestead. The taste of iron that meant family. His father. His father's trade. And it filled him with a fury so strong that it carried him across the open ground, running hard behind one of the red soldiers who was trying desperately to get a foot in the stirrup, to swing into the saddle, as his horse bolted away. He brought the *iklwa* up, over his head. Not the cutting up-thrust that he would normally use, but a ferocious downward hacking that sank the blade deep through the soldier's spine with a splintering, bone-snapping impact.

'USuthu!' called Shaba as the fellow released his grip on the pommel and was propelled forward for several steps, though quite dead, by his own momentum.

To Shaba's left, the warriors that Mnukwa had sent to act as the left horn were coming up fast, trying to join the fray, to head off the last of the retreating horsemen.

But it was all over.

The riders, those that had survived, bolted down the far side of the narrow valley, leaving their dead behind them. Five of them. The fellow killed by Mnukwa's throwing spear. One shot through the neck. One killed by

Langalabelele. The one with the *iklwa* buried so deep in the body that Shaba could not easily pull it free. And the red-coated *induna*. Though this latter was not dead. He was curled tight on the ground, making a noise as though he were straining with the belly gripes, gripping his right arm with left hand just above the place where the spear shaft, slender and quivering, had impaled the limb, pinning the soldier to the ground when he fell from his horse. The AmaSwazi stood over him, prodding the officer's side with the points of their own spears, laughing, taunting him. One of them lifted his weapon, intent on finishing him off, but Shaba brought up the barrel of his rifle to prevent him.

'Stop!' he said. 'The Great King has ordered that we should take prisoners. We will take this one.'

Shaba would have been equally happy to kill the white man too, but he saw another opportunity. The prisoner would be his. One white *induna* shot by the Giant Slayer at eKhambule. Another taken captive here. He would become a legend.

'Whey, Zula,' replied the warrior in his own language – but the form of IsiSwazi employed by those along the border, closer to Shaba's own dialect than the true *siSwati* spoken elsewhere in that neighbouring and troublesome kingdom. 'It was we that the red soldiers were chasing. This one's soul belongs to us.'

'You would all be dead,' snarled Mnukwa, 'if we had not intervened. It would have been this red soldier claiming *your* soul. This is the land of the Great King, Cetshwayo kaMpande. And everything in this land belongs to him. Including this thing.'

'You mean everything in the land that the red soldiers have not pillaged from you,' said the Swazi. 'And we carry tidings to your King. We could take this thing with us if you truly want him as a captive.'

'Tidings?' said Mnukwa. 'To where would the bakaMswati be carrying their words?'

'To oNdini.'

'To the capital? What can be so important that you make such a journey?'

'The tidings are evil,' said the warrior. 'For our Prince, the Blessed Mbilini kaMswati is dead.'

These were evil tidings indeed. The Prince was admired throughout the Kingdom for his deeds, his loyalty to Cetshwayo though he was not of his kinfolk.

'How?' said Mnukwa. 'How, dead?'

The Swazi smiled.

'As a Prince should die,' he replied. 'Fighting these white invaders.'

He put his foot on the red soldier, pressed downwards so that the officer screamed with pain.

'Leave him,' said Mnukwa. 'And you men…' The *induna* nodded towards

Shaba and Langalabelele. '...Pull him free. See what you can do with that wound. We need to keep him alive if it's possible.'

Shaba looked at his companion, who shrugged, bent to grasp the spear shaft while Shaba himself knelt at the white man's side, setting down his shield and rifle.

'We will take this out,' he said, knowing that the soldier would not understand yet speaking slowly and trying to sound reassuring. He pulled the thin wooden snuff spoon from his hair, placed it between the man's teeth so that he could bite down on it. His father had carved it for him. It was a sad loss. But as he went to place his hands on the man's arm, the fellow spat out the spoon, kicked hard, caught Shaba on the knees with his metal-studded boots, sent him sprawling backwards. At the same time, the soldier's left hand reached under his body, grasped the revolver that had fallen beneath him and twisted onto his back, even though his other arm was still spiked to the ground. For a moment, Shaba thought to speak to him. Perhaps his reassurances had not been sufficiently persuasive. To tell him that Cetshwayo would care for him as he had done for the hapless Frenchman. Such a foolish thought.

The gathered warriors all took a couple of defensive steps backwards. The revolver fired. Once. A bullet to the Swazi's chest that bowled him backwards. Twice. But failed to find Langalabelele, his target. Then the soldier lifted the thing and placed it to his own head. Shaba moved snake-fast despite the throbbing of his knees, reached across the man and swiped his hand away. The revolver spun across the dirt. The red soldier glared at him, shouted some form of curse, then rolled back on his side and gripped the impaled arm once more. *Perhaps he did not understand that we were trying to help*, thought Shaba.

'Damn him!' said Mnukwa. 'But at least we still have a prisoner.' He put a restraining arm across the other two Swazis who were plainly intent on revenge.

Shaba rose painfully to his feet, picked up his rifle. He realised that he was full of self-recrimination. He felt stupid. Guilty at the same time. This man was an enemy. An invader. He deserved nothing. But they had tried to save him, albeit at the behest of the Great King. And this was how they were repaid. Then he thought of Umdeni. That last time he had seen his friend. Shaba lifted the rifle, gripped it with both hands. And before *induna* Mnukwa could stop him, he brought the butt crashing down into the red soldier's face. Red. Red. Red.

He listened as the surviving AmaSwazi told the story of Prince Mbilini's death.

'After the fight at eKhambule,' one of the pair said, 'the Prince gathered our people together again. Until we had enough to form an *impi* of our own to strike back at the whites. Then he led us up the Bhivane Valley to attack their farms. Most of the whites had fled. But we caught some and killed them. We also took many of the cattle that they'd left behind.'

'And the red soldiers,' said Mnukwa. 'Did you see their army?'

'Their main force is still at eKhambule,' replied the other Swazi. 'But their camp is even bigger now. There are more of them. And the Prince took some prisoners of his own. Some of the Basuto slave-boys who run with them. And a few of our people fighting for the whites.'

The warrior spat upon the ground.

'What did the Prince learn?' said Mnukwa.

'That the white iNkosi – the one they call Wood, who led them at eKhambule – has orders to gather still more men, then march to oNdini. They plan to attack Cetshwayo with a beast of their own. Chelmsford with the chest and loins. The others forming the left and right horns.'

'When will this be?'

'We did not learn this thing. But it cannot be long. They are already dismantling the camp at eKhambule.'

Mnukwa nodded.

'So what happened to the Prince?' he asked.

'He had sent many men away with the cattle we had taken, but we continued to raid. Then we found horses. A lot of horses. We were driving these home too when the red soldiers attacked. The Prince was shot. Here...' He pointed to the top of his right shoulder. 'But it came out again here...' He patted his left hip. 'A terrible wound. And the thing must have ripped through his innards as it went. He was in such pain.'

'Then he did not die straight away?'

The Swazi laughed.

'You did not know Prince Mbilini kaMswati well then, Zula?' he said. 'Or you would certainly not have asked such a foolish thing. With such a wound, *you* would certainly have been dead. Any of us would have been. But the Prince lived for a full seven suns more. Travelled all the way back to Mbongweni. To die with those that loved him.'

They all fell silent for a while until, finally, Mnukwa looked towards the west.

'There is still work to do here,' he said, 'and the shadows grow. Those horsemen will bring more red soldiers if we stay here too long.'

The warriors knew it. Shaba knew it.

There were four of the AmaSwazi dead. And six of Mnukwa's Swarm. The ten bodies were therefore laid together in a depression near the side of the stream, their shields covering them, stones placed loosely on top. The souls would be placated this way, at least for a while. Then there were the whites to deal with. It was generally accepted that they had not fought well, not like the lions they had faced at eSandlwana. So there was little enthusiasm for the *ukuhlomula* – the honour cuts – on this occasion, though there were a few who thought it worthwhile to stab the red soldiers again, even if only to show that their killing was a collective achievement. But, valiant or not, if left untreated the souls of these devils would be trapped there, unable to find their way safely to the afterlife. And if they were prevented from making that journey, the spirits would surely remain to haunt whoever had been responsible for the killings.

Shaba had heard terrible stories of warriors who had not taken steps to free the spirits of those they had slain, how those demons had entered the warriors' own bodies, first causing nightmare visions, then total madness and, finally, a swelling of their stomachs. Bigger and bigger until they burst apart. He had not been able to observe this necessary ritual in relation to the rancid fat soldier he had slain at eKhambule, nor the red soldiers' iNkosi that he had shot there, and he had indeed been afflicted for some days afterwards while he was staying at the cleansing houses until his treatment by the *izinyanga* was complete. The medicine men had told him that his affliction would have been much worse if the spirit of Umdeni had not been watching over him. So he was careful to follow all the ceremonies today, to begin the process afresh of cleansing both body and mind. For, until the cleansing was complete once more, his companions would be in fear for their own souls, in fear that they might somehow also become infected by the spirits of Shaba's dead.

Thus he went first to the fellow he had stabbed in the back, stood on him and used both hands to retrieve his spear. Then, after they had stripped the coats and shirts from all five whites, he went to the dead officer, used the blade of his *iklwa* to open the man's stomach, dragged the point upwards until it jarred upon the rib cage, and thereby freed the red soldier's essence. The innards were beautiful – purple and blue, crimson, grey and pink. They reminded Shaba of life renewed. The colours of birth. The colours of calving. So he swept away the instantly gathered flies, touched the spear tip into the renewed trickle of blood, lifted it to his lips and, though his own tongue remained swollen, numb, he savoured the taste of the white man's iron mingling with his own, mingling also with the metal of his father's blade. *Blood of my foe*, he thought. *Body of my foe.*

He repeated the process with the other that he had killed, knowing that while he himself would remain fouled by the day's blood, he would have done enough to protect his own essence until the war doctors could complete the process. Meanwhile, until that purification could take place, he might ward off further evil by observing the *zila*, by taking and wearing something belonging to his slain. *But what shall it be?* he wondered. He despised the white men's scraps of cloth, their coats and shirts. Yet he must wear something.

In the pockets of the officer's trousers he found that large square of white cloth which, it was said, these dirty folk used to collect the snot from their noses. It was a ritual that nobody understood and, normally, such rags were left untouched. But this one seemed entirely clean, so Shaba fastened it among the civet tales of his kilt. The other soldier was more difficult, but he eventually pulled off the man's boots to reveal the woollen things that the whites wore inside their shoes. In this case, they were a sad discovery, holed in several places and smelling foul. He amused the others, momentarily, by lifting the civet furs and pulling one of the woollen things over his plaited penis sheath, although Mnukwa upbraided him both for delaying them and for making a mockery of the *zila*. So Shaba, suitably shamed, decided that they would have to suffice, and the objects were soon also attached to his cow hide belt. He thought of Amahle, of course, and became ashamed all over again.

'Now,' said Mnukwa when each of those who had killed completed their ceremonies, 'these bakaMswati must be sent onwards to oNdini. To the Great King. To tell their story. Somebody needs to go with them. To show them the way. To confirm that the Frenchman has been released. And to take word of those things that Prince Mbilini learned of the red soldiers' plans. The rest of us will continue to shadow their army here in the north. Until we receive fresh orders. I can see no reason why it should not be you, Giant Slayer. Then you can also inform the Great King that he would have had a second prisoner. A red soldier *induna*. Except that one of us killed the captive when there was no need. Tell him that, Shaba. And try to sound remorseful when you break the news. Try to avoid sounding as though you cry with one eye.'

'But iNkosi,' said Shaba, lifting a finger to his left cheek, the sightless socket, 'do I not *always* cry with just one?' And his companions laughed.

Chapter Five

Friday 25th April 1879

'I can't remember the last time we had such terrible rain,' said Griffin. 'It's unseasonal, sir. Unnatural.'

'And how long have you farmed here, Mister Griffin?' Carey asked.

He was sitting on the verandah of Griffin's white-washed house, watching through a metallic mesh of drizzle to the sloping fields of cowering sugar cane which slowly filled with reluctant Indian labourers, ankle-deep in a sluicing terracotta sludge.

'Twelve years,' Griffin replied. 'We took advantage of the Scheme once the cane industry began to develop. Moved up-country. Built the house.'

It was similar to many that Carey had seen on the journey, built of sun-dried brick. Fifty feet in length, with three main rooms —a central living area flanked by two bedrooms. This wooden verandah around all four sides provided both shade and shelter, although the front porch had been altered by the addition of two smaller rooms, one at each end. The roof was steep, double-pitched, hipped and rough-thatched. Outside, and just to the rear, stood the separate cookhouse and, on the eastern side, a cluster of outbuildings with a narrow barracks from which, even at this distance and despite the weather, there emanated the rank odour of latrine laced with grease and garlic.

'I don't know how the crops survive,' said Carey. 'It's a miracle they're not washed away.'

'The advantage of using the hillsides, Lieutenant. If you pick the right ones, that is. Many of the neighbours down on the flat have been flooded. But the dongas here carry most of the water away. Most of it. And we stuck with the hardy varieties. Bourbon Purple and Natal Green. They yield about four tons per acre. Bad slump in the early years but it's recovering now.'

'You're a canny farmer then, Mister Griffin. In your blood, I expect.'

Though he did not match Carey's image of a traditional farm owner. Griffin was in his late fifties, stocky, a full beard, but his face showing few traces of exposure to the elements. The man snorted.

'Pa tried his hand at it for a while but it didn't come easy to him. He was a gunsmith by trade. They came out with Bailie's party on the *Chapman* in 'Twenty. Brought five children with them. Then had another four of us when they settled. On the Great Fish River. Sixty-four one-acre lots, Lieutenant. Cuyler Town.'

'The Cape Emigration Scheme,' said Carey.

'As you say, Lieutenant. Pa accepted the land grant, set down his deposit and picked up his supplies. But after a couple of years, he and Ma had their fill of it and built a small store in Port Elizabeth.'

'Back to his old trade?'

'No,' laughed Griffin. 'Set himself up as a shoe-maker.'

'And you learned the trade too?'

'Not exactly. Pa was keen that we should all make something of ourselves. They came from Whitechapel, Lieutenant. Most of Bailie's party were the same.'

'That's why he named his settlement East London.'

'Of course. Anyway, I trained as an accountant. Good at it. Married Janey. Thirty years next year. Moved to Durban. Ten kids. All survived. Little Charlie will be ten soon. But Durban's overcrowded now. And when this came up...'

Here is a man, thought Carey, *who understands what it means to take life by the heels and shake forth its bounty.*

'But I've never seen so many Hindus, Mister Griffin.'

'More Indians in Natal than whites now, Lieutenant. It's the problem with the Zulu, d'you see? Thinks himself too good to be doing honest manual work. Too high and mighty. Not a decent labourer among them. Damned blacks. So we had to bring in these fellows. All indentured. And their families too, of course. I expect it will bite us in the arse one day, but what can you do?'

'They live over there?' Carey wrinkled his nose towards the barracks.

'Yes,' said Griffin. 'Sorry about that. Wind in the wrong direction today. We've got used to it, I suppose.' Carey made a quick calculation. The number of men he could already see – just about – in the fields. Doubled the figure to allow for their families. Measured the result against the size of the barracks, barely twice the size of Griffin's own house. 'Anyway,' the farmer continued, 'it's the reason we need you fellows, isn't it? Lick those bloody kaffirs into shape. Now, won't you join us for our reading?'

Carey stood, left his cloak on the porch, took a last glance at the tents on the higher ground above the house. A ragged row of white fangs, gnashing against their guy ropes through the wind-driven rain. Colonel Davies had decreed that the drafts would remain in camp today until the storm passed, although Carey himself would likely be required for scouting duties later. So he had seized the opportunity offered by Griffin that the officers' mess might join his family for morning prayers. Yet only Carey had accepted, risen early. No need to shave, of course, since he had given his whiskers free rein over the past weeks so that he now sported a full growth, wide and bushy as a Mopani tree. The sun was barely risen but the farm was already alive with its Indian labourers, and Griffin's family gathered – squeezed, rather – into the living room. It was an amusing replica of an East End parlour, complete with Aspidistra. Yet it also touched something profound within Carey, recollections of his own family's daily prayer sessions. Matthew Six, Verse Six.

'"But thou,"' intoned Griffin, '"when thou prayest, enter into thy closet, and when thou hast shut thy door, pray to thy Father which is in secret."'

Then thanks given. For the continued good health of the children here gathered, including the three older boys – Tommy, Edwin and Alfred – all volunteers now serving with the Victoria Mounted Rifles. Protection sought also for their guest, Lieutenant Carey, and for all those brave soldiers gathered near this place on God's good work.

'You were making the point,' said Carey, when the final prayers had been offered, 'that the blackies need licking into shape, sir?'

'Can you doubt it, Lieutenant?' said Griffin. 'The Zulu is the stuff of our very worst nightmare. Their borders are no more than seventy miles from here, as the crow flies. No more than that. You can't imagine what it's been like. Sleeping on a volcano. Zulus quite out of hand. Crossing the borders whenever they choose. War parties on the rampage to settle their family squabbles. Quite outrageous. Then one of our surveyors seized and assaulted. It's a very necessary war, Lieutenant, wouldn't you say? And I thank the Lord that he has sent you all to deliver us from the savages.'

'I met a Dutch gentleman,' said Carey. 'Mister Van der Byl. When we came ashore. Decent fellow, on the whole. But thought the war had rather been foisted on the Zulus. A pretext, he believed.'

'It's an old chestnut, Lieutenant. And the Dutch would say such a thing, eh? Thought they were going to have the Cape for themselves. The whole of South Africa if it comes to that. Well, they've had their eye wiped, and no mistake. And why not? It's the British that will bring true civilisation to this country, Mister Carey. We'll make Christians of them yet!'

'I hear there are some among the British community who would be happy with Van der Byl's view as well.'

'What?' said Griffin. 'The Colensos?'

Carey recalled his father's fury when the Bishop of Natal published the first of his treatises calling into question whether certain beloved books of the Old Testament should be considered as either literally or historically accurate. Although, ironically, Reverend Adolphus Carey would have been perfectly comfortable with John Colenso's advocacy on behalf of the Zulu. Carey's mother, on the other hand, had praised the Bishop's enquiring mind, his search for truth, in relation to the *Pentateuch* and the *Book of Joshua*, yet condemned him as a Darwinian mountebank for his opposition to the war against Cetshwayo.

'Yes,' he replied. 'Among others.' *Good grief,* he thought, *it almost sounds like I share their views.* 'Though my mother sees him for what he is. A damned traitor.'

'It makes me shudder now,' said Griffin, 'to think of the support we all gave when the Church attacked him for his views. Defended him to the hilt all through the court case when they were trying to get rid of him. He was our man, after all. That's what we said. Even when they tried to set up MacRorie as a rival bishop in 'Maritzburg. Boycotted the fellow in favour of Colenso. But that's all gone now. He still has his followers, of course. Though mainly his family. A few friends. If they love the bloody Zulus so much, they should go and live with them, that's what I say.'

The sentry's challenge was the merest formality, the soldier cocooned in his rain-battered greatcoat like some pupa clinging to the bole of the only African pine on the encampment's edge, and Carey returned his salute with an equal lack of enthusiasm before ducking through the flap of a tent he shared with young Farrer. He shook a shower of silver droplets from his cape, picked up his rosewood writing slope, then put the cloak over his head to protect both himself and the precious Parkins & Giotto gift from his mother before sliding through the mud to the officers' mess.

'These boots won't last the month,' he said, attempting to stamp some of the mud from them.

'Be careful, old boy,' laughed Brander. 'You'll get the damned stuff everywhere. Oh, by the way, this is Alderton. He's just come up from Durban.'

Carey identified the fellow as an Assistant Commissary, technically equal in rank to his own lieutenancy. But he had been schooled to believe that you should not rely on a Commissariat officer. They were never gentlemen and, therefore, an inferior breed. *And this one*, thought Carey, *looks more inferior than most*. The fellow was deathly pale, shivering with fever.

'On my way to Bethlehem, of all places,' said Alderton. 'To purchase horses.'

There were predictable quips about stables and mangers.

'You'll be messing with us, Alderton?' said Carey, aware of the disdain in his own voice. He might, himself, be long overdue for promotion but this fellow must be almost fifty.

Alderton coughed into his kerchief.

'Afraid not,' he said, wiping spittle from his lip. 'I've lost two days already. Doctor Taylor, you know? Insisted I stayed in bed until the fever broke. If I crack on, I can get to Estcourt by nightfall. Then Bethlehem tomorrow.'

'You're planning to go on in this weather?' said the Surgeon-Major, setting down a well-thumbed copy of the *Cape and Natal News*. 'And in your state of health? I should strongly advise against it, sir. Strongly!'

But Alderton insisted that he would be fine. An hour's respite and...

Carey set out the writing slope, took a sheet of paper, opened his ink.

'Letter to the good lady wife?' asked Brander. He was enjoying a cheroot, studying one of the sketch maps that Carey had completed just the day before.

'Thought I'd take advantage of the rain,' Carey replied, and leaned the photographs of Edith and baby Pelham inside the open pen tray.

'And how long married, Carey? Almost nine years, didn't you say? She must be a very special lady to keep you at the letter-writing after all that time. Where did you meet?'

'Falmouth.'

'Ah, sweet West Country.'

'No,' said Carey, fixing his gaze quickly upon the blank page so that he might avoid both Brander's quizzical expression and, hopefully, any further questions. 'Falmouth, Jamaica.'

My own treasure, my dearest Annie,
I am writing this letter to you in high spirits, seated at the very fine writing slope which Mama gifted to me before I left. I have in front of me the portraits of darling Edie and our little soldier, Pel. But I still grieve that I have no such remembrance of Jahleel junior. We are presently encamped upon the property of a most amiable gentleman, Mister Stephen William Griffin – though he is commonly known hereabouts as 'Bill.' I am quite jealous since God has granted him ten children and allowed him to keep them all. He must have led an entirely blameless life to be so blessed.

'According to your sketch, Carey,' said Brander, 'Mister Alderton would need to get across this Bushman's River to reach Estcourt. Is it passable, d'you reckon?'

'It looked bad enough yesterday. Though I didn't check all the drifts.'

'I'm sure one of the locals will point me in the right direction,' said Alderton, sipping at the most efficacious brandy that the mess and its Surgeon-Major could provide, the Grants Morella Cherry.

Carey smiled.

'Yes,' he said. 'They're sure to be helpful.' He dipped the nib of his Fairchild once more and returned to the writing.

Still, my own one, I am determined that this campaign shall be the making of your poor husband, though I am still lacking news of promotion. I was assured before sailing that Johnson was to be appointed Paymaster and would have to resign his commission in order to do so. Colonel Sceberras could not promise me the step, naturally, but he gave me to believe that seniority would apply so that, by rights, the captaincy should be mine. Still, I must bear the thing patiently, I suppose, knowing that the Adjutant General's Office has greater priorities just now than a single appointment within the 98th.

Farrer was involved with some of the others in learning the rules of poker, a game which Carey associated with American iniquity, though it seemed to have become popular with the British court these past few years.

'Good Lord,' said the young man, 'have you ever heard rain come down so hard?'

It howled like a hundred banshees against the canvas of the marquee.

'In Honduras,' said Carey. It was an absent-minded comment, instantly regretted, followed by that familiar image of a jaguar pursuing him through dripping forest. He shook his head to clear it.

I have been out on patrol almost every day, scouting the roads ahead and rooting out decent camping ground, all of which I enjoy. There is a freedom here, dear Annie, that you would greatly savour. A true Garden of Eden. But there is a price to pay also, for which God, I trust, will forgive me. It is a wicked thing, but I have frequently been out so early in the morning that there has been no time to say my prayers, and I am often on duty throughout Sunday. Why, even Easter — two weeks ago, already — was a solitary affair. How I envy Reggie his service on the Triumph where, I know, they must rig for church every Sunday regardless of sea-state or other concern. I envy him his silver medal too, of course. From the Royal Humane Society indeed. My own reward from France seems positively modest by comparison! But Reggie also honoured for saving lives. Well, my sweet darling, you should know that your own husband has also been engaged once more in a similar endeavour. In truth, I merely helped to pull one of the men back into our little boat when we were escaping from the Clyde. Hardly a feat of great daring, though the fellow could have been eaten by sharks if I had not acted so. Yet he is considered such a worthless cove that my fellows here have ribbed me for not throwing him back. Hahaha! Eh bien, at least the rain today has allowed me to partake of the Griffins' bible gathering this morning.

'There's a mention of Jamaica here in the paper,' said the Surgeon-Major. 'The *Pelican*, Carey. Been ordered from Port Royal to join the Pacific Station. This spat between Peru and Chile. All those nitrate mines of ours to protect, I suppose. D'you know her?'

'The *Pelican*? No, I don't think so. Who's her skipper?'

'Henry Boys, according to this. Says she's a composite sloop, whatever that means.'

'She'll have an iron frame but a hull still built with timbers, teak most likely,' said Carey.

'You see, Alderton?' Brander laughed. 'Carey is our resident expert on all things naval. A long line of admirals. His mother's side of the family, I think.'

'Anybody famous, Carey?' said Alderton. He was a heavy-set man, with an extravagant moustache and a deeply dimpled chin.

'Sir Jahleel Brenton's probably the best known, isn't he?' said the Surgeon-Major. 'Fought some notable actions with his squadron against Old Boney, I recall. Naples, I think. Was he ever here, Carey? In South Africa?'

'He served a spell as Commissioner of the dockyards at the Cape,' replied Carey. 'He died before I was born.'

'Never tempted to follow in his footsteps?' said Farrer.

'I had my heart set on the army,' said Carey.

Papa has never forgiven me for it, he thought. *One would imagine it might be mother's ambition. The navy's in her blood, after all, not his. Yet because Pa wanted it so badly, she did everything in her power to discourage me.* There were sounds of splashing in the mud outside, muttered curses, and the entrance flap drawn aside to reveal the Colonel's drenched servant, Taylor.

'Forgive the intrusion, gentlemen,' he said. 'But Colonel Davies requests the presence of Lieutenant Carey.'

Carey confirmed that he would join the Colonel in his tent immediately, then added a couple of hasty final lines.

Well, my dear treasure, Colonel Davies wishes to consult with me, so I will try and let you know a few words more over the coming days. Good night, my own one!

The manservant, Taylor, had a limp that Carey had not noticed before and was clearly in some pain.

'Did you check on the horses?' Colonel Davies directed the question towards the ceiling of his own marquee and Carey saw Taylor roll his eyes, exchange a glance with his fellow-footman, Joshua James, who was busy working on a pair of his master's boots, supervised by the Colonel's regimental orderly.

'Which we did, sir,' James replied. He had an odd manner of speech, which turned each 's' into a strident sibilance. 'Not half an hour past. Can't be too careful, sir. Not with all them Hindus about.'

'As you say, James,' said the Colonel. 'Good man. But half an hour, was it? Best have another look, I think. Make sure that Limerick is warm enough. Didn't like the look of the old fellow last night.'

James muttered something, set down the boots and went to collect a rain cape from a stool near the entrance. He too was limping.

'Blisters, sir?' Carey asked the Colonel.

'Who, James?' said Davies. 'Yes. Surgeon-Major is a good fellow but doesn't seem to have a cure for the common blister. Strange, eh?' There was a walking stick – stout, dark patina, baboon carved at the grip – leaning against the arm of the Colonel's own campaign chair. He picked up the stick. 'Here, James,' he shouted. The fellow turned and Davies threw the thing towards him. James caught it.

'Thank you, sir,' said the servant. 'Which it is very kind.'

He lifted the flap and ventured out into the storm.

'Need to look after them, Carey,' said Davies. 'Horse and servant both. Horses mainly though. Can always find a decent servant, eh?'

'Taylor has blisters too?' Carey asked.

'Taylor? No. Rheumatism in his case, I think. Isn't that so, Taylor.'

'All this rain, sir,' said Taylor. 'Mustn't grumble though.'

'"Do all things without murmurings and disputings." That's what the Good Book tells us.' The Colonel stroked his sandy moustache. 'And here's the thing, Lieutenant. My weather eye tells me that this filthy stuff will break this afternoon. I'm never wrong about these things. So the men will have to be on the road at first light tomorrow. We must try to make up the time we've lost.'

'You need me to go out, sir?'

'We could rely on the maps you drew yesterday but I need to make absolutely sure of the crossings. Find us a good one, eh Carey? And decent ground at Estcourt too. Have to press on. Estcourt will put us half the way from Durban to Dundee. So Ladysmith in a few days.'

'And Dundee four more after that, sir. Then hopefully some action at last.'

'Maybe a cure for all these damned blisters too. Half the draft seems afflicted with them. But you make it sound like I'm not working you hard enough, Lieutenant.'

Carey felt deflated. Patient hard work was, after all, his trademark. *God waits*, he thought. It was the way in which he compensated for all the natural gifts which the Lord had so far failed to bestow upon him – the gifts which God seemed to have distributed so lavishly among the other members of his family.

'"Whatsoever ye do,"' quoted Carey, '"work heartily, as unto the Lord."'

'"And not unto men,"' said the Colonel. 'Isn't that how it ends, Carey? Colossians, I think. As unto the Lord, and not unto men. I fear that in the service we must sometimes balance our duties to God with those to our commanding officers, eh?'

'I was thinking of action against the Zulu in particular, sir. Shame to come all this way and find that it's over by the time we reach the column. There seems to be a common view among the settlers that Cetshwayo will surrender now. After Khambula.'

'Wood performed very well,' said the Colonel. 'Very well indeed. Hardly a scratch on him. A score killed. Fifty wounded. Poor Hackett blinded, of course. They say that he still had that old pipe of his clenched between his teeth when he went down. A lucky shot from the blackies, I imagine. Unlucky for Hackett, of course.'

'The Zulus still seem to have plenty of fight in them, sir. Don't you think?'

'Chelmsford will keep them on the run now. Any fight they have left will be sheer desperation. You're right though. Shouldn't underestimate them. Not again. Keep them on the run, that's what we need. Stop them gathering together. Stop them settling down in their own kraals. I don't think it will last much longer. But don't worry, it will be just long enough for us to be in on the kill. Think of yourself as our best huntsman, Lieutenant. Find the right track for these hounds of ours. Get them on the scent of our fox, eh?'

'I'll do my best, sir.'

'I'm certain of it, Carey. It seems that I'm rarely able to write a report without mentioning your name. It's a mystery to me that you've been overlooked for so long.'

And the Colonel's dispatches, Carey knew, this being a time of war, would each appear in the *Gazette*. His own sweet Annie would undoubtedly see them there and be proud of her husband. She would read them, he was certain, to the children. He was grateful to the Colonel, of course, though there was really only one item that he desired to see confirmed in the journal's columns.

'I wrote to my wife earlier, sir. As it happens, I mentioned to her that my company captain is likely to be accepted by the Army Pay Department. It might provide an opening, I hope.'

'Indeed, Lieutenant. Well-deserved. Good luck with it, old man. And speaking of letters, I must write to young Harry. My son. He's at Eton, you know. Good luck with the patrol, Carey.' He was dismissed, saluted the Colonel, collected his own cloak. 'Oh, and Lieutenant,' said Davies. 'Take that Commissary fellow with you. Point him in the right direction.'

'Alderton, sir? Yes, of course.'

The rain cleared, precisely as Colonel Henry Fanshawe Davies had calculated, a little after midday, though the wind still smothered them with the scent of wet clay.

'And after she went down?' said Alderton.

There were four of them in the party. Carey riding an appaloosa mare, one of the mounts loaned by Mister Van der Byl; Alderton himself; and two horse-tailers, stockmen – both Dutch – hired by the army to handle any strings of beasts purchased by the Assistant Commissary during his travels. Apart from Carey's own mount, the others rode the hardy Cape *boerperd* ponies.

'We spent most of the following day on the beaches,' said Carey. 'Until the *Tamar* arrived. In response to the messages we'd sent. She put her boats ashore and we managed to get everybody safely on board. Though the sea was much rougher than the previous day. And there was no possibility of re-embarking the horses. The Colonel was all in a funk about it, naturally. But in the end Mister Van der Byl promised to see them safely overland to

Simon's Town. Taylor and James went with them.'

'And you all sailed back to Simon's Bay.'

'That's about the size of it. Then the *Tamar* took us on to Durban. We finally arrived there on the Eleventh. We've been on the road ever since. And what about you, Alderton? What brings you to the Army Service Corps?'

'My pa indentured me to an army grocer. Scots Fusilier Guards. I was at Sebastopol – but after it was all over. The only fighting I saw was against the weather, old fellow. Never known cold like it. Chaps freezing to death by the dozen. I got my Commission in '70. Rose through the ranks. Proud of it. But this feels like the first *real* thing that I've done. You wouldn't understand, I don't suppose.'

Oh, I understand perfectly, thought Carey. *You join Her Majesty's forces, imagine all manner of possible outcomes. All outcomes except boredom. The life of the* Boomvogel. *And then, when action does come along...*

'Understand what, Alderton?' he said. 'Our soldierly quest for action?'

'Not action alone, no. But the valour which must accompany it.'

'Ah, valour,' said Carey. 'It is a precious commodity. To be used sparingly, don't you think? Valour is that which a man may practise when he is certain of survival. In all other circumstances, he shows discretion. It is, after all, valour's better part.'

'You believe that?'

'Simply being provocative. But I *do* believe this. That officers have a responsibility for the men under their command. And a uselessly dead officer cannot fulfil that duty.'

'Yet he may inspire them.'

'You think we will have much opportunity to inspire and lead from our own respective roles, Alderton?' said Carey.

'James Langley Dalton,' replied Alderton, his face flushed with pride.

Dalton's name was now known far and wide for his conspicuous bravery in the defence at Rorke's Drift back in January. There was even talk of a Victoria Cross.

'And Dalton was only an *Acting* Assistant Commissary,' said Carey. 'Why, there's certainly hope for you then, Alderton. But look. There's the fort.'

The muddy track they were following was, in truth, the main road north from Durban to Ladysmith, and it ran here through the veld in all its rich variety. It smelled sweet today, after the rain. Yet Carey had also experienced its dryness in the weeks before, the metallic scent in his nostrils whenever the dust rose. The eery and ubiquitous *haa-daa-daa* cry of the local ibis too. And the rusting taste of Natal's earth would soon return to his tongue, he knew, for they swam still in a spectral mist which reached their girths straps as the sun began to burn away the wetness.

A wide and wild moorland marched away on either side and ahead of them, mostly tall grass and scrub. It might have been the Cumberland Fells. Or one of the Welsh valleys. Except that, at times, among the clusters of trees, giraffe could be glimpsed. Sometimes kudu and impala. Several miles away, on each flank, the ground rose upwards, giving way to the Thornveld, shorter grass but studded with sharp Acacia. Higher still, the Knob Thorn and Buffalo Thorn of the Sourveld. And then, finally, the slopes folded over to embrace the sparse uplands of the Highveld. The track curved towards a gap in the hills, although the gap itself was partially filled by a flat-topped eminence, crowned by the squat bulk of a sandstone fortress with two square towers.

'Fort Durnford?' asked Alderton.

Carey detected the merest hint of distaste in the way that the Assistant Commissary spoke Durnford's name. Durnford – then a Major – had been responsible for the fort's construction six years earlier in the aftermath of a rising by Hlubi tribesmen. It was during the rising that Durnford had also been in command of a battle at Bushman's Pass – one in which he had displayed personal bravery though apparently poor judgement. Even so, he had subsequently been promoted to the rank of Lieutenant-Colonel.

'Ah,' said Carey. 'I sense that you're in the Durnford-to-blame camp then.'

'For Isandlwana?' Alderton replied. 'Well, who else *would* you blame? He was the senior officer at the camp, after all.'

'As you say, Alderton. Lord Chelmsford certainly seems to hold him accountable. The newspapers too.' But the word *scapegoat* came to Carey's mind. It was somewhat academic anyway. For Durnford lay dead. Among the other twelve hundred who had perished at the hands of Cetshwayo's Zulus. Their bodies still unburied these three months later.

They drew nearer to the fort and were met by a patrol of Natal Mounted Policemen, part of the small garrison here.

'You're back, sir,' said the sergeant in command of the troop. Carey encountered him on the previous morning, just before the rain had so badly disrupted his map-making. He was a grizzled fellow, wearing a peaked forage cap rather than the white, brass-spiked sun helmet of his constables, their uniforms of such dark grey woollen cord that they seemed black.

'The Colonel is keen to get the draft moving again,' said Carey.

'I wish we were coming with you,' said the sergeant. 'Scores to settle, Lieutenant. You understand?'

He understood. A score or more of the Force had perished with Durnford and the rest.

'How are the fords?' he asked.

'Only as you'd expect, sir,' said the sergeant, 'after so much rain. It *never* storms like this in April. Never!'

'But can we pass, man? Can we pass?'

'The lower drift should be clear by morning, I think. But not today, sir. Not on foot anyway. And not much better mounted either, if it comes to that. Supply wagon came across from the village a while ago. Only just made it though.'

'I've no choice, Sergeant,' said Carey. 'Need to find a decent campsite beyond the village. But Assistant Commissary Alderton might appreciate the hospitality of the fort for tonight.'

'Not on your life, Carey,' said Alderton. 'We're going to press on. I can be in Bethlehem before dark.'

The sergeant puckered his nose and lips, scrutinised Alderton. There was widespread contempt, Carey knew, for the Commissariat. *All the same, he's an impertinent fellow*, he thought. *But I know what's on his mind. Alderton certainly doesn't seem precisely at home in his saddle.*

'Well, gentlemen,' said the sergeant, 'at least we can show you to the drift.'

He maintained a steady commentary for most of the ensuing two miles, pointed out the slopes of Makabeni Hill, confirmed the distance to the next crossing upstream – the Wagendrift, where the Voortrekkers had fought the Zulu for three days in '38. And when they had skirted Fort Durnford itself he showed them the two fords which the thing had been built to command. Its hill-top plateau stood in the centre of a long north-pointing meander, with one drift to the west, the other to the east. But even at this distance the water was cocoa dark, menacing against the green background, while across the river sat the scattered dwellings of Estcourt village. A church just up from the farther bank; a mill; some solid stone two-storey buildings; a spread of houses; an active bakery – from the scent that wafted towards them – and, beyond, a second church.

'That's your path, sir,' the sergeant said to Carey. 'To the right, Lieutenant. You'll find the lower drift beyond that clump of trees. But the offer is still open, gentlemen, if you'd care to stay at the fort.'

'I can assure you,' bristled Alderton, 'that we shall do perfectly well.'

Carey reached the farther bank without incident or damage apart from soaking his already deteriorating boots. He had bought them from Peal and Company in Duke Street, just off Grosvenor Square, in the previous Autumn and, despite the care he had attempted to lavish on them, there was no doubt they were almost spent. He turned the appaloosa on firm ground just below the church and nodded an acknowledgement to the Boer horse-tailer who had accompanied him on the crossing. It had, all things considered, been easier than he imagined. Just one deeper section towards the middle of the drift where the water had been past his ankles. But, as the sergeant had said, by tomorrow they should be able to get the men across without too much difficulty. The river looked nasty, of course. Fifty yards wide here. It sounded enraged, wounded. A filthy shade of brown. Froth and tree debris rushing past, though nothing large. Still, he would come back early, perhaps with the small party of engineers, and rig some safety lines. Apart from that...

'Very well, Alderton,' he yelled, standing in his stirrups. 'Across you come!'

The Assistant Commissary hesitated then spurred his horse forward, alongside the second of the horse-tailers but a few yards downstream from him. Alderton's feet and stirrups were well above the flowing surface, but his knees were bent at an odd angle, as though he were trying to keep them even further clear of the water.

'Perhaps we should find another crossing,' he shouted, and urged his mount back towards his Dutch companion.

'It's safe enough,' Carey replied. 'Need to take it steady though.'

Alderton said something to the horse-tailer and, as he did so, their horses almost collided. Carey saw him jerk the reins, pulling the pony's head sharply to the right, trying to turn it. But the beast slipped sideways. It snorted, then squealed, finally throwing up its head and screaming. Then it seemed to lose its footing, shied and caused Alderton to fall backwards. Yet, surprisingly, he managed to hold on to the reins, grabbed for the saddle, held it, as the pony tried to regain its feet. And so it was that, initially, they were swept away together.

Carey and the Boer put spurs to their horses' flanks and began to canter along the broken riverbank in pursuit. Then Alderton's pony shook itself free of the water's grip and Carey was satisfied that all would be well. Until, for a reason he would never understand, the man seemed to simply relax his hold, slipped backwards, gave a cry, and was gone. The chase began once more, Carey shouting Alderton's name. The Assistant Commissary's hands came briefly out of the water and Carey urged his horse towards them, then thought better of it, calculated the river's speed, headed further downstream in an effort to intercept the fellow. But the river was narrowing again, growing deeper, Carey's horse almost swimming now, and still no further sign of Alderton. Nothing.

The horse-tailers had stuck to their respective banks, so made better progress, and Carey saw them both ahead, jumping from their ponies and splashing into the shallows. He did likewise, up to his waist but maintaining his footing, casting about him. For he had no fear of water. *Valour is that which a man may practise when he is certain of survival.* Yet the combined efforts of the three men revealed no further sign of Assistant Commissary Thomas Alderton.

The lantern cast an amber light across one side of the Colonel's face and set the other in deepest shadow, a Caravaggio study in *chiaroscuro*.

'You should not have allowed the fellow to cross, Lieutenant,' said Davies.

'It was perfectly safe, sir,' Carey replied. 'I made the crossing myself.'

'Safe?' said the Colonel. 'How can it have been safe when the man drowned?'

Captain Brander coughed with discretion.

'I've questioned the horse-handlers myself, sir,' he said. 'They confirm Carey's account to the last farthing. If anything, he seems to have played down his own part in trying to find Alderton.'

Brander was trying to be helpful, but Carey found that he resented it.

'Well they *did* find him, Captain, did they not? Unfortunately, the poor fellow was dead. And what now, Carey? You expect us to take five hundred men across the same river, in full spate, tomorrow?'

'With the greatest respect, sir,' said Carey, 'it is very far from being in full spate.'

'Then can somebody please explain to me how we have managed to lose one of Strickland's Commissary Officers? His adjutant, in fact.'

'He was not sitting his horse very well, sir,' said Carey. 'Perhaps the fever. I'm not sure. He'd seemed perfectly competent until we reached the river. But I think he may have caught his spurs in the pony's flank. Startled it, perhaps.'

'Did it seem skittish?'

'No, sir. Not really. He was riding a *boerperd*. They're generally very steady.'

'There's another possibility, Colonel,' said Brander. 'I saw a similar accident once, at home. Water not too deep but, at the wrong angle, the beast's tail washed under its back legs. They often react badly when that happens, sir. Imagine that it's a branch or some other obstruction. It can panic them.'

'I need no lessons on the behaviour of horseflesh, Captain,' said Davies. 'Rotten luck though. We survive the shipwreck with not a man lost. And now this! The fellow not even one of our own. We'll have to collect the body, of course. Take it to Ladysmith.'

'What about sending him on to Bethlehem, sir?' suggested Carey. 'He was determined to get there, after all. There's a doctor in town – Taylor – who says that he'll make the necessary arrangements.'

Davies considered, visibly relaxed.

'Quite so, Lieutenant,' he said. 'Full military honours, of course. And you can help me pen a letter to the man's family. Append a report of your own perhaps. Eye-witness account. I assume he was married? Expect his widow will be somewhat consoled by the fact that he met a soldier's death in dedicated pursuit of his duty.'

'And I should personally like to commend Lieutenant Carey for his diligence, sir,' said Brander. 'I believe he could not have done more for poor Alderton. His efforts in the river verged on the heroic, I understand.'

'I'm afraid, sir,' said Carey, 'that I lack the essential attribute of the hero. Since I do not consider myself indestructible.'

Chapter Six

It was all a matter of accountancy, this issue of how the tally of one's wives might be reconciled.

There were his current assets to be considered, the nine that Cetshwayo had already bestowed upon him and now this additional girl. The fixed assets were well-established. But when it came to the other side of the balance sheets, the liabilities, these included the four women that he had inherited from John Dunn.

With the noise of his latest wedding celebration disrupting his calculations from the room behind him, McTeague stood on the verandah, took stock of the four harpies while sipping at his favourite whisky, the Encore, all the way from Bernard & Company's Leith distillery. It was highly recommended by *The Lancet*. By the *British Medical Journal* too. A host of eminent physicians. It had travelled well, he thought.

The women sat in a half-circle in front of one of the dozen huts that fringed the yard and its outbuildings. All but one had children and several of the infants were pale-skinned, though they had all sprung equally from the loins of John Dunn. All three mothers had a younger child swaddled to her back by a thin grey blanket knotted above her breasts, while older sons and daughters played in the dirt among them. The fourth woman knelt a little to one side, stick-thin, a porridge bowl on the ground before her, as though she were a beggar. She was naked, naturally, apart from her leather kilt just visible beneath the woven loin-dress that marked her status as a married woman, iNkosikazi. The only item that she seemed to wear in common with the other three was her topknot, the red ochre mound of hair, stiffened with straw and ox-fat, preserved and protected by a wide head-band of otter fur.

Why does she have no children? he wondered, but he also made a mental note to add seven *pequeñitos*, as Maria Mestiza might describe them, to the list of his liabilities. Piccaninnies, of course, in McTeague's eyes. *And what*, he thought, *if one of these should lay claim to my estate? In the absence of any heir of my own?* There was the question of space, too. Could he reasonably put his new bride to the discomfiture of sharing accommodation with these other women? For Maria Mestiza had established herself at Emoyeni as McTeague's

Supreme Wife, mistress of the fine house, tolerating the presence of his lesser wives on the premises but never permitting them to live under her roof. He had been required to explain the constitution of the realm to each new acquisition in turn, reminding them that they must only visit the bungalow when they had been summoned to do so while, as Supreme Wife, as his Queen, Maria Mestiza held the honour of being able to enter his presence whenever she chose. *As if*, he thought, *I could ever stop her!* It seemed an acceptable arrangement, one which John Dunn's Great Wife, Catherine, had imposed before them, although, in her case, she had consistently refused to see her husband's Zulu women as anything other than savages, whereas Maria viewed them more as subjects.

He took another sip at his glass. *But the worst thing*, he thought, *is that none of them has been taken in holy Christian matrimony.* Dunn had seemingly engaged only in some heathen bonding with these women. It would be an outrage in the eyes of God if McTeague himself maintained the pretence of marriage to them when they were, in fact, no more than deferred liabilities, carried over to the current page of his accounts. *Deuteronomy 7: 1-4, is it not? The prohibition against marriage with a heathen?* Perfectly acceptable where the lady has first been baptised, of course, as today's bride had been. But these…

He put down the whisky, set his monocle firmly in place and walked across the yard, past a group of his workers enjoying the beer he had provided for them, past a second clutch of women – his legitimate wives – to the whitened mud brick hut that served as McTeague's tack room. And there, among the saddles, bridles and carriage harnesses, he found his riding crop, a Beven, its black handle topped with an ornate cap of finely wrought silver wire, a collar to match, the whole whip covered in braided black baleen. He flicked the tightly-wound cord tress twice against his boot, then strode back to the four women, spoke to them in a slow and deliberate IsiZulu.

'Is any of you a *kholwa*?' he said. 'Have you taken the water? To become a follower of Jesucristo?'

The three women with the children stared at him blankly. The fourth looked at the crop, smiled at him.

'Do we no longer please you, *uMyeni*?' she said. 'That you come to whip us like dogs?'

'I am *not* your husband,' McTeague replied. 'Jantoni was your man. But now he is gone, He has abandoned his people. Abandoned you also. It is time for you to leave.'

'And where would you have us go, lord?' said the woman. She was attractive. McTeague had to admit that. Broad cheek bones. Intelligent eyes. Tiny breasts, but firm and uplifted. She had spirit. It would not be such a *great* sin to keep just one of the women, perhaps. If he was honest in his confession to the Almighty, he was sure to be forgiven. But on his wedding day?

77

'You can take food and return to your own homesteads. Or you may follow Dunn. Follow Jantoni.'

'And would you shame our families by forcing them to repay the *ilobolo?*'

'Your dowry is between you and your husband,' replied McTeague. 'If you do not wish to shame your families, then go join him.'

'And if we choose to remain?'

The workers in the yard heard the remark and laughed. The three older women looked aghast. And McTeague was enraged. A little spirit was one thing...

He lashed out with the crop so that the short tress caught her cheek, split the skin. She scrambled back, out of range, but held his gaze with her own mamba eyes.

'Take your belongings and go!' he yelled.

The others gathered the children, retreated to their hut, while the fourth rose carefully to her feet, glared at him with contempt.

'You may live to regret this day, white man,' she whispered.

A trickle of blood ran defiantly, unstaunched, towards her chin.

'There are always accounts to be settled,' said McTeague. The woman troubled him, and he considered applying the whip once more. You could never be too sure whether these tribal women possessed some witchcraft. But, if so, that simply meant that he had served the Almighty twice by the one action. Expelled the faithless heathen from among his household and rid his estate of potential wizardry. He hoped that the Lord would be pleased with the way he had spent his day. After all, the only critical balance sheet was that which Gladstone had recommended. *"An account book to God for the all-precious gift of Time."*

'She is an admirable young woman, McTeague,' said Pastor Jago Jupe. 'Admirable, sir.' The funereal grey of his clerical suit bunched and shifted in several places as though trying to adjust to the Pastor's spreading bulk which itself seemed fed, nurtured, by an internal irrigation system of sweat running down the channels of his flesh.

'Do you think so, Pastor?' McTeague replied. 'I only agreed to take her out of courtesy to Cetshwayo, truth to tell. But at least we have another soul saved for the Lord.'

Yet admirable she was! Her name was Amahle and he guessed that she was not yet sixteen years old. He had expected timidity, reluctance, though her laughter now bathed his kitchen in the orange warmth of a second dawn and, as she shifted on the small chair which her family had brought to the ceremony, she seemed to shimmer like a heat haze. She took a moment to straighten the knee-length black kilt, the *isidwaba*, its leather pleats perfumed with the fruit of Bird's Brandy and, as she moved, the bright beads of her breastband jounced and tinkled aside to reveal her elegant nipples, while the red gossamer shawl, fastened at the cleavage between them, whispered terrible temptations. Much of her face was hidden by a veil of woollen mesh, the woven strands of which were coloured to match the beads, and the same greens, yellows and blues had also been threaded into the base of Amahle's coiffure – from which the veil was suspended – so that her topknot was exaggerated into a full *isicholo*, the scarlet inverted cone which at first glance looked like a hat but which, on closer inspection, was plainly fabricated by sewing together and stiffening the girl's own hair.

The preliminaries had been mercifully brief. A royal messenger had taken the news to Amahle's parents at Hluhluwe that she had been favoured by the Great King. She would be wed to his white brother, KaMtigwe, who in turn had then followed normal custom by inviting the bride's family to Emoyeni – happily just a short walk – and a date agreed for the wedding to take place during the following week. McTeague had presented the necessary *ilobolo*, six handsome cows – including one simply to gain acquiescence to her baptism – and then, this morning, he had slaughtered two more for the feast. A goat in the bargain. There had been the strange ritual to observe, by which everybody in the house was required to pretend they had not noticed the bridal party's arrival, Amahle's entrance to the kitchen wrapped in a blanket, and her setting of the bridal seat near his hearth. It was difficult *not* to notice them, however, for her relatives had filled the house. Admittedly, they brought gifts. Some blankets. A fine mat. Two brooms. Three clay pots. A collection of well-crafted iron farming tools, wrought personally by McTeague's new father-in-law. But then they had spent most of Amahle's brief christening, the subsequent recital of the wedding vows, suitably abridged and adulterated by Pastor Jupe, in avid exploration of the villa, despite the protests of Maria Mestiza.

In the building's central passage, three muscular young men in full ceremonial attire, all leopard skins, ostrich feathers and cow-tails, pushed and pulled at his William Robb long case clock – left behind by John Dunn – ears pressed to its mechanically beating, though now somewhat discordant, heart. In the four larger rooms flanking the corridor, groups of women, distinguished in age and status by their costume but all resplendent in festival colours, rummaged respectively among his Wedgwood dinner services; among the bonnets, dresses and items of millinery abandoned by Dunn's one white wife; among his collections of Thackeray, Mill, Macaulay, Kingston, Arnold, Carlyle and Dickens; among his vases, cheese bells, shaving mugs, ornamental potteries and platters. They laughed hysterically at the lace antimacassars which clothed the backs and arms of each chair and couch. They drew tormented protests from an already tuneless and therefore misnomered harmonium. In the hipped roof-space, several older men scattered his collection of curios – mirrors and manuscripts, shells and stuffed birds, gems and fossils – until one of them finally came crashing through the ceiling into the kitchen, landing in a writhing heap at Amahle's feet.

'Yes, one saved,' said the Pastor, 'but so many more still to be shriven.'

'Then the Almighty be praised that you have remained among us,' McTeague replied, 'when so many others have forsaken their posts.' For when the mission stations of Reverend Adams, or the Norwegian Schreuder, or the Swede Otto Witt had been left empty with the outbreak of war, Pastor Jago Jupe had been persuaded to remain at Emoyeni, under a dispensation granted by Cetshwayo at McTeague's personal request. 'And mark my words,' he continued, 'we shall rue the day. Leave an opening like this and the Papists are bound to fill it!' He had strong views on the subject. But the Pastor was, at least, not the only white guest at the event, and a rancorous accordion burst – undoubtedly one of the Portuguese – from the front parlour seemed to suddenly remind the Zulus that they had not yet celebrated the marriage in their own fashion. So the guests were marshalled away from their various distractions and filed into the enclosed yard with the recently vacated hut, which would now serve as Amahle's bridal suite. Slices of sizzling beef were served. More sorghum beer. More blankets gifted to McTeague's "family" members. Amahle herself led out on to the verandah by her matrons of honour, grass switches waving to sweep away any presence of evil.

McTeague and his household, his friends, his retainers, were persuaded to form a line in front of the hut, heavily outnumbered by the Hluhluwe Zulus who danced, sang and ululated towards them across the intervening dust. It was clear that something was expected of them but McTeague's previous marriages had been mere formalities in comparison to this one, so he felt himself lacking in respect to the necessary ritual and etiquette.

'We are required to reject her, iNkosi,' shouted the warrior at his shoulder, appearing as he always did, apparently from nowhere.

'Reject her?' grumbled McTeague. He felt a moment of panic. 'Don't want to do *that*, Klaas!' He used the name that the warrior claimed had been given him by the Dutch who raised him.

'It is expected,' said Klaas. 'Part of the ceremony.'

The fellow smiled, though the gesture did little to improve his scarred features, while the wisps of chin hair lent him a permanently piratical air of insolence. And he used that characteristic skilfully now, raising his small shield, his spear shafts, dancing forward towards Amahle's extended family to menace them, to send them back in mock confusion, in full retreat. To the porch, where they rallied once more. Began the process for a second time.

On this occasion, McTeague's supporters – many of them suffering from an excess of alcohol – managed to grasp their role in the performance, though they failed to match the swirling, stamping elegance of Klaas the Skirmisher as he led them forward. And it was Klaas who signalled to them also when it was finally time for the two groups to halt, to hold their respective lines, while Amahle advanced alone, making intricate bird patterns in the red dirt to the rhythm of her family's singing. McTeague was pushed forward too, to meet her in his own overweight mimicry of her steps, holding his monocle in place while Klaas set out the straw mats which would form a path, a bridge, to carry the new bride to acceptance and her new home.

'Where have you been, warrior of the uNokhenke?' McTeague asked him, as more of his meat was devoured by an apparently growing crowd of guests, now including Cornelius Vijn and a bodyguard of men arrived from Emahlabathini.

'Watching the red soldiers,' replied Klaas, tearing at a strip of equally red beef with his teeth.

'And where are they now?'

'Burning huts in many of the valleys. But they are gathering, iNkosi KaMtigwe.' It was a name that McTeague cherished, for the prefix captured the same sense as the Gaelic use of *mac* – the sense of being somebody's son, but also part of a wider family, a clan.

'It is an interesting name,' said Vijn. 'McTeague. Is it Irish? Or Scottish perhaps?'

'I owe it to my adoptive Pa,' said McTeague. 'They say that blood is thicker than water, though it's all nonsense. Except in the literal sense, of course. Take my own case. Natural parents unknown. Left on the doorstep of a very respectable Edinburgh family. No name. No prospects. It could have been the workhouse. But they gave me a home. An education. A veritable character. I feel no affinity with any family but they. I was permanently concerned that the bubble might burst, naturally. That the old gentleman would desert me. He was a Manxman by birth, incidentally. "My dear child," he would rejoin, moved I think by the sudden warmth of my appeal, "you need not be afraid of my deserting you, unless you give me cause." And I would interpose, "Oh, sir, I never will!" What d'you think of that, *Mijnheer* Vijn?'

Cornelius Vijn smiled. Whatever he thought in truth, McTeague doubted that the fellow would have read much Dickens. Not *The Parish Boy's Progress*, in any case. Though the link between his tale and that of the lad, Twist, seemed almost incidental at that moment. The book had such a turn of phrase that it always proved hard to resist extracting from it, as was his wont, while the factual truth of his childhood remained buried in those deeper recesses of McTeague's mind that no key would ever open.

'He is a liar,' said Maria Mestiza, swaying from the effects of the whisky bottle that she carried. 'He is the bastard son of a *cabrón*.' She made a sign of the horns. 'A *cabrón* who trusted his wife. Trust! What good is trust to anybody?'

McTeague was stung. *Good Lord*, he thought. *Has she learned nothing? It was the villain's lack of faith in God that caused him to be cuckolded. Divine justice for his heresy. More the heathen than most of those here gathered. May his soul burn in Hell. Mother may have been a whore, but she was an honest whore at least. And bequeathed me that most honourable of qualities.* But it was an uncomfortable subject for him. And he preferred the mythology of his Twist-like adoption by wealthy benefactors.

'Gathering?' he said. 'Where precisely are the red soldiers gathering, Klaas?'

'One large *impi* at Gingindlovu.' He pointed south. 'Another at eHlobane.' He pointed west. 'And the *amakhanda* of the Great King in between.' He stabbed the blade end of a throwing spear into the ground at his feet.

'It was always Chelmsford's plan to attack Ulundi,' said Vijn.

Cetshwayo's Royal Kraals will be caught in a pincer movement, thought McTeague. *But the old boy can still win, surely? One way or the other, we need to end up on the right side, eh?*

'And will you care, iNkosi?' said Klaas. 'If the AmaZulu are blown to the four winds? So long as you can still make gold? So long as you can hold our lands? So long as your missionaries can bring us their bibles?'

'Klaas!' said McTeague. 'I am shocked. Shocked. You must take no notice of my skin. Nor yet the sort of clothes that I wear. For I am now a Zulu. Like you. And Pastor Jupe may be a friend, but I have nothing to do with those things that the missionaries preach.'

He knew that the Almighty would forgive him this minor transgression. After all, had he not gained significant credit today by bringing that sweet girl into the Lord's fold? *Everything for the greater good. But, all the same, there may be friends here that would bring Willie McTeague more profit from their loss. Some friendships blossom better once buried.*

'Then, if you would be one of the People of Heaven,' said Klaas, 'you must learn to share our sorrows as well as these blessings.'

'I see that the war goes badly.' He wondered whether he might have been just a little over-enthusiastic in his efforts to fan the flames in the first place. Given Chelmsford and Frere just *too* much cause to pursue the thing so hotly. Yet the *Cape and Natal News* had so avidly accepted his various pseudonymous fabrications about Zulu barbarity. There had been the reverses too. At Isandlwana. At Intombe. At Hlobane. So much slaughtered English pride to be avenged. *And where would I have been without the war? Still playing second fiddle to people like Dunn, that's where!* 'But the Great King may still win, my friend,' he continued, brimming with false optimism.

'It is Cetshwayo who has brought us this shame, iNkosi. And now Chelmsford has rejected his offer of peace yet again.'

'The guns?' said McTeague.

'Chelmsford did not even send him a reply.'

'And…?' He was about to say, *And my own message?* But he thought better of it. Yet Cornelius Vijn caught his drift.

'The Frenchman, Grandier,' he said, 'was delivered safely back to the English lines ten days ago. Eleven maybe. We have heard nothing since.'

'So, yes, iNkosi KaMtigwe,' said Klaas, 'the war goes badly. And, as I told you, things will not be the same at its end. Not for the People of Heaven. But for you, white Lord? With your oiled hair and your eye of glass? I doubt that much will change. You will still have your money. The fine wife that Klaas has brought. The wife for which I have still not been paid.'

'Ah,' said McTeague. 'The gold. Yes, of course. The gold.'

'Stick fighting,' McTeague explained to Maria Mestiza, 'is no different from fencing. Boxing, for that matter. They help to prepare a fellow for war. The instincts for thrust and parry, or feint and footwork. They're all the same.'

She swayed at his side, the only woman who had been permitted to follow the men folk down the hill to the natural arena carved by the wind and spirits into the sandstone rocks below eMoyeni.

'Stick fighting,' she repeated, and spat on the ground. 'Then what are they eating?'

'The brown stuff? Some sort of stimulant, I think. Concoction of the medicine man.' *I wouldn't say no to a snort myself*, he thought. *All that dancing. Takes it out of a fellow.*

There was quite a gathering, the younger men already taking turns to display their skills. Shadow battles. Right hand gripping the reversed shaft of the *iklwa*. Left hand using the longer body of a throwing spear as the blocking stick, an *ubhoko*, as well as a miniature version of the war shield.

'Perhaps we should all try some, my dear,' said Simeon Cornscope, one of McTeague's cronies.

Now here is a case in point, thought McTeague. Cornscope purported to be a medical practitioner but was, in truth, no more than a purveyor of quack unguents. A plausible rogue. And useful enough when McTeague and Maria first arrived at the Cape. *Wonderful exponent of the Glimmer Drop. One of the best Magsmen I've ever seen.*

'I don't think the rules permit its use by the spectators,' said McTeague.

'They have rules for this?' said Cornscope in dandified surprise.

'It's a gentlemen's game here. Strict protocols. The old *induna* there will regulate the whole thing.'

'Ah, regulation,' said Twinge the freightmaster. 'The curse of modern society.'

They watched as the wizened umpire checked each spear shaft for fair play, while the onlookers chanted the praises of every potential fighter and the first challenge took place. A young unmarried man circled the ring, shaking his shield until he set eyes on another, bounded towards him.

'*Nansi inkunzi*,' he yelled. Here is the bull!

'And here is another!' replied his opponent, accepting the challenge, jumping forward into the open space.

'We haven't done too badly from the regulation here, old boy,' McTeague said to his freightmaster. 'In fact, I'm wondering whether we should modify our prices somewhat.'

'Time to put them up again?' said Twinge. It seemed strange to see him so well dressed. Scented to disguise his normal odour of oxen and mule.

'Oddly, Mister Twinge, I was contemplating the possibility of offering Her Majesty's government some discount.'

'Over my dead body,' said Twinge. 'Discount? Why would we give a bloody discount?'

'You should see it as an investment, old fellow. We have the freight contract only between Botha's Hill and Pietermaritzburg at the moment. Correct?'

'That's because we only own the one set of sheds. The ones at Botha's Hill. But we'll clear £20,000 from the business by the end of the year all the same.'

'Exactly, Mister Twinge. The train only runs inland from Durban to Botha's Hill. We own the depot at Botha's Hill. To ship freight any further, it has to be stored in our sheds, conveyed on our wagons. Or left there to rot. And we charge the Commissariat the same for that privilege as the competition elsewhere. Three shillings per hundredweight.'

'Then why cut the price?'

'Because, Mister Twinge, when the war is over, trade will flow. It will most certainly flow. So imagine, good sir, that we used some of our profit to invest in further equipment. Klaas tells me that there are still perfectly good wagons lying abandoned at Isandlwana and other places. A few modifications. Lick of paint. How would the Commissariat ever know? And a new depot perhaps. At Pietermaritzburg itself. Or Ladysmith. And an offer to the army that our expanded enterprise has brought us economies. Economies that our patriotic duty requires us to pass on? To keep our own wheels greased. Those of the Commissariat too. And then, Mister Twinge, we can always add the occasional sweetener here and there. What d'you say, sir?'

Twinge did not, in fact, say much at all. He merely shook his head in disbelief. *Perhaps another case in point then*, thought McTeague. *And what was it the fellow had said? 'Over my dead body.' Was that it?*

'Going at it hammer and tongs now,' said Cornscope. 'Just look at them. Why did he challenge that particular fellow, d'you imagine?'

'Probably some bad blood between them already,' said McTeague.

'And we are required,' said Klaas, 'to settle all such disputes so that they do not spoil the ceremony.'

'Speak now or forever hold thy peace, eh?' McTeague smiled while, in the open ground, the two warriors completed their initial sparring of shields, each now satisfied that he had smoked any weakness in the other's defence.

The stick fight begun in earnest. Both crouched low to the ground, their white cow-tail leg ornaments kicking in the dust. The flurry of shaft on shield, the crack of wood upon wood. Then the sharp slap as one of the men's weapons made contact with his opponent's flesh. A wound to the calf that he would feel for many months to come. They separated, circled again, the successful strike greeted by renewed singing among the crowd, jeering laughter from its perpetrator. Crouching once more, each moving remarkably fast in this unnatural position. Strike, parry. Counter-parry and riposte. Cross and cut. Feint and envelopment. Lunge and retreat. *Touché*. Another hit scored.

'How long will they go on?' said Cornscope.

'It could go on for some time,' McTeague replied. 'And then there will be more challenges. More fights. We might be here all afternoon. But I have promised to take my new bride on a tour of her new property.' He glanced at Maria Mestiza. 'And I trust you will accompany us, my dear?'

'Stick play ends whenever first blood is drawn,' said Klaas, 'so that the *induna* may declare a victor. Or when one of them says he has had enough, that he recognises his opponent as the chief bull. In which case, the victor is required to accept his surrender with humility. You see, my friends, that the People of Heaven have learned to fight so that we might win – or at least so that we might lose with good grace.'

From the highest point of his lands at eMoyeni – the low ridge where his wealth lay hidden, just beyond the house – the veld sloped gently down towards the east and, while the coast itself was not visible, he could easily discern the distinctive outline of False Bay and Lake Saint Lucia, eight miles away, just inland. The edges of the forest too. Lines of broken hills to the north and west.

McTeague had expected the ceremonial cart to impress Amahle and her family. It had, after all, been a principal symbol of Dunn's status and McTeague believed that it should have bestowed the same significance upon himself. The thing itself was impressive enough. A four-wheeled sienna-yellow shooting brake, its longitudinal rear seats allowing a dozen passengers to sit *dos-à-dos*, and a fringed canopy to protect them from the sun. The red leather reins and traces, breeching and back straps, collars and bridles. A team of eight zebra. Eight as a minimum. For he had discovered, as Dunn had before him, that while the beasts could be at least partially domesticated – so long as one was prepared to commit sufficient quantities of blacks to the ordeal of nasty bites and broken bones in bringing them to the halter – they lacked the strength of either horse or mule. They had a wayward nature too, so would frequently refuse to move at anything above an amble, or sometimes to even move at all. At others, they would take the carriage on an erratic canter in company with the family of ostrich that frequently ran about the place. But their least appealing attribute was an absolute refusal to submit to grooming so that, though they maintained an instinct to bathe themselves in dust, they were never quite free of the dung scent that accrued from confinement within the enclosure of their thorn *bhoma*. Yet the smell of the zebra seemed to move Amahle no more than the shooting brake itself. The smile that had illuminated McTeague's kitchen, the dancing ceremony which followed, remained fixed upon her features. She exchanged no word with new husband to her left nor with mother to her right. Nor with Maria Mestiza, cradling a hunting rifle on McTeague's farther side. Nor with the female relatives on the *banquette* seat behind her who chattered sufficiently to drown even the rasping wing-song of the crickets.

'What do you think of your new home, my dear?' He spoke to her in IsiZulu, using the word *sthandwa* to express his new-found affection.

'My daughter is honoured to marry a lord with such wealth,' said Amahle's mother, a large and perpetually jovial woman.

'Has the girl no tongue of her own?' said Maria Mestiza, though the words were so slurred that nobody but McTeague understood her.

She is usually more amusing that this, he thought. *The whisky normally mellows her mood.*

A large monitor lizard lumbered across the track ahead of them and the driver attempted, unsuccessfully, to persuade the zebra team to turn aside from a collision course. Luckily, the reptile was capable of prodigious acceleration when it so chose, and with a scrabble of claw on gravel, it was gone into the bush. McTeague had discovered that the local blacks were equally uncomfortable with the administration of rein and bridle as the zebra with bearing them. *Unlike the English-speaking negro of the West Indies*, he thought. *Docile and malleable fellows for the most part, especially when given good leadership. Like... well, like my own.* He was certain that the Almighty would forgive his lack of modesty. *Just a pity that my subordinates never followed the same example. Things could have been so different.*

'My daughter,' Amahle's mother continued, 'also finds herself married to a great lord whose chief wife is also a renowned *inyanga*.' She turned towards Maria Mestiza, but kept her eyes fixed firmly on the floor boards of the carriage. 'We see you, lady. Your fame as a shaman stretches across the land.'

'That,' said Maria Mestiza, 'is because I am *from* this land. My spirit has crossed the wide oceans, been born and raised again, far away.' McTeague prayed that God would also forgive her heresy. 'A stranger on strange shores,' she continued.

'But now returned to the home of your ancestors, sweet one,' he said, then regarded both Amahle and her mother. 'To build a kingdom of our own. Under the dominion of the Great King, naturally. But a kingdom, none the less. What say you, ladies?'

There was a stagnant pool below them, shaded by Butterspoon trees, and six Cape buffalo wallowed there, surrounded by a cordon of white egrets at the water's edge. Amahle regarded the beasts with the same inscrutable smile.

'We are blessed, iNkosi,' said the mother. 'But my daughter wonders whether your chief wife can help her locate the soul of her brother, my son? He is with the Great King's *impi*. Gone to fight the red soldiers.'

Maria Mestiza swayed in her seat as the shooting brake startled a herd of nyala away across the veld.

'I see your one-eyed son,' she intoned, as though entranced. Amahle and her mother both gasped. The relatives were silenced. 'I see him praised by the Great King Cetshwayo kaMpande himself. Exalted for slaying a white iNkosi. A new rifle bestowed upon him in honour. New Praise Names conferred. And a reward. Cattle of his own. Cattle that he will bring to the homestead of his father, Ndabuko Iron-shaper.'

It did not seem to occur to them that Maria Mestiza might have actually witnessed the scene, and their amazement at this revelation kept the Zulu women silent for some time. They were moved neither by the view of a crocodile feeding frenzy by the river, nor by a distant sighting of the lion pride clustered around the sandstone base of Anvil Rock, a pair of cubs draped across its back and bathing in the afternoon sun. *It is so unlike Honduras*, thought McTeague. *Yet there is a wilderness grandeur that they share. The hand of God so evident in them both!*

'I was thinking about Honduras,' he said to Maria Mestiza.

'You want to be a major again?' she cackled. 'Marching with the red soldiers? Up and down. Up and down.'

'I found there was little profit in holding the Queen's Commission.'

Yet she had touched a nerve. All those years with the Regiment, five of them as a major.

'They treated you like a piece of dung. But you deserved it. Court of Inquiry!' She spat over the side of the wagon. 'I could have told them some things.'

'Ah, Kingston. Jamaica. Now there's a place!' *Oh, the glorious sights and smells of Harbour Street.* 'You know, my dear, that it seemed glorious to me even on *that* day.' Jamaica had still been in the grip of the Morant Rebellion's aftermath. *You could hardly blame the blacks, I suppose. Thirty years past emancipation and neither food nor work to show for it.* And he was glad that the Fourth had played no part putting the thing down. No, the Fourth had been stamping out flames elsewhere. In Honduras. 'And *what* would you have told them, sweet one?'

'How you ran away, of course! When we attacked your pretty soldiers at San Pedro.'

If only the men had stood, he thought again, for the thousandth time. *I would have stood with them. Of course I would!*

'You know very well that I had little choice. Once those two young cowards broke...' Yet there was the small matter of the Civil Commissioner who had been with the expedition. 'And you never *did* tell me exactly how Mister Rhys met his end, I don't think.'

'You don't want to know,' she replied. *No*, he thought, *I don't suppose I do.* Rhys had disappeared without trace. McTeague had heard about the reprisals though. Another force sent into the Yalbac Hills. Three *campesino* towns burned. A thousand Indians butchered, according to the reports. He had seen some of the devastation for himself. For Honduras had called him back. God had summoned him there. It was written that way. His meeting with Maria Mestiza. A reunion, really. Though he had not known at the time that she too had been at the San Pedro rout – on the other side, of course. But that was after the Court of Inquiry. After he had done the deal. The surrender of his Commission. In exchange for exoneration. And a modest purse of gold, naturally. A bargain for his silence. No blot upon the pages of regimental history.

'The other two were entirely acquitted,' he mused, hardly realising that he spoke the thought out loud. 'My so-called lieutenants. Ferguson. And the other fellow, young Carey...'

'From what I could see,' said Maria, 'they were a long way behind you.'

She stood, lifted one foot to brace herself against the shooting brake's side board, wound the rifle's sling around her left arm, lifted the trapdoor receiver and slipped a bullet into the breech. Then she tucked the butt's heel and toe tightly into her shoulder. An American weapon. Springfield. 1870 model. McTeague followed the line of the barrel to a place almost five hundred yards away where, with concentration, he was finally able to discern the slender and camouflaged outline of a male cheetah, tail raised, marking its territory against the bark of a desiccated tree stump, and apparently staring back along the gun's sights with an intensity, focus and defiance that matched Maria Mestiza's own. A straight line between the feline's high-set amber eyes, reaching back to the rifle and Maria's shoulder. A perfectly steady axis around which every other part of Maria's body wavered and lurched in the way that he had seen marksmen perform their skills aboard ship – in their case to compensate for a pitching deck, in her own for the befuddled effects of inebriant liquor. She made a slight adjustment to the sights and squeezed the trigger.

The report was like the raucous exhalation of breath knocked from a gut-punched pugilist. Almost an echo of itself. The barest hint of smoke but the air sharp with cordite. The Zulu women starting in alarm. Songbirds too, flocking skywards all around them. The Springfield remaining on target, firm as the proverbial rock while Maria Mestiza's head lifted drunkenly to one side, a puzzled snarl curling her lip. For the cheetah had not moved, stood as still as the gun. The whole scene seemed frozen. The flies no longer whined. The rasping cricket song ceased. Then Maria reached to her bandolier, drew out another .50 calibre cartridge, and was ejecting the spent round when the cheetah suddenly slipped sideways and collapsed into the yellowing grass.

McTeague stood on the threshold of the hut he had cleared for his new bride. He was nervous.

They had returned triumphant from their excursion, the bridal matrons awed in equal measure by Maria's powers of divination on the one hand and her hunting prowess on the other. Word had spread quickly among those still within the villa's precincts, though these were mainly the wedding party's women, for the men folk remained immersed in the stick fighting, away down the hillside, and a small crowd had assembled to see the cheetah's corpse lifted from the shooting brake. So, while the heart-shot beast had been carried off for skinning and butchering, Amahle's maids of honour had danced and chanted their way across the yard, escorting the new bride, proudly carrying the upturned miniature spear that represented her purity, to the alien wedding bed that McTeague had provided for her.

He was sweating profusely. Partly due to the effect of afternoon heat, his recent efforts and his corpulence. Partly to the heady mix of Amahle's musk and Bird's Brandy perfume that still filled his nostrils. Partly to the recollection of her form seen through the diaphanous scarlet of her wedding cape. Partly to her public pronouncement that he had turned her heart as white as the milk of her dowry cattle – a compliment, he was certain. Partly to the doubts that filled his heart. Not doubts about fidelity, naturally. He had prayed to the Almighty for guidance, and the Lord seemed to have responded positively enough. Maria Mestiza also showed scant concern about wife number ten, so long as the girl followed the normal prohibition from the house once the ceremony was concluded. Indeed, Maria seemed only pleased that there were a few less mouths to feed now that Dunn's four concubines had been driven away. She had taunted him, of course. Drunken jibes about his virility. But they did not trouble him. No, it was the recollection of the difficulties which had followed the consummation of his previous marriage that caused him such concern.

McTeague's breath came in short gasps. There was a tightness around his chest. Yet he could not discern whether he was actually experiencing these sensations or merely reliving the symptoms of his earlier debility. *Take it steady, old fellow*, he thought. *That's the way to do it. Almost sixty, after all. And wouldn't some of the younger chaps give their eye teeth to be so blessed as this?* He had a momentary vision of Amahle heavy with child. *His* child. A son and heir. He reached for the door, while the matrons giggled behind his back.

There was a shout from across the yard. One of his field-hands running towards him.

'You must come, iNkosi!' the man shouted. 'The stick fighting...'

Damn them, he thought. *Too much sorghum beer, I imagine. The whole thing out of control. Somebody injured.*

So he followed, while the Zulu babbled about an intruder, an unwelcome guest at the wedding. McTeague tried to seek some clarity but failed miserably. Yet by the time they were part-way down the hillside, the sandstone outcrop below them, the semicircle of flat ground that the rocks sheltered, he could see for himself that something was wrong. The disciplined ring of spectators had broken down into fractious and argumentative groups. The fight captain, the old *induna*, was restraining Klaas, shouting at him. And behind him was Amahle's father, Ndabuko. He was remonstrating with a warrior who stood defiantly on a flat boulder.

'It is the tradition,' yelled the warrior. 'That where there are differences between guests at a wedding, they must be settled before the ceremony is over. You cannot deny my right to challenge this man.'

'I recognise no difference between us,' Klaas replied. 'But I will accept his challenge anyway. It is not the first time that I have needed to teach this cub a lesson.'

McTeague looked again at the newcomer, recognised him. He recalled Maria Mestiza's prophesy about Amahle's brother. That he would bring cattle to the homestead of his father. *Well*, he thought, *it's more than just cattle he has brought. And I, too, now see the one-eyed prodigal son.*

Chapter Seven

Sunday 27th April 1879

He thought that his shield arm must surely be broken – and the fight had barely begun. Shaba cursed himself for even being here. He cursed himself for the time he had spent on his return to the Great King's *ikhanda* with the Swazis, with news of Prince Mbilini's death, news of the red soldiers' movements, news of the Frenchman's release. He cursed himself for the censureship he had endured on his confession that he had slain a potentially valuable prisoner. He cursed himself for the days spent in isolation during his cleansing. He cursed himself for his failure to speak out when he finally received word that his sister was now betrothed to the white man, KaMtigwe. He cursed himself for the loss of face, the paucity of his kills that had allowed this Skirmisher with a Dutchman's name, this Klaas, to lay claim to Amahle – not for himself, it turned out, but as a broker of her marriage to the fat trader. He cursed himself for his foolish wager of his sister in the first place. He cursed himself for allowing, even then, the honour cattle that he received from Cetshwayo kaMpande to beguile him more than the need to return quickly, to prevent this thing. He cursed himself for the delays experienced while driving the cattle eastwards to his father's homestead, yet forgetting the remarkable fortune which, despite his confession and censureship, had left the beasts in his possession at all. He cursed himself for his shock at finding the *umuzi* empty, the wedding ceremony already under way. He cursed himself for the shame he felt in the realisation that most of his family members – his mother, his father, even Amahle herself – were willing partners in this charade.

He sprang back, rising from the fighter's crouch and spinning around, raising the wooden haft of his *iklwa*, his stabbing spear, as though to say, '*See? I am unharmed by this man.*' But he could not have raised the shield arm so. Despite the *ugwayi* that he had snorted from his neck bottle. Despite the battle-heat he had raised within himself. Despite his focus on defeating this Skirmisher, with his scars, his goat's face, his goat's beard. It was all he could do to maintain his grip on both the small shield's spine-stick, as well as the blocking *ubhoko* – the shaft of his throwing spear – let alone lift them back into the defensive position that he would need in order to continue his challenge.

The grizzled fight captain stepped forward during the lull.

'Well?' said the *induna*. 'Do you see the bull, Tshabanga kaNdabuko, Giant Slayer?'

It was an invitation to graciously admit that the blow to his arm was significant, that Klaas had bettered him. A chance to lay down his grievance in a manly fashion and accept that it was now resolved, that the marriage was inevitable. He had not shamed his family by speaking this grievance aloud, naturally. But the men here assembled all knew well the root of his challenge. Yet was it sufficient reason to fight? And to what end? Even if he had not suffered the injury, even if he had been victorious, could he have changed the outcome?

'I see no blood,' Shaba replied. 'And I see no bull.'

The spectators laughed, or cheered his defiance, glad that the contest would continue. The *induna* shrugged, stepped backwards, and Shaba turned once more to face Klaas, falling back into the crouch and using the movement to mask manipulation of the shield, lifting the left arm with his right hand, planting the blade of his throwing spear in the ground so that its blocking stick shaft stood vertically, forming a crutch to support the useless limb and around which he might still pivot a decisive attack. It was a subtle manoeuvre, but the flicker of a smile on the lips of his opponent told him that Klaas had seen it, understood it.

'Is your wing broken, little bird?' asked the Skirmisher.

'It is well enough, Izimu,' Shaba answered. The insult literally implied an eater of human flesh, a cannibal, but it also conjured images of the evil trickster, the ogre of tales told to children, the wicked character that preys on the weak.

Klaas feinted to the right. Shaba flinched but managed to turn quickly around the upright spear without taking the bait.

'If I am Izimu,' Klaas hissed, 'how have I tricked you? Did I not win your beautiful sister fairly?'

Shaba scurried forward towards his own shield, keeping low, bringing his attacking stick round in a fast arc that was instantly parried. But before the spear shafts had even touched, he had lifted his own into an over-arm blow that Klaas barely managed to block. There was a flurry of strikes, stick cracking on stick, but no successful hits.

'To win her for yourself may have been one thing,' panted Shaba. 'But to deliver her for marriage to this white dog, that is another. What happened Izimu? Were you well-paid?'

'If I am Izimu,' said Klaas, 'how do you see yourself, little bird?'

As Hlakanyana, of course, thought Shaba. As the half-human dwarf of their folklore. the hero who uses intelligence, the forces of nature, to defeat the evil trickster. But the thought cost him dear.Klaas took advantage of the distraction, scampered around Shaba's undefended right side, lunged inward with his stick.

Shaba danced away, but only so far that he could still hold on to his support. He realised that here was another feint. His stomach churned. He tried to swerve away, to bring his attacking stick into play defensively. But Klaas had already outflanked him. And the blow, when it landed, was another punishing one, to his lower back, that sent him sprawling forward, his full weight falling onto the already injured left arm. The pain was excruciating, unquenched by the *ugwayi*, so violent that it cascaded ice water on the fires of his battle-frenzy. The weight of it pressed him into the earth, made Shaba helpless in its grip, as though trapped and battered by the breakers of the coastal surf. He tried to rise but managed only a futile scratching of toes in the sand. And even when he finally lifted himself on his good elbow, the ground would not entirely relinquish him – great clods of red dirt clung to his sweat-streaming body – nor would the flooding tide of his agony turn to ebbing relief.

'I have received no payment,' said Klaas from somewhere just behind his shoulder. 'Not yet. And it seems to me that it is *you* who pays the price... Giant Slayer!'

His mocking laughter receded into the background as the *induna's* face swam into focus close to Shaba's own.

'Do you see the bull *now*, warrior?' he said.

Shaba spat the metallic dust from his mouth, cleared his nostrils of the blood and burning stink that filled them, listened as even his few supporters in the crowd chanted his downfall.

'See the bull,' they sang, 'and smells his balls.'

It is useless, he thought. But he recalled the wisdom of the leopard. The patient stalking of its quarry. The use of sudden speed to close for the kill. The reserves of strength upon which it relied to finish the thing. *I shall be like the leopard.* And his fury began to build once more.

'See the bull,' cried the spectators.

'Well, do you see him?' asked the fight captain.

'It is over, Warrior of the Evil Omen,' Klaas laughed. 'Your sister is already married. Time to let the beast go free.'

'I truly can smell the bull's balls,' whispered Shaba, 'and I shall chew on them before this day is through.'

He lifted his *iklwa*, used it to struggle to his knees.

'I could end this now,' said the *induna*, 'and you would obey me.'

'There is still no blood,' Shaba managed to say, 'and therefore no end.'

I have an advantage too, he thought. *For I have a reason to fight. While this Klaas Izimu has none.* He pulled himself upright. Unsteady, but upright. It was difficult to lift his head. He fought to master his hurt, to channel it through his hatred for the trickster. But he knew that he must make a sorry spectacle. Unable to crouch, he succeeded only in leaning clumsily on his throwing spear, flinched as he lifted the shaft of the *iklwa*.

Klaas took up his own fighting stance again, circled, keeping low, forcing his opponent to hobble around, to follow his stamping steps. And, in doing so, Shaba noticed the trader, KaMtigwe, puffing and panting his way down the slope to the arena. He saw the afternoon sun gleam golden on the white man's oiled hair, caught his gesture as the fellow placed a disc of glass in his eye. *Does the glass eye-piece hold magic?* he wondered, turning again to keep Klaas in his own vision. *Has he entranced my whole family?* And it seemed that his spirit ancestor shades answered him for, when they had each completed another half-revolution, he saw how the tumbling sun shone on the white trader's monocle, cast a dazzling burst of light against the eyes of Shaba's enemy. *Now!* he thought, knowing that there would be no further chance for him. He mounted the anguish in his back, his buttocks, his arm, and rode it forward. He lunged. Lunged again. Seeking the opening that he needed. The shafts smacked together. Twice. Three times. Klaas countered but was falling back, dropping his guard completely so that Shaba pressed on to deliver a sure strike to his enemy's skull. Whatever happened, he knew that he must draw blood.

But the assegai wood sliced only empty air. Klaas had skipped lightly to the left. It was Shaba's blind side, and he was hardly aware of the blow that found the crown of his own skull, even though it was delivered with even more force than those he had suffered previously. *Ah, Izimu the Trickster*, he thought as he fell. *Now, at last, there is blood.* For it was seeping down to fill Shaba's good eye.

The witch woman frightened him. For, difficult as it might be to grasp, and even through a half-clogged eye, he could see that this *was* a woman. The woman of KaMtigwe. His chief wife, it seemed. Though her face more resembled the monkey, *nkawu*. Yet even the monkey smelled better than she did. The stench of one who had consumed too much *utshwala*.

'He is awake,' said the woman. She spoke the tongue of the People of Heaven. Spoke it well enough for him to understand. There was a wailing in the background but he could not turn to see its source. The pain was too great. He had heard tales of those whose backs had been broken, who could no longer move any part of their bodies. Those who must sometimes be left to die in the bush. And he was afraid. Above him was a white expanse. Not the sky. Not the interwoven dome of a homestead hut. Just white. Perhaps the place where departed ancestors dwelt. For the expanse had corners, and the ancestors loved nothing more than a corner in which to hide themselves.

'Do you have the herbs to ease his pain?' It was his mother's muffled sobbing. 'Do you know how to throw the bones so that we can judge the medicines he needs?'

'Shall I travel to the spirit world also?' said the woman. 'To find out what is ailing him? Or shall I try to work it out for myself? Perhaps I could ask your son whether anything out of the ordinary has happened to him today. Something that may have caused these strange symptoms.'

'You mock me, holy one,' said Shaba's mother. 'But even the greatest *inyanga* must know the nature of any injuries within. Those that we cannot see. And how can these be known without throwing the bones? Without the trance? Or can you match the skills of our best diviners? Those who can sit close to their patients and simply sense the aura that rises from them, to perceive the very root of their problems.'

'Will he live?' he heard Amahle say from somewhere across this place of the dead.

Oh, I shall live, he thought. *But no thanks to you, little sister.*

'For what should I live?' he whispered. 'To see more friends die at the hands of the red soldiers? To see our lands stolen by white thieves like this one? To see yet more shame heaped on the name of our Clan?'

'Thief?' hissed the wife of KaMtigwe. 'I have blood in my veins as royal as that of your Great King.'

Blood filled with white man's liquor, more like.

'He needs food to strengthen him,' said Shaba's mother.

'There is broth,' the witch woman replied. 'There, on the stove. Dragon lizard meat.'

He knew that he needed strength. To settle with the white trader and the scar-faced Skirmisher. For the deal they had done. The selling of his sister. But the shame of his recent defeat filled him with bleak despair.

'We call it *inyama yembulu*,' said Amahle. 'We use it to treat those who are lame or palsied.'

'In the land from which I come, it is *iguana*, but its use is the same. And we must turn him soon. Rub his spine with snake fat.'

'Only the fat of the mamba will do,' said his mother. 'And the powdered horn of rhinoceros to give him strength.'

'This too,' said the wife of KaMtigwe. Shaba saw her hold aloft a sprig of oval leaves, deepest polished green. 'What do you call this here?'

'*Buchu*,' said Amahle. 'That is *buchu*. For the bruising?'

'Yes,' said the woman. 'For the bruising. That is, for the bruising that we can see. The bruising of his pride may be a different matter.'

'Oh, my brother's pride knows no boundaries,' said Amahle. Her voice was clearer, as though they at least now shared the same world once more. 'He has boasted about it often enough.'

Shaba lifted his head gently, shook it with care. To test the thing. It hurt. But he could move it.

'My pride,' he said, 'would not permit me to sell myself to the whites.'

The witch woman took his skull in both of her hands.

'How long since he lost the use of this eye?' she asked.

'When he was a boy,' said his mother. 'A stick fight with a friend.'

Umdeni, he thought. *I could not protect him. Nor Amahle. Nor even myself.* But the chief wife of KaMtigwe was laughing.

'Stick fight?' she said. 'It has never been one of his better skills then. Has he ever won one?'

'His boastful pride,' said Amahle, 'sadly exceeds his skills. And I did not sell myself to KaMtigwe, older brother. As I recall, it was *you* who wagered away my future. But fortunately it is a future I welcome. My husband is a growing light in the land. And when the war is over...'

'We will rule side by side?' said the witch woman. 'Is that what you think, girl?'

She loosened her grip on Shaba's head. He tried to sit. But it was too soon. *What is it you imagine, Amahle? That the war cannot still be won? That if we lose it, life under the whites will be kind to us?*

'Can you fix his eye?' asked his mother.

'I do not need her magic, Mama,' he said to her.

'It is an old injury,' replied the witch woman. 'But there are these.'

She took a milk-coloured pitcher from a shelf, poured some of the contents into her grime-streaked palm.

'The bean of the *umkhoka*,' said Amahle. 'Their juice is poison.' And she fingered one of the same, beaded into her breastband, bright red with a vivid black spot at one end.

'Yes, a deep poison,' said the witch. 'We call them *Ojo de Cangrejo*. But if we infuse them with spirit of sugar they can heal many things. Sometimes an eye becomes clouded like this because its parts have been displaced. But sometimes the cloudiness is no more than swelling around the injury. Like a scar. But after so long...'

He looked around, saw that he was in the cook-house of KaMtigwe's strange household. The walls as white as the ceiling. Cauldrons of copper hanging from hooks. Plates lining a rosewood rack, each one intricately patterned. And a monster of scorched black iron, a stove, across the room from the table over which he had been laid. Before the stove, seated on mats, a huddle of his female family members, still crooning and wailing while, at their centre, on a pair of the white man's slender chairs, his mother and sister. Amahle was beautiful in her wedding finery. He felt a tear run down his cheek but he could not find the power to wipe it away.

'Why have you done this thing?' said Shaba. 'Why has my father permitted you to marry the white man when you could have taken a great warrior of our people?'

'Because the Great King decreed it,' his mother replied. 'You gave your sister as collateral for your wager. The wager was lost and our daughter would have become the property of the one they call Klaas. That Skirmisher knew the lord KaMtigwe was seeking new wives who might bear him sons, told him of his new possession. And KaMtigwe asked the Great King's permission to marry Amahle. The great King decreed that it should be so.'

'Did you think,' said his sister, 'that your way was better? That I should simply have been taken by this Klaas?'

'At least he is one of the People of Heaven,' murmured Shaba. 'He is strong.'

For a trickster, he thought.

'Strong?' said Amahle. 'You mean stronger than *you*, brother? So what did you prove by challenging him on my wedding day? What did you think you would change? You thought only of your injured pride.'

'I thought that father would stop it,' he replied, though he knew it was a foolish comment.

'All that you did was to shame him,' said his sister. 'And me also.'

The witch woman had returned to her shelves, lifted down another container. A small glass bottle. Blue. She smiled, turned to him once more. It was disconcerting to watch her. For when he had regained consciousness, he had imagined his vision and balance badly impaired. Everything slanted at an angle. Though he now realised that it was only this strange woman who was tilted, out of kilter. As though she moved permanently on a sloping ledge. The effects of the liquor.

'Well,' she said to him, 'will you accept my gift?'

'I want nothing from you, witch woman. And where is my father?'

He had not seen him since before the stick fight. His father's furious face pressed close to his own. The spittle between his teeth as he cursed Shaba for his stupidity, as he spat upon his son's challenge.

'He is gone,' said his mother.

'But I brought cattle. To the *umuzi*. To Hluhluwe. They are still there. Five fine beasts. And one of them I have pledged as a token for my father.'

'He does not want your cow, my son.'

'Then let him tell me that himself.'

He saw his mother's jaw tighten, as though steeling herself.

'Nor will he see you,' she whispered.

A cold fear gripped his innards, dulled his pain at last. For this was no simple statement that his father would not meet him but, rather, that he was no longer recognised in his father's eyes.

Each separate step had been a trial, somehow made worse by the burning in his left eye socket. For the witch woman had applied the *umkhoka* spirit regardless of his objections, then covered it with a patch of leather, forbidden him to remove it until the moon was full again. But he had to admit that her broth, the unguents that she had applied, had freed his muscles sufficiently so that, within a couple of hours, he was able to ease himself from the table,

97

standing as clumsily as a new-born calf. And by sunset he had struggled back to the homestead at Hluhluwe, leaned now against the open entrance to the outer palisade, beneath the flame that still burned above the gateway. His father kept it lit, even in this time of war, so that the spirit shades of the Clan would always find their way home. For old Ndabuko was wise enough to know that it was most often during the hours of darkness that one needed the souls of the deceased to intercede with uMvelinqangi, the One Who Came First, that which has no name since it is beyond human understanding; that is more than creator but is, rather, the very nature of all that exists. That essence so far removed from the People of Heaven that no person had ever seen it, nor communicated with it, nor held ceremonies in its worship, since only the spirits of the dead had those privileges. But while the flame might provide succour and direction for his ancestors, it held none for Shaba.

And nor was he encouraged by the procession of other lights that blazed like a sky serpent in a wavering line from the furthest upper zone of the homestead. A slender, silent column of uncles, cousins, more distant male relatives, adopted and indentured herd boys attached to the *umuzi*. At their head, the homestead's diviner, the *isangoma* Mutwa, without the trappings of his office tonight and thus resembling the scampering baboon familiar that accompanied him, its back bald, stripped of hair by the shaman's practise of riding the beast, it was said.

'I see you, Baba,' said Shaba, noticing Ndabuko, further back in the line.

'But he cannot see *you*, Tshabanga of the Evil Omen,' replied the diviner.

'I am, above all other things, Tshabanga, son of Ndabuko. Now called Giant Slayer. My father may not see me at this moment, but he shall not deny my name.'

'You have shamed our headman,' said Mutwa. 'You have denied his will, his authority. Brought misery to your sister on the day of her marriage. For these reasons Ndabuko the Iron Shaper does indeed deny you the right to bear his name any more.'

Shaba could no longer distinguish the pains of his head, his back, his leg, from those of his deepest soul.

'I think that you are laden with lies, Mutwa Spirit-Speaker. If these things are true, let my father tell me so himself.'

'Let it be known,' cried his father, 'that every word spoken by the *isangoma* is the truth.'

Shaba glared at him. He was hurt and desperate, lurched forward with difficulty, snatched the burning brand from Mutwa's shrivelled fingers and pushed his way through a knot of the leading men folk to reach the wall of the cattle enclosure. He thrust the torch up to shed light on the animals within.

'But I have brought cattle to the homestead,' he shouted. 'If you cannot see me then at least see these beauties. For they are the pick of the Great King's own herd. Each one I have named. See this most noble of the five?' The yellow glow flickered across the dappled chestnut of a wide-spanned heifer. 'She is *Forest Floor in Leaf-Light*. And that one, called *Bountiful Portion*. Here is *Hut Cluster*.' The white hide with the sharp ebony mottle was so pure that it illuminated its surroundings even without the torch. 'This one, *Lark's Egg*. And the best of all, *Ancient Cloud Stabber*. See? The horns are almost upright and the hide could eventually furnish a fine shield for an *induna* of my own regiment, it is so noble.' Mottled, venerable grey.

His father murmured something that Shaba could not hear.

'Ndabuko the Iron Shaper says that he already has a surfeit of cattle. Including the six that he has received as *ilobolo* for the hand of his daughter to the white trader. He does not need these thin creatures that the stranger, Shaba of the Evil Omen, has brought here. He says that they should be taken away from this place.'

Thin creatures? It was a wound more cutting even than his father's rejection of him.

'Thin?' he said. 'Only a Basuto running dog of the whites would fail to recognise the perfection of such stock. They are each without flaw or blemish. More elegant than any wife could ever be.'

'If they have such value,' said Mutwa, 'you should take them and go. But they give you no right to question your father's decision in the matter of his daughter's betrothal. Nor to gainsay the will of the Great King.'

'Since when did a son that is also a grown man not have the right to have his voice heard?' replied Shaba. 'Did my father not teach me that a child who does not cry will perish silent in the sling? And so far as the will of the Great King is concerned, I am also a warrior of the Evil Omen. I fight for the Great King, received my honour name from him. But I see many here that should be with their regiments yet hide at Hluhluwe while the people bleed.'

There was an outcry of collective rage from those close enough to hear, more challenges made.

'The ancestors speak to me,' said Mutwa. 'And through me they inform our headman. They bring word from the One Who Came First to say that this war will soon be over. That we must tend our beasts and crops so that the People of Heaven can survive when it is done. For those who fall asleep while tending their herds will wake to find the enclosures empty, their cattle stolen.'

'The only threat to our herds will come from the red soldiers,' said Shaba. 'And hiding here while the war is fought will not protect us from them. Nor marrying our daughters to the white men. For what manner of calf may such a coupling bear?'

Shaba believed he saw doubt for the first time on his father's face. His words had struck a nerve, it seemed, and the old man began a heated debate with some of the other elders. Yet Mutwa's posture remained aggressive, his baboon familiar rushing forward, screeching, swiping at Shaba's shins.

'All the same,' said the shaman, 'you are banished from Hluhluwe.'

Banished from my own homestead? thought Shaba. *What evil has Mutwa woven to turn my father against me so?* He loved this place. Its chestnut and cabbage trees. The thorny poisonous climbers that gave the area its name, that grew in such profusion along the river banks. The slender spiked stems of the plant that he and Umdeni had cut as boys so they might muzzle the calves when it came time to wean them. The perils he had faced from lion, cheetah and leopard while watching over the herds. The winged creatures that filled its skies, ibis, stork and vulture, cuckoo and guinea fowl, drongo and widow-bird, hornbill and lourie.

'And shall my father never see me again in life?' he asked, his voice low, almost trembling with emotion.

'Is growing old not supposed to be a blessing?' said Ndabuko to the elders gathered around him. 'It is no blessing to be cursed with a child who knows no respect. May the spirits help to hasten my end, that I should not be so afflicted for long.'

'I am as you have made me, father?' murmured Shaba. 'Fashioned me as surely as you shape the iron. Every stream has its source, don't they say so?'

But his father was not listening. By some shared yet unspoken consent, the elders had turned away and begun to climb back up through the huts that circled the enclosure. Shaba caught Ndabuko's words, carried to him on the dung-scented breeze.

'He is like a knife,' said his father. 'Sharp only on one side.'

Mutwa the *isangoma* scuttled across to him, the baboon still dancing at his side. The shaman reached up, snatched back the torch from Shaba.

'Now go from here,' said Mutwa.

'I have my belongings to collect,' said Shaba. I left them earlier.'

'Then collect them and leave.'

So Shaba turned back towards the entrance, crossed it to the huts shared by the unmarried young men. He thought about the times he had stood watch here, guarding the gateway, stopping visitors to check their business, entrusted with the judgement to either turn them away, or make them await an audience, or usher them immediately into his father's presence. It all depended on the importance of the visitor, their relationship to the Clan. And for those allowed admittance, the gatekeeper's second duty. To perform the *Siyakhuleka ekhaya*, the welcome song in praise of the headman's attributes, his honour names. Well, he would sing them no more.

'Where will you go?' said one of his cousins as Shaba gathered his possessions.

'How is that your concern?' he snarled. But it was a good question. Where *would* he go? He needed to rejoin his regiment as soon as possible. Or, at least, to rejoin Mnukwa's mixed Company, his Swarm. Yet where to leave the cattle? Not here, that was certain. And he could not lose more face by returning them, even temporarily, to the Great King's herd. The logical alternative was to drive them south, to KwaMbonambi, the muster barracks of the Evil Omen and home to his new *induna*. Indeed, it was possible that he might find Mnukwa himself there, since there seemed to still be a lull in the fighting. So he took the regimental shield, removed its spine-stick, rolled the stiffened hide as best he could into a broad drum, marching fashion, to form a bundle that would protect the rifle and his spears, tied it with leather thongs. He filled a pouch also, with pieces of sweet cane, for the journey.

All the cow-tails, furs and feathers of his ceremonial attire must be left of course and, for a moment, he also considered leaving behind those items which, in happier days, Amahle had made for him – the loin cloth, the civet tail kilt, the headband – but which now made him feel unclean. But replacing them would require either trade with his cousins or theft from them. And he could be bothered with neither option. *I would sacrifice the calf for no more than the price of its hide*, he thought. A pointless exercise. *Anyway, I have fatter prey to hunt.* The stain of banishment to erase. His father to be released from whatever spell the old shaman had woven around him. The shame of his sister's marriage to the white trader to be wiped clean. Revenge against Klaas to be planned and savoured. And all his old dreams to fulfil. More cattle. Glory in battle. A worthy wife. More fame as a shaper of iron than his father could ever imagine. Yet still he ached from his injuries. From the spirit, too, that the witch woman had poured into his eye. Involuntarily, he touched the leather patch, almost failed to notice his father enter the hut.

Shaba experienced a surge of excitement. *I knew it*, he thought. *He could not renounce me so readily.* But his father did not spare him even a glance, looking instead at Shaba's cousins.

'I found this old kaross,' said Ndabuko. 'It no longer pleases me. And the winter nights are becoming cold. Especially for those with journeys to make. I thought that one of you might be able to use it.'

Yet he threw the sheepskin cloak purposefully upon Shaba's belongings and, without another word, ducked back through the low opening, disappeared into the night.

Chapter Eight

Saturday 17th May 1879

Voltaire had said: "Every man is guilty of all the good he did not do." The fellow's Faith may have been questionable but Carey had been unable to shake this observation about culpability from his mind ever since Alderton's death. It was, he believed, his mother's fault. For she had inculcated in him that most Catholic of beliefs – that we must all stand guilty of any evil that happens in our vicinity – even though she was not, herself, a Papist. Perhaps something to do with the time she had spent in France. Yet it was ingrained in him. Bred in the bone. Indeed, it was so strong within his soul that Carey frequently managed to feel guilty even when things were going well. And they were, indeed, going well!

He had received almost a hero's welcome when news of his vain efforts on Alderton's behalf were conveyed to Colonel Davies, and the two men had parted on the very best of terms when they finally reached Dundee almost two weeks before, on the Fourth. They had been met there by two officers of the 24th, Upcher and Clements, who had re-organised the drafts to form five new companies and thus bring their battalion up to strength for the first time since Isandlwana.

Carey was therefore free, at last, to join the Commander-in-Chief and take up his new duties for Lord Chelmsford, though he had one last escort responsibility to discharge beforehand. There had been a civilian waiting at Dundee for somebody to guide them onwards to Utrecht and, since this was also Carey's destination, the responsibility naturally fell upon his shoulders. And it was this individual who, he thought, might be assailing him today with a secondary guilt, one that he shared with the impressive column of soldiers that had formed before him – the sick parade.

He had set up a folding campaign table and rosewood writing slope outside his tent, and he was superficially engaged in producing a fair copy of the map he had sketched on the previous day. But his table and chair were sited as strategically as the strong-points detailed on his chart. To Carey's front, the mixed line of malingerers and modestly infirm formed a solid connection between the tents of Lord Chelmsford's Headquarters and those of the imposing hospital marquee, recently established here under Doctor Fitzmaurice. Beyond the hospital, the single-storey houses of Utrecht were scattered loosely around the web of tracks that met and crossed in the heart of the hamlet, against the backdrop of the Balele Mountains. No more than two hundred white inhabitants in total, plus a similar number of tame Zulus, living in the huts that fringed the settlement – the village to which Cetshwayo's brother, Prince Hamu kaMpande, had come in March to desert the Zulu cause, surrendering himself to Landrost Rudolph, the local magistrate.

Carey could see the Landrost's house from here and, very close to it, the bungalow and store owned by the hamlet's only Englishman, James White. And it was White's store that was the true object of Carey's vigil that morning, the source of his guilt, in fact, and that of the Company-strength sick parade too. For it was not actually the store itself that fascinated the camp so much as its most recently arrived resident, Carey's companion on the road from Dundee. He knew, even without looking, the moment when she had crossed White's threshold since the assembled line of soldiers gave vent to a collective roar of excitement that was, at once, both lecherous and adulatory. Carey shared neither sentiment, naturally. Rather, Sister Janet Wells inspired in him a similar level of awe, of respect for the gifts of the Almighty that he had felt when first exposed to the glories of Delacroix at the unveiling of that majestic central ceiling panel in the Louvre's restored *Galerie d'Apollon*. Indeed, she could have stepped, nymph-like, directly from the artist's brush strokes, though garbed in the grey ward dress, scarlet cape, white apron and coif of her profession. She was not yet twenty years old, yet the lettering on her armband identified her as one of the angels of mercy sent here by the Stafford House Committee, and he knew from the time he had spent with her that she had learned her trade the hard way, serving in the Balkans, seconded to the Russian army's medical team in that country's particularly cruel war with Turkey the previous year. She held no other fascination for him, of course. *Yet it would be churlish*, he thought, *should I not at least bid the young lady good morning and enquire about her health.* After all, she had been made less than comfortable by the considerable time spent in the saddle on her journey up-country. So he set down his pens, sauntered across to the line of soldiers.

'Make way there,' he said, and forced a path for himself towards the hospital's entrance flap, where Sister Janet was receiving her instructions from the doctor.

'All the normal problems,' the doctor was saying. 'More blisters. Lots of them. But you can instruct the orderlies to de-roof them. Dress them in salt, yes?'

'Yes, doctor.' It was a demure response, without any hint of irony, though Carey was certain that Sister Janet would be fully capable of dealing with no amount of blisters. All that experience in the Balkans. Her lone journey across two hundred miles of open veld to reach this most far-flung of Zululand's medical outposts.

'Apart from that,' said Fitzmaurice, 'still more cases of rheumatism. Too much time in the rain and rivers. Soaking wet uniforms. And half of them still showing signs of rickets from their infancy, of course. Doesn't help, does it. Then there's our old friend, *tinea cruris*, of course. The dreaded Dhobi itch. Another outbreak of fungal infections too.'

'They've not been following instructions then, doctor?' said Carey as he reached them. Sister Janet's recommended cure for the ailment had caused amusement throughout the camp. Foot infection was rife wherever the British army marched in warmer climes, as he well knew. But her recommendation that it could be cured by a simple expedient of the soldiers urinating in their boots at night, then leaving them to dry while they slept had divided opinion about the young woman. Half gave her credit for a miracle cure, the rest for being the best prankster they had ever met.

'Lieutenant Carey,' said the doctor. 'I was about to advise Sister Janet that a goodly half of these fellows appear to have no symptoms whatsoever beyond their fixation with the rare presence in our midst of an English rose. I trust that you are not similarly affected, sir?'

Well, damn the man's impertinence, thought Carey.

'I understand,' he replied, 'that the young lady has also helped fill the daily services as well as your sick parades, doctor. I trust that you will not similarly query my Faith should you see me there at my prayers?'

'I expect that Lieutenant Carey has come to enquire whether I am recovered from my ordeal,' said the nurse, with admirable composure. 'He was gallant enough to travel with me from Dundee.'

'You have no ailment to report, Lieutenant?' snapped Fitzmaurice.

Damned if I do and damned if I don't!

'None, sir. I am perfectly well.'

Actually, it was a lie. Carey had been feverish for some days. Since Dundee, in fact. Some vague malady, reminiscent of his illness in Jamaica, but one that he could not fully define. He had, in truth, intended to share his symptoms with Fitzmaurice but now entirely lost that inclination. There was a cloud of dust in the east, distant hoof beats, the guard instructed to stand-to at their allotted places around the camp's entrenched perimeter. The usual nervousness, the ever-present possibility of a Zulu counter-attack. Another massacre.

'Harrison's patrol?' said the doctor.

'The Prince,' murmured Sister Janet, and she blushed. For though that most renowned member of Chelmsford's staff might be fond of visiting the daughter of Swart Dirk Uys, one of the hamlet's burghers, there was no secret about the Dutch girl's lack of interest in the French Prince Imperial, while Sister Janet's open fondness for Louis Napoleon seemed, in turn, completely unrequited.

Louis had arrived here before Carey. His father, Napoleon the Third, had been defeated in that disastrous war with the Prussians eight years earlier, and

Carey had his own reasons to recall that conflict particularly well. But with France in chaos, yet another revolution, a Republic declared once more, the deposed Emperor and his family, including Louis, had taken refuge in England. Kent. Chislehurst, of all places. Then came the Emperor's death – a bungled gallstone operation, Carey recalled – and Louis proclaimed as his heir by Bonapartist supporters. An emperor without a realm, *prétendant* to a vanished throne. So the young man had immersed himself in British society, entered the Royal Military Academy at Woolwich. He would become expert in ordnance, as his great-uncle had been, though as a foreign prince he was denied the opportunity of taking up a commission. All this was public knowledge. So too was the manner in which, with the news of Isandlwana, Louis had begged permission to join the forces here in Zululand. His mother's personal intercession with Her Majesty. The Queen's intervention with Lord Chelmsford. And, hence, Louis Napoleon's presence as part of the Commander-in-Chief's staff – officially as an observer, albeit a celebrated and active observer.

'Have you ever seen a man sit a horse like our good Prince? The finest horseman in all Europe, don't they say?'

It was Longcast at his side. *Mister* Longcast, since he was Lord Chelmsford's principal interpreter. Though it grated. He may be part of the staff, but he was a Zulu when all was said and done. Half-Zulu at least. Half-caste. Longcast. Was it a jest? He often wondered. Though he had seemingly been given the name by Reverend Robertson, perhaps in a moment of Dickensian inspiration, when that godly gentleman had taken the young and orphaned Henry under his wing at the Magwaza Mission. Perhaps a jest within a jest, as Carey was convinced would soon be made apparent once more.

'He is a positive centaur, Mister Longcast. A centaur, sir.'

A centaur, it seemed, who had been using his time on patrol to learn a new song in English.

'*We don't want to fight but, by jingo, if we do,*' Louis sang, lustily.

Carey had heard the Great MacDermott sing it for the first time, at the London Pavilion during the previous year.

'*We've got the ships, we've got the men, and got the money too.*'

Carey preferred George Leybourne, despite his age. Past his best now, but *Champagne Charlie* could still bring the house down. Superficially, the licentious lifestyle that the song portrayed was deplorable to Carey, yet he saw its satirical qualities. There was something of Hogarth about the lyrics that he admired.

The patrol had been out for about five days, but was now considerably larger than when it began. There were two dozen Basutos who had ridden as the original escort, with Louis in their midst, on the bay called Fate rather than his favourite, a grey. Then a cluster of officers. Colonel Harrison, Lord Chelmsford's

Acting Quartermaster General – to whom Carey was directly responsible – commanding the patrol, along with Mister Drummond, the Head Adviser. A few others that Carey knew reasonably well by this time. And with them the now renowned figure of Colonel Buller, a thick-set figure with a beard almost as rampant as Carey's own who had made quite a name for himself by carrying several fugitives to safety at considerable personal risk during the headlong retreat from Hlobane. Colonel Harrison's group, Carey knew, had been given orders to meet up with Buller's men for a strong reconnaissance in depth, and these now formed an extended line of horsemen bringing up the rear of the column.

Lomas, the Prince Imperial's valet, hurried from the tents to help his master dismount. But Louis simply passed him a slender spear that he had been carrying, then vaulted easily from the saddle.

'You see, Henry?' Louis said to Longcast. 'I have found another with which we can practise. Give it to him, Lomas, will you?'

'Should you not like to rest first, sir?' said Lomas, a well-groomed little man, a Royal Engineer, with his oiled hair centre-parted and his moustache waxed.

'We shall have all eternity to rest, Lomas,' smiled the Prince. 'For the moment, I need some exercise. To stretch my muscles after so long in the saddle.' He drew level with Carey, whispered to him in French. 'Ah, Carey, I seem to find myself in some disgrace also.' He grimaced, gave the slightest movement of his head towards Buller and Colonel Harrison. It was obvious that they were, indeed, discussing the Prince Imperial, Buller seeming especially agitated.

'Your Highness,' Carey replied, also in impeccable French, 'whatever happened?'

'The Zulu,' said Louis. '*That* is what happened.'

'You were attacked, sir?'

'I wish it had been so. But no. We saw them several times. But always in the distance. In the end I took matters into my own hands.' He patted the hilt of his sabre.

'What exactly…?'

Louis swatted aside Carey's question before it was even fledged.

'There was one of them on his own. On a hill, I chased him away. Nothing more. He was so frightened that he dropped one of his spears. You see?' he pointed at the weapon now balancing in Henry Longcast's grip. 'There was never any danger.'

'You followed the Zulu alone?' said Carey. But Louis had already taken Mister Longcast by the arm and, as Lomas led Fate away, the two men strolled to the edge of the perimeter trench. The early morning sick parade queue was still moving slowly towards the hospital, and those in the line turned to watch the spectacle. Louis had drawn his sword and Henry was walking away from him, pacing out thirty yards, then forty, and finally fifty. Several of the other staff officers gathered around Carey.

'I wish he would not,' said William Molyneux, Lord Chelmsford's Aide-de-Camp.

Two years younger than me. A captain for the past year. An ADC already.

'I understand he is not in Colonel Buller's good books.'

'Making a report to His Lordship as we speak, Carey. Chasing after the hostiles on his own, I gather. Waving Boney's sword like a mad man.'

Boney's sword. That was the whisper around camp – that the sabre had once belonged to Bonaparte himself. Louis was waving it now also, to signal Longcast that he was ready. Then he adopted an *en garde* stance and waited while Henry, at the fifty yard mark, backed away several steps further, hefted the spear and ran forward. His arm came back, then launched the thing with a force that Carey could hardly credit. It hung in the air for a moment, seemed to oscillate before it hurtled down towards the Prince's position. The spear fell fast and true, would have skewered its target with ease but, at precisely the correct instant, Louis flicked his wrist, struck the shaft with the fuller of the precious blade, just at its balance point, near the guard. It must have jarred the young man's arm terribly but the spear spun harmlessly away.

'Again!' cried Louis, and Longcast – who had truly lived up to his name – ran forward to retrieve the assegai.

The spectators were joined by Paul Deléage, the South African correspondent for *Le Figaro* who shared Carey's tent.

'Did he injure his wrist?' said the Frenchman, breathing on his spectacles and cleaning the lenses with his kerchief, a small sketch pad clutched under his armpit.

Louis was lifting a finger to smooth his pencil moustache.

'He took it cleanly enough,' Cary smiled. 'He's very good at this.'

'Closer this time!' Louis shouted.

'You can't help liking him,' said Molyneux. 'But what's he doing here, Deléage? He has no position, so he can't even be mentioned in dispatches. And will the French love him any better for it? Heaven forbid that he should be wounded, yet I suppose that a limp might at least buy him some sympathy from your damned revolutionaries.'

'I don't know why he's here, Captain. He loves the English, though your comrades seldom seem to deserve his admiration. He was telling me last week, quite candidly, about an incident in which a group of your officers and gentlemen were standing outside his tent, very loudly discussing the same topic, apparently arguing about how many French each Englishman was worth. Five seemed to be the consensus.'

'That would have been an example of our strange British sense of humour, *monsieur*,' said Carey. 'Do you not think?'

'Oh, he thought it neither amusing nor offensive, Lieutenant. He was a little hurt, I think, but merely advised me by way of a lesson in life. He told me that I should not, myself, be disturbed if I heard such things. Simply a manner of speech, he said. The way that the English think – that they are superior to all other nations. I told him that I could understand why your presence here is so despised by the natives and the Dutch Boers alike.'

Longcast's second throw covered a distance of forty yards and, being closer, had less trajectory and thus far more velocity than its predecessor. This time, the Prince's sword struck the spear shaft with a loud crack, and the force of the impact caused Louis to grasp and rub his wrist. The onlookers grimaced but the Prince simply waved cheerfully at them.

'One more time, Henry,' he called.

'We're here to bring some civilisation to the heathen, Deléage,' Molyneux protested. 'And the Prince Imperial is not exempt from feelings of superiority, you know? Did you not see him with that poor fellow Grandier? The Frenchman who escaped from the kaffirs? Spoke to me about him afterwards. The best he could say about him was that – and I quote – he was not exactly *la crème de la crème.*'

'And it's hardly as though your own people have been kind to him,' said Carey. 'You're a Republican yourself, *monsieur*, are you not? I read some of those bitter articles that Ernest Blum wrote about him. And that awful caricature!'

It had depicted Louis as a mewling infant in an over-sized military uniform. *'Baby goes to war!'* it had declared.

Yet here was no spoiled child. A man grown, receiving the third throw of the spear from just thirty yards. Longcast had not spared him, hurled the missile with his full strength so that Carey had found himself forced to avert his gaze, unable to watch. But he heard the shaft whistle down the wind, the musket-shot report as it crashed against the sword, and a ragged cheer from the sick parade.

'I may be a Republican, Lieutenant,' smiled Deléage, 'but I admire that young man. His exuberance. His *joie de vivre.*'

Deléage was present also when the trader's wagon arrived late in the afternoon. It was a jawbone, one of those used by the Voortrekkers when they left the Cape and headed into the wilderness during the '30s, much longer than the carts employed by the army, and drawn by a span of sixteen oxen. Its hardy timbers and side-chests were dust-grimed green, its wheels daubed with red lead paint, and the internal hoops supporting its canvas cover – even the bamboo stretchers that held the canvas taut – were hung with an assortment of larger commodities, mainly farming implements, scythes, hoes, riddles, intermingled with an array of pots and pans.

The beasts had been released from their yokes and allowed to graze on the open ground near the hamlet's small arrow-shaped cemetery, final resting place of some of the town's original Voortrekker settlers.

'Are you looking for something particular, Lieutenant?' said the correspondent.

'A tin of condensed milk would be heaven, *monsieur*,' Carey replied. And was rewarded with that very thing, though it cost him a shilling. The label was peeled and the base rusted. But there it was, alongside the Cadbury's Cocoa – for "Strength and Staying Power," of course – the Royal Talcum Powder, the canned peaches, the bottle of Camp Coffee, the Seidlitz Powders, the bath salts, the Carr's Table Water Biscuits, the Cape cheeses – and the butter.

'My goodness,' said Sister Janet to the vendor, 'can this be correct? Eightpence an ounce?'

'Dear lady, the war. It is hard to believe the number of scoundrels seeking to profiteer from its pursuit. Why, we are almost giving our goods away these days.' The man was corpulent, immaculately dressed in a vivid waistcoat of yellow silk. He had two companions. A whip man, wizened and filthy, who remained leaning against the wagon, a clay pipe clamped between his rancid teeth. And a Zulu, thin, scarred, sparse beard. 'But since we share the same profession,' he continued, 'I am happy to dispense some of this finest butter at cost-price, Sister. Sevenpence ha'penny.'

'That's still almost ten shillings a pound. Oh, very well. I shall take two ounces.'

She turned to the others in the queue. 'I can't believe it. One shilling and thruppence for two ounces of butter.'

'Did I hear him say that he is also a medical practitioner?' said Carey. 'Even more incredible, don't you think?'

'I would take Mister Cornscope with a fair pinch of salt, Lieutenant,' she whispered. 'Though I wonder how much he might want for that jar of strawberry preserve. And an ounce of pipe tobacco, perhaps.'

'I could not imagine you smoking a pipe, Sister Janet.'

It was a feeble jest, for the whole camp knew that she spent the best part of her limited income on luxuries for her patients.

'And you, *Monsieur* Deléage,' she said, 'does anything catch your eye?'

'I was dreaming last night of Saint-Émilion, a Belair, *mademoiselle*. A '71, before the blight. But I cannot see any.' He smiled.

'I was hoping they might have a fresh copy of the *Gazette*,' said Carey.

'Expecting news, Lieutenant?' said Deléage.

'For several months now,' he replied, though he did not elaborate.

He had received word from the Regiment that Johnson had resigned his captaincy to enable his appointment to the Army Pay Department. *He must have taken up the post by now, surely. And I have seniority for the step.* So why had he heard nothing? Promotion within the 98th was almost guaranteed to follow the pattern. Johnson himself had been gazetted that way only last September. Yet there was always that chance that something might intercede with routine. Favours to be bestowed. Or obstacles to intervene. Some black mark on one's service record. He thought about Honduras...

'Now, gentlemen!' cried Cornscope. 'How else may we serve you this fine evening? Toiletries perhaps. A stick of shaving soap. A bottle of Bay Rum – the finest hair tonic that money can buy. And, speaking of tonics, we have on offer today my very own elixir. A powerful prophylactic against dyspepsia, dementia, diarrhoea and general debility.'

Molyneux had joined those gathered around the wagon, William Drummond too, though neither seemed especially interested in the trade goods.

'Mister Cornscope,' said Molyneux when there was a brief respite to the brisk business, 'might we have a word?' And he extended an arm towards the camp by way of invitation, or instruction, that Cornscope should join them. 'You too, Carey, if you please.'

Carey had been appointed as Deputy to the Acting Quartermaster-General, Colonel Harrison, to help resolve the absolute dearth of road reports or terrain sketches for the country – a task for which Prince Louis had also been loaned to the section – but it was unusual now for such patrols to depart without a briefing from the Honourable William Drummond. Yet Drummond remained a shadowy figure and Carey was always struck by the fact that he could never quite recall the fellow's features, even just a moment or two after leaving his company. So he studied him now. He was a little older than Carey, tall and slim, with the careful gait of a game hunter. Cornscope maintained a lively but nervous monologue, and Carey followed them to Drummond's tent. It stood next to Lord Chelmsford's and, like the Commander-in-Chief, Drummond was quartered entirely alone.

'Well, gentlemen,' said Cornscope once they were seated within, 'I am exceedingly pleased to have this opportunity. It is no mere chance that brings us here today.'

'It is Saturday,' said Drummond, 'is it not? And don't your trade wagons arrive *each* Saturday, Mister Cornscope?'

'Yet they rarely bring myself nor Mister Twinge in person, sir. Indeed not.'

'McTeague sent you?' said Drummond. He seemed somewhat unsteady, had a certain reputation for strong spirits. 'Does the old renegade have another meaningless message for us?'

'Ah,' said Cornscope, 'then I assume Trooper Grandier managed to escape safely. Mister McTeague was fearful for the poor fellow's life after they dragged him away to goodness-knows-where.'

'Escape, you say? Well, the story might serve for the rank and file, Cornscope, but between ourselves I suspect we all know the truth. We find him wandering just a stone's throw from our lines, conveniently carrying messages. One from old Catch-em-alivo himself. And the other from your good friend, McTeague.'

'You smoked him then, gentlemen?' said Cornscope. 'Well, it would never have done for the whole world to know his mission. And we had our own fellow as part of the escort. Just to see that the Frenchie came to no harm.'

'The kaffir who's with you today?' asked Molyneux.

'The very same.'

'Then we might have use for him,' said Drummond who, Carey knew, already kept a thriving team of Zulu spies on his private payroll. 'Does he speak English?'

'And Dutch too, sir. Raised by the Boers, he claims.'

Drummond nodded.

'Well,' he said, 'I'm not sure what that says about his loyalties but, Carey, you can fetch him in a moment and we'll have a little chat with the fellow. Now, Cornscope, we have a few other tasks for McTeague. But first, "no mere chance" you said. Your meaning, sir?'

Carey had heard mention of McTeague. One of the many whites who had been living within the borders of Zululand before the war but, unlike most of the others, McTeague was still there. But it was the name itself that gave him cause for concern. Common enough, he supposed, but all the same...

'And where exactly *is* Mister McTeague these days, Cornscope?' Molyneux interrupted.

'He made a strategic advance,' said Cornscope, 'as you military gentlemen might put it.'

'You mean he sequestered Dunn's place at Emoyeni,' said Drummond.

'The house was vacant, sir,' Cornscope protested. 'And it posed an excellent vantage point from which to observe the enemy's manoeuvres.'

'And Catch-em-alivo simply let him do it, I suppose? McTeague clearly takes his duties seriously in that regard though,' Drummond laughed. 'We hear he's taken another darkie to his bed.'

If Cornscope was surprised by Drummond's knowledge, he did not show it. But Carey was appalled. He had come across no end of stories like this. There was plainly some moral deficit among settlers at the Cape. Or, at least, settlers of a particular sort. And this fellow Dunn of whom they spoke had ridden into camp barely a week ago, bold as brass, a troop of his own volunteers at his tail, to join the mounted units already spread between Landman's Drift, Doorn Berge and Kopje Allein. Carey had been impressed, until he discovered that the cove had no less than four dozen Zulu concubines – wives, Dunn claimed, though Carey refused to grace them with any status of holy matrimony.

'Indeed, sir,' said Cornscope. 'I was a witness at the wedding. Divine young creature. For a blackie, of course. And I do indeed bring word from the lucky bridegroom. He was most distressed, gentlemen, that his offer in relation to King Cetshwayo seems to have been ignored. The Major maintains...'

'Major?' said Carey.

'Mister McTeague,' Drummond explained, 'once held the Queen's Commission, Lieutenant.'

'He was with the West India Regiment,' said Molyneux. 'The 4th, I think. Didn't you say that you served in Jamaica too, Carey?'

'With the 3rd, sir,' Carey replied, though he felt as though the ground had suddenly swallowed him. He tried hard to keep his voice casual, level. 'We saw very little of the 4th.'

'All the same,' said Drummond, 'it might be an interesting connection.'

Interesting? thought Carey. *It is the stuff of my worst nightmares.* There could be little doubt about it. This was the same McTeague. Come to haunt him. Or worse. He barely heard the ensuing conversations.

'And you were saying, Cornscope?' Drummond continued.

'Well, gentlemen. Three items really. First, he can indeed assist you in ensuring the return of those field pieces so unfortunately lost in January. Second, he believes you may be interested in his suggestions about bringing Cetshwayo to justice. And, third… well, it is a matter for the Commissariat, I suppose, but I am instructed to confirm that there may be an opportunity to re-negotiate the freighting costs between Botha's Hill and Pietermaritzburg.'

'How much are we paying now?' said Drummond.

'I'm afraid I have no idea, old man,' said Molyneux. 'As Cornscope says, it's a Commissariat matter.'

'I think you'll find, Captain,' said Cornscope, 'that the commercial rate is three shillings per hundredweight.'

'And McTeague's offer?' said Drummond.

'Two shillings and ninepence.'

'In exchange?'

'Agreement that, when the war is over, the territory around Emoyeni will remain under his jurisdiction, sir. Second, a simple endorsement of his plans to open a further freight depot at Ladysmith. And, third – a sensitive subject, gentlemen – but we understand that an expedition is imminent, to recover the remains of those unfortunate souls lost at Isandlwana. There are wagons there, too, are there not? So perhaps the opportunity for a mutually beneficial transaction?'

Drummond lifted a hand to silence him, considered briefly.

'Lieutenant Carey,' he said. 'I think we may need…' Carey realised he was being directly addressed at the same moment Drummond noted his lack of attention. Carey apologised, and Drummond continued. 'I was saying that we may need to discuss these matters confidentially with Mister Cornscope. If you don't mind, perhaps it might be a good time for you to go fetch the kaffir. Bring him here, would you?'

*

Carey was annoyed at this peremptory dismissal but delighted to leave the tent. Was it truly possible that this McTeague might be the same man? He had heard nothing of the *other* Major McTeague since Kingston. There had been rumours, of course. Smuggling, they said. Other illicit activities. It did not surprise him, for he had rarely encountered such a propensity for self-delusion in any other human being. Carey remembered his first encounter with the man. A detachment of the 4th under Major McTeague had been dispatched on a punitive expedition against Marcus Canul's Indian rebels after their attack on the Bravo River logging camp – and Carey, thirsting to make a name for himself as a warrior, had volunteered to join them. McTeague had provided a briefing to the officers, intelligence about Canul's strength, location and disposition. It all proved to be entire nonsense, of course, and they had walked into a trap. At the subsequent inquiry, Carey had realised that McTeague did not lie, exactly. The truth on the one hand and McTeague's version of facts on the other were magnetic poles that seemed the same yet each repelled in a contrary direction by the physical nature of the other. And could this be him? An entire hemisphere away?

There was an unusual level of noise from those still gathered around the traders' wagon. Indeed, the crowd seemed to have swelled considerably. There was often a certain lack of discipline at this time of day, Carey had found, here at the Headquarters camp, that would not have been tolerated elsewhere. But there were limits and, on this occasion, he could see that the line had been crossed. For there was an absolute prohibition against the sale of intoxicants. Yet here was Cornscope's white companion, Twinge, brazenly dispensing bottles of whisky, rum and square-face gin as fast as his Zulu assistant could free them from their crates. And the liquor was plainly already flowing fast among their customers. Carey was furious, looked around for assistance and saw a sergeant-major of the 90th emerge from his tent to also investigate the commotion.

'Sergeant-Major!' Carey yelled. 'Is there *nobody* in charge of those men?'

The 90th were garrisoned here, ostensibly to provide infantry protection for the Commander-in-Chief.

'I think we assumed, sir,' said the sergeant-major, 'that since the gentlemen are being entertained by Mister Drummond...'

'What?' said Carey. 'That this gives them authority to sell the devil's brew? For the men to imbibe same? Call out the guard, Sergeant-Major. At once. Disperse the men and clap that fellow in irons.'

'The kaffir, sir?'

'No, *not* the kaffir. The other. Twinge.'

But Twinge was not to be arrested so easily. The guard was duly turned out, and the soldiers of the 90th, their purchases subject to confiscation, confined to their tents, while Twinge protested that he neither knew of any such proscription against the sale of alcohol to off-duty servicemen nor, indeed, any under which he could be detained by the military for this alleged offence. And when the sergeant-major tried to action the detention, an enraged Twinge — he was a muscular fellow, as befitted the driver of a sixteen-strong span — flattened two men with a long-handled shovel. In the absence of any other senior officer, Colonel Wood was called, a flogging parade convened in which the miscreant would suffer two dozen lashes and be expelled from the camp, with his name posted on the door of the Landrost's Office so that all might know the purpose of his punishment.

'You will forgive me, I hope,' said Sister Janet, 'but the practice of flogging is barbaric, Lieutenant. The fact that this particular case involved a civilian only makes it more so.'

'It was a particularly heinous crime, Sister,' Carey replied. He had strolled across to the hospital to assist with her late-evening ministrations to the more acute patients, as was his wont. Some of them had been injured at Rorke's Drift, at Hlobane, at Khambula. Amputees. Those recovering from bullet wounds and broken bones. Many suffering the advanced stages of dysentery or rheumatic fevers. And no less than twelve other men who themselves had been flogged during the past couple of weeks, principally charged with insubordination or theft, dereliction of duty or drunkenness. 'It is critical that we maintain discipline, miss. Out here. The Commander-in-Chief endorsed the punishment personally.'

'I doubt we shall ever agree on this topic, Lieutenant. But would you care to help me read to the men? Something from the gospels again, perhaps.'

'As it happens, I brought this with me.' It was his mother's prized copy of *The Song of Hiawatha*. He opened the book, held it towards the lantern so that she could see Longfellow's signature. 'He rather admired her verses.'

'Carey's *maman* is something of a celebrity in my country.' Louis had entered the hospital without them noticing. 'Whole anthologies of fine poetry. One of them a tribute to the Imperial Academy of Caen. She had a vested interest, of course.'

'I was educated there,' Carey explained.

'You lived in France?' said Sister Janet.

'For a while.'

'And he came back again, did you not, Lieutenant, in my country's hour of need?'

Carey held up his hand in an effort to stop the Prince continuing.

'Please, Your Highness!' he said.

'He is a modest fellow, Sister Janet. But you should know that Lieutenant Carey is something of a hero. During our war with the Prussians he volunteered to serve with the English Ambulance Service. Did you know? Risking his life on the battlefields. And captured. How many times, Carey? Twice?'

'Three times, sir. It seems that I made a poor prisoner too, for they kept releasing me.'

'They released him, Sister Janet, because he had such a reputation for providing succour to each side equally. As you would have done too, *mademoiselle*, I think.'

Sister Janet had a certain reputation indeed, maintaining a separate enclave where she happily also treated the various injuries and illnesses of the local Zulus. They called her Mrs Sekhukhuni – one who moves about in the dark.

'You are too kind, gentlemen,' she said. 'But we should attend the patients now. I am not sure though, Lieutenant, that a heathen tale like Mister Longfellow's is precisely what they need.'

'I shall concentrate on the story's ending, Sister,' Carey replied. 'In which Hiawatha welcomes the Black-Robe to his camp so that the godly man might bring the Word of the Lord to his tribe, and the Christian message is accepted by the chief's warriors.'

'That sounds most appropriate,' she agreed. 'And I will take my own turn in due course. But I must attend to Gunner Burslem first. His new cork leg arrived today – though you should never guess the cost. Fourteen pounds and five shillings!'

She hurried away between the row of cots.

'And you, sir,' Carey said to Louis, 'should you care to read something for the men?'

'Nothing would give me greater pleasure, Carey,' said the Prince. 'But I understand that His Lordship is holding a small *soirée*. To discuss the expedition.'

'The dead to be buried at last.'

'Three months is a long time. But I suppose there would have been considerable risk of another attack had they gone sooner.'

Personally, Carey doubted that. He believed it an offence against God to leave decent Christians to the ravages of the wilderness all this time, as they had been at Isandlwana.

'You will volunteer to join them, Your Highness?'

'Frederic will not agree,' said the Prince, with that unique familiarity that allowed him first-name terms with Frederic Augustus Thesiger, Second Baron Chelmsford. 'He has seemingly promised Colonel Buller that I shall not be allowed out in future without strict control. I shall try to insist, though, that you are always part of the escort, Carey. The rest of these fellows are so dull.'

Carey smiled, knowing that the Commander-in-Chief was unlikely to agree such a request. And he was not unhappy.

'Well, enjoy the *soirée*.'

'Oh, I shall. And then I am planning to visit a certain young lady in the village.'

'Well, *bon chance*!'

Carey had been reading to one of the patients for perhaps fifteen minutes.

'From the farthest lands of morning came the Black-Robe chief, the Prophet, He the Priest of Prayer, the Pale-face, with his guides and his companions.'

But thoughts of the Indians brought back visions of Major McTeague, the ambush at San Pedro. He tried to focus on the verse, though it did nothing to banish his ghosts.

'Oh, has the Prince gone?' said Sister Janet, now at his side and wiping her hands on a cloth impregnated with diluted carbolic.

'A *soirée* with His Lordship,' said Carey. 'And then a private assignation, it seems.'

He had not needed to make this latter comment but it pleased him somewhat to see the disappointment it inspired. But she said nothing and wandered away, leaving him feeling a scrub. In any case, if he had hoped that she might spend some time with *him* instead, it was Carey's turn to be disappointed. And so, asking the Almighty to forgive his hypocrisy, he turned his thoughts to home, to Annie, to the children. Memories of them tumbling among entirely distinct recollections. Of Honduras. Of crimes committed and penalties paid. The death of little Jahleel Junior. The Lord had taken him, Carey was certain, as a judgement. They would meet again, he hoped, at the Day of Reckoning. But the interval between was long. So cruelly long. And, meanwhile, there was the Prince Imperial, Napoléon Eugène Louis Jean Joseph, heir to the throne of France. He would assume that throne, of course, one day. There was no doubt about it. This further French flirtation with Republicanism could not last. And when sense was restored, so too would be the Bonapartes. A golden age, thought Carey. France and England in a bright alliance of shared cultures. Peace in Europe for generations to come. Such a future!

And against it, Carey weighed his own prospects, tried to analyse his feelings, and felt himself surprised.

For he was jealous.

Chapter Nine

Wednesday 21st May 1879

McTeague could smell the place long before they crested the final rise and rounded the flank of the Ithusi Hill. The stench of decay that was, at once, both sickly sweet and sour. *How can that be*, he wondered, *almost four months to the day since the massacre?* And the sphinx-like outline of Isandlwana itself was still two miles away across the intervening veld, at the farther end of this broad valley flanked by mountains both to north and south.

They had seen more recent death, of course. At the local kraals. The horse soldiers, said the survivors, had appeared with the first glimmer of dawn, scouting parties making a broad sweep around the ridges and valleys, presumably checking that there was no *impi* waiting to ambush them once more but taking the opportunity to burn everything they could find, torching huts and palisades, driving off cattle, or simply slaughtering them where they stood, leaving families to the mercies of the veld, killing any who resisted.

So the Zulus that had run beside McTeague and Maria Mestiza, all the way here, two days from Emahlabathini, had indeed wanted to attack the invaders. They numbered almost an entire regiment – an escort, Cetshwayo had said, to make sure that McTeague arrived safely with the King's new messages for the white iNkosi. The Zulu commanders had been instructed that they must not engage the enemy, of course, despite all the temptations they were bound to suffer. For this was now almost sacred ground, the Hill of the Little House itself, the valley which it guarded, not only the scene of their greatest victory over the whites but also close to the final resting place of so many Zulu dead. The opportunity for a second victory was almost too great to ignore. And there were the ravaged homesteads to be revenged. The souls of the slain to protect. For the red soldiers who had come to finally bury their own dead would not respect the remains of their enemies. They never did. On the other hand, it was clear that Chelmsford was sending an expedition in force – an expedition composed solely of horse soldiers, for whom the Zulu regiments held no fear but certainly a healthy respect. They had still been debating the issue when McTeague and Maria Mestiza left them, made their way down towards the eastern extremity of the battlefield.

The message from Cornscope had arrived two days earlier, brought by

Klaas to Emahlabathini, where McTeague had been summoned again by Cetshwayo. It was a mixed message. Cornscope had been in negotiations with Drummond, Lord Chelmsford's Chief of Intelligence. They seemed to have been progressing well. Until, that is, Twinge had begun selling rot-gut to the soldiers and been flogged from the camp, the negotiations then taking a decidedly different turn. *Damn the fellow's soul*, thought McTeague. *He's becoming a real liability.*

Maria Mestiza looked at him with disdain, straightened her bandoliers, and medicine satchel.

'Ride, old man,' she shouted. 'By the time we get there, they will have gone.'

'I hope they have,' he replied. 'We'd do better to catch up with them at Utrecht. I don't relish the prospect of this place. The stink! Even from here.'

McTeague knew that he was not in the best of conditions to spend two full days in the saddle. Too old. His mare was a gentle enough beast that maintained her own rhythm, a walk, trot, canter style, going very much as she pleased but keeping a steady pace that did nothing to pacify Maria's impatience.

At the base of the hill, they found the first of the dead in some long grass, a heap of yellow, damp-looking human bones, and two dead mules among the boulders. A metal tripod too, left standing with its metal trough still intact, a case of nine-pounder Hales' rockets to one side, the contents strewn about the surrounding terrain.

'Rocket battery,' said McTeague. 'I met an old *induna* who was here. Told me it made a hell of a noise. Great screeching thing, he said. Only managed to fire one of them. But didn't kill anybody. Then lifted up his blanket and showed me the burns. The fellow looked like a hyena. White blotches everywhere. From the sparks, apparently, as it flew overhead.'

'It stinks here,' said Maria. 'Like *un matarife*.'

A knackers' yard, thought McTeague. He recalled a humorous piece he had read in *Household Words*, about the travels and observations of the mythical Mister Booley, including just such a charnel house. But even the inimitable Dickens could not have imagined this scene.

They continued westwards until they encountered the first of the outlying picquets, a couple of cavalrymen. The 17th, newly arrived from Durban. Dark blue tunics beneath the sun helmets and chin straps, long bamboo lances with wicked steel points, red and white pennons.

'Good morning, sir,' said one of the troopers. He looked uncertainly at Maria Mestiza. 'You have business here?'

'My wife and I are looking for a Mister Drummond,' said McTeague. The soldier looked even harder at Maria, shook his head slightly. 'We have intelligence for the Commander-in-Chief.'

'And have you seen anything of the enemy, sir?'

McTeague was momentarily taken aback. *The enemy…?*

'Ah, the Zulu!' he said at last. 'I'm sure they're not in force within fifty miles of here. Now, my good fellow, where might I find Mister Drummond?'

'I'm afraid I don't know, sir, but there are some civilian gentlemen with General Marshall's party. You'll find them just to the west. About a mile, just past that conical hill. They think they've found Colonel Durnford, sir.'

McTeague had met Durnford some time ago, liked the Irishman, thought he had something of the theatrical about him.

'I liked him too,' said Maria with that uncanny ability to read his mind. 'He was a man.'

But he was a man who had been largely reviled since the disaster as a major contributor to its cause, allegedly for failing to follow Chelmsford's orders and defend the camp when, instead, he had taken a significant part of the command and taken them on the offensive, splitting the available force and leaving it vulnerable. He had been similarly criticised six years earlier for the *débacle* at Bushman's Pass. *Of course*, thought McTeague, *it was Chelmsford who had split the column in the first place*. More than half his force led off on a wild goose chase. *These poor blighters left behind to their fate.* The Zulus he had met who helped lure them away had thought the red soldiers insane to fight a war this way. Durnford had come back when he realised his mistake, of course. Back in this direction, he imagined, fighting a rearguard action ahead of the left horn of the Zulu horde.

'Damn'd fool, he could have just ridden away!' said McTeague.

'Like I said,' Maria replied, 'he was a man.'

The path of the dead was growing wider. At each spruit and donga a further abandoned crop of remains, as though Durnford's men had kept halting, firing, inflicting casualties among the Zulu. They followed the trail for almost a mile until McTeague's heart was lifted by the sight of some distant wagons which, he assumed, marked the site of the camp.

'I had no idea there would be so many,' he said, his mind calculating a reasonable price that he might offer for any that the army no longer wanted. But between McTeague and his potential profit there was considerable activity. Uniforms of red and blue and buff hurrying here and there among the dead and debris. Immediately to their fore, on a rock-strewn knoll where the ground began its climb towards the heights of Isandlwana itself, there was a further cluster of lancers, a small cart, some Basutos, a knot of officers at their centre, peering down into a particularly wide donga.

'Is it him?' McTeague heard one of the officers ask.

McTeague and Maria Mestiza halted towards the near side of the gulley. There were many bodies. More bones, of course. But frequently the features of the fallen were quite distinct, hair and beards still intact, though sparse and lank, bleached by the elements. Tanned leather hide stretched taut over the skeletal remains beneath. Blackened orifices. Grinning faces mocking the insanity of their own final moments. Maria murmured something under her breath.

'How are they like this?' said McTeague.

'Gutted,' she whispered. 'It helps preserve them. Like…' She struggled for the word. 'Like *momificados*.'

Gutted by the Zulus to free their souls, McTeague knew. So the spirits would not haunt their killers. But he doubted the British saw such mutilation thus. He kicked his mare gently, trying to move her towards the very rim of the donga but, like all the other horses here, she was beginning to fret, becoming difficult to control in this place of death.

'Yes, it's him,' said a voice from below, choked with emotion.

McTeague could see now that two other officers were down in the dry river bed. One of them he recognised. Young Shepstone, was it not? Yet it was Durnford who drew his attention. There could be no mistaking him, despite the corruption that had rotted his corpse so badly. It was those absurdly long moustaches. And the sling, still tied around his neck, that had habitually supported a left arm paralysed at Bushman's Pass. The sling fluttered loose, filthy now, and the arm was flung out at a strange angle. Uniform trousers and boots still intact but his patrol jacket missing, the remains of a shirt bunched up around his upper torso to allow his disembowelling.

Shepstone – McTeague was relatively certain that it was Shepstone – felt gently around the trouser pockets, discovered a small penknife. He held it up, showing it to a mounted colonel, who nodded.

'For his family,' said the colonel. 'And those rings, Captain. Can you get them off?'

Shepstone looked at the withered hand, gingerly slid each of the two signet rings from their respective fingers.

'You see?' said Maria. 'He died with his men. And his men died with *him*.'

She was trying to make a point, of course. Yet it was true. The scene told its own story. Many of the bodies had been stripped but others were more easily categorised. The dark blue of Durnford's volunteers, the Natal Mounted Police, the Carbineers, others that he did not know. But similarly uniformed groups of the living were gathering their own, searching for signs that would help them identify friends, family, brothers-in-arms. Local men, all of them. Cape settlers. The remains were being lifted with care, on blankets, carried to a shallow and communal grave just a little distance away. *Too shallow*, thought McTeague. *Two months of rain and the poor devils will all be tumbling about the veld again.*

'These are the same fellows who cursed him for the Bushman's Pass affair,' McTeague replied, but the irony was lost on his principal wife.

'We'll bury him here,' said the colonel. He turned to a subordinate who seemed to be in charge of the Basutos. 'A tarpaulin if you please, Lieutenant. Then get those blackies to dig a grave for Colonel Durnford. Down there. We'll mark the place.'

'And the dead kaffirs, sir?' said the lieutenant.

'Leave them where they lie, of course.'

'I think these belong to us, sir. Native auxiliaries.'

'Can you tell the difference, Lieutenant?'

'Well no, sir.'

'Then leave the buggers where they lie.' The colonel looked up, noticed the new arrivals for the first time. 'You, sir!' he yelled. 'Why are you here, eh?'

McTeague straightened himself in the saddle, ran a thumb along his moustache, reached inside his coat, fumbled for the monocle, pushed it slowly into place and squinted through the glass.

'Me, sir? How dare you address me in that tone!' Nothing worked quite so well in dealing with the military boor, he had found, than the assumption of higher authority. 'I answer to none but the Commander-in-Chief and the Almighty Himself. Now, sir, you will direct me to Drummond, if you please.'

The colonel fulminated for a moment more but finally instructed a lancer sergeant to escort "these gentlemen" to the General's party. The route took them a little north, a little west, a little higher. More death. More stench. Belts and torn pouches.

'This seems to be the line along which the 24th was deployed, do you not think so, sir?' said the sergeant, with a deference due to this fellow who, unlikely as it might appear, seemed to outrank even the irascible colonel.

McTeague nodded. You could almost identify where each company had taken up its initial position facing the Inyoni Ridge. Beside him, Maria still bristled at the colonel's insult.

'If I meet him again, I will take his *cojones*,' she murmured, though there was no force to her venom. In fact, he thought, she seemed subdued, fearful. 'Can you see them, she asked?'

He gazed ahead, past their companion, as they picked their way carefully now, the horses still nervous, to the bare ground of the crest, beneath the mountain's bulk.

'The wagons?' he said, but knowing that she referred to something else, something more spiritual.

It was the site of the lost camp, an almost pastoral scene from this distance, for crops had sprouted in great profusion around the area, new life sprung from the grain sacks spilled here, nurtured and fertilised by the fallen. The stems embraced history too, froze time. For the wheat and long grasses trapped all the bric-a-brac of former owners as though they would soon return to claim them. Tent canvas, naturally, and guy ropes too. Kitchenware. Personal letters, official documents, books and journals. Playing cards. Sheet music. Chess pieces. Tins of meat and milk. Bottled pickle. Toilet bags. Brushes of every variety. A forge and bellows.

'Damn me,' said the sergeant. 'A survivor?'

He pointed to the shadows beneath one of the wagons. There was a man there, head resting on his saddle, soundly asleep and nestled comfortably under a blanket.

'It's been four months, man,' said McTeague. It was absurd that anybody *could* have remained in this place so long. 'More likely one of your chaps taking a break.' Though that seemed equally improbable.

But the sergeant had dismounted, squatted at the wagon's side and reached a tentative hand to the fellow's shoulders. As he did so, the man's skull fell sideways at an odd angle and the sergeant recoiled, pulling the blanket away. He was quite dead, the desiccated body riddled through with spear wounds. Yet the final dregs of his will seemed to have brought him here, to settle himself for sleep and peace.

On the gentle slope the grass was also long. But it did not whisper as it was supposed to do. Rather, it rattled. A continuous chattering noise as their hooves disturbed the ground, or as the many burial details passed by. The clatter of dried bones. A serpent's warning of mortality. More wagons, scores of them shattered beyond repair but, spread across the crest as a whole, perhaps three dozen that still seemed serviceable. More than could be said for the teams that once hauled them, countless numbers of butchered ox carcasses, all those that had not been driven away. *Fine beasts*, he thought, *those that survived*. For McTeague now numbered many of them within his own stock.

'General Marshall's party, sir,' said the sergeant, although the advice was largely unnecessary. There was a small laager on a square of cleared ground, Twinge's jawbone wagon prominent on the near-side, Cornscope in conversation with some troopers and, at the laager's centre, a conference of senior officials and a few civilians.

'Is that General Marshall?' asked McTeague, and the sergeant confirmed that it was, indeed. The General was exceedingly tall, slim and ramrod straight, moustaches, and a beard trimmed in that French style that allowed it to grow from the full width of his lower lip yet kept his chin clean-shaven. Enormous eyebrows and the crown of his head almost flat.

Cornscope came to greet them and they bade the sergeant farewell.

'Well, Simeon,' said McTeague, 'how is he faring?'

'Suffering considerably, I fear. Flayed the skin from his back in places.'

'No less than he deserves. He's in the wagon?'

'I made him as comfortable as possible. But it rather disrupted the old negotiating process, I'm afraid. And Klaas? He obviously got through with the message.'

'Of course. But he wouldn't come here. He says there is no guarantee that the souls of those he killed aren't still at large. He'll meet us back at Utrecht. Now, is the time right for introductions, my friend?'

'They seem to be in something of a funk at the moment. Can't find Pulleine's body, it seems.'

'Pulleine?' said Maria Mestiza.

'Another Colonel, my dear,' said McTeague. 'We never met him. Commander of the First Battalion of the 24th here. Well, the whole force, as it happens. Chelmsford left him in charge. Big mistake, I suppose.'

'They say that some of his friends,' said Cornscope, 'identified him when they were here in January just after the disaster. But now…'

'Scavengers have scattered them,' said Maria. 'See?'

Just beyond the areas of activity, beyond the cavorting vultures, beyond the circling buzzards, there were dogs. A small pack, perhaps a dozen strong, prowling back and forth, keeping low to the ground. But not the feral dogs of the veld. These were domesticated – or they once had been. The former camp dogs, abandoned now and still surviving on whatever edible booty remained. And at night they would compete with the hyena, with the bush pig, with a score of other species. It was one of God's miracles that *any* of these corpses could still be named.

'Apart from that,' said Cornscope, 'they can't agree on what's to happen with the dead of the 24th itself.' He pointed a thumb at some of the uniform jackets, once scarlet, now weathered to faded rust. 'It seems their C.O., Glyn, is insisting they should only be buried by their own.'

'And why should it not be so?' said Maria.

'Because, my sweet one,' McTeague replied, 'he has no soldiers from the 24th here to do the thing. So these poor fools will have to lie here a while longer, I suppose.'

'The honoured dead,' said Maria.

'To the other ranks they are, indeed,' said McTeague. 'But to General Marshall over there? To Chelmsford? To the War Office? I often wonder at the role of burial details like this. To harvest the honour of heroes? Or to disperse the detritus of defeat? Hypocrites, my dear. The very reason that I resigned my own Commission.' He caught the mocking glance she gave him. 'What?' he said, though he did not pursue the matter.

'One way or the other,' said Simeon Cornscope, 'it may not be the best time to interrupt them.'

'Perhaps not,' McTeague replied. 'But show me which is Drummond.' Cornscope indicated the civilian with sandy hair and unkempt beard, tweed suit and waistcoat, white wing-collared shirt and neck cloth, riding boots and a grey slouch hat. 'And the other?'

'With the sketch pad?' asked Cornscope.

'The very same,' said McTeague. The second civilian could have been a younger version of himself. Plump, sideburns, monocle.

'That's Melton Prior, William. He's with the *Illustrated London News*.'

'Ah, the celebrated Mister Prior. You think the *News* would be interested in our story, my dear?'

Maria Mestiza snorted with derision.

'You want me to doctor Twinge?' she said.

'Ease his suffering?' suggested McTeague.

They climbed a few planking steps into the back of the jawbone, set its pots and pans swinging and singing all a-shimmer, its casks and cartons to oozing vapours of warm whisky, sulphuric soaps, odious unguents. A space had been cleared in their midst and a filthy palliasse laid on which Twinge was sprawled, face down, his upper back bare except for some pieces of gauze that had been applied and through which a mixture of blood and iodine had seeped.

'There's a sweet little thing at the hospital in Utrecht,' said Cornscope.

'A real beauty,' Twinge groaned, 'except for her tongue.'

McTeague thought about Amahle. He had finally consummated their marriage, picked his time carefully and been amply rewarded.

'Gave us a veritable lecture,' said Cornscope. 'The effects of flogging. Always made worse, apparently, by general ill-health, unclean habits and drunkenness.'

Twinge flicked a cow's tail whisk over his shoulder, scattered the flies that tried to settle on his lacerations.

'Risk of infection,' he said. 'Spread on the air or by these little buggers.'

'All modern *mumbo jumbo*, of course,' said Cornscope. 'Always some new theory being promoted in my profession.'

'She reckoned,' Twinge grimaced, 'that infections can quickly infiltrate the lungs or the heart.'

McTeague caught Maria's eye, raised a quizzical brow.

'Those wounds need fresh salve, clean dressings,' she said.

The flies clustered once more and the whisk scattered them.

'Well, my old friend,' said McTeague, 'Simeon tells me you rather queered his pitch.'

Twinge laughed.

'Bloody nonsense,' he said. 'Discount!' He spat. 'Over my dead body.'

'You already said that,' said McTeague, as Maria eased the gauze from Twinge's back, took some small pots from her satchel, gently daubed a cream into the deep wounds.

'My poor friend,' said McTeague, 'they cut you very badly, did they not?'

'A pair of damned drummer boys trying to make a name for themselves. But I remember their faces. Bastards will pay for the privilege, and no mistake.'

'You need to rest first,' said McTeague. 'But I really can't have you disrupt my efforts to make a deal with these gentlemen. I have responsibilities, don't you know? For all our futures.'

'Bollocks!' said Twinge.

'We have an excellent hand. But we must not over-play it. What do you think, Simeon?'

Cornscope agreed.

'Tired,' said Twinge. 'Need to sleep.' The fly whisk moved, but barely brushed his shoulder.

'Capital idea, old fellow,' said McTeague. 'We'll leave you in peace.' He steered Cornscope to the back of the wagon, down the steps, as Maria placed a square of clean linen on Twinge's back, then joined them outside. The officers' conference seemed to be breaking up. 'Ah,' McTeague continued, 'excellent timing, it seems. Be a good fellow and ask Mister Drummond whether he could spare us a few moments of his time now.'

'It is done,' said Maria, as Cornscope left them.

'What did you use?'

'Squeezed bulb of the Poet's Daffodil. Rare here. Brought by the Dutch, I think.'

'It will bring him peace?'

'Of course. If you had wanted pain I would have used the sap of the thing they call Bushman's Poison. For protracted agony, the extract of castor bean.'

'How long?'

'Five minutes to paralyse him. Another five to stop his heart.'

Everything for the greater good, he thought. *And friends that would bring Willie McTeague more profit from their loss.*

'He would not have wanted a lingering demise,' he said. 'And we shall ask Jago Jupe to pray for his soul.'

It was plain that Drummond did not like him, though McTeague could not fathom the reason.

'The sale of army transport is not really within my purview, McTeague, though I'm happy to provide you with a note to Commissary-General Strickland. I know he wishes to dispose of those wagons which may no longer be viable for our purpose and I'm sure he would appreciate the opportunity to use some of your beasts for the return trip. We seem to be somewhat under-resourced in that department.'

'And my offer on freighting costs?' said McTeague. 'A confidential matter, sir. For His Lordship's ears alone, don't you agree?'

'I doubt that he will be concerned one way or the other. Within a year the railway will be extended all the way to Pietermaritzburg. And by then the war will be won.'

'*This* war may be won, Mister Drummond,' whispered McTeague, 'but what about the next?'

'I don't follow you, sir.'

'We've both lived among the Zulu, old boy. If you take away their Great King, what d'you suppose will happen? Chaos, sir, that's what. Her Majesty's forces will be back here before you can blink, trying to impose some form of order. And then there's the Boer, Mister Drummond. The whole Cape knows that, sooner or later...'

'You have a solution, I suppose?'

'I am a modest fellow, sir, as the Lord is my witness. A humble servant of the Crown. But I have been fortunate enough to be granted a certain insight of the Zulu's mentality. Why, my household remains in Emoyeni at some considerable risk, and many of them held hostage there now, pending my return after delivering Cetshwayo's message. But we settled there, remained there, simply so that we might be of service when the time was right. And this, Mister Drummond, is surely that time.'

Why, damn the fellow! He looks at me as though I'm a liar.

Drummond lit a cheroot, looked north beyond the protective confines of the laager. A pair of seven-pounders stood there, brought by the column for its own protection and similar to those lost here in January, now gracing Cetshwayo's kraal at Emahlabathini.

'The devil still has our guns,' said Drummond. 'Catch-em-alivo.'

'I *could* help to get them back, sir,' McTeague replied. 'The Great King is still offering to surrender them as a gesture of goodwill.'

'He expects too much in return, McTeague. He had a chance to avoid this war, sir. To disband his regiments. I respect the Zulu, of course, and Heaven knows I do not personally want to see them destroyed. But once the ultimatum deadlines were past, the dice were down. And this...' He gestured towards the surrounding scene of a battle lost. 'It must all be paid for. Accounts to be settled in full.'

'We both know Cetshwayo could never have accepted the ultimatum, Mister Drummond. But I know he would give up the field pieces for no more than the chance to open lines of communication. That's the very message that I bring for His Lordship.'

'Communication, you say? Do you know, McTeague that the N.G.R has plans to extend the rail line far beyond Pietermaritzburg? Within five years, six at most, it will have reached Ladysmith.'

'I should very much hope so, sir. I have shares in the company.'

'And the field telegraph too. Lines will link every township of the Cape. Then from the Cape direct to London. It is communication, civilisation, that will bury the Zulu.'

'But in the meantime, who will transport the line, Mister Drummond?

And the poles? Who will provide the freight wagons so the N.G.R can convey its tracks, its sleepers, its ballast, to the rail head?'

'At two shillings and ninepence per hundredweight, McTeague, I assume that *you* shall. But why would this concern Lord Chelmsford?'

'Because it's the early bird that catches the worm, sir. I need to consolidate my position. And soon. I can do so by securing early endorsement to re-locate our southern depot to Pietermaritzburg. And a second depot at Ladysmith. I know full well that this is not within His Lordship's gift either, but it would help considerably if he might simply smile upon the project. And his personal involvement in achieving significant savings on the Commissariat costs would do no harm to his reputation, I dare say. Besides, I envisage admirable profit to be derived from such an enterprise. Enough to ensure that lucrative appreciation is shown to all involved. Eh, Mister Drummond?'

Drummond took a silver hip flask from his tweed jacket, lifting it to his lips. *But not a drop offered to a poor former soldier,* thought McTeague.

'You cannot expect Lord Chelmsford,' said Drummond, 'to associate himself with a confederation of whisky drummers, McTeague. Surely?'

He was looking at Cornscope and Maria Mestiza, both sitting some distance away with a group of soldiers.

'You must not confuse my legitimate business associates with fellows like Theophilus Twinge, sir. He was merely a contractor to my enterprise, no more. I am deeply ashamed that his outrageous behaviour in Utrecht should have brought my enterprise into disrepute but...'

'Was?' said Drummond. 'You said he *was* merely a contractor?'

'The contractual arrangement between us is now dissolved, Mister Drummond.'

Well, by now it should be, thought McTeague. Drummond nodded.

'And your colleague, Cornscope, mentioned the possibility of bringing Catch-em-alivo to justice?'

'Indeed, sir. When the time and the rewards are propitious, I will make sure that His Lordship knows exactly where to find his fox.'

'Very well. I will convey your proposals to Lord Chelmsford, with a recommendation that these logistical suggestions be nurtured, as well as your availability to provide intelligence on the old devil's whereabouts – as you say, when the time is appropriate. Meanwhile, you will return with us to Utrecht while we ponder this latest overture for peace from their so-called king – this attempt to open up a line of communication.'

'Oh, I think that might be difficult, Mister Drummond. Cetshwayo awaits my return. My household might be at risk.'

'You're coming to Utrecht, McTeague. And there's an end to it.'

'Then in the long-term, Mister Drummond, my land rights? To the Emoyeni territory? Her Majesty will need trusty folk to rule these lands once they are under the control of the Crown, after all. A number of suitable satraps who can govern sizeable tracts of land in her name?'

'An interesting idea, McTeague. But we're a little ahead of ourselves, I think. Governorship of Zululand's various zones is very far from our agenda at the moment. But, as you say, it's the early bird that catches the worm.'

'Yet an opinion from you, sir. You do not think, for example, that Dunn might be a rival contender?'

'He may lay claim to Emoyeni again, I suppose. But possession is nine-tenths of the law, don't they declare? And I am not aware of any discussion with Dunn or other parties on the matter.'

What were the words, thought McTeague, *that Dickens had put into the mouth of Jaggers? "Take nothing on its looks. Take everything on evidence." Why do I believe that you are dissembling, sir?*

'How very reassuring to hear you say so, Mister Drummond,' he exclaimed. 'My own thoughts precisely. But the guns, sir. You haven't mentioned the guns.'

'They're obviously no use to old Catch-em-alivo,' said the Honourable William Drummond, 'else he'd have deployed them by now. And I doubt very much that they will have any further value for His Lordship. But they might be a useful way to keep stringing the Zulu along. Just for the moment.'

'I checked on him just a few minutes ago,' said McTeague. 'Sleeping soundly. May be best if we all sit up-front. Leave the dear fellow in peace.'

'We go back to Emoyeni?' said Maria, climbing onto the jawbone's chest bench.

'I fear not, my dear. Further negotiations to take place at Utrecht.'

Cornscope froze with one foot on the bed board, the other on the step.

'Oh, my goodness,' he said. 'It was difficult enough driving the team here. I could not possibly...'

'I will drive,' said Maria Mestiza.

It was a much easier team to handle in any case, half of the span having been loaned to Captain Evans as a supplement to his transport animals. The wagons began to move, hauling themselves over the crest where troopers of the Natal Native Police were still collecting and burying their own dark-uniformed dead. And while progress was not rapid, there was an urgency almost palpable in the column's activity, its desperation to be away.

'It's only a little past noon,' said Cornscope, glancing at the sun. 'Will they leave the rest?'

'They think they're tempting providence by staying here even this long,' said McTeague. 'They think it cursed, for all their science and logic.' Chelmsford had been forced to bivouac here when he had finally returned to the scene on the evening of the massacre. And McTeague had heard the ghost stories of those forced to spend that awful night on this field of death. Tales of the speed with which the army had moved on again the following morning. 'Nobody can stay here long anymore,' he observed.

But Melton Prior was still there, seemed untroubled by the prospect of being left behind. For he was engrossed in his sketches. He remained in the same spot even when they picked up Lieutenant-Colonel Black's companies of the 24th Regiment's Second Battalion that had been posted at the head of the Batshe Valley to protect the column, rather than look after their own fallen. Eyes were averted as they passed a shattered ambulance wagon overtaken during the retreat, though its butchered occupants had now been mercifully laid to rest, a shallow grave, a small mound of stones to mark the spot. But no such courtesy had been shown to the perished pair of artillery horses, still hanging from their harness, dangling over a deep gulley with the limber itself upturned and balancing on the lip.

McTeague could rarely recall such a profound silence among such a throng. All was muted. The wheels made little sound on the track that traders' wagons had etched into the landscape over so many years. Leather and chain fell to a reverential whisper. Ox and horse lowered their heads, trod quietly upon the road. Men ceased their chatter, cast careful glances back over their shoulders, averted their eyes from everything else but the sloping path. Past the paths to the place they now called Fugitives' Drift, the rock-strewn slope to their left with its ravine beyond. The only possible escape route for, on the day of the battle, those trying to flee in this direction, along the wagon road, had run headlong into the waiting assegais of the Zulus' right horn. This was the trail of defeat. And he was glad when they finally left the place behind, came down to the scene of Chelmsford's salvation, the mission station at Rorke's Drift which the otherwise victorious Zulus had been unable to capture following the debacle at Isandlwana.

'Look at them,' said Maria, nodding towards Black's redcoats. 'Happy to be back in the safety of their barricades.'

A deft movement of her wrist sent the whip's thong spiralling outwards, just catching the shoulder of the lead beast.

'Can't blame them,' said Cornscope. 'This place has become a talisman for protection, a safe haven, as surely as Isandlwana is cursed, a symbol of dread and danger.'

They came to a halt alongside the ground which had served as the mission station's gardens, now back under cultivation again by the garrison, and across from the storehouse in front of which the defenders had built their mealie bag walls. To their right were the remains of the house which had once belonged to James Rorke, and thus endowed upon it the name by which the Zulus still knew the place, KwaJimu. The house had served as the garrison's hospital, though there was little of the building still standing, of course, for it had been largely destroyed by fire during the attack. But the garrison had been strengthened now, a new defensive perimeter established, tents neatly arrayed within.

'Her Majesty needs a sacred shrine here,' said McTeague. 'It's the reason she plans to award so many of her tuppenny crosses to the defenders.'

That's all they're worth, after all. Nation's highest military honour. And made from bits of cheap bronze. Captured cannons, melted down.

'You can't help but admire their bravery,' said Cornscope.

'Bravery?' said McTeague. 'What else could they have done? Do you not think they would have run if there'd been somewhere to go? Of course they would! But I'll give them this. That in a hundred years, when Chelmsford is forgotten, when Isandlwana is forgotten, gentlemen in England then a-bed will remember the name of Rorke's Drift.'

'I'm sure you're correct, dear fellow,' said Cornscope. 'But had I not better wake Twinge?'

'Gently then,' said McTeague, as Cornscope clambered over the back of the bench. Maria Mestiza smiled, then jumped down to the ground.

'Oh, good gracious!' cried Cornscope.

'Whatever's the matter, Simeon?' said McTeague with as much drama as he could muster.

'Better come see for yourself.'

So McTeague eased his bulk over the seat, shifted aside the pots and pans hanging from the hoops.

The blood-stained palliasse was still where they had placed it, but of Theophilus Twinge there was no sign whatsoever.

Chapter Ten

He drove the cattle south and the further he went, the closer to the lands into which the whites had made incursions, the greater was the devastation.

Shaba reached KwaMbonambi after four days of continuous pain, hoping to find *induna* Mnukwa and the rest of his Scout Swarm. But he found there only the smoke-stained songs of mourning, winging on the wind like the harsh cry of the *hadeda* bird; the scorched wreckage of wattle, thatch and palisade; the ruin of warriors, walking or crippled wounded; the barest remnant of families, fatherless infants and weeping widows. Time and again he would crest a ridge, or traverse the edge of a gulley, only to find small clusters of women, of children, of cattle, hidden in the folded ground beyond, he and they each suffering simultaneous shock, alarm, at the discovery. Then the shared conversation, repeated at each encounter, sometimes the chance for respite, two of the nights spent in such company, Shaba huddled in his father's kaross but each night surrendering the thing to help keep the little ones warm. So he slept badly, cold and uncomfortable, sharing the tales that his father had taught him when sleep also eluded the children.

And no tale was more beloved than that which told how stories themselves had come to be. '*Kwasuka sukela…*' he would say. Once, long ago…

'*Cosi!*' whispered the children. Tell us!

'There lived a woman whose name was Manzandaba who had many fat and happy children. A husband too – Zenzele the Wood Carver. And they all lived on the edge of the Great Ocean. During the daytime, life was full of wonderful things and they rejoiced. But at night, when it grew too dark for weaving and carving, for playing with the crabs along the seashore, yet too soon for dreaming, the children would become fretful. "We want stories, Mama." But neither their parents, nor their neighbours, nor the wind, nor the ocean had any tales to tell.

'So the day came when Zenzele instructed his wife that she must go in search of some stories, and Manzandaba packed food, kissed the children, set out upon her quest. On the road, she came across Hare the Trickster, who pretended to have stories but possessed not one. Then Baboon the Spiteful, who scolded Manzandaba for wasting her time. And Owl the Night-Dweller,

131

who did not wish to be disturbed during the daylight hours. Then Elephant the Bountiful, who knew no stories but referred her to Fish Eagle the Vain, so that Fish Eagle carried her to his great friend, Sea Turtle the Creator. The Sea Turtle took Manzandaba upon his enormous shell, carried her to the Land of Spirits, deep in the ocean's depths, where the King and Queen of the Spirit Folk promised her stories – if only she would bring them a picture of her home, of the Dry Lands, where their people could not venture. She pledged that she would return within the next moon to bring them the picture and Sea Turtle was charged with carrying her home to her family.

'The following night, when the children begged for stories, she was at least able to recount her adventures. But the children were not satisfied because, they said, these were just things that had happened in Manzandaba's real life. So next day, Zenzele began to carve the picture for her. She watched him as his fingers brought the wood to life, with images of all their kin folk, their cattle, their homestead, the beasts of the plains, the birds of the forest. And with the next full moon, she returned to the Sea Turtle who carried Manzandaba back to the Land of Spirits. There, the King and Queen praised Zenzele's art and rewarded her with a gift. It was the most elaborate shell she had ever seen. "This shell," they said, "holds the magic of imagination. Whenever you want a story, simply hold it to your ear and you will be inspired." She thanked them and made the journey home.

'When the sun went down, when it grew too dark for weaving and carving, for playing with the crabs along the seashore, yet too soon for dreaming, she called together her children. Then she called together all the other children of the homestead, every person of the village, in fact. And they lit a huge fire.

"Tell us a story, Manzandaba!"

'So she set the shell to her ear, listened to the inspiration it gave her.

"*Kwasuka sukela…*" she said. And that is how stories came to be.

'*Cosi, cosi, yaphela,*' whispered Shaba. 'And thus ends my tale.'

But, as the children's eyes grew heavy, he knew that his own tale was far from run. His dreams were fitful, fraught with his father's rejection of him, with prey that he sought but could never catch, and with visions of a white man's weapon – the slender blade of an elaborate sword.

At KwaMbonambi itself, they pointed him west, certain that Mnukwa and the Swarm were following the Emakhosini Valley – the Valley of the Kings – towards Nondweni, for there had been many such groups and entire regiments, marching in that direction. But there was no food to spare so, when he had left the place far behind and the sun was high, he pressed the cattle into a blind gulley, bolted the gulley's entrance with some thorn bush, stowed his bundle of shield-wrapped possessions within, and scattered snares in the way that he and Umdeni had learned as boys. Cords of twisted gut taken from his pouch

132

and fashioned into the running noose, the free ends anchored firmly to well-embedded sticks and strategically sited where there was the most spoor of rabbit and guinea fowl. It was a good run. Almost perfect, for the ravine to which the gulley belonged was also home to a colony of the *sambane*, the Ant Bear, whose burrows yawned along the length of its sides. Shaba chose one, high on the bank with a dense clump of Num-Num bush above, where he could crawl among the shiny green leaves. Then he waited, with just a single throwing spear. Patiently. For patience, said his people, was the mother of a beautiful calf. And the calf delivered of his patience, in this instance, was actually a young female *iphiti*, the tiny Blue Diver antelope that savoured nothing more than to shelter from the noon heat in the den of its friend and ally, the Ant Bear. So when the sun began to slide down the western sky, a small head appeared suddenly below him, cautious, quick movements to left and right, nostrils twitching, then inching forward until her shoulders were also free of the den. It was at that moment that Shaba's spear, the shaft cushioned on the slope above, stabbed downward, snake-fast, to make the kill. He saluted his ancestors for this bounty and broke from the cover of the bush.

He laughed when he found that one of the snares had also been effective, for the noose was tight upon the leg of a scrub hare, scrambling in panic to escape. Shaba broke its neck, used the cord to sling it from his cow hide belt, to dangle among the civet fur tails of his kilt, then quickly plaited some grasses so that he could whip together the legs of the *iphiti*, tossing it across his shoulders. It was not proper hunting, of course. For that, you needed dogs. His father's dogs, the dogs of his people. Though this implied ownership was not strictly true. For the AmaZulu had shared this land with the Hunting Hound since the time before memory and neither called the other master. Yet there was a mutual loyalty, and the men of his homestead were never seen too far from the beasts. So Shaba added a following of dogs to the list of his other life's desires. He saw them in his mind's eye. Not the mongrel breeds of the whites but compact and muscular, long-snouted, wedge shaped heads, pointed ears always alert, a faint ridgeback, curled tail. He would take them out to the bush, with the other men, have them catch the scent of some animal, run with them through the long grass to a place where the prey was brought to bay, finish its misery with a sharp blow from his *iwisa*, the hunting club, the bone-breaker. So there would be fresh meat for the families. They would share the strength of the slaughtered creature. But the first hunt would be for Umdeni. To follow the custom. For was it not spoken that, after the death of *any* young man, there should be a hunt in his honour? Yet how could the custom be followed when so many young men had died? Still, he would make sure that Umdeni kaMthinga had his due.

He loped back along the ravine, knowing that he must make haste now, cover the ground to catch Mnukwa. But before he even came in sight of the gulley enclosure once more, he froze. It was the sound that hit him. The whooping cry, *buwo, buwo*. And then that absurd noise that sounded like nothing so much as the white man's giggling laughter. In the background, the terrified sound of his cattle.

Shaba squatted close to the ground, shuffling forward until he could see. Three of them, circling outside the thorn *boma* that he had built. The spotted wolf. Hyena. *Impisi*. The Purifier. He despised them, these thieves that often came in the night to take the homestead's goats and lambs. But he respected their role in keeping the land clean, and he did not under-estimate them either. He had seen them on more than one occasion get the better of a leopard full-grown with the bone-shattering, disease-ridden pressure of their jaws. And if they were hungry, he doubted his ability to easily drive them away.

One of them scrambled up the bank of the ravine, and the cows responded with even more high-pitched bellowing. But the hyenas did not venture to attack from above and Shaba could imagine the tossing heads, the wickedly sharp horns. *Buwo, buwo*, howled the hyena. *Yes, cry*, he thought. *Hairless ones. Eaters of all decaying things.* He sprang from cover, but remained in a crouch, his shoulders hunched in mimicry of the hyena's profile, his legs bent, hands upon the ground. Two of the beasts scampered away, startled by his sudden presence, though they rapidly returned, while the largest of the three stood its ground, turned to face him, bared its mocking fangs, bristled and snarled. Shaba sniffed the air.

'Well, ugly ones,' he shouted, 'you think you can take my cattle? You who share the hole with the wart-hog.'

He rattled his throwing spear, stamped forward several paces, roared out the barking cough of a lion. The more timid pair edged backwards but the pack's leader advanced, began to circle around him. Shaba held its stare, unslung the corpse of the *iphiti* from his shoulder.

'See what I have brought for you, dung dogs?' he yelled, gripping the binding with which he had tied the antelope's feet.

He straightened, lifted the small carcass from the ground and spun around, once, twice, building momentum until, when he released the thing, it spun over the head of the most aggressive predator. The others seized upon it immediately, ripping at the fur and flesh, dragging the body away, and away, while their leader danced an angry pirouette, gnashing its jaws at him. But it was distracted, deprived of meat yet again. *Buwo, buwo*, it whooped. And, in its distraction, Shaba hefted the spear, concentrated all the power that his damaged muscles could muster, launched it, flexing and whistling its own name – *isijula* – to take the hyena in the shoulder, the blow knocking it from its feet. Abandoned by its fellows, it pushed itself upright, drooling saliva from its lips and whining. It side-stepped, unsteady now, while Shaba grabbed for a rock, sprang after the creature, slamming the boulder down upon its skull.

Again. Again. Until his arms were drenched in its blood and it lay dead at his feet. He pulled out the spear. Then stopped, shocked. For, momentarily, he experienced the strangest sensation, saw in his hand that same elaborately fashioned sword.

The following day, he reached the southern extremity of the Emakhosini Valley. More accurately, he reached the Mthonjaneni Mountain from which the valley stretched away north-westwards. He had eaten the scrub hare but not the hyena. It was one of the taboos. That you should not eat the flesh of a beast which itself eats the flesh of men. Yet it was the thirst that troubled him. The cattle too. But as he crested a low ridge on the mountain's flank, he saw a pleasant pool, part-shaded and fed by a spring which babbled from a cascade of rocks. The herd needed no persuasion towards the water and Shaba was soon among the trees, hands cupped to catch the sweet nectar.

A woman's voice startled him.

'Do you not know that it is death to drink here?' she said.

He rolled onto his back, the water splashing across his face, trying to focus on the female form silhouetted against the morning sun and dappled by its light falling through alder leaves.

'What manner of vision is this?' he replied.

There were tales of secret springs, protected by spectres of the dead.

'Perhaps one that is incomplete.' She lifted a hand to lightly touch her left eye. His own fingers aped the gesture, brushed the leather patch.

'I see you well enough, Guardian of the Spring,' he said. 'But the image might be clearer if you stepped from the sun's glare.'

'It is not for *me* to move, warrior. Not I who drinks from the Forbidden Pool.' She glanced at the rolled hide of his shield. 'But warrior of what? The Evil Omen?'

'You have a sharp eye.' *And a tongue to match*, he thought.

'As sharp as your own for the cattle, it seems, despite the theft of your eye. But where do you take them, warrior? There are few stupid enough to herd their beasts *towards* the red soldiers.'

Her allegation of stupidity stung him but he chose to ignore the jibe, decided that honesty was his best policy.

'I am trying to catch the Swarm of Scouts to which I am attached. I hoped to find them at KwaMbonambi and leave these children there. But the *ikhanda* is stripped bare. I feared the loss of my herd if I left it there. And the children are beautiful, are they not?'

She took two paces towards the pool and, for the first time, he could see her clearly. Tall, yet despite the depth and severity of her voice, her apparent authority, she was no older than Amahle. And he could also hear that she was not alone. Giggling, back among the trees, barely visible shapes studying him.

135

'Pay them no heed,' said the girl — for she was no more than that. 'My sisters and I are only here to collect water for the homestead.' She gestured towards the others who, one by one, broke from cover and carried their clay gourds down to the muddy margin. There were a dozen maidens, the youngest little more than children.

'So the water is only forbidden to strangers?' he said.

'It has been that way since the days of Dingane,' replied the girl. 'Our homestead was once a barracks for the warriors who guarded this place. The waters are pure. They bring long life, it is spoken, to those who take them. So, every day, young women came from the Royal Enclosure at the Place of the Elephant...' She pointed away up the valley. 'Two thousand young women, warrior. Two hours to walk here, collect water. Two hours to walk back. Every day of their lives. And death for any of them if they allowed the water to become sullied. Thrown from the cliffs of Execution Hill. Death too for anybody else who touched this pool.'

The lore of their people listed Dingane as ninth of the great AmaZulu kings, successor to his half-brother Shaka, the Bull Elephant himself, and for whose death Dingane was responsible. And Dingane overthrown in turn by another half-brother, Mpande — father to the Great King Cetshwayo. Shaba sang the genealogy in his mind, back beyond Shaka, son of Senzangakhona, son of Jama, son of Ndaba, son of Mageba, brother of Phunga, son of Gumede, son of Zulu kaNtombela — the founder of the clan now grown by conquest and alliance to an empire that must surely rival the domains of the red soldiers' Fat Queen. Yet the tale did not even begin with Zulu kaNtombela since, beyond him, there was a different saga altogether. Lines that stretched back through the forest mists, through all the long-sires of the Land. Six of the kings buried here in this valley, their regal shadows mingled with all those countless generations of the departed, a potent protective force for the area. He could taste it.

'Then I should know the name of the Guardian to whom my life is now forfeit,' he said.

'It need not be forfeit should you pay for the water. With one of these fine animals perhaps.'

'Whey! A cow for a swallow of water?'

'Without the water they would have died. A fair price, isn't it? To save four at the cost of one. Now, which shall it be? The dapple perhaps, so it may remind me of this place.'

'That one is indeed named *Forest Floor*. But she is not for you. Nor any of them. My cattle have already drunk their fill and I doubt you are able to exact your price. Not even with the help of all these fighters at your tail.'

'You should not underestimate them. My sisters are strong. Do they not have to break the earth? To plant and sow? To harvest? To carry firewood and water? And the shades of great women stand here with us.' She pointed

136

a clenched fist towards the north. 'The Queen Mother of Shaka the Elephant sleeps in the ruin of KwaBulawayo.' She turned west. 'And there, the resting ground of the Great Princess, Mkabayi kaJama. Did she not stand as regent for her brother? And alongside Senzangakhona, did she not become the spirit leader of our *impi*? Did she not inspire the warriors before battle? Did she not protect Queen Nandi when her brother rejected her? And therefore protected the Queen's son, Shaka – the blessing of the Sky Lord be upon him. Was she not then counsellor in turn also to Dingane and to Mpande? Her blood runs with our blood, Warrior of the Evil Omen. And though you be a warrior, we see that you are not yet a man.'

She gestured towards his head, the absence of the marriage ring, the *isicoco*, without which, despite the number of his summers, he must remain *insizwa* yet a while.

'When the war is won, my regiment's turn will come, as last year the honour fell upon the Dust Raisers.'

But this year there had been no such announcement at the First Fruits Ceremony. No massed marriage between the favoured regiment and age-guild of ripened girls. All the focus then had been on the threat of invasion.

'If there was a man,' she said, 'and that man had means, honour too, then I would speak with my family, ask them to celebrate my *umemulo*, so that I could cut stems cleanly for the Reed Dance when the winter ends.'

The laughter of the younger women mingled with the spring water's own mirth.

'And how would you find the fellow, living in this desolate place?'

'Oh,' she said, 'I saw such a man once. At KwaNodwengu. Before the great battle when we wiped the red soldiers from the nose of the Earth Mother.' She blew on her fingers. 'Before the moon bled. As I remember, the Great King had called out both the Evil Omen and the Skirmishers. And this warrior was elected to *giya* for the Mbonambi. He was a great dancer, that warrior. With one eye the colour of finest milk. If I remember correctly, he even wagered his sister's future on his own prowess. So he must have been a fine fighter, I think. A worthy man. Though I have no idea whether he is still among the living. I imagine that, if the Lord-of-the-Sky has protected him, he must now be famous. Blessed with rich rewards from his exploits.'

'Such a warrior would not have time, I expect, to waste his days in idle chatter with girls.'

'No, I expect not. Though perhaps one day, when the fighting was done, he would find time to visit the Valley of Kings again. Then travel to watch the maidens gather for the Reed Dance and perhaps select one that he thought beautiful enough to rival his prized cattle. And if the warrior's regiment held enough sway with the iNkosi Cetshwayo kaMpande, they might be allowed to marry that season's age-guild of virgins.'

'And what if the Great King chose, instead, to marry those maidens to some other regiment. A regiment of old men, perhaps?'

'Then the warrior's betrothed would suffer the Great King's wrath and go to join the shades of her family like the women of the iNgcugce.'

Only three years earlier, Cetshwayo had given permission for the older men of the Black Mambas to wed the maidens from that year's age-guild, though many of the girls were already betrothed to young warriors from the Bender of Kings, from the Savages, and even from the Evil Omen itself. And many of those girls ignored the decree, so that Cetshwayo had sent two regiments to find and execute the defiant, along with their suitors, leaving their bodies to rot upon the roads as a warning to others.

'That is dangerous talk. The commands of the Great King must be obeyed. Or we have nothing.'

'So you would see your own betrothed wed to an old man? What if the warrior who danced the *giya* at KwaNodwengu had lost his wager and his sister had been ordered to marry such a grey-beard?'

'I expect that such a warrior would have honoured the traditions that have made the AmaZulu so respected. I think that he would have wept bitter tears for a sister lost to him but done his utmost to wipe clean his boastful error, even if it meant disinheritance from his family, from his own father. I believe he would have been amazed that his own valour in battle, the great deeds that he had performed, were not enough to prevent such a loss, but that he would have pledged himself to even mightier feats in the future. Feats that would make his name renowned throughout the nation. And I see a vision that, in doing so, the Sky Lord would smile on him, bring him to a place where he might meet a maiden with whom he could share the rest of his days. Raise fine children in a land free of the whites. Become head of their household. Breed many cattle. Perhaps become a great worker of iron, like his father before him.'

'And what is the name of this warrior's father?'

'He is Ndabuko kaMahanana, iNkosi of Hluhluwe.'

'Then it is a good thing, for is Ndabuko not also the name of the Great King's brother?'

'Not especially good. Not if the warrior has been disinherited by that father. For how would he arrange the *ilobolo*?'

'Yes, that is a problem. But let us suppose that this warrior was upon the road alone with his cattle. And near the *umuzi* of the woman that he hoped to wed. He would not be foolish enough to marry into a family that he did not trust. So, if he trusted this maiden's family, he could speak to her father – or her grandfather should the father be away with his regiment. He could speak with her family and ask them to keep safe his fine cattle. Against the day when he might come to claim her. Or, alternatively, should the betrothal not happen as they might wish, he should simply come to reclaim the beasts.'

'A warrior would certainly have to trust such a family. To know their history well. The father's regiment. His name.' The girls had filled their pots and were waiting beyond the pool.

'It is reasonable,' said the girl. 'Then that warrior should know that the father's name is Mandla kaSibusiso, *induna* of the uMxapho, the Mongrels, the Shower of Shot, kinsman to Zibhebhu kaMapitha.'

'Zibhebhu is commander of the Swarms. There can be no greater honour than being his kinsman. And does the daughter of Mandla kaSibusiso have a name?'

'Do you not know that he has many daughters? Which one do you mean?'

'Let me see. This would be a maiden of sixteen summers, perhaps seventeen. She is tall, with the neck of a giraffe. She carries herself with all the grace that one might expect from the daughter of a great *induna*.'

'I know the maiden you mean, warrior. That one is called Zama. The Trial. She is well-named. For when she was conceived her parents were trying to have a son. She has been a trial for them ever since, they say. And several suitors have already tried to win her. But she is waiting for the right man. A man that has means, honour too. If there was such a man, she would speak to her father about him. But she would look foolish if she did not have even a name for him.'

'She could say that he is called Tshabanga kaNdabuko, with the honour name Giant Slayer. But the father's regiment is far to the north. It may be a long time before this maiden might speak with her father.'

'Ah,' she said. 'Those who are upon the road might often be without the latest news. They may not be aware that the Great King has decided that the symbol of our people, the *iNkatha yeSizwe yaKwaZulu*, shall be returned to eSiklebheni on the night of the next Full Moon. There will be a great muster there. The uMxapho regiment shall be in attendance. The Evil Omen too, I hear. All the *izinduna*. Every Swarm and Company.'

'Ten days away.'

'Ten days. I wonder whether that is sufficient time for a warrior of determination to rejoin his Swarm, to heap more glory upon his shoulders in such a short time.'

'But first he must leave his cattle with a family he can trust.'

There were no gatekeepers on duty at Zama's homestead, nobody to determine whether they should be admitted, none to sing the *Siyakhuleka ekhaya* and praise the honour names of her father. For the place was all in turmoil, the lookouts intent only on the assault taking place among the huts that fringed the cattle enclosure.

It seemed that a large colony of bees had taken up residence during the summer months inside the trunk of an ancient Mopani tree and, despite many warnings that honey should only be collected from hives well beyond the *umuzi*'s precincts, a group of enterprising but foolish children had determined that there would be little risk. For the winter had come and the colony was now much smaller, intent on keeping the nest warm and safe, eating voraciously within the hive and therefore seemingly inactive.

There was no shortage of honey within the homestead, naturally. But like Gingile the Hunter, the children had not yet learned the lesson about greed. So they had made fire sticks, climbed the Mopani to reach the cleft which sheltered the hive cells. Yet they had also failed to grasp another thing. That a hive in such a position was notoriously difficult to plunder, for bees always stored the honey in the upper section of a comb – in this case the part that was high up within the cleft and beyond both reach and sight – while the lower levels held, in turn, the pollen stores, the worker and drone cells with the pine nut-shaped queen chambers at the very bottom edge. And even the most foolish of creatures would know that you should never poke sticks into that portion of a bee nest, even when you might think that fire sticks and smoke had driven away the occupants. So while the hive may indeed have been smaller than usual at this time of year, there were still several thousands of its colonists prepared to swarm in protection of their queen.

Shaba could see the black mass of them from the gateway, a roaring cloud that rose and fell and flew between the huts, ardent in its pursuit of those who had breached its sanctity, hunting down the miscreants as they fled. Some of the children had been seized by their mothers, and the mothers knew there were only two ways to safety – either to keep running, as fast and as straight as they were able, or to take shelter inside a home, darkening the interior to disorientate any of the insects that might follow them inside. But for the infants without such maternal protection, without sanctuary, there were only the harsh lessons of the Earth Mother. That those who do not protect their faces from angry bees shall surely be stung in the eyes. That those who swat at the creatures will attract more and more simply by that highly visible activity itself. That those already stung will carry upon their skin the banana scent secreted by the bees and enticing still greater numbers to the target of attack. That those who do not run hard, spear-straight and into the wind will surely be caught. And that there is an undefined limit to the number of stings which one small body can tolerate.

The boy lay dead in the aftermath. A few dozen bees still circled wildly around the Mopani while the rest had returned to the task of repairing the damage done to their hive. It would be fruitless, of course, for the men of the village would now take steps to destroy the thing properly, to appease the shade of the lost child. But, for the time being, there was just the weeping, the keening, the wailing of grief-gutted family, the clustered matrons and maidens of the child's clan, while mothers elsewhere, more fortunate than these, scraped away the stinging barbs from the skin of survivors.

'It is a grievous thing when a child passes in this way,' said Zama's grandfather.

The old man squatted on a stool outside the entrance to his hut with five other veterans who had introduced him without excessive formality as Sibusiso kaBheka. The barest minimum of praise names, a nod towards his kinship with the renowned Zibhebhu.

'Will you stay for the child's funeral feast?' said one of Sibusiso's companions, scratching in the dirt with a stick.

'The boy needs to rejoin his Swarm,' said Zama's grandfather.

Thirty-five summers and he still calls me a boy, thought Shaba. It made him smile. For the first time in many days.

'It is true,' he said. 'If we may settle this matter of my cattle, Lord?'

'I am loathe,' said Sibusiso, 'to interfere in the matter between a man and his son. But this marriage of your sister to the white trader, KaMtigwe, it is an abomination. What will happen to the People of Heaven if our blood is diluted in this way? Mixed with the thin spirit of the AmaNgisi. And what is he become, this KaMtigwe? Is he lord of Hluhluwe now?'

Shaba thought of his lands: the plentiful game that filled their plains; the richness of their soil; the bounty of the forests that filled the higher northern parts; the clean rivers that laced the valleys; the metallic ores that graced the rock faces.

'A rich prize for the whites,' he said. 'It seems that the Great King has a fondness for establishing white *izinduna*. First Jantoni, that had eMoyeni first. Now this KaMtigwe.'

He saw Amahle once more in her wedding finery. *'Oh, my brother's pride knows no boundaries,'* he heard her say again. But he felt no pride today. Only shame for her, his self-respect flattened and battered by his banishment from the *umuzi*. He knew that all those close to him were bewitched. By that trickster Klaas. By the white devil KaMtigwe. By the *isangoma* Mutwa. And he knew that those he loved must be freed, though the manner of their release still eluded him. Still, there was also Zama kaMandla. Fate may not have been kind to him in other ways, but if it had not led him here...

Zama and her sisters emerged from a neighbouring hut bearing a water bowl for their hands, a jug of sorghum beer, and a plate of maize and bean that they passed between them. She was beautiful.

'Well, we shall care for your cattle, warrior,' said Sibusiso. 'As best we might. But the herd boys bring word that the horse soldiers grow bolder every day. They draw closer. You have been on the road to the south. What did you see there?'

Shaba told them about the devastation, the burned-out settlements. Worse even than that which he had seen in the west.

'But I saw none of the whites,' he said.

'When Cetshwayo brings the *iNkatha* home to eSiklebheni it will protect us from them. And let us hope that, this time, he may show the respect it deserves. That we should suffer no further misfortunes.'

Shaba had heard the whispered criticism elsewhere. For, when word had been carried to the Great King of the engagement at eSandlwana, Cetshwayo had immediately followed his duty and locked himself in private communion with the Sacred Coil, that wide hawser ring plaited by Shaka from all the smaller *iziNkatha* of the peoples forged together to form the AmaZulu nation. One ring now, an arm's length across, a hand's span deep, which bound all the lesser rings of their people. And Cetshwayo had sat upon this thing, channelling its energies to help the *impi* in its battle. He had held vigil with the *iNkatha* until the runners brought him news that victory was close. Then he had broken his link with the Sacred Coil, left his quarters. But the matrons had wailed at him, since the battle was not yet done so that, when they heard that some of the regiments had been driven off by the red soldiers at KwaJimu, the old mothers scolded him, continued to blame him for all subsequent set-backs.

'The Great King's wisdom cannot be open to our judgement, can it, Lord?' he said. 'And the whites may have stolen total victory from us at KwaJimu, yet it was hardly a defeat. After all, we wiped the soldiers again and again afterwards, whenever we followed the King's words and avoided attacking them behind their walls and in their holes. For the cornered rat may wound even the most fierce of our hounds.'

'Yet if we had followed the guidance of my kinsman, we may never have stirred up the AmaNgisi hornets' nest in the first place.'

'But Zibhebhu is not king and we cannot judge his wisdom, wide as it may be, above that of Cetshwayo kaMpande.'

'Judgement? You lecture me on judgement, puppy? I have served this Kingdom since the days of the *Mfecane*, the Tempest Wars by which Shaka the Bull Elephant united our people. The rivers ran scarlet with the blood of those who opposed us. Great forests of the impaled sprang up at our passing. Widows wept whole oceans. But we became a nation. So I do not judge Cetshwayo. I sing his honour names, knowing that it is too easy, this game of challenging the wisdom of others, forgetting to recall their glories until after they are gone. The mothers may blame him for our defeats but they are women. What do they know? Did he not take us to victory at eSandlwana? At eHlobane? We may have fallen at eKhambule and kwaGingindlovu. But what do women know of these things? Did he not bring us two of the white soldiers' big guns? The women may say that the guns are useless to us, but surely this was the act of a King favoured by the shades of our departed. How could any disagree? I had barely eighteen summers when I fought my first battle. At the Hill of Gqokli. Over yonder. I stood at Shaka's side that day. Facing the traitor Zwide and an army twice our size. Twice our size, boy. But by cunning and strategy we beat them.'

'And you doubt our ability to beat this enemy that is so much smaller than we are?'

'You have fought it, this red thing of the Fat Queen's.' He used the form of speech that expressed the highest degree of contempt. 'You have seen into its soul. What do *you* think, boy?'

'I have stared into its face,' said Shaba, 'and I think that it can still be defeated – with leaders like Zibhebhu to command us in the field.'

'And afterwards?' said Sibusiso.

But Shaba's imagination could not see the future, simply the past. And some strange past too. For he conjured visions of the red soldiers, though they were not fighting his people. They stood on a field of golden, waving grass and they faced another force. Soldiers like themselves, though dressed in blue. A force that transformed itself at will, with the art of the *isangoma*, into another cloud of angry bees.

'Afterwards,' he said, 'we will see that which is left.'

The old man nodded.

'Then, meanwhile,' he said, 'serve your own Swarm with distinction. Obey your *induna*. Keep faith with his lord, my cousin. For he will need loyal warriors even when the war is done. *Particularly* when the war is done. Warriors worthy of my son's daughter.'

The future, however, was still not visible. Not in any real sense. Only an image of himself, a darkened enclosure, a dozen globes of fire at his feet that hid from his eyes an invisible multitude that split the blackness with a noise like thunder.

Chapter Eleven

Sunday 1st June 1879

The sabre that the Prince Imperial balanced so precociously across his knees was the very same blade – as he so frequently reminded them all – that his great-uncle had carried during the Ulm Campaign, subsequently gifted as a wedding present to Ney, the bravest of Bonaparte's Marshals, and later again presented by Ney's grandson, the Duc d'Elchingen, to Louis before the Prince went into exile in England.

'Shall it bring me luck, Carey, do you think?' he said. The Prince's obsession with the sword was beginning to grate.

Carey saw the younger man's tall silhouette in the tent's opening as the sun rose above the veld. He smacked impatiently at a fly that had landed on his neck and before it had a chance to escape beneath the mohair-braid collar of his blue patrol jacket.

'Luck, Your Highness?' said Carey. 'I'd rather have settled for those damned Basutos. Where the devil did they get to? Division's already on the move and we've not even started. How shall we look? More ragging in the mess, I expect.'

He was irritable, had been so since his previous reconnaissance, when Chelmsford had poured scorn on Carey's suggested route for the coming few days' march.

'Blame your superiors,' said Louis. 'They will insist on providing me with nursemaids. Everywhere I go. But a twelve-man escort would have been excessive, don't you think? Simply so that we can draw a map? Don't worry, Carey. We are enough.'

'The orders were very clear, sir.'

The sort of orders, thought Carey, *around which reputations are shaped or shattered.* They spoke in French and English, transferring between the two languages according to the Prince's imperial whim.

'You think me impetuous also?' said Louis. He rose from the borrowed chair, the portable writing desk, with some difficulty, pulling at the crotch of his breeches. 'This damnable itch,' he complained, setting the sabre back in its scabbard and looking around the tent that Carey shared with Paul Deléage, the *Figaro*'s correspondent. Carey imagined that he saw disdain in the Prince

Imperial's eye, despite his obvious discomfort, the surroundings distinctly less opulent than the brace of houses that the Prince himself enjoyed in company with the Commander-in-Chief. 'Never mind, I shall be obedient today. You see...?' He brandished the letter on which he had been working. 'I have made it clear to *Maman* that the escort is under Captain Carey.'

'Regrettably still a mere lieutenant, Your Highness.' Carey studiously avoided any mention of the Dhobi itch. It did not seem proper, though he knew that Louis had been suffering with the ailment for at least a week. But the Prince Imperial waved aside Carey's correction, sealing the note inside its envelope.

'A detail, Carey. Nothing more. You still expect to be gazetted captain, do you not? It will seem so much more acceptable that I am under the protection of a senior officer. Anyway, by the time she receives my note, it will be true, yes?' Louis signed the letter with a flourish. *Napoléon*. His regular affectation, Carey knew, as the Prince ripped the page from his note book and called for his valet. 'Lomas! Lomas!'

The dapper orderly from the Royal Engineers appeared immediately, ducking below the flap.

'Sir?' he said, showing proper deference to the Prince Imperial's status even though he held no military rank.

'Make sure this letter goes out with the mail, would you? Mister Forbes is returning to Landman's Drift this morning, I think. Perhaps he would be so good as to visit the camp post office. And is my horse ready?'

Lomas took the letter, tucked it inside his tunic.

'I've saddled Fate, Your Highness. Beggin' your pardon, sir, but the grey's acting up even more than usual this morning.'

'Show me,' said Louis, and Carey followed them out of the tent, fastening the shoulder strap for his holster. It was a fine day, crisp and clear, though he was grateful for the dishevelled spread of his beard given the exceptional early morning chill, bitter even for South Africa's June mid-winter.

'He seems steady enough to me, Lomas,' said Carey, surveying the breast-high pegs and air-rope of the picket line and settling his gaze on the largest beast – the grey for which Louis had apparently paid seventy guineas to Bennett in Durban. Bennett had named him Percy, though the Prince, unhappy with his pronunciation, had re-christened him Tommy.

'Thank you for your observation, Lieutenant,' said Louis, 'but I will take the advice of my groom. Tommy will rest here today, Lomas. I will take the bay, as you suggest.'

Carey began to regret volunteering for the patrol. The command should have been Bettington's. But the Captain had been called to duty elsewhere. So the command fell to Carey. And there was just the possibility that the thing might provide him with an opportunity to vindicate his proposed route – the route that Lord Chelmsford had so readily dismissed. Yet command of the heir to the now vacant French Imperial Crown had its own double-edge. And the Prince had barely set hand to Fate's harness than Bettington's men returned, leading their own mounts. Six troopers in total. Wide-brimmed hats and buff corduroy in contrast to the blue jackets of Carey and the Prince Imperial. Mostly weather-worn local farmers, generally retired veterans of British service in the Crimea or across the Empire. And they had company. A scampering white fox terrier they had adopted. A friendly Zulu too, almost indistinguishable from the enemy apart from the thin line of red cloth tied around his head.

'Have the Basutos still not shown, sir?' said the troopers' corporal to Carey. But he had no chance to answer.

'I fear they may have reported to the wrong place,' said Louis. 'But we are enough, I think. We are not going too far. And they can follow on. In any case, it seems we have a guide of our own.' He nodded towards the Zulu who was squatting in the dirt, fondling the terrier's ears. 'But does he have a horse?'

'He's a Zulu, Your Highness,' said Carey. 'They can outrun our cavalry over considerable distances.' He conjured the ubiquitous nightmare image, of the way the Zulus had pursued and butchered the horsemen attempting to flee the massacre of Isandlwana back in January. Before the months of stalemate. Before this second invasion of Zululand that was now finally begun. The main column – the Second Division – had crossed the Blood River into Zululand on the previous morning with the intention of marching directly on Cetshwayo's capital at Ulundi, while the First Division would support them from the south.

'All the same,' said the Prince Imperial, 'we shall make better progress if he is mounted. He can ride, I suppose?'

The corporal – Carey recognised him as Jimmy Grubb – spoke to the guide. Fluent IsiZulu. The fellow nodded.

'Excuse me, Your Highness,' said Lomas. 'But you think he'll be able to handle Tommy, sir?'

A moment of uncertainty, a sudden doubt, almost of fearful premonition, passed over the Prince Imperial's face and then vanished as quickly as it had appeared.

'Here,' he said, 'he may take Fate. I shall ride Tommy after all. Change the saddle will you?'

Carey felt rebuffed yet again. Diminished in his authority. Yet he found himself struggling for a way to reassert himself. He was not at his best in any case. The rebuff from Chelmsford. The feverish remnant of his lingering malaise. His self-doubt about its nature. The lasting effects of the shock which perpetually jolted his innards each time he recalled seeing William McTeague enter the camp at Utrecht with the returning burial detail. His shame at having hidden himself away until the Major – he still *thought* of McTeague as the

Major – had left again with his little band of renegades, seemingly on some errand for Drummond. The incredulity that gnawed upon his soul, that their paths should so nearly cross again after this amount of time, this distance. And almost before he knew it, they were all mounted and making their way out of the laager, past the Scotch wagon barricades, past the well-wishers who always appeared whenever Louis put himself on show. And Deléage was there, naturally.

'Do you have time to wait for me to saddle?' said the correspondent.

For a self-professed Republican, thought Carey, *he has an astonishing fondness for this particular member of the royalty.*

'There'll not be much of interest for *Le Figaro* today, *Monsieur,*' he said. 'Only seven or eight miles. Find a spot to pitch the next camp. That's about it.'

'You can join us there,' said the Prince, shifting uncomfortably in his saddle. 'And Carey is correct. This little excursion will not be very interesting. Not for you anyway, Deléage. You have already been much further into Zululand than I have. Still, I shall try to inspire something exciting for your dispatch.'

Carey worried that it should not be anything *too* exciting. He began to feel more relaxed, however, when they came up with Lieutenant-Colonel Harrison and one of the infantry majors, both of whom fell in alongside them.

'Ah, Carey,' said Harrison. 'It seems that Shepstone's Basutos have paraded in the wrong place. You should wait while we find them for you.'

'We'll carry on slowly, sir. Do you think somebody might instruct them to follow and meet us *en route*?'

'Certainly,' Harrison replied, and relayed the instruction to his own orderly. 'In any case, Major Grenfell and myself will join you for a while. At least as far as Thelezeni.'

It took them an hour to cover the seven miles from Kopje Allein to the site chosen for the army's first camp at Intelesi. A pleasant hour. Distraction from his woes. Chat about Wimbledon – Hartley would win, surely. Gossip about the Grace brothers, the scandal of their expense claims – a gentleman ought not to make a profit from playing cricket, after all. The Prince Imperial's affection for Trollope – the latest two-volume novel an absolute delight. So that Carey began to relax once more. He may only have known Louis for a couple of weeks but he admired his dash, despite the jealousies. It had been amusing during their previous patrol together, just a few days before, to see him charging away alone in pursuit of fleeing Zulus, despite Colonel Buller's earlier admonition. But the Prince's *élan* assumed an entirely distinct complexion now that they would be alone within this patrol.

At the Intelezi camp site, Harrison was keen to get about his business, to ready the place for the arrival of the Division's main force.

'By the way, Carey,' said the Colonel, 'if you still want to verify your sketches of the next leg, there should be enough time. Just as far as the Ityotyosi perhaps. But you will wait for Shepstone's fellows, won't you?' And Carey agreed that he would, delighted that he would, after all, have the chance to reconnoitre the route that Chelmsford had declared impassable. Though the Acting Quartermaster-General had barely left them before Louis, without any word being exchanged, spurred the grey and headed on. The troopers looked confused for a moment, then followed him. Carey cursed silently, touched his dust-coloured helmet in salute to the Major and did likewise.

'Take care,' shouted Grenfell. 'And don't get shot!'

The Prince Imperial turned in his saddle.

'Oh no,' he called. 'I'm sure Carey shall take good care of me.' And he trotted on. Superficially, it was a pleasant enough retort, but Carey thought that he detected contempt in his voice.

Carey fumed as they made their way up the spine of the ridge above the Ityotyosi Valley, from the highest point of which they would be able to complete their drawings and route maps in line with the clearance given them by Harrison. The day was becoming warmer, the vague scent of wood smoke and damp grass. The silver chime of curb chain on cheek piece. Creak of leather. Raucous cry of the ibis. Talk between the troopers and the Prince Imperial was all about their farms now; about their fear of the Zulus – and their respect for them too; about the damned Boers, who had mostly stood aside as spectators to the war even though a few of them had chosen to fight alongside the British; about whether they might get the chance to capture some Zulu cattle while they were out here; about their sense of belonging – a sentiment that Carey, in common with much of the invading army, certainly did not share. So he lifted his voice to the Lord. Proverbs Three, verses twenty-three to twenty-five.

'"Then shalt thou walk in thy way safely, and thy foot shall not stumble. When thou liest down, thou shalt not be afraid. Yea, thou shalt lie down, and thy sleep shall be sweet. Be not afraid of sudden fear, neither of the desolation of the wicked, when it cometh."'

Grubb came alongside him.

'We heard about your exploits at Dyer's Island, sir,' said the corporal, as though it were some sort of consolation. 'Fine show, sir, if you don't mind me saying.'

A pity about Alderton though, thought Carey. The incident at Bushman's River still weighed heavily on him.

'You see?' shouted Louis. 'Already mentioned in dispatches. You might spare a little glory for the rest of us!'

He means, thought Carey, *for the great-nephew of Bonaparte*. But Grubb's reminder of his abilities as an officer helped to buoy him in turn as they reached a pan-flat section of the ridge, the vantage point he had been seeking.

'Prepare to off-saddle...' Carey shouted, but Louis looked at him, seemingly puzzled.

'Here, Carey?' he said. 'But surely we will not be staying long enough. A few sketches and then back to the camp, no? We shall simply loosen the girths for a while.'

Once more the troopers looked to Carey in some consternation. It was a feeling he shared. On the one hand, Louis was correct. And there was little point in making the men off-saddle simply to prove a point. They would not thank him for it. Yet his authority was again at stake. And not for the first time.

'Loosen your girths for now,' he said. 'We can always off-saddle if we decide to stay longer.'

He knew that he should at least make his feelings known to the Prince Imperial. But even this seemed like a weakness. And, anyway, he was trapped. He liked Louis. Yet he had seen him on more than one occasion pay mere lip service subservience to those in true authority – though it seemed to Carey that the Prince Imperial always in truth considered himself *their* superior, rather than the reverse. And Carey, son of the Vicar of Brixham, had been raised in that rigid class structure that bred unquestioning respect for royalty in each of his bones. So he settled, mute, beside the Prince while they sketched the valley and river crossings below. It was the ground that he had already surveyed, the same ground about which Chelmsford had stung him, but he was no more certain now about its suitability than he had been on the previous day. All that long grass made it difficult to judge. But then his thoughts strayed back to his father, remembering that this was Sunday and feeling himself accursed that he was missing yet another Church Parade. He checked his watch. 2.40pm. And they had still not eaten, nor had a brew.

'Right men,' he called. 'Time to off-saddle and make some tea.' Then he turned to Louis. 'A shame though,' he said, 'that we can't take a closer look at the terrain down there. More of an adventure too, perhaps.'

'*Eh bien*, Carey,' said Louis. A smile played on the lip below his boyish moustache at the mention of adventure. 'This is such a dull place. And if we need to take a closer look, well, there is a kraal down there.'

He pointed to the spot, perhaps two miles away. Carey thought he recognised it, for it lay just to one side of the route he had proposed to Chelmsford. But he was suddenly unsure of himself. It was, after all, considerably beyond the limit that Harrison had set them. Yet the Prince Imperial was already tightening Tommy's girth and the troopers began to follow suit. *Dammit!* thought Carey. *They've assumed that I've agreed this. Now I'll just look a fool if I seem to be changing my mind.* But Carey had noticed earlier that the Prince's saddle was hardly in the best of condition. The strap holding the pommel wallets, for instance, looked fit to fall apart. Perhaps a chance to reassert his authority.

'Your Highness,' he said. 'With respect, some of that stitching seems to be coming undone. And that strap looks like it's made of paper. Perhaps you should change the saddle for a fresh one when we get back to camp?'

'Thank you for your observation,' replied the Prince. 'But it is perfectly satisfactory, Carey. It was my father's. At Sedan. And what possible harm can there be? Besides,' he whispered, 'you cannot scold me for the condition of my leather when you cannot even care for your own boots!'

Carey glanced down involuntarily at the dilapidated state of his footwear, felt himself rebuffed yet again. Diminished. A boor for even raising the matter of the saddle. And almost before he knew it, Louis was leading the way down the slope, though stopping often to adjust his breeches, to ease the painful itch. Across a spruit, through a dry gulch, closely followed by the Zulu guide, then the line of troopers with their adopted terrier running to heel and, at the rear, Carey himself, knowing that the Prince Imperial had somehow subverted his command.

A mile or more through the tall grasses of the open veld, picking their way between the termite-hills which made much of the countryside so hazardous to horsemen. There was a donga that carried a thin stream southwards into the Ityotyosi and Carey stopped at its edge, satisfied himself that there were no serious impediments for the army's wagons here, despite Lord Chelmsford's views. Then, with the dried seedheads of local *tamboekie* brushing and sighing against his poor boots, he trotted towards the kraal itself – a cluster of six beehive huts around a central, empty stone cattle enclosure, beyond which stood plantations of man-high mealies.

'Corporal Grubb,' said Carey as they approached, 'does the kaffir know this place?'

The Zulu seemed edgy, answered Grubb's fluent IsiZulu in a low whisper.

'He says that it's the *umuzi* of Sobhuza.'

I'm not sure, thought Carey. *It could be the same kraal.* They all looked pretty much the same, of course. And so did the land. But he had at least been to a similar place only a week earlier. With Watson. And the words of advice stayed with him.

'*Only off-saddle half your men at any one time. The other half should remain mounted while the rest eat. Then swap them over. Oh, and avoid mealie fields at all costs, won't you, Carey? You could hide an entire regiment of Zulus there.*' But Louis had already ordered the whole troop to dismount. They were in the process of knee-haltering the horses when the Zulu emerged from one of the huts, clutching some charred sugar canes.

'He says they're still warm, sir,' said Grubb. 'He doesn't like the feel of the kraal either. Reckons he heard a dog. Zulus are never far from their dogs, sir.'

'We saw no sign of a fire when we were up on the ridge,' said the Prince

Imperial. 'And it was probably just your terrier that he heard. Anyway, are we completely sure we can trust him? He's one of them after all, isn't he?'

'He hates Cetshwayo as much as we do, Your Highness,' Grubb replied. 'Same as all the native contingents we've got fighting for us.'

'That will do, Grubb,' said Carey. 'Let the men eat but make sure they keep their eyes open.'

Coffee and tea were brewed. Each pair of men shared a small tin of bully and a couple of stone-hard biscuits. Talk turned to a piece that somebody had read in the *Illustrated London News* about the luxuries enjoyed by their troops in the Afghan Campaign. Lucky bleeders, somebody grumbled. *I should speak to the Prince*, Carey thought, *before we head back*. But Louis was already asleep in the afternoon sunshine. So he pondered instead their wider situation. Not really a soldier's place to do so, of course, but he had found himself caught up the same as everybody else with Frere's insistence that the war was necessary – civilisation against savagery; villainous warlike Zulus; the need to bring them the Bible and European justice. But then it had become clear that there was no Government authorisation for the war. Indeed, little justification for it at all. But now that they were here, the task had to be completed. And Isandlwana avenged, of course.

He checked his watch again. 3.20pm. They should move soon. But he could still not quite bring himself to shake the Prince Imperial awake. So he sat beside him. Clumsily, until Louis stirred.

'I was dreaming about my great-uncle,' he said. 'Have you studied his campaigns, Carey? Egypt. Italy. Marengo. The creation of the Empire. The glory. The victories.'

The whole of Europe under Bonaparte's heel, thought Carey.

'I always thought he was lucky at Marengo,' he said. 'It's a poor commander who sits in his headquarters all day with his army strung out along a six-mile front. They were in full retreat towards San Giuliano by the time he arrived on the field. At what hour? Three in the afternoon? If Desaix hadn't arrived...'

'But Desaix *did* arrive, Carey, did he not? And my great-uncle *knew* that he would arrive. You know what he said, don't you? In war, luck is half of everything.'

Louis patted the sword at his side.

'I seem to recall that he was depending on Grouchy's arrival at Waterloo also,' said Carey. 'Perhaps he should have kept hold of that fine blade instead of giving it to Ney.'

'Perhaps. But it is a strange irony that, without his downfall, we should not be here, you and I.'

They had discussed this previously, the Congress of Vienna's decision in '15 to give control of the Cape Colony to Britain.

'We need to move,' said Carey.

Louis took his own elegant gold pocket watch from his breeches, flipped open its case and wound the mechanism.

'Oh, just ten minutes more,' he said. 'And I promise to obey your every command on the way back, Lieutenant.'

Carey nodded, wandered over to check his own mount, looking forward to their return to camp, to vindicating his choice of route, and was almost instantly surprised to hear the Prince Imperial calling to the men.

'Collect the horses,' shouted Louis, and the troopers instantly began to pack their belongings, to knock the dottles from their pipe bowls, and to begin gathering the mounts that were now scattered across the kraal. The process took only minutes, but long enough for Carey to seethe at this further undermining of his authority. And across this fretful concern, other elements began to play themselves slowly through Carey's consciousness once more. The dead ground of tall and waving 'boekie grass. The dog abandoned by its owner. The still warm embers. Watson's warning…

'Prepare to mount,' Louis commanded. And the troopers each placed their left foot in the stirrup. All except the Zulu guide whose bay mare, Fate, was still knee-haltered. No sign of the fellow.

'Where…?' Carey began.

He heard the guide at the same moment as he saw him, the splash of red from his head-band, breaking from the mealies and waving his arms, eyes wide and white. Shouting something.

'Mount!' shouted Louis, turning to see what was happening.

Ripples in the grass. Smoke. A single shot. Then a ragged volley. And a mass of Zulus burst from the tall grass, some with rifles, the rest with shields and assegais. It was chaos. The Zulus screaming USuthu! USuthu! The horses terrified, bucking and plunging. Carey the only one already in his saddle, his mount rearing. Clinging to the pommel, trying to recover the reins as the beast broke into a run towards the donga. He glanced back, saw two of the troopers following him but another, still on foot, speared in the back. Rogers, he thought. Then Grubb and another man who could not quite get his feet in the stirrups. The Channel Islander, Le Tocq, on the move too but only with his belly over the saddle. The Zulu guide down on the ground. The rise and fall of assegais.

And where was Louis?

There! The big grey in a dead gallop for the gulley, but off to the right, the Prince Imperial still running alongside, running with difficulty – the Dhobi itch, Carey assumed – gripping the pommel wallet, the Zulus almost upon him. Even so, he was sure that Louis would make it. The Prince was the best of horsemen, was he not? So he looked ahead, checked that they were still following a course for safe and higher ground. Almost there. Another glance backwards at the grey and, as he did so, he saw that bloody strap break, the pommel wallets fall loose, and Louis thrown to the ground, his arms trampled by Tommy's hind hooves. The Prince rolled. Over and over. But then he was up, sprinting awkwardly for the donga.

Alongside Carey, one of the horses had been shot, dropped in the dirt, its rider thrown over the beast's neck and left winded, senseless, on the ground. But still his own mount was beyond control, plunged over the rim of the donga, veered to the right, spittle flying, snorting with the effort, until it found a path of escape. And at least the remaining fugitives were also now out of the donga, heading up a rise, allowing them to regain control of the horses so that, among some rocks, on an open hillock, they reined in, turned about, while Le Tocq slid from his saddle, intending to mount properly. Yet he did not do so immediately. Instead, he looked up at Carey.

'Shouldn't we…?' he began.

But Carey could see that it was too late. And a chasm of ill-fate opened.

Louis had made it as far as the donga but was still two hundred yards distant. They could see him clearly enough though. He turned at bay, his back towards a steep grassy bank. He reached for the sword. His great-uncle's sword. But the scabbard was empty, the blade lost during the Prince's tumble. Worse, it was now being brandished by one of the warriors. The other trooper – the one whose horse had been shot – was dead too. Stabbed over and over again. So that Louis was alone. Entirely alone. They saw him reach for his pistol. A dozen or more Zulus within yards of him. He fired. Missed. And a throwing assegai embedded itself in his left shoulder. He tugged it free. Fired. Missed again. Hit by a second spear.

'Dear God,' said Grubb, 'should we not go back?'

'Five of us?' said Carey. 'We'd never get there in time.' *All die for nothing too*, he decided. 'Look!'

The rest of the Zulus were now much closer. Another twenty or thirty, and rolling towards them like a threshing machine, flattening a swathe through the grasslands.

Anyway, thought Carey, *isn't this the moment of glory that Louis has been craving?* But Louis was running again. A further ten yards. Fifteen. Then he stopped and fired once more. Yet another miss. While a third spear caught him in his left thigh. He pulled it free, tried to turn, to use it as a weapon – and stumbled backwards, tripping on a tussock of grass.

The Zulus were on him in an instant. And from somewhere came the terrier, yapping and snarling.

They finished them both at the same moment. The dog speared to the ground, and Louis pierced by one assegai after another until, finally, a warrior forced his spear-point down through the Prince's face.

*

The troopers scattered, putting as much distance as they could between themselves and the rapidly approaching enemy. But Carey stopped for a final moment. *Is it my fault?* he wondered. And he saw the way that the press would portray this day's events. The tragedy. The notoriety. The disgrace. Fourteen years service, twice mentioned in dispatches – all for nothing. And what would his Annie think? He must write to her as soon as he was able.

He caught the chant that drifted towards them up the donga. But Carey found his gaze locked with the fellow who now held the Prince Imperial's sword – Bonaparte's sword.

'*Shall it bring me luck, Carey, do you think?*'

Yet it was a very different question that he imagined on the Zulu's lips. He was noteworthy too, this warrior, distinguished from his fellows by the patch that covered his left eye.

The Zulu hefted the sword skywards, a holy cross gleaming in the afternoon sun.

All fortune has today deserted the last hope of Imperial France, thought Carey. *As it will soon desert the entire Zulu nation. And me too. May God have mercy on us all!*

Chapter Twelve

Wednesday 4th June 1879

It was two weeks since McTeague had seen the charnel house of Isandlwana. A couple of days as the "guest" of that cove, Drummond, in Utrecht, then sent back like some messenger boy to Cetshwayo's capital with the unpalatable news that the Great King's overtures for peace, while not openly rejected, were certainly not even close to acceptable either. Just enough, Drummond had said, to keep the old fellow guessing, to dance him on a string while Chelmsford completed his deployments. The hostilities would continue meanwhile, of course, but Drummond expected that these would amount to no more than a few skirmishes, Cetshwayo being reluctant to engage in a further open encounter while even the most slender possibility of settlement might be in sight – and the King had pursued that possibility by immediately dispatching another delegation to Chelmsford's camp.

But in Tennyson's immortal words, *"Someone had blunder'd."* For in one further skirmish, just days ago, the pride of Queen Victoria's army had lost something of very peculiar value. And it had thrown this gathering, summoned by the Great King at the sacred hold of EsiKlebheni, into some disarray since the diviners seemed split in their interpretation of the portent.

'They left him there, iNkosi,' cried the old *induna*, spreading his arms wide in the same theatrical style with which he had relayed the entire tale to the assembled thousands, his words repeated and spread among the regiments like seed cast upon the winds. 'They left him and we did not then know his significance. Yet the earth sang to me. There was something abnormal here, that they should abandon the man so easily.'

McTeague understood the Zulus well. They were naturally valiant, and where natural valour might fail there was always the threat that cowardice in battle would be rewarded, first by public humiliation and, second, by public execution. Yet they were a logical folk who would no more think of sacrificing themselves needlessly in a lost cause than of standing in the path of stampeding elephants – though, ironically, that was exactly the behaviour that they had come to expect of the red soldiers. They had seen many examples in the past months, could not truly fathom them, but were amused by the eccentricity.

The cult of personal sacrifice was more familiar to McTeague, of course, though he spurned it as fiercely as did the Zulu. He did not believe that any person was simply hero or coward according to strength or weakness of character but, rather, would fight or fly dependent upon an astonishing spectrum of diverse circumstances. He had seen acts described subsequently as heroic that derived from nothing more than the blind terror of the protagonist. And he counted some of his individually best moments as those when he had braved mindless opprobrium to run from certain death.

Well, there is this interpretation, I suppose, thought McTeague. *That somebody saw this as a convenient way to rid the British Empire of any possible problem with a revitalised French Imperial rival.*

'Is that not your foolish brother?' he said, over his shoulder. 'Was he there?'

McTeague had brought three of his wives with him, along with Maria Mestiza, of course. But it was Amahle whose company he craved most.

'As you say, lord,' said the girl, 'he is foolish. For it was he, they say, who struck the blow that killed the iFulentshi Prince, rather than taking him prisoner.'

'And the Great King will doubtless execute him in turn for his stupidity,' said Maria Mestiza.

Cetshwayo was seated upon a throne of ivory tusks, some distance away in the midst of his counsellors and chief ministers, the white shield of state held high behind him, sheltering him from the sun while, symbolically, also protecting his people from harm. He held the ceremonial axe in his right hand, listening to the *induna* while slapping his left palm impatiently, repeatedly, against his knee. Before him stood this leader of the scouting party involved in the skirmish and behind the *induna* the warriors involved were arrayed in a couple of ranks, two dozen men in total. McTeague thought he could identify some of their regiments – iNgobamakhosi, uMbonambi and uNokhenke, among others. The heads were all bowed, but Shaba was easily distinguishable by his eye-patch.

'It seems that your medication did little to heal his ocular problem either, my dear,' whispered McTeague.

'I think that may not be his greatest concern just now,' Maria replied, leaning towards him and infusing the air with the stink of sour liquor.

'And who,' bellowed Cetshwayo, 'were those who struck the death blows?'

The *induna* pointed in turn to each of a dozen men from his command, calling their names, bringing them forward to stand apart from the rest, Amahle's brother one of them.

'These were the chest and loins of the attack, iNkosi,' said the old chieftain.

Cetshwayo looked down at the bundle of possessions at his feet. A blue uniform tunic, tan trousers, sun helmet, shirt, pistol belt and holster, boots, and an elegant sword in its scabbard.

McTeague was a trifle too far away to see clearly but it seemed a sparse collection, no personal items in evidence.

'Who struck the first blow?' he demanded.

'Langalabelele kaBandile, iNkosi. The man fired at him many times. But the bullets could not touch him. But we did not then know who he was. This warrior showed great valour, Lord.'

'And the last blow? Who struck the last blow?'

'Tshabanga kaNdabuko, iNkosi. The man had his gun. He was wounded but still firing. This warrior showed great valour too, Lord. It was he that brought you the blade.'

'It would have been better if he had brought me the man,' cried the King. 'Why can nobody obey the order to take prisoners? And especially *this* prisoner.'

What a bargaining chip he would have made, thought McTeague.

'I saw it all, Great King,' said the *induna*. 'It would not have been possible even if the iFulentshi had then been recognised. He fought like a lion, Lord.'

'Have him come forward,' said Cetshwayo.

Amahle's brother fell to his knees and crept towards the King, his face close to the ground. And from Cetshwayo's counsellors an ancient appeared, withered and ugly. McTeague heard Amahle's gasp.

'What *is* that?' he whispered.

'The *isanusi*,' she said. 'A diviner who can smell out evil. He is old. From the family of kings. He has served them all.'

The creature snuffled around her brother, touching him, sniffing at Tshabanga's sweat. It seemed to take forever, while the gathering held its breath, complete silence in which even the crickets fell still. But it was finally done, and the diviner reached into a leather bag, scattered small white stones upon the ground to the collective murmur of the crowd.

'What are the stones?' said McTeague.

'Not stones, lord. Bones. Knuckle bones. Five from a man, five from a woman.'

The diviner scampered around the pattern that they made in the dust, an almost perfect circle.

'What does that mean?' said Maria Mestiza.

'It means that my brother is safe. The bones are *izikhombi*, pointers used by the shades to speak with the *isanusi*. Ten because that is the number of life. And if they fall in a circle thus, they speak of health, an absence of evil intention.'

The diviner edged sideways, to rest at Cetshwayo's feet.

'The warrior shall bring me the sword,' said the King, and Tshabanga crawled to the Prince Imperial's possessions, lifted the scabbard in both hands and moved forward on his knees, head still bowed. Cetshwayo passed the ceremonial axe to a small boy, took the sword and drew it slowly, exposing half of the steel and allowing the sun to dazzle the faces of those before him. Then he rattled the blade home, handed it with reverence to one of the Ministers, speaking soft words that none could hear but those closest to him. The group behind him parted to allow the passage of an old woman, almost as wizened as the diviner. But she was tall, her bearing still erect.

McTeague did not need to ask her identity, for he knew that this would be Queen Langazana, a prominent wife of Senzangakhona seventy years earlier and, since the days of Shaka, Guardian to the *iNkatha* here at the EsiKlebheni Palace. She was, they said, already a hundred years old. She brought forward a heavy brass bangle, which she dutifully bestowed upon the kneeling warrior, sliding the armlet over his wrist. It was, said Amahle, a singular honour, granted only to the most valued of men.

'And my brother,' she smiled, 'is now such a man.'

McTeague had seen the French Prince Imperial at Utrecht. He had no great love for the Frenchies in general and had seen this particular specimen as a typical braggart, engaged at the time in some form of vulgar display, cleaving apples in mid-air which were thrown to him by a Basuto manservant of Chelmsford's. With that very sword, he assumed. Indeed, it was McTeague who had brought the news to Cetshwayo, believing that it might have some value. But like most of his efforts recently, this one had also gone unrewarded. Yet it had given the King a chance to relay word of the "AmaFulentshi iNkosi" to his units when they received the final summons to attend here. So he mulled now upon his own position while the rest of the dozen who had been involved in the killing were brought forward, each in turn, and subjected to the scrutiny of the *isanusi*.

Drummond had conveyed to him that Lord Chelmsford had no views one way or the other about the planned development of McTeague's freighting line, but would graciously accept the reduced cost to his Commissariat. He refused, therefore, to pronounce publicly upon the project, but he would certainly do nothing to hinder it. His Lordship similarly declined to be drawn on the matter of land rights at Emoyeni. A civil matter, he claimed, to be settled once the outcome of the conflict was resolved, although the Crown would not be ungrateful, of course, to those who had shown loyalty during the conduct of the war. *Well, how could they doubt my loyalty?* he wondered, with only the slightest discomfort, the niggling and deeply buried recollection that he might at some stage have pretended towards wholehearted support for the Crown's enemies. After all, what did Proverbs say on the matter?

"The tongue of the wise useth knowledge aright. But the mouth of fools poureth out foolishness."

Yes, the Almighty had sent him knowledge, the ability to see beyond any momentary confusion. And if McTeague was honest with the Lord God about any earlier lapse in prudence, well, it was surely not for a fellow like the Honourable William Drummond to challenge divine judgement. And the final proof of his loyalty would come, surely, with Cetshwayo's eventual capture. He had delivered Chelmsford's ambiguous message, the offer to return the captured ordnance acknowledged – though without any thanks – and the suggestion of an open line of communication left under consideration. Cetshwayo had been angered at the lack of progress but not entirely disappointed, and seemingly had no sense of being kept dangling, although this was precisely the view of several of his closest advisers. Meanwhile, Drummond had pledged that McTeague's part in any capture of the King would be properly recognised and, when Klaas had later come loping into the Utrecht camp, the Zulu had been inducted into the intelligence chief's team of native spies, a willing participant in the plan – so long, of course, as there was gold at the end of the line.

Quite how the capture might be achieved was a matter for further deliberation, but Drummond had insisted that the final *dénouement* must now be imminent and that with "Catch-em-Alivo" defeated it would simply require Drummond's agents and McTeague's associates behind the lines to remain vigilant of the King's whereabouts in the almost certain eventuality that he would seek refuge in some place of supposed safety.

'It is done,' whispered Amahle, and McTeague saw that the *isanusi*, having sniffed and pawed at each of the twelve men singled out by the *induna* as having attacked the Prince, and after throwing the knuckle bones for every one of them in turn, sometimes twice where there had been any hint of doubt, had found no trace of evil in any of them.

'And you, Mnukwa kaBhekithemba, when did you arrive at the place of death?' demanded Cetshwayo.

'Just after he was slain, iNkosi. We had chased the horse soldiers away, across the river. When we returned, I remembered the words we had received from you, Lord. That very morning. Yet it did not occur to me that we would have come across the iFulentshi so soon. Then I found this.' He reached among the monkey tails of his kilt and pulled forth a dark scrap, held it aloft. McTeague had already seen the thing. Before the ceremony began. A blue sock, embroidered with the emblem of Imperial France and, below, a single letter 'N' in gold thread.

'And from this you knew him?' said Cetshwayo.

'I suspected that it might be him.'

'And you told this to your Swarm?'

'I did, iNkosi.'

'He was already cut?'

'Honour cuts from those who had taken part in his hunting, Lord.'

'And then?'

'And then, before I could prevent it – for it seemed to me that you would want it prevented, Lord – one of the warriors opened him, released his shade.'

'Not one of those who killed him?'

'No, Lord. Another.'

'So that you would all be cleansed?'

'He said so, iNkosi. Yes.'

'Which is this man?'

Mnukwa turned to the rest of his company, pointed.

'Hlabanatunga kaWandile,' he said.

The warrior looked terrified as, without prompting, the *isanusi* sniffed him out, turned a toothless grin towards the King and produced the bones. They were scattered upon the earth and Hlabanatunga took a step backwards. Cetshwayo signalled to his bodyguard who rushed forward, seized the warrior's arms.

'They show the presence of evil,' said Amahle. 'Now the *isanusi* must throw them again.'

The creature did so, and the warrior cried out.

'No, Lord,' he screamed. 'I have no evil. And none towards you, Lord.'

'That is not what the shades tell us,' said Cetshwayo. He stood. 'Now, listen well, my people. These others, these who slew the iFulentshi Prince, they are blessed in my sight. For they killed an enemy in good faith, not knowing his importance. But this one...' he stretched out a finger towards Hlabanatunga, the most deprecating of gestures, 'this one had evil in his heart. Towards your King. The red soldiers do not understand the *qaqa*, will think that this Prince was opened out of malice and cruelty. And that, in turn, shall steal from us a chance to make an honourable settlement with these invaders.' There was a tremor of discontent, since most of those assembled here wanted nothing less than the invaders' destruction, not some miserable settlement, but Cetshwayo ignored them. 'So this one will die that we might appease the AmaFulentshi with our justice.'

Hlabanatunga struggled uselessly to free himself from his captors, but Mnukwa took two steps to stand in front of him and, careful to keep his eyes averted from the King, the old *induna* spoke.

'Lord, the fault was mine. I should have been quicker. To stop him. He is also a brave man, iNkosi. But...'

The blow from a knobkerrie shattered Mnukwa's skull, spilled his brains, with one blow from the bodyguard at Cetshwayo's signal command.

'Mnukwa was always a man of wisdom,' said the King. 'He was right. They both deserved to die. And for this one, *ukujoja*.'

Execution by impalement had fallen largely into disuse, McTeague knew, though it had been almost a daily occurrence in Shaka's day. But a public execution was also a public duty and none dared avert their gaze, while it was entirely impossible to shut out the animal squeal and screech of the Zulu as he was held spread-eagled, the sharpened stake hammered, forced up through his nether parts, his innards, until his killers stood the stake upright in a post hole, leaving Hlabanatunga's own body weight to complete the process. But it took a long time, more than an hour, before the point finally stilled the struggle.

Through it all, Cetshwayo sat in the shadow of that unnatural tree, holding court with his commanders and gleaning intelligence on the deployment of the red soldiers. And McTeague was summoned to join them, quaking at his proximity to the horror but none the less welcoming the reprieve it offered to turn his back upon the scene.

'The scouts tell me,' said the King, 'that yesterday a great body of horse soldiers joined together with the rest of the Fat Queen's army on the Ityotyosi. Tell me, KaMtigwe, about their *impi*. Details of each regiment. All that you know.'

So McTeague recalled all the detail he was able from Utrecht and the assembled column. The 80th, 94th and 58th Regiments of Foot. The 90th and 13th Regiments of Light Infantry. The Natal Native Contingent. The Royal Scots Fusiliers. Even units of the Naval Brigade. The cavalry too. The King's Dragoon Guards. Natal Native Horse. Frontier Light Horse. And the dreaded 17th Lancers. Almost five thousand European troops and a thousand native auxiliaries.

'We can put five times that number against them, Lord,' said Chief Ntshingwayo kaMahole Khoza, hero of Isandlwana.

'And what good were your numbers at eKhambule? You think I have forgotten your defeat there? But you have not mentioned their *mbayimbayi*, KaMtigwe,' said Cetshwayo. 'How many big guns?'

'They have some like those captured at eSandlwana, Lord. And some bigger too.'

'The *mbayimbayi* did us no harm at eSandlwana,' said Ntshingwayo. 'Nor even at eKhambule. Why do we listen to the white man? Why do we honour him, Lord, by heeding his words thus?'

But you did not face Gatling guns at Isandlwana, thought McTeague, and decided not to mention them. He had seen them in action. Terrifying. But he thought it likely that they might seal the Zulus' fate.

'Because he serves our purpose,' said the King. 'Because he knows no true master but the prevailing wind. Because, at the moment, the wind blows in our favour. And because, if the direction of the wind changes, there is always this to keep his loyalty...' And he gestured towards the still moaning thing that twitched on the stake above their heads.

And the old fellow is always careful to make sure that whenever he lets me off the leash, the bulk of that which I hold dear remains in his possession. He won't repeat the mistake he made with Dunn, giving him time to pack up all his wealth and sneak across the border with it.

'Loyalty!' said Ntshingwayo. 'What do the whites know of loyalty? Of honour? Where are the pledges they made to us at your coronation, iNkosi? Where...'

But Cetshwayo stopped him, held up his hand, looked towards the distant gateway where his sentries were signalling.

'The Dutchman,' he said, 'and the other emissaries that I sent to Chelmsford. They are back.' He waved permission for them to approach, waited while they crossed the parade ground expanse between the regiments, sat almost motionless except for the slightest tapping of his left hand fingers against his hefty thigh. 'Well,' he demanded when they were finally in his presence, 'what word?'

But Cornelius Vijn could barely respond, his eyes straying always to the impaled body. So it was Klaas, sent at McTeague's suggestion as part of the delegation, who broke the news.

'The word is not good, Lord,' he said.

'You met with the white iNkosi, Chelmsford?'

'No, Lord. But we met with his mouth. The man they call Drummond. He is a powerful Minister to Chelmsford.'

'Such arrogance!' said Ntshingwayo.

'He met us at the camp of the horse soldiers, Great King. At the Nondwini River. We set out the terms of your offer carefully, Lord. The *mbayimbayi* to be returned. The cattle as a settlement of good will. The things of the iFulentshi Prince to be returned to them.'

'And they did not want them? There must be power in those things. The sword...'

'They say, Lord,' said Klaas, 'that the body of the Prince is already on its way back to the Land of the Fat Queen. There was a great cleansing, two days ago, when they found him. And immediately afterwards they began his journey, first to the ocean and then on one of their boats back to eNgilandi.'

'Did they speak of the *qaqa*?'

'They were very angry, Great King. The man Drummond said that we are evil savages. That this thing will be revenged.'

'They have no respect for our rituals,' said Ntshingwayo. 'Do they not realise that we have freed the man's soul? What would they do, leave his shade trapped inside the body, all the long way back to eNgilandi?'

'I am certain,' said Cetshwayo, 'they will be appeased when they know the warrior responsible is executed. One day I will sit in person with the iNkosi Chelmsford and I can explain these things. Lighten his darkness. But they rejected all else? Did they offer nothing?' Klaas fell silent, turned to the Dutchman. 'Well?' said the King. 'Speak!'

'Drummond said…' Cornelius Vijn spoke in his high-pitched version of IsiZulu. 'He said that they would speak about negotiation when all the horses, all the oxen, all the weapons and all the ammunition captured by the AmaZulu during the war… when it has all been returned to them, Great King.'

Cetshwayo's Chief Ministers erupted like a smouldering crater.

'Silence!' cried the King. 'Let us hear these words. Of horses we have no need. Nor the oxen. And more rifles and ammunition can be supplied to us by KaMtigwe.'

'Whey!' said Ntshingwayo. 'More of the useless old guns that the white trader gave us before the invasion. We must not do this, Lord.'

No, thought McTeague, *nor give them back my damn'd oxen, neither.*

'I am sure we can prevail upon KaMtigwe to find a source of new guns,' said the King. 'After all, he has much to lose here too.'

'There is more, Lord,' said Vijn. 'I fear that there is much more.'

Silence fell.

'Then speak,' said Cetshwayo.

'Drummond says that here is the new word from Lord Chelmsford. That Lord Chelmsford's word comes directly from the Fat Queen herself. And this is her word. Apart from the horses and oxen, the captured guns and ammunition, the Zulu King must surrender one more thing.' He paused, looked around, his eyes blinking back tears of anguish.

'Speak!' bellowed Cetshwayo.

'Chelmsford – the Fat Queen too, they say – demands, Lord, that you surrender entire, to be held as hostages, all the warriors of your greatest regiment.'

'It is a strange twist of the fates, is it not?' said Maria Mestiza when the sun was setting; when the auspicious Full Moon was already climbing in the evening sky; when Cetshwayo's fury and frustration were slowly ebbing; when the fire pits were being lit; when the feast was being prepared; when the *iNkatha* was about to make its processional return to the kraal.

'There seem to be several such twists at the moment, my dear,' replied McTeague. 'To which do you refer?'

He had not seen her touch a drop of intoxicant all day but she frequently astonished him by that ability to hide liquor bottles about her person and consume the contents unnoticed. But these days it took only the smallest quantity to rekindle her inebriation.

'The way the soldiers left that young Frenchie to die.'

'Boney's great-nephew? Damned careless of them.' He knew what she was thinking, of course. She loved to tease him with this thing about abandoning Rhys, the Civil Commissioner, in Honduras. Nonsense, naturally. 'I imagine,' he continued, 'that whoever was in charge faced the same problem that

I, myself, had to endure. Once you know that your men won't stand, once the rot has set in, it's all *sauve qui peut*, my sweet one.'

Amahle was watching the exchange, straining to catch some thread of their foreign tongue.

'Did you know,' Maria said to the girl, switching to IsiZulu, 'that your husband was once a great iNkosi of the red soldiers?'

But much of the statement was lost between slurred pronunciation and Maria's hysterical laughter.

'Great warrior,' said McTeague, beating his own chest, then removing the monocle to polish it.

'How could it be otherwise, Lord?' said Amahle. 'But I was thinking about the iFulentshi Prince. I believe that you would have stayed at his side. At the end. In the way of your people.'

'My people only tend to do so when they have no choice, dear girl.'

'I spoke with my brother,' she told him. 'He says that the horse soldiers did not even stay long enough to count our spears. He says that two of them acting boldly could have saved the Prince. Would you not have acted so?'

More laughter from Maria Mestiza.

'Always difficult to stand in another man's footprints, my sweet. Especially with death staring into our eyes.'

He felt the cold grip of a poem around his heart. Dickens, of course.

"Brave lodgings for one, brave lodgings for one,
A few feet of cold earth when life is done."

And death turned his thoughts to Twinge. *How did the bugger get away?* he wondered.

'Your brother is now reconciled with your family?' Maria Mestiza was saying to Amahle.

She had insisted that the dose had been sufficient to finish an ox – which, in the case of Twinge, was highly appropriate. But he had escaped all the same. McTeague glanced around, as though expecting to see the fellow, sensing some evil gathering in the flame-seared twilight.

'My father will not see Shaba,' said Amahle. 'But *this* is my family now. And while my brother speaks to me, he has not forgiven me. Nor the Skirmisher, Klaas. Nor my husband.'

So what now for young Willie? thought McTeague. *It could all have been so very different. If Cetshwayo had only finished the job when he had the chance.* But now McTeague's dream of creating the kingdom which he and Maria Mestiza so badly craved was slipping away. He saw it plain. Emoyeni as its capital. The house built afresh. A veritable mansion, with a library to rival anything outside London itself. A palace, founded upon the wealth which he had begun to hoard there, beneath the marker stone on the low ridge, the highest point of his domain, with the views out towards False Bay and Lake Saint Lucia. The territory extended to encompass all of Hluhluwe. The mineral wealth. He must guard his fortune this time. Enough to wipe out the godless infidelity of his mother, the blight of her cuckolded husband, too stupid to prevent young Willie's illegitimacy. He would keep Maria at his side, of course. After all, he could never have made the journey without her, and he loved her for it. She should have her kingdom therefore. But it would be young Amahle who would bear him the heirs that he sought. She was baptised, was she not? A fitting bride. And he felt sure that the Almighty would spare him long enough to see those sons, prevent him from becoming useless just a while more. He shook away the thought that he was already almost sixty.

Yet he had depended too much on Cetshwayo and it seemed inevitable that Cetshwayo would be thrown down. The English would certainly not keep him on the throne once he was defeated. Why should they? So it was upon Chelmsford that he must now rely. And what could he offer Chelmsford that would give him the leverage he needed? Cetshwayo's capture? There would be plenty of runners in that particular field. No, something more. But what?

The feasting continued until the Full Moon had reached its zenith and, all that while, the *iNkatha yeSizwe yaKwaZulu* was being prepared. Then, at full dark, a thousand blazing torches had appeared in the distance, a fire snake that slithered up the hillsides, its sibilant song becoming clearer with every sinuous change of direction until, at the gateway, the beast fell silent, the flame of its scales swaying, sucking at the air in the gathering wind. The gatekeepers had taken up the chant, honouring the Great Coil with the names of each king and every clan whose essence had come together in its forging, craving admittance for this soul, this shade, of the Zulu Nation.

Cetshwayo had bidden welcome to the *iNkatha* in a simple rhythmic ritual, at the end of which the regiments, all the women and families gathered here too, had taken up the refrain, so that the burning serpent was welcomed, bearing the Coil back to its sacred home. And they pressed forward, hoping for a glimpse of the thing at close quarters, the heavily stuffed tube of stitched and rope-bound python hide, before it disappeared for renewal by the medicine men, the shamans, the diviners, within the inner sanctum of Queen Langazana's Royal House.

'It is always so,' said Amahle. 'Whenever a new campaign is about to begin. The *iNkatha* must be strengthened again.'

In the centre of the parade ground, a shallow pit had been dug and around its edge stood the same warriors – Amahle's brother included – who had earlier been identified as having killed the French Prince and, more important, as being free from evil. An *inyanga* brought them a gourd from which each of them drank deeply, quickly causing them to retch the contents of their stomachs into the pit.

'This is *umbengo*, is it not?' said McTeague.

'The vomit will be mixed with new elements that will cause the *iNkatha* to grow and thrive,' Amahle replied. 'Hair and skin taken from the red soldiers. Grass trampled by this year's new calves. Earth and blood from the field at eSandlwana. All those things that speak of our greatness.'

A portable Westminster Abbey, thought McTeague. He had no real faith in such collective idolatry, of course. In the end there was simply the individual and there was the Lord God. In everything that he did. You paid your due to the Almighty by a simple honesty with Him about your actions – *all* your actions. And, in return, he would protect you. As a father should. Either in this life or the next. Honesty. Yes, that was the thing.

'And so long as the *iNkatha* is renewed, kept intact...' said Maria Mestiza.

'Then the AmaZulu remain one people,' said Amahle. 'Intact also. Under the Great King. So that none may defeat us.'

'But now, inside the Royal House, the elements of the *iNkatha* are taken apart?' said McTeague.

'Yes, Lord. While the *iNkatha* is born anew. So we hold our breath under the Full Moon that is a blessing on our actions.'

She spoke the words bravely, but fear lay beneath them.

'I see a terrible thing,' said Maria Mestiza. 'A thing that must not come to pass. The elements of the *iNkatha* thrown apart for a hundred years. The Royal House of the AmaZulu divided against itself.'

McTeague thought that it was a piece of theatre, fuelled by cheap liquor, but then he realised that the two women were sharing the same vision, a nightmare that did not dissipate until the *iNkatha yeSizwe yaKwaZulu* was presented, whole once more, to the frenzied gathering, with an outpouring of collective relief.

'These are the words that you will write,' said Cetshwayo, touching the Dutchman none too gently with the head of his ceremonial axe. They were gathered in the most private section of his dwelling here in EsiKlebheni. It was long past midnight and the King had a striped blanket about his shoulders. 'Tell them that I would make peace.' There was a growl of discontent from Ntshingwayo and some of the other ministers. 'But ask them how this can happen when the Fat Queen's army is capturing my cattle each day, burning our homesteads, killing my people. Tell them that if they leave our country, there will be peace. But if they proceed then I see a great calamity before us. And if the red soldiers die in such a calamity, they will say that the fault belongs to Cetshwayo kaMpande whereas, in truth, the fault may be with them.'

'And how should I reply to Lord Chelmsford's demands, Great King?'

said Cornelius Vijn. 'The surrender of all the horses and oxen, the guns and ammunition? The surrender of a regiment?'

McTeague saw the Dutchman wince as he spoke this latter sentence, expecting some violent backlash.

'Tell them that, of all those things they lost at eSandlwana and elsewhere, very little came to myself. Tell them that most was carried off by individual warriors and would take a great time to gather again. So far as the horses are concerned, I know of none that we possess. But the oxen are a different matter, though many of them were sickly beasts that died of their lung fever. All the same, I am sending one hundred and fifty back to them.' The King looked quickly towards McTeague, smiled at him benignly. 'Do not look so worried, KaMtigwe, the oxen will not come from your herds.'

'And the surrender of the regiment, Lord?' said Vijn.

'Why do you press this nonsense?' cried Ntshingwayo. 'Of course there will be no surrender of our warriors. What sort of foolishness would that be?'

Cetshwayo held up his hand.

'Of course we will not respond to that demand,' he said. 'And remind them of this. That all those things that were taken by my people were not stolen during a raid on *their* territory. It was the reverse. They were taken when the red soldiers invaded our country for no good reason. If they had come to me and spoken man to man about any differences between us, I would have reached agreement with them. But they send me demands. Threats. For the rest, I will speak more with my Council. But meanwhile, they can have these also as my token.'

He slapped his hand on his thigh and eight young warriors appeared, carrying between them the longest elephant tusks that McTeague had ever seen.

'And the guns, Lord?' McTeague reminded him.

'The guns,' said Cetshwayo. 'Always the guns. We will not delay the letter but tell Chelmsford that the *mbayimbayi* are being sent to him in any case. For, in truth, they are no use to me.'

'But they may be useful to the red soldiers, iNkosi,' said Ntshingwayo. 'I do not fear the *mbayimbayi*, but why make a gift of more guns to our enemy?'

'You think me a fool?' cried Cetshwayo. 'That I would simply send them the big guns? But the offer might buy us more time. The Lord Chelmsford does not have either the desire nor the ability to destroy us. These are simply the posturings of commanders. Tactics. When he thinks the time is right, he will negotiate.'

'And who will deliver this letter, Lord?' said Ntshingwayo.

'I will send KaMtigwe,' the King replied. 'And four warriors of my choosing.' The Chief Ministers grumbled among themselves and there were some openly angry exchanges. 'Silence!' Cetshwayo roared. 'I have spoken. Now, leave me.

Only KaMtigwe shall remain. I must have a private word with him.'

'You do me great honour, Lord,' said McTeague when they were alone. But I wonder whether I might beg another. Perhaps my wife might accompany me...'

'The Witch Woman remains here,' said the King. 'With all your other wealth. Including that which you guard so carefully at eMoyeni. So there will be no distractions.'

McTeague had never intended to take Maria Mestiza with him, for it was Amahle whose company he craved. But there seemed little point in pressing the issue. In any case, he was more concerned that Cetshwayo apparently knew so much about his hidden treasure. How could that be?

'Of course, Great King,' he said. 'But there was another matter you needed to discuss?'

Cetshwayo pulled the blanket closer about his shoulders.

'I begin to feel the cold, my friend,' he said. And, to McTeague, the King seemed suddenly to grow old, the habitual smile falling from his lips.

'You think that Chelmsford *does* mean to destroy the Kingdom, Lord?'

'And my Diviner tells me he has the power to do it. So you will take him a second message, KaMtigwe, though you will speak not a word of this to any other. Or I shall surely kill you. Do you understand me?'

McTeague nodded.

'I understand, Lord.'

'Then you will tell them this. You will deliver a private message to Chelmsford, KaMtigwe. To Chelmsford and nobody else. You will tell him that, over and above the words in this letter, I accept his terms.'

'All of them, Great King?'

'All of them. If they will agree to negotiate, face to face, then I will indeed surrender my greatest regiment. The iNgobamakhosi. They must be treated with respect, naturally. But it is time to end this thing. Before it is too late.'

'Yes, Lord,' said McTeague. He bowed, left the hut in consternation.

This could be a disaster, he thought. *The one demand that Chelmsford could not have dreamed would be taken seriously. The one offer that could bring a peaceful settlement. It simply won't do!*

He found the Dutchman near the hut to which they had been allocated.

'That letter,' said McTeague. 'We need to add a wee codicil of our own, Dutchie. Just in case. A private note from you and me. Tell them that, regardless of anything they might be told, the Zulus intend to fight. Tell them that they've just renewed the *iNkatha,* that it's the heart of the nation. That if they want to break that heart, they should come here – to EsiKlebheni.'

168

Chapter Thirteen

Monday 9th June 1879

'He was a good man, a great man,' said Shaba.

'Then he should not have stood between the King and his kill,' laughed the warrior at his side.

This was true, though Shaba still regretted the death of Mnukwa. About Hlabanatunga he cared less. The man had been a fool, taking delight in opening the iFulentshi Prince even after the old *induna* had told them that the body should be left untouched. So he deserved his fate. Even the *ukujoja*. But the death of Mnukwa required the Swarm to be disbanded, dispersed, and Shaba had gladly received the instruction to rejoin his own regiment. He returned with his prospects still in the ascendancy. His cattle were safely protected among the herds at Zama's *umuzi*. Zama herself was pledged to him, so far as such a thing was possible pending some permission from the Great King for the uMbonambi to wed among her age-guild. He had been recognised once more, this time by Queen Langazana from whose hand he had received the *ingxotha* that he now wore around his right forearm. One more praise name had been bestowed upon him so that he was now Tshabanga kaNdabuko, Giant Slayer and Sword Taker. Due deference was shown to him by those within the regimental division to which he was now attached, the Red Calf, and it was spoken abroad that he might one day be granted recognition as a chosen *iviyo* company leader, perhaps even a junior *induna*, responsible for the training of young boys and cadets. Meanwhile, he had spoken with his sister at eSiklebheni, found her surprisingly happy and properly treated by the white trader. He could still not bring himself to accept the situation and his hatred for the Skirmisher, Klaas, continued to scald him. But his enmity towards his sister had dissipated as soon as he saw her.

'Ah,' she had said, without any form of greeting nor any sign that there may have been dissent between them, 'I see that you still wear the *umutsha* I made for you. The headband too.'

He had touched the tube of leopard skin.

'It is a good headband.'

'Does the girl like it also?'

'Girl?'

'Whey! The one who follows you with the eyes of a new-born cow. She is called Zama kaMandla, they tell me.'

'Ah, she guards the sacred spring at Mthonjaneni, I think. What about her?'

'Fool! It is said that you have seen the grandfather. The father too. He that is *induna* of the Mongrels and kin to Zibhebhu.'

'There are many seedlings to be nourished before that crop can be thought safe.'

So many things that might go wrong, he thought. *So many possible false turns. How would it have been if the whim of the Great King had considered the slaying of the iFulentshi Prince in the same way as Hlabanatunga's opening of him?*

'And which crop is that? The girl or her *ilobolo*?'

'Her family favours me. But it is a difficult thing. They favour me because my reputation grows.'

'You must be pleased to have so much about which you can boast. Before, you sang your own praises when you had done nothing. Except talk and perform the *giya* dance.'

'So, Bitter Tongue,' he had smiled, 'the white man has not drawn your venom. But here is my problem. My reputation grows through this war, yet it keeps me too from those things that I truly desire. Tending our herds. Following my father's craft.'

'Growing old and fat with Zama kaMandla at your side?'

'That too. When I am no longer bound by the cleansing. But most of all to have my father see me once more.'

'He did not see you at eSiklebheni?'

'He would not.'

'You spoke with him?'

'I told him that I had once heard a story – about a warrior kept warm on the road by a kaross that an old man had thrown aside. That the warrior was grateful. But our father did not seem to enjoy the tale. And still he did not see me!'

He would have spoken with Amahle about many other things if he had known that, on the following day, his company, the whole of the Red Calf Division of his regiment, in fact, was going to be marched towards the west to shadow the red soldiers' advance. But also to accompany those that the Great King was sending to speak with the white iNkosi – the delegation that included his sister's husband. And the cur had sought him out, used whatever authority had been granted him to demand Shaba's presence during this third day of their journey.

It was familiar territory. The same that he had travelled when they came to set free the other Frenchman, the prisoner. It seemed like yesterday. It seemed like a lifetime.

'You have no fear of the red soldiers in this place?' asked the white trader.

'It is *you* that has the fear, old one,' Shaba replied, running alongside the horse. 'I hear it in your voice.'

'But look at all this...'

They had been marching through that wilderness the invaders had plundered so many times from their camps to the west. More homesteads abandoned and burned.

'They only come here when there are no regiments to oppose them. They are cowards. Good at fighting women and children. Old men. Then they ride back quickly to the safety of their walls. But they never venture beyond the Sbhokwe.'

The river lay ahead of them. And beyond the river, the eZungeni hills, sprawled like a slender lizard, basking in the sun against a fierce blue sky.

'Hot work, all this running!' said the trader.

They had begun just before dawn, eating the ground quickly, beating the grass flat with the oxen that they drove as an offering to the Fat Queen, through the clay-coloured stains that the Sky Lord's fingers spread across the disappearing dark, through the anger-shot fiery eye as it climbed the early hours, and into the liquid clarity of the day's core.

'We will stop soon,' Shaba told him. 'So that you may fill your belly.'

Once again there was little food but there was bound to be sufficient for this stealer of young girls. In any case, the real purpose of the halt would be to send him and the King's messengers on their way, to the white iNkosi, while Shaba and his Division would cross the river, make another half-day's forced march.

'They say that the Great King's regiments can run the whole day around and still fight a battle at the end of it,' said this KaMtigwe.

That was true also, yet it was buried inside a man to know and understand the strength, the pain, that such a feat required.

'But the regiments of your Fat Queen can do no such thing.'

'I serve only the Great King, Cetshwayo kaMpande,' said the trader. His face was blotched scarlet with unhealthy, bulging veins, and grease-riddled sweat dripped from beneath his hat, the glass eye-piece swinging from a cord around his foetal neck. It seemed like a great effort for him to keep pace, to keep talking, even though he was mounted and they on foot.

'The regiments of your people are like mongrel packs. Old men mixed with young.'

'Not my people,' said KaMtigwe.

'Yet you were once an *induna* in their army.'

'No longer.'

'You are still not too old to fight. You see that warrior who leads our Division? He is past seventy winters. He has more scars that I can count. Yet he is still here, serving his King.'

'I too serve the King,' said the trader. 'In my way. And the regiments of the Fat Queen are not so far different from your own. Each raised in a particular part of the land, named for that area, as your own are sometimes named for the *ikhanda* at which the age-guild boys are mustered. One regiment distinguished from another by the markings on the necks and wrists of their coats – like the colours and patterns of your shields.'

But this was too simple, Shaba knew, to explain the Zulu military system. In his own case, he had belonged to an age-guild of boys born thirty-five summers and winters past. They had become boy servants, *udibi*, at the age of fourteen, carrying the food and weapons of family and clan members. Then, at seventeen or eighteen, they presented themselves at one of the twenty-seven royal barracks scattered across the realm, to take the King's Milk – a token payment to them from the udders of the royal herds to signify and confirm their willingness to serve, to train as cadet warriors, guardians of the King's cattle and his crops until such time as he deemed the numbers sufficient to form a new regiment. Thus it had come to pass that, when he was twenty-one, all those of his age-guild were summoned to the capital and their regiment established, its warriors issued with the King's shields, hides of grey in every shade and mottled white. They would be based at the *ikhanda* of KwaMbonambi, taking both its name and also its significance. For the place implied an Evil Omen, a Fearsome Aspect. It suited the King's sense of humour, they said. This new regiment would strike terror into any of his enemies that beheld it. But there was this also – that in the years when they became *udibi*, the nation had been afflicted with a terrible outbreak of the white man's pox that had killed many boys and left most others with the scarred faces, the evil aspect, that typified those who survived.

'It is told,' he said, 'that the red soldiers do not see the sun in their own land. Because the places in which they live are so full of smoke that it blots out the light.'

'In the big *imizi*. Where there are countless thousands living. But many others come from green lands. Like these. Very much like these.'

Shaba despised himself for the conversation. Yet this thing held him in its spell.

'If they have green lands of their own, and so many people, why do they come here?'

'They are never satisfied with what they have. They cannot rest. They always want more.'

'Can they not simply steal what they need from the AmaFulentshi that live nearer to them?'

'The French are no better than the English. They have been stealing from each other for longer than either tribe can remember. And now they each steal what they need from other parts of the world.'

'Will the French continue to steal now they have lost their Prince? Or will they be swallowed up?'

'He was the last of their royal line. But they will not be swallowed up. They too are a proud people.'

'Made so by their great iNkosi. The one-armed warrior with the huge hat.'

The white trader spoke a word that Shaba did not understand. It sounded like *Bhoni* but he could not be sure.

'And the young prince died well?' continued KaMtigwe.

'Well enough for an iFulentshi.'

'You brought back all that belonged to him?'

'Mnukwa kaBhekithemba made sure that it was so.'

'There was nothing else?'

'You think I am a liar?'

He felt the thing press against the top of his thigh where it was tied among the civet furs of his kilt, wrapped in the white nose cloth of the one soldier he had killed, stuffed inside the woollen foot sheath of the other. That small thing of shining yellow metal with the bee engraved upon its shell. He had been convinced that it was an omen, the shade of the iFulentshi Prince speaking to him as though he should have understood when the swarm had killed the small boy at Zama's *umuzi*. Indeed, when he found it, the thing was still talking, making the small noises of the Death Beetle that he could not fathom. It was silent now, but he feared that it may begin to whisper anew, to alert this fat white man.

'You are my wife's brother,' said KaMtigwe. 'Too honest for your own good, she tells me. But the possessions of the French Prince are a powerful medicine.'

'He has passed,' said Shaba. 'He no longer has possessions.'

'Even without those possessions, he is a powerful medicine still himself. His shade. Have you spoken to the Lord-of-the Sky about this?'

'Only the shadows of those departed may speak to the Sky Lord. Or do you mean the Jesucristo that you and the *amakholwa* hold so dear? The Jesucristo that you forced my sister to obey before she married you?'

'I suppose the name does not matter. There is only one Creator. And I did not force your sister to anything that she did not already desire. We must each be honest with the Almighty.'

'I do not see this Jesucristo.'

'Ah,' said KaMtigwe. 'Your eye. My chief wife tried to heal it for you, did she not?'

'The Witch Woman. She is no *inyanga*.'

And this was *less* than the truth. For there were times when he lifted the patch from his eye and there was light. There was indistinct shape. He wondered whether another dose of the *umkhoka* would produce further improvement but he would not put the question. You should, after all, never be too greedy in life.

'No,' said the trader, 'she is not. But she knows a great deal about healing. And it's healing you need, is it not? For your woes if not your eye.'

'I need healing only for those close to me. Those afflicted by evil brought to them by that trickster Klaas who runs at your tail. Or by the *isangoma* Mutwa who has poisoned the soul of my father against me. Or by you, Sister Husband!'

He watched them disappear into the distance after KaMtigwe's party – with the many oxen and the elephant tusks – took the valleys that would lead them finally, according to the local men who guided them, to the newest of the fortified camps that marked the red soldiers' slow progress towards oNdini and Cetshwayo's capital. It was less than one day's march westward, they said.

And then their own march continued, a simple plan. Around the lower slopes of the eZungeni hills lay the cluster of larger homesteads that the red soldiers had left untouched because of their size. But they also sat close to the route that the Fat Queen's army seemed to be taking – a good place from which to observe them and then, keeping hidden from their scouts, to follow them, to seize any proffered opportunities to raid and sting their ponderous column. But with the river finally before them, they were shocked to discover that, on the near bank, guarding the drift which they had intended to use for their crossing, yet one more soldiers' camp was already in the process of being established. So the Division halted in a broad *udonga*, fed itself on thin porridge and observed the red soldiers at their work.

'It is the horse soldiers,' said Langalabelele. 'With the horses they can move almost as fast as we can.'

'They must still wait for those on foot and their ox wagons to catch up,' said Shaba. 'He pointed to a small group of horsemen patrolling beyond the edge of the camp. Blue coats. White Helmets. The longest spears he had ever seen with small red and white flags near their points. 'But those are new.'

It took them some time to reach the next drift downstream, then sweep around towards the heights on trails that would keep them away from the soldiers' view and allow them to reach the homesteads unseen. Yet, by then, the situation had changed dramatically. The first *umuzi* they reached, a place of perhaps one hundred dwellings, was in turmoil. Its garrison of warriors, though not small, was plainly insufficient to meet the threat gathering in the distance, back across the river. For the horse soldiers were advancing to the drift.

Shaba could see his Division's commander just ahead, consulting with his two *izinduna* and, it seemed, the headmen from the homesteads, while the three hundred warriors of the Red Calf waited in silence. There had been a cleansing after the *iNkatha* had been restored to EsiKlebheni but it hardly prepared them sufficiently for battle. Yet it was to battle that they seemed destined. The commander was resplendent in his regalia, full cow-tails, a ball of red-crested lourie tufts at his forehead and a single long white ostrich feather, but he cut short the conference after only a short time, waved a sweeping signal with his spear and lifted his voice, that it would carry both to the Division and also to their enemies away below them.

'We stand here!' he called. 'The breath of our life will protect the People of Heaven.'

He chanted this thing slowly, over and over again, while the *izinduna* led the warriors out of cover, down the slope a short way, then lined them along some open tussocks, a ridge, so that from the river they would be silhouetted against the skyline. And as each man reached his place in the line, he turned to face the horse soldiers, took up the song so that it seemed to flow down the hill like the rolling volleys of the white men's guns, its rhythm set by the beating of *iklwa* shaft against the taut hide of their shields.

'We stand here, Johnnie!' they sang. 'Breath of our life! Breath of our life!'

It seemed to have the desired effect too, since the horsemen had halted after splashing across the drift. He could see them more clearly now, and these were not the blue-coats with the long spears he had seen earlier. Nor were they the black-coats they had fought at eSandlwana. No, these were the soldiers in dung-coloured jackets, the same that had drawn out the iNgobamakhosi, the Bender of Kings, at eKhambule. Their turn to consult now, to calculate the risk, to think about their own cleansing. And Shaba wondered how the red soldiers' rituals might differ from their own. *I should have asked the trader*, he thought, then scolded himself for the foolishness of the idea.

The dung-jackets were on the move, spread in long lines that they tried to keep in close formation as they advanced. But the ground was too riven by gullies to allow them any true precision, so that they were soon broken into smaller groups although, in total, their numbers seemed equal to those of the Red Calf. And when they were perhaps four or five spear-throws away, most of them dismounted and opened fire.

'Here we stand, Johnnie,' chanted Shaba's companions, the refrain gathering pace, the drumming of their shafts beating a new urgency until some of their number began to fall.

'Breath of our life for the Earth Mother!' sang the commander and, as one body, they slipped down behind the ridge. Some of their names were called, Shaba's among them, and these edged forward, captured rifles at the ready. They were the Division's most accurate marksmen, though Shaba greatly regretted that they had not taken better instruction on the weapon's use. Still, he had at least learned to hold the thing steady, to sight carefully, to control his breathing, to pull the butt-end tightly into that gap between neck and shoulder bones, to squeeze the trigger. But he wished that he better understood the small knobs, the white soldiers' symbols, that adorned the blackened metal device along which his eye now squinted.

They did little damage. Not a single dung-jacket touched so far as he could see. Then the soldiers were in their saddles again, urging the mounts up through the rocks and scree until they had halved the distance. *Perilously close,* thought Shaba. For the horse soldiers, of course, since a downhill charge by the Division would, in all likelihood, catch them unawares. Like eHlobane. There would be losses among the warriors, naturally, but...

He looked back at the commander, fully expecting the order to advance, but the old one kept his place.

'Burn them, warriors of the Evil Omen!' he cried. 'Burn them!'

Shaba and the others took aim once more, fired a ragged volley. It was well-timed since the dung-jackets were closely bunched, caught in the act of forming their own firing line. Several fell. A horse also. It screamed, kicked up red dirt and small stones, all a tangle of foam-flecked teeth, stinking sweat spray and twisting leather straps.

'*USuthu!*' went up the word, while those still in cover began to beat their shields anew.

He felt his blood rise, the frenzy build, until he thought he recognised the soldiers' iNkosi. A heavy man, though nimble enough when mounting or dismounting. A man like a bull. A man with a beard that covered his entire face, more expansive than even that of the fellow who had left the iFulentshi Prince to die. He remembered that other one, the way he had sat so impassively on his horse, watching as Shaba had picked up the sword. This soldier was similarly dressed. A coat of blue rather than the earthen shades of his men. But he wore the same broad hat as they did, a ribbon of red around its crown.

This is the man, he thought, *that I saw at eHlobane. We were trying to kill him, but he kept coming back towards us, taking up others of his kind who had fallen on the mountain, carrying them to safety. We thought he was mad, that he would surely die. But he did not. How different from the soldier at the* umuzi *of Sobhuza. Or* perhaps not *so* different. For this iNkosi seemed uncertain now, shouted wildly at his men. There were more shots exchanged, but by the time the white smoke cleared, the dung-jackets were in the saddle again and urging their beasts back to the river. *Now,* thought Shaba. *Now we must surely fall upon them.*

'You think me stupid, Johnnie?' called the commander. 'We have seen the Trickster's dance before, Johnnie!'

Shaba felt ashamed. Had he not himself identified these as the same men who had made fools of the Bender of Kings, lured them to their doom? The commander looked back at the homesteads and Shaba did likewise. They seemed deserted now, only the distant image of women, children and the old far above, beyond the tree line, escaping to safety.

'We have done here,' said the commander and, at his beckoning, the Division clambered from the shallow ridge and, shields above their heads, moved steadily upwards, past the now abandoned thorn-bush palisades.

Clouds of acrid woodsmoke clawed at them, the shades of those who had lived here long ago, taken solid form once more. The palisades burned and a million amber sparks danced the *giya* together, more numerous than the holes in a night sky, leaping from wall post to thatch. The sparks roared in triumph, lifted rolling black arms upwards with each hut that collapsed on itself. Flames chattered and spat, the heat pushing and clawing at Shaba's face even at this distance. White flakes floated in flurries of mountain snow above the main homestead and also above the two smaller settlements away to his right, higher up the slopes. The flakes settled on the line of warrior faces, as though they also were now shades of the departed. The flakes fell upon lip and tongue so that each of them tasted the *umuzi*'s death. In places, even the bush itself was burning, dry grass smouldering. But the commander had made no attempt to save the homesteads, nor to offer any explanation of his strategy.

'It is enough that we helped the people get away,' said Shaba. He pushed forward the rifle's lever, drew one of the precious bullets from his pouch and pressed it into the breech.

'We should have saved the homesteads too,' Langalabelele grumbled.

Shaba waited for a dark shape to materialise from the smoke, aimed and fired, but hit nothing.

'The old one knows his trade,' he said. 'For once, we have the walls – and it is the red soldiers in the open.'

They had been here for some time, on ground higher than the homesteads, higher than the enemy, ground that was a warren of stream beds and thorn scrub, tumbled rock faces and darkened cave openings. From time to time, the dung-jackets ventured from the smoke, from their own cover, but they were easily driven back each time.

There was a respite, while each side drew breath, and the *inyanga* from the larger *umuzi* came among them, splashing them with holy liquid from gourds carried by small boys. Shaba was uncertain about the efficacy of this particular medicine, thought that the falling ashes might be a stronger potion, but he accepted the blessing with due deference, supplemented the thing by dragging the spoon from his hair, pouring the *ugwayi* from its neck-bottle and taking the powder through his nose to help stoke the battle-heat.

'Now we wipe them!' cried the commander, and Shaba saw that the dung-jackets were finally leaving the homesteads in true retreat.

So two companies of the Red Calf would advance, the third would stay hidden.

'We are coming, Johnnie!' shouted Langalabelele. And they were up,

177

swallowing the slope, war chants creasing the air, splitting the smoke, so that each warrior understood how they must seem to the enemy, as though their numbers were multiplied many times over.

There was no resistance. Once again, as at Sobhuza's *umuzi*, an enemy preparing to leave the field had already set aside its ardour, and valour quenched could not be easily kindled anew. Thus, the warriors screamed through the flaming desolation of gut-ripped huts, the roasted carcass of the homestead, emerged on the far side to find the bulk of their foes riding hard for the river, a rearguard offering only a token threat. Bullets whistled this tune and that, high overhead, songbirds in an early spring. Shaba thought he could see them in flight, their leaden progress slowed, while his own movements seemed faster, his body greased by the rime of sweat-moistened flakes that still swirled about him. He barely heard the instruction to halt, almost failed to heed it. *We could kill them now*, he thought. *Kill them all. Then follow the river west to the next of their camps. The one after that. All the way back across the borders of our lands.*

'Wait, Giant Slayer!' It was Langalabelele, gripping his arm, touching the brass *ingxotha* by mistake, pulling back his fingers quickly from the thing that still bore the warmth of royal blood.

They were back near the ridge where they had formed earlier, and while the dung-jackets were still falling back, more horse soldiers had come up in their support. Three groups of the Long Spears. Behind them, a sizeable body of mounted red-coats. And something rigid about these, some grim stillness that spoke of the toughest metal.

'The Fat Queen has kept her best fruit until the season's end,' murmured Shaba, as the Long Spears came on.

Most of the Division's rifles – Shaba's included – were back in the trees and caves, but the horsemen were just within throwing range, still moving slowly as they kicked the beasts, muttered foreign words to them, the animals ill-equipped for climbing over boulders. Jingling and snorting. Shafts cut through the air but achieved very little.

'Time for the Red Calf to now become the Tricksters!' yelled the commander. 'Back, my sons! Back!'

They understood, began to sprint up the hill again, some of them cavorting in a ridiculous pretence at fearful flight. Back through the homestead, with the riders at last on less broken ground and therefore keeping pace to the rear. Yet, to Shaba's amazement, before him stood a warrior in the red soldiers' path. He had dressed in every item of his ceremonial manhood, a head-dress of black feather, a broad collar of leopard skin. His beard was peppered with grey and white, and Shaba did not even know his name, though he had seen him earlier, in consultation with the Division's commander and the *izinduna*. He was the headman of this place. Or he had been when it existed. And now he stood alone, his tall shield, also black, erect before him. Alone in the upper section of the central enclosure where he might once have placed his seat of authority, in the midst of the dwellings that still burned at his back.

'Come!' said Shaba. 'They are close.'

But he regretted the words before they were even spoken, and the headman ignored him entirely. He was already in some other place, his family's shades gathered close about him.

Shaba was punished immediately, stepped unseeing onto a tangle of smouldering timbers and, hardened as his feet might be, his flesh was seared. But he hobbled onwards, watching back over his shoulder as the headman, still entirely on his own, took the first of his throwing spears, three short steps, and loosed towards the horsemen. He struck no target. None that was tangible. But it shook the soldiers all the same. Two of their mounts shied, stepped sideways and collided. The scene froze briefly. *Should I stand with him?* Shaba wondered. He would have done so gladly, he realised. But there were times when a man must be left to his destiny. And he suddenly felt an affinity, a fellowship, with the bearded one who had stared into his face when the iFulentshi fell. Perhaps he, too, had simply allowed fate to run its course.

'*Ji!* Bring me your blades!' The headman's war cry was defiant. He beat his own spear twice against the back of his shield, stamped two paces forward. 'Bring me your blades! We have shown you how we can fight. Now I show you how we die!' Two paces more.

A soldier pressed his horse between two others. He was an iNkosi, Shaba assumed, from the sword that he carried and the authority that he exercised, though he seemed no more than a boy. He shouted something at his men.

'Bring me your blades!' the headman spat at them.

And they did. Three of them levelled their shafts, bamboo shafts with white strapping that looped around the soldiers' arms, so that they should not lose their weapons, and they spurred the horses to a trot. There was rifle fire in the background now, from the Division's shooters up in the trees. *I must move,* Shaba thought, *or I may be killed by my own people.* But he could not simply turn his back on the scene.

He saw the headman spread his arms wide.

'Bring them, invaders!' shouted the warrior one last time before the first of the blue-coat spears pierced him, pushed him back, the point protruding near his spine. The soldier tried to pull it free but the headman gripped the bamboo, tore at the red and white flag, refused to fall, staggered, seeming to drag his enemy back with him. A second horse came forward, a second spear tearing into the headman's flesh. But still he stood. As though he might, by his own will and nothing more, absorb every blade that the Fat Queen's army had to offer. Yet it could not be so, and the first soldier raised his boot, kicked against the warrior's chest, levered the spear free, forcing the headman to his knees. Shaba thought that, even then, he would stand again, until the young iNkosi of these soldiers came forward, sheathed his sword and took out a revolver. He fired twice and the headman spun backwards, fell and lay twitching, though still trying to rise.

Shaba ran then, at last, as two more shots rang out.

He was stuck fast, the thorns of the bush piercing his right arm and side, others snatching at the fur tails of his kilt. He had stumbled — the fault of his burned foot — when he had only just cleared the ruined homestead, fallen on his shield, then become entangled when he tried to free himself.

Behind him, the Long Spears had abandoned their beasts and formed a firing line, using whatever cover was available to them and those short rifles that the horsemen seemed to favour. The shortness of the gun, however, bore no relationship to either range nor accuracy. And worse, the demons were advancing.

Bullets whined around him, random, careless things from both directions that entirely dispelled any final benefit of the *ugwayi*. He was tempted to stay, to let fate alone decide whether he had a future here, between the shadow lands. But the ancestors of the place reminded him that he had much for which to live, that perhaps he should remain a while longer. So he dragged the shield towards him, caught the familiar warmth of its hide on his nostrils, the worn grip of its centre-stick in his fist, until it was beneath his chest. Then he pushed down hard upon it, one-handed, lifted his weight on that arm alone and rolled himself free, though the thorns ripped and cut painfully at his right wrist, pulled the *iklwa* from his fingers, caused serious damage to the fine kilt that Amahle had fashioned for him.

He was on his back, the grey mottled shield held close above him. More bullets were drilling the dirt, one so close that earth and grass showered his face. The stabbing spear seemed firmly tangled in the thorns still, so that he could not risk its rescue and, by craning his head to one side or the other, he could see the blue-coats slowly making ground towards him.

Shaba used his heels, found a purchase and slid himself less than a pace towards his own lines, grass scratching against his back, some small stones. Another push. And another. Ash was still falling. Bullets too. Yet something was missing.

He pushed once more, risked a glance beneath the shield. The thorn bush looked bigger from here. He felt a fool again for falling into the thing. It was now providing shelter on the far side for two soldiers, as well as the young iNkosi who had shot the headman. He was paying little attention just now, however, to the engagement. And Shaba could see the thing that held his gaze. A pair of civet tails were caught on long barbs of a branch. They fluttered a little in the slight breeze. Amahle would be angry with herself that she had not made them strong enough to withstand her brother's clumsiness. But she would have been as puzzled as the white iNkosi by the object tied to the tails themselves. It was a thing of blue wool, a knot in one end. She might not have recognised it before her marriage to the white trader. Yet Shaba was certain that KaMtigwe must also wear such strange garments inside his boots of leather. He was certain, too, that this iNkosi of the Long Spears knew what it was.

The woollen thing itself was unimportant, of course. But that which it concealed had become precious to him. The time-counter of the French Prince with its bee image. He had heard of such items being found on others of the Fat Queen's soldiers but he had never heard of one so finely wrought nor one with such potent magic. And he could see the way that the white iNkosi was being drawn to that power. The man stood, stretched his hand across the branches, cursed as a thorn pierced his wrist, and grabbed at the knotted blue wool while, all around him, his men loaded and fired in spirals of acrid smoke, ducked and ran, hither and thither, dodging the whining bullets of the Red Calf.

There was a bugle call, down and away, in the manner that the soldiers sent messages one to another in music, this one causing the Long Spears to cease their slow advance. The iNkosi waved his revolver, gestured towards the river, shouted in each direction, so that he and his men began to retire, though still slowly, still firing as they went, towards the homestead and their waiting horses. *It will be lost*, thought Shaba, stricken with grief. He had not surrendered the time-counter to the Great King as he knew he ought. But the King had asked only for the Prince's clothes and weapons. Nobody had mentioned other things. And Shaba had been drawn to possess this particular treasure, had seen himself carrying it home in triumph to Zama's *umuzi*, to impress her father, her grand-father, when he went to claim her. So he rolled over, crouched still, looked back to his own lines, to the trees and rock cliffs. There was no sign that the Division would pursue the soldiers, though they were still firing at them. The blue-coats were getting away – and the time-counter was going with them.

He was unsure about the thing that drove him, yet found himself on his feet, still with his shield but no other weapon and leaping down the hill, past the thorn bush, no more than a spear's throw behind them.

'Whey, Johnnie!' he cried. 'I am Shaba kaNdabuko.'

The young iNkosi saw him, fired at him and missed – exactly as the iFulentshi Prince had done. It was the time-counter, he was sure, that protected him. For the whites almost ignored him, looked this way and that, yelling at each other, seeking the rest of the horde which, they now seemed sure, must be at Shaba's heels. And there was yet more magic. For the iNkosi's helmet flew from his head and he spun backwards. A bullet from above had pierced the boy's eye, his left eye, the same eye that afflicted Shaba. Surely this must be the Sky Lord's retribution, some deeper meaning here. He stood among the soldiers' panic and their grief. For this iNkosi was plainly dear to them. But Shaba stood before them, beating the back of his shield with his fist.

'USuthu!' he chanted, again and again, almost tripping on the dead man's boots as the soldiers pulled the corpse away. He thought he heard one of them call the name of their Jesucristo, though the rest of their frantic shouting was unfathomable. A bullet holed his shield. Another carried away his head-band. A third passed cleanly through the rest of his civet tails. But he suffered no hurt except that of his singed sole, the scratches from the thorns, though he was still no nearer to retrieving the woollen sheath clutched in the iNkosi's lifeless fingers.

The Division was coming at last, however. He could hear them, the war cries behind him, the panic more evident among the blue-coats as they gained the ravaged homestead, much of it still flaming and crackling, smoke billowing, ash settling. A soldier came at him with a blade attached to his rifle, feinted at him. But Shaba moved in close, hit the fellow with his shield. Twice. Three times. Until the blue-coat dropped the weapon and ran for his horse as his companions were doing.

Shaba turned to see where the iNkosi was being taken. He was there, alongside the body of the fallen headman, both of them dead now. *Surely the work of the Lord-in-the-Sky*, Shaba thought. They were trying to lift him onto a horse. They would escape, he was certain. Yet the Sky Lord's benevolence was not complete for, as the Long Spears heaved their man's body from the ground, Shaba saw the blue foot sheath catch on the centre-stick of the headman's shield. It caught and it held.

They followed the column of horsemen on a similar course, but some distance to the north, keeping the river between them and always on the higher ground. The Long Spears had escaped safely enough when their reserve *ibutho*, those iron-hard horsemen in the red jackets, had come up to support them, allowed them to bear away the body of the fallen iNkosi. *But at least they carry him away without my time-counter*, Shaba thought as they came in sight of the enemy's main camp. He touched the woollen thing, now safely back among his civet tails. It warmed him, for the evening was chill, the sun beginning to settle upon the distant tips of the Great Barrier, but the light still sufficient to understand the size of the place, the row upon row of white tents, the lines of horses, the countless wagons, the many enclosures for the oxen, the ramparts of earth and stone that enclosed it all.

He saw the long column reach the wall, the way that men spilled forth, the silence that settled as the soldiers came home with one more fallen hero. He saw the reason that he had been wrong earlier, why wave after wave of his people would have broken themselves in futility against this fortress should they have attempted to take it, or any of those like it. He saw the conceit of the Fat Queen's generals explained, the reason that they felt able to make such outlandish demands upon the Great King of the AmaZulu.

And he saw one final thing. He saw a runner approach the encampment. Not a Basuto dog in the employ of the red soldiers. Nor one of the party sent by Cetshwayo to negotiate with the Fat Queen's iNkosi. But one of the People of Heaven, all the same. There was no obvious reason for him to be here. Yet there was no mistake. The lean build, the wisp of beard at his chin. It was the Skirmisher, Klaas. But why was he here?

Chapter Fourteen

Friday 13th June 1879

Carey was effectively under arrest, confined to his quarters pending the opening of the General Court Martial's second day. He had not slept, of course. His attempt at a further letter to Annie had ended in tearful frustration. What would he say to her now? The fancy Fairchild pen with the Number Four Mabie Tod nib remained mute on the matter. That which he had written immediately after his return from the disastrous patrol had been addressed with excuses, dated with indignation, bore a salutation that pleaded sympathy, was lined with inevitability, stained and blotched by tears of half-truth, incredulity, despair, and signed with a flourish of self-loathing. He regretted having sent the thing, as he regretted a great many others. How different might it all have been? He remained relatively certain that his captaincy must, by now, at last have been confirmed and that his step upon the rung towards further seniority would have been accelerated by the previous exemplary conduct so frequently mentioned in dispatches, his valour a matter of record; his wife and remaining children proud of him; an atonement for the loss of Jahleel junior. The Lord God finally satisfied. But now? The Almighty seemed to be waiting once more. This time for him to clear his name. *And only the Court Martial,* thought Carey, *can do that. It must remain the focus for my efforts.*

Through the muffled canvas of his tent flap, he heard the sentry speak. 'I'm sorry, sir, but the Lieutenant is permitted no unauthorised visitors.'

'Och, I have authorisation,' said another, indistinct, the accent strange, though with a clear hint of the Scot. 'From Mister Drummond himself.'

Carey was expecting a visit from his defence advocate, Crookenden, the artillery captain, even if the fellow had been little use yesterday; left him largely to conduct his own case. But this was not Crookenden.

'Very good, sir,' the sentry was saying. 'All seems to be in order.' There was a slight movement of the flap. 'Beggin' pardon, Lieutenant,' said the guard. 'Visitor for you, sir.'

'Send him in, Corporal,' Carey replied. 'And see if somebody might rustle up a brew, would you?'

The flap was pulled all the way back. The sky was still dark, though dusted with the first scarlet streaks of South Africa's dawn, quickly blotted out again by the bulk that filled the entrance. Carey turned up the lamp wick so that he might study this early bird better then took a step backwards with the shock of recognition.

'Sweet Lord of Mercy...' It was a genuine prayer, not a blasphemy.

'Surprised, old boy?' said McTeague. 'Just thought I'd drop by and offer a few wee words of comfort. Not the most auspicious of days, eh?'

Twelve years had passed, but Carey would have recognised him anywhere: those amiable rust-red cheeks; the dancing eyes; the comfortable paunch. They all spoke of cherubic *bonhomie*. The heavily oiled hair and moustache, on the other hand; the monocle; the most immaculate of clothes, regardless of location, yet always doused in the cheapest of colognes, these things all chimed a different tune. He should have known, of course: all the fuss about Cetshwayo's latest peace envoys, the white trader as the King's chief spokesman.

'I heard your name mentioned,' said Carey. 'Never imagined... but no, Major, not auspicious. Yesterday did not go well.'

Despite himself, he found that old deferences to rank died hard.

'The Court Martial?' said McTeague. 'Oh, I'm sure it will be all fine. No, I simply meant that it is Friday. The thirteenth. Inauspicious for us all. You seem to be bearing up though. A little peaky perhaps.'

Carey had trimmed the full beard away, cut it back to the sideburns and moustache again. But whenever he looked in the glass he realised that the attempt at military smartness had done him no favours. For while the sun had tanned the area around his nose and cheekbones, the permanent use of a helmet had kept his forehead white, and the beard had done the same for the sides of his face. The overall effect was a false pallor and the semblance of sunken eyes.

'I don't wish to seem rude, Major, but why are you here? I've a busy day ahead of me.'

'Oh, to be sure, Lieutenant,' said McTeague. 'And strange the way that years slip past, history repeats itself. When I heard it was you, Carey, I thought: such irony, this could be Kingston all over again. Don't you think?'

Is that it? Carey wondered. *Will he offer himself to them as a witness?*

In truth, Carey had no idea how much of the Honduras affair was detailed in his service record. He imagined that it was little or nothing, based both upon the general deficiencies in the administrative systems of the West India Regiments and also the dearth of references to the incident during any subsequent posting.

'Is this an opportunity for me to purchase your silence, sir?' he said.

'My dear chap, how can you imagine such a thing?'

'Perhaps your reputation precedes you. Trading guns to the Zulus. Inflated freight charges to the army. Illicit liquor to the men. Kaffir wives almost as numerous as those of that rogue, Dunn. What else am I, except the source of further profit?'

'Why, Lieutenant, you offend me! I sold weapons to old Cetshwayo only when he was on friendly terms with Her Majesty – may the Lord grant her a long and happy life – and mainly at the insistence of her Government. My freight charges are no higher than the commercial rate and, to tell the truth, I have recently offered Lord Chelmsford a substantial reduction. The only freightmaster in the Colony who has done so. No, sir, it is the livestock traders that have so shamelessly cheated our Commissariat. Have you any idea, Carey, how many oxen and carts His Lordship was forced to purchase here? After the campaign began?' Carey was forced to admit that he did not. 'Then I shall tell you, Lieutenant. More than two thousand oxen and three hundred carts. Inflated prices. An outrage, sir, both that the Commissariat should have been so ill-prepared and also that anybody should have taken such unscrupulous advantage of the situation.'

'You would not have done so, Major, naturally.'

'As the Almighty is my shield and my witness, Lieutenant, I would not. And so far as the sale of liquor goes, I deplore the very existence of strong spirit. The fellow who was guilty of that crime was a renegade who deserved every lash that he received and more. No longer in my employ neither, devil take him. For the women? Well, sir, I take as my source Kings One, 11:3. *And he had seven hundred wives, princesses, and three hundred concubines: and his wives turned away his heart.* Ah, the wisdom of Solomon. King David too, of course. Yet I would beg you to speak of those ladies with more respect, Lieutenant. They are my wives, after all, in every sense of the word. Baptised Christians each and every one. My conscience clear in the eyes of God.'

Carey was shocked to feel himself shamed, then recalled his previous dealings with Major William McTeague, the man's plausibility.

'Then if not profit, Major, what else? Revenge?'

'For that little *contretemps*, twelve years ago? You may have acted the Nose as my good friend, Doctor Simeon Cornscope, might put it, but I'm certain you only told the Court of Inquiry that which you believed to be correct. Trade must flow, eh? We must all do what we need to keep going. Of course, if I *was* to be called as a witness...'

'You appreciate that it is, in part, your fault that I face this predicament, I suppose?' said Carey.

'Mine? Gracious, no. I have been blamed inappropriately for many things in my time but I cannot say that I had any hand either in the Prince's sad demise, nor in your own rather questionable actions, sir, though the thing hardly merits a General Court Martial, naturally.'

'Then you must be the only one in the entire camp who thinks so. Nobody could have regretted the loss of poor Louis more than I.' Carey paused, unsure whether that was actually true. 'But when we escaped and met up with Colonel Buller, he told me I deserved to be shot. Colonel Harrison said as much too.

186

When I led the search party to recover the Prince's body the next day nobody spoke to me. All the way there, at that pitiful place itself, and all the way back. Not a word, Major. Nor at the service they held for him. Nor when they set off for Durban to take the coffin home. Back to England, that is.'

'And Chelmsford?'

'His Lordship was the only one who offered any crumb of comfort. Blamed the Prince. His lack of discipline. Refusal to follow my orders. Or, at least, in the beginning that was Chelmsford's stance.'

'Politics, dear chap. You know what Dickens said. *Sudden shifts and changes are no bad preparation for political life.* And since then, I suppose, all the other fellows have followed like sheep?'

'To a man. That damn'd scoundrel Robinson too, from the *Telegraph.*'

'Ah, the gentlemen of the press. Unlikely to be kind. But my fault, you say?'

'I remembered Honduras, Major. The way you responded to the tittle-tattle after Mister Rhys was lost.'

'You demanded a Court of Inquiry too?' said McTeague. 'Thought they would exonerate you? Put an end to the gossip?'

'As they had done with yourself at Kingston.'

'And you, Lieutenant. You were blamed also, as I recall. Young Ferguson, as well. But different strokes, eh?'

'How, different?'

McTeague examined the nails on his overfed fingers.

'I knew one or two things about the inquiry's president,' he said. 'You should never pick a fight unless you know the outcome beforehand, Carey. Did they not teach you so at Staff College? No, I suppose not. And plainly it did not go well for you. Who was the convening officer?'

'General Marshall.'

'That explains a great deal,' said McTeague. 'I saw him with the burial detail at Isandlwana. Not even enough balls to stay and finish the job. And a pity for you that the inquiry took place before the mess he made at the Ntinini. The 17th blame him entirely for the death of young Frith.'

Carey had witnessed the skirmish at the eZungeni hill, been present when they had brought Frith's body back from the skirmish just four days before, shot through the head by a Zulu marksman after Buller had burned some kraals and Marshall had sent in the Lancers to support him. Lancers! Uphill over broken ground.

'It's rather academic, don't you think?' said Carey. 'Chelmsford has stripped him of responsibility for the Cavalry Brigade anyway, so he certainly would not have given him responsibility for a Court of Inquiry. No, the real pity is that everybody decided to turn a blind eye to the *fracas* on the following night.'

'Can't blame the sentries, Carey.'

'Then what about the officer on watch? Chard of all people! Hero of

Rorke's Drift. Will get the Victoria Cross, so they say. And allowed the guards to run amok, spooked by a few noises in the dark. Thousands of rounds wasted. Seven men wounded by our own fire. Five horses dead. And not a word of opprobrium.'

'He's so much shorter than I expected. Chard, I mean. But welcome to Fort Funk, Lieutenant. You know the difference, of course?' Carey was not sure that he did. 'Plain as the nose on your face,' McTeague continued. 'Mister Chard's losses included not one single heir to the French Imperial throne.' And an orderly arrived, brought them tea.

Crookenden insisted on going over yesterday's old ground yet again. He was younger than Carey. Of course he was younger. Were they not all younger than he? This rash of captains come to join the fray. Even Frith. Just a lad really. Yet not only a captain in the 17th but also their Adjutant. And popular. You could tell that from the almost universal mourning that his death had inspired. He had been a mascot for the Lancers. Crookenden seemed not much older, arrived in May with the Royal Artillery reinforcements and now chosen for this strange responsibility. His defence advocate.

'He says that he will attend as a witness, Carey. A character witness. It's clear from the manual that we're entitled to call him.'

'It would be a mistake,' said Carey.

'But you served with him. You were under fire together, he says. In Honduras. It could be important.'

'We were serving with the West India Regiments. In some eyes that, in itself, is sufficient to condemn a man, sir. Apart from that, I was with the 3rd, Major McTeague with the 4th. We were barely acquainted. Even a superficial cross-examination would confirm that. I fear it would smack of desperation.'

And anyway, he thought, *I cannot guarantee that he would not betray me. Why should he not?*

'Forgive me for saying so, Carey, but you have nothing to hide, I suppose?'

'If you should prefer it, sir, I am happy to conduct my own defence. The Court Martial would simply put it down to another piece of recklessness on my part, I'm sure. No reflection on yourself.'

'I have a duty to carry out, Lieutenant, and shall do so to the best of my ability. If you choose to represent yourself, well, that is entirely your affair. But I should caution against it. It is generally frowned upon, I am told, and may lead the Court to certain conclusions. No, Carey, I was simply advised to check against the possibility of any nasty surprises – whether, perhaps in your younger days, there might have been any impropriety…'

'Of a moral nature, you mean? Because I served in Jamaica, perhaps?'

'No, I suppose not. And they tell me that you are a good Christian fellow. Devout, they say.'

'Oh, the son of the Vicar of Brixham, no less. That should be character reference enough for the Court, don't you think? Anything else, sir, is between myself and the Almighty.'

'Yet McTeague made a remarkable claim.'

'This nonsense about being married to the sister of the Zulu who killed Louis, who picked up his sword. You don't believe him, surely? And wouldn't that rather spoil the effect? That he is a self-professed renegade, living under Cetshwayo's protection, married to a string of native concubines?'

'He says that he spoke to the fellow in question. On the way here. That Cetshwayo provided this peace delegation with an escort, including his... well, his brother-in-law, I suppose you would say. If what he says is true, it could shed considerable light on the situation you faced. He claims the Zulus almost had your party surrounded. A few more moments and you would all have been dead. Massively outnumbered. What does the Court of Inquiry indictment say again?' He rustled through the sheaf of papers on the writing table. 'Here, "...a lamentable want of military prudence." But that is a criticism which should, at least, be shared by your superior officers, Carey. The entire command assumed that this was territory largely free of the enemy.'

'I face a court, sir, composed of senior officers. An assortment of colonels, lieutenant-colonels and majors. Might they not see the criticism aimed at themselves? They are hardly likely to be sympathetic to such an attack, I dare say.'

'Attack is, usually, the best form of defence, is it not?'

'I'm not certain whether that applies in the case of military jurisprudence, sir.'

'Then we should try to focus on the positives. Turn their attention from those that were lost to the men that you saved. Four of them, Carey. And, as we now know from Major McTeague, against impossible odds. Plus the intelligence that you brought back to the Column. Invaluable evidence. That, contrary to common belief, the terrain to our front was *not* clear of Zulus but infested by the devils. Imagine the disaster we might have faced if Colonel Buller's troopers had set off on their expedition to establish the further camp, destroy the local kraals, without the support of Marshall's Brigade. Support only provided as a result of your own experience.'

'The Court of Inquiry's conclusion does not really concern itself with the *what ifs*, sir. Simply that I made no effort to rally the escort, nor to show a front to the enemy. The impossibility of the odds would simply reinforce the fact that they expected the entire patrol to sacrifice itself on the Prince's behalf.'

'Then we should at least recall some of yesterday's witnesses. There were so many discrepancies. The corporal, Grubb. They made great play of his evidence that you gave no order to rally. Yet he admits that you were all spurring away from the kraal. Nobody in his right mind would attempt to rally until you were clear of immediate danger. And, by then, it was obvious that the Prince was down and lost. You couldn't have known any earlier. The Channel Islander, Le Tocq, said as much.'

'I fear, sir,' said Carey, 'that this is all icing for the cake when, sadly, we do not have a cake on which to spread it. My own statement must be the rock on which we rest our case, Captain. I am certain that the Court Martial will hear my account with sympathy. To be fair, I did not give them the best of myself at the inquiry. I see little point in recalling any of the others. And the day ended on a positive note, don't you think? They clearly took a shine to Trooper Cochrane. An old campaigner, experienced soldier. His opinion that no rally could have been made is a good place from which to start today. If that damn'd Prosecution Attorney will give us the opportunity.'

'Very well, Lieutenant,' said Crookenden. 'We'll play the thing your way. Yet is there anything else?'

'Yes, sir,' replied Carey. 'You might pray with me, if you would.'

It was Brander. Prosecution Advocate Brander. Captain Brander who was five years his junior. Five resented years. Brander with his condescending approval of Carey's actions during the evacuation of the *Clyde*; Brander who had not even been able to keep his boats together; Brander who had sneered at his service in the West India Regiment; Brander whose grudging respect following Alderton's death still rankled; Brander who, despite his late arrival at the Cape, had secured a Special Services prime position as an *Aasvogel* while Carey was still confined to *Boomvogel* tasks, sketching, escorts. Escorts! Brander the captain while he, Carey, no longer had any rank at all, his position suspended pending the outcome of this trial. And now Brander the Prosecution Advocate. Was it chance? A random selection? Or had the swine volunteered for it?

He was seated at a table away to Carey's left, a table that he shared with an orderly responsible for keeping an accurate record of the proceedings, a member of Lord Chelmsford's secretariat. On the far side of the tent was a longer table, Colonel Glyn presiding in the middle, dwarfed by the other members of the Court Martial on each side of him, Colonels Harness, Courtney and Whitehead on one flank, the Majors Anstruther and Pleydell-Bouverie on the other. The tent flap was to the right and, between Carey and his judges, a single chair, set at something of an angle and currently occupied by Sergeant Willis. *The rather ineffective Sergeant Willis, as I recall*, thought Carey, though the Sergeant was giving a good enough account of himself now. A good account – and an imaginative one.

'You say that the Prince may have been dragged by his horse to the place in the donga where he was found, Sergeant?' said Brander.

'Yes, sir.'

'And how far was that?'

'From the kraal, sir? Maybe seventy-five yards, sir.'

He's talking nonsense, thought Carey. *That runs against all yesterday's evidence that the Prince was on foot in the donga. Long after he fell from the horse.* He turned to Crookenden, expected him to intervene, but the Defence Advocate was absorbed in his paperwork.

'And do you think that a rally might have been made, Sergeant? To save the Prince?'

'Yes, sir, I do.'

'Where, Sergeant? How far from the kraal?'

'Sixty yards, sir. Perhaps seventy.'

The Court Martial judges turned their heads in unison, as though they were joined by some invisible string.

'Perhaps you'd like to reconsider, Sergeant,' said Brander. 'You said that the Prince was dragged about seventy-five yards. A rally to save him would have needed to be made *beyond* that point. Near the other end of the donga. Perhaps ten or twenty yards from that end, surely?'

'Objection!' cried Crookenden. 'Captain Brander is leading the witness.'

'Quite so,' said Colonel Glyn. 'Strike those comments from the records, will you?'

The orderly scribbled enthusiastically across his most recent notes.

'I will rephrase the question, sir,' said Brander. 'Now, tell me, Sergeant Willis, how far from the end of the donga – the end furthest from the kraal – might a rally have been made?'

'Oh, from *that* end, sir? Well, I should say twenty yards.'

There was a short adjournment after Brander declared the case for the Prosecution now closed.

It was quite deliberate, Carey decided, *to call Surgeon-Major Scott as his last witness.* A harrowing image to leave in the minds of the judges. His description of the body, the manner in which it had been discovered. The Prince stripped, lying naked on his back. On examination, five separate assegai wounds that could have caused his death but a further twelve, some of them causing lesser injuries – two to his left forearm, for example, indicating a prolonged struggle in self-defence – the rest probably delivered *post mortem*. Not a single bullet wound, and every injury received to the front of his body. In relation to items recovered from the scene, only a gold chain about his neck, with attached medals, a single blue sock embroidered in gold with the insignia 'N', and a pair of spurs. Nothing more. A most ignoble and lonely end. And when asked by the Court whether the body had been eviscerated, the Surgeon-Major had been reluctant to respond but finally confirmed that, yes, it had been so.

The Major of the 17th Lancers, Pleydell-Bouverie, resplendent in his full-dress uniform, the white plastron of his blue jacket dazzling against the discoloured mildew of the tent wall behind him, had caught Carey's eye, a look of such disgust, such open accusation of betrayal, that Carey had recoiled from it. Yet he still believed that his own statement would be pivotal and now, as the case for the Defence was opened, Crookenden announced that, apart from Mister Carey, only two witnesses would be called. *All part of the theatre, of course,* thought Carey. *The Court already knows our case exactly.* He was not entirely naive, naturally, understood that witnesses must be made available at the appropriate time. But, all the same, he suspected that it would be normal protocol for the Defence Advocate to share the shape of things to come, at least with the Court Martial President. *But not even Crookenden knows the substance of my statement.*

'With the Court's permission,' said Crookenden, 'I should like to call Lieutenant-Colonel Harrison once more.'

And there he was, as though by magic, straight as a spruce.

'Colonel,' said Crookenden, 'perhaps I might begin by summarising the main points that you made earlier?'

Crookenden studied his notes, while Harrison studied the face of Colonel Glyn. But if he was seeking confirmation that he should accede to the Defence Advocate's suggestion, he was disappointed.

'If you says so, Captain,' he replied. 'Though my comments are already a matter of record, I think.'

'Of course, sir. But perhaps for my own benefit.' He referred to his notes again. 'Let me see. You said that Lieutenant Carey was the senior combatant officer on the patrol and this placed him in the position of seniority?'

'Indeed.'

'That the Lieutenant had volunteered to join the patrol so that he might verify some of the sketches that he had already made of this particular terrain?'

'Yes.'

'That the Prince Imperial had been ordered to go so that he could report more fully on the ground?'

'Did I say ordered? I do not recall saying that he was ordered to go, Captain. But his role was to report in more detail, certainly.'

'You were fully aware that the Prince Imperial was part of the patrol, sir?'

'Yes. I said so!'

'And he had formal duties to perform?'

'Yes.'

Crookenden shuffled his papers.

'Let me see,' he began. 'Ah, yes. Here, sir. The Court asked you to confirm that the Prince was officially attached to your Department. And you replied in the affirmative, sir?'

'Of course.'

'And then you said, I think, that it had been suggested the Prince might not be treated as a royal personage. In the matter of escorts, for example. But, rather, as any other officer. Taking due precaution against any possible danger.'

'Exactly the point, Captain,' replied Harrison. 'I already covered this ground. In my view, Lieutenant Carey was guilty of failing to take due precaution at the kraal. And then, to make matters worse, of failing to rally his men and attempt a rescue. Leaving that poor fellow behind. No officer should ever be left behind, Captain, don't you agree?'

'It is the word *officer* that seems to be causing some confusion in my mind, Colonel.'

Harrison turned to Colonel Glyn.

'Dammit, sir!' he said. 'Is this some lawyer's trick? We all know what I intended, I think.'

'Not at all, sir. I was merely trying to establish that the Prince Imperial – perhaps because he *was* the Prince Imperial – was treated as though he were an officer.'

'The Prince Imperial,' Colonel Glyn interrupted, 'held no military rank whatsoever, Captain Crookenden. None.'

'Yet many times yesterday, sir,' said Crookenden, 'and today also, we have all fallen easily into the use of the word *officer* to describe him.'

'Semantics,' said Glyn. 'Simple semantics.'

'I hope not, sir. Perhaps if I could put the question direct to Colonel Harrison?'

'If you insist, Captain.'

Crookenden turned to Harrison once more.

'In your opinion, Colonel,' he said, 'do you consider that most of your Department treated the Prince Imperial as an officer, or as one of the other ranks – or perhaps as neither of those things?'

'As an officer and a gentleman, of course!' Harrison snorted. 'How could the Prince Imperial of France not have been treated with the deference that he deserved?'

'Thank you, Colonel. And on the fatal day itself, I understand that you accompanied the patrol yourself, for some distance.'

'About seven miles. From Kopje Allein to Thelezeni.'

'You spoke to the Prince, sir?'

'Well naturally I spoke with him.'

'Do you remember the subject, sir?'

'Is this really relevant? We talked about sport, I think. His family. And about books. His love of Trollope, I recall.'

'Did you speak much with Lieutenant Carey?'

'I don't believe so. He was chatting mostly with the troopers.'

'Might I ask for your assessment of Lieutenant Carey's general ability, Colonel? Before this incident?'

Lieutenant-Colonel Harrison coughed, considered a moment.

'I had every confidence in Lieutenant Carey.'

'You considered him your deputy, in fact?'

'I did.'

'Yet on the ride to Thelezeni you spoke only to the Prince Imperial.'

'Is that a question, Captain?'

'If you wish, sir. I suppose my question should have been this. That since Carey was your deputy, and yet you chose to keep company only with the Prince, might that not have implied a certain seniority on the Prince's part to the rest of the patrol?'

'That question is impertinent, Captain,' said Glyn. 'It will be struck from the record. Now, sir, do you have a more relevant point?'

'Yes, sir,' said Crookenden. 'Just one. You say, Colonel Harrison, that Carey volunteered for the patrol?'

'Yes.'

'And had he not done so, who would you *then* have considered to be in command? Or, rather, who would you have considered responsible for the Prince Imperial's death?'

'This witness is dismissed!' said Colonel Glyn.

This is a mistake, thought Carey. *A serious mistake.* Colonel William Bellairs was Lord Chelmsford's Deputy Adjutant-General. And Carey had avoided him like the plague since he arrived in Utrecht. He was a man of considerable reputation, born in Honfleur and thus also something of a Francophile. He had repeatedly arranged various *soirées* to help entertain Louis, and Carey had frequently been on the guest list. Yet Carey had excused himself from every one. For he shared something with Colonel Bellairs.

'I am correct in assuming, Colonel,' Crookenden was saying, 'that you have been responsible for the arrangement of today's proceedings?'

'Yes, Captain. That is the case. His Lordship asked me to attend to the details.'

'And has His Lordship already reached a judgement on this case?'

'I rather thought that it was the task of this Court Martial to pass judgement.'

'Indeed, Colonel. Then could you explain why Lieutenant Carey was relieved of his staff appointment before the Court Martial even took place?'

'Normal procedure, Captain, wouldn't you say? Have you not read the Regulations? Carey stands accused of misbehaviour before the enemy.'

'On Sunday, the first of June?'

'Yes, Captain, although the charges were not confirmed until after the Court of Inquiry – convened at Carey's own insistence, you'll recall.'

'The charges confirmed then, sir, on what date? The fifth?'

'Yes, Captain. The day after the inquiry, I believe.'

'Yet Lieutenant Carey was not deposed from his duties until the day before yesterday. The eleventh. I wish to put it to you, Colonel, that in the intervening period the Commander-in-Chief had already pre-judged this case.'

Colonel Glyn slapped the table.

'This is outrageous, Captain,' he said. 'A slur on the integrity of this Court Martial. You will retract that statement, sir.'

Crookenden wavered. If he was honest with himself, Carey had never expected him to go so far. To have so much bottom.

'If I might be allowed a word, Colonel,' he said, and stood to attention.

'This is irregular, Lieutenant,' said Glyn. 'I trust that you do not intend to make the situation any worse.'

'No, sir, I do not. I fear that Captain Crookenden is pursuing a chance remark that I made, believing that my removal from duty was a punishment inflicted in advance of the Court Martial's decision. Heat of the moment, sir. I intended no slur upon the Court itself. Regret the remark. And I am certain that Captain Crookenden intended no such slur either.'

Carey sat again.

'Do you retract, Captain Crookenden?' said Glyn.

'I do, sir,' replied the Defence Advocate.

'Then the witness is excused,' said Colonel Glyn.

Bellairs rose from his seat, straightened his tunic, walked past Carey's table. Then he stopped.

'It is a pity, Lieutenant,' he said, 'that we were unable to be better acquainted earlier. I'm sure we would have had much to discuss. A great deal in common, they tell me. I understand that we both served in the 3rd West India. Not at the same time, of course. But I should have enjoyed reminiscing about Kingston. And Honduras, perhaps.'

'If there are no more witnesses, Captain,' said the diminutive Colonel Glyn following a short respite, 'I assume that we will now hear from Mister Carey? Will you examine him, sir?'

'He has a prepared statement, sir,' replied Crookenden.

'Very well. Lieutenant Carey — as soon as you're ready, if you please.' He opened his pocket watch, showed it to Harness, Lieutenant-Colonel of the Royal Artillery. They both grimaced.

Carey carried his written statement to the chair, uncertain whether he would even be able to read. Was the Honduras affair so plainly upon his record? Or did the previous service of Bellairs with his former regiment give the Colonel some separate arcane knowledge of the thing? Bellairs had left the 3rd West India ten years before Carey had even joined it, went to fight in the Crimea. But had he maintained his contacts? Would the newspaper reports have caught his eye? Or was it simply coincidence and a genuine desire for reminiscence that caused the remark? Worst of all, there was an annoying tune running through Carey's mind. The tune to a ditty about the Colonel, a play upon his surname. Yet the words would not come to him, and this piece of trivia was driving away his need to focus.

'On the thirty-first day of May...' he stammered, 'Colonel Harrison informed me that the Prince Imperial would be riding on the following day over the same ground I had already mapped and recommended for the advance of the column. The Prince's task would be to select a camping ground for the second of June.' Carey paused. He had expected to create drama but his account sounded flat, heavy; the delivery mechanical, dull. He continued, 'I therefore at once suggested that I might accompany the Prince, so that I might verify certain points of my previous surveillance.' He stressed the word *accompany* as best he could, then paused, expecting that somebody might ask him why such verification was necessary, why they had descended to the kraal at all.

I will explain, he decided, *that there would have been no need for us to venture so far in the first place if His Lordship had accepted my original survey.*

But there was no such question. So he simply proceeded, explaining that Colonel Harrison had consented, reminded him that the Prince was undertaking this work at his own request. Carey paused again. He realised that the statement was unclear. Did the phrase "at his own request" imply at Colonel Harrison's own request or at the Prince Imperial's.

'Yes, Lieutenant?' said Colonel Glyn.

Perhaps it does not matter, thought Carey. *Or I can return to the point later.*

'At his own request,' Carey repeated, found his place again. 'And that I was not to interfere with him in any way.'

He stressed this phrase also, looked up to see its effect. Nothing.

Carey carried on reading out his statement, giving details of the promised escort, the failure of the Basutos to turn up; the Prince Imperial's insistence that they should proceed at once, without the full escort. Their arrival at the ridge. Carey's further suggestion that they should wait for the Basutos. The Prince's insistence that the patrol was quite strong enough without them – or words to that effect. Their halt on the highest point of the ridge. The sketches.

'From here,' he read, 'the country was visible for miles, and no sign of the enemy could be discovered.'

He described the descent into the valley, then realised that he had not explained his own tentative suggestion that they might do so, nor the Prince's ready acquiescence to the thing. Carey found himself glancing ahead. *Let me see*, he thought. *Entering the kraal. Off-saddled. Knee-haltering. The kraal surrounded by mealies. No danger in encamping. Ah, here it is!* Too late. His tongue had overtaken his brain.

'If any blame is attributable to anyone for this,' he heard himself reading, 'it is to me...'

His judges all looked up at the same time, the cord that joined their heads moving them together once more. They were nodding.

'…As I agreed with the Prince,' he hastened to add, as loudly as he could, 'that we were perfectly safe.'

But the heads had all fallen again.

Carey pressed on. He had been over the area twice before. Seen nobody. And after one of those excursions, the Brigade-Major of the Cavalry Brigade had laughed at Carey for taking such large escorts with him. The Brigade-Major himself had covered the ground with only two or three men. It was supposed to be a decisive point, but it seemed to go unnoticed.

'We had with us a friendly Zulu,' he read. But he thought, *Though I never discovered his name.* 'A friendly Zulu,' he repeated, 'who, in answer to my inquiries, said no enemies were about. I trusted him.' *Did I? I'm not sure that I paid him any mind, one way or the other.* 'But I still kept a sharp look-out, telescope in hand.'

The image was intended as heroic, graphic. He looked towards Brander's table. The orderly was writing furiously but the Prosecution Advocate himself only yawned, scratched the back of his hand, not even taking notes.

'In about an hour,' Carey went on, regardless, 'that is, at 3.40 p.m., the Prince ordered us to saddle up…'

He had forgotten to say that he himself had wanted them to move on twenty minutes earlier, but Louis had been asleep. *And I was not to interfere with him in any way. Is that not what they'd told me?* Yet the rest of the account was coming out wrong too. *How can words that seem so accurate when viewed upon the paper sound so false when read aloud?* There was this section about the guide seeing a Zulu in the distance. The Prince's horse saddled first, the other men not quite ready; Louis waiting for them to finish saddling then the order given – the Prince Imperial's order, mind, not Carey's. *Did they catch the importance of that?* he wondered. Then Louis with his foot in the stirrup, his discomfort… *should I have mentioned the Dhobi itch?* The other men vaulting into their saddles and then the volley from the mealies; twenty black faces, only thirty yards off. The war cries. '*USuthu!*'

'There was a stampede,' he said, more by memory now than rigid reading. 'Two men rushed past me, and as everyone appeared to be mounted, I dug the spurs into my horse, though he had already started of his own accord. I felt sure no one was wounded by the volley, since I heard no cry, and I shouted out, "Keep to the left. Cross the donga. Rally behind it!" I shouted as loudly as I was able.'

He looked at the notes, to check that he had recited this section accurately. It was near enough. And at least he had remembered to use the word *rally*. That was important. Back to the reading, though it sounded even more stilted now.

'At the same time I saw more Zulus in the mealies on our left flank. They were cutting off our line of retreat. I crossed the donga behind two or three men, but could only get beyond one man, the others having ridden off. Riding a few hundred yards on to the rise, I stopped and looked round. I could see the Zulus after us, and saw that the men were escaping to the right, and that no one appeared on the other side of the donga. The man beside me then drew my attention to the Prince's horse, which was galloping away on the other side of the donga. He was saying, "I fear the Prince is killed, sir!" And I immediately said, "Do you think it is any use going back?" The trooper pointed to the mealies on our left, which appeared full of Zulus, and said, "He is dead long ago, sir. They assegai wounded men at once." I knew from experience that he was correct.'

Of course I knew. I could see it all. Why have I not said so? To leave a question mark over whether Louis may still have been alive is absurd. *And why does this all seem so weak?* But in his mind he saw a familiar vision. The face of a man being chased through a forest. By a jaguar. But to whom did the face belong? To Louis? To Commissioner Rhys? *I must clear my good name*, he thought, then realised that the Court was waiting for him once more. It was growing warmer in here. He could feel sweat in his armpits, hear the hooves of horsemen passing outside, smell the latrines, the grease from the cooking pots.

'It was useless to sacrifice more lives,' he went on. 'I had but one man near me, the others being some two hundred yards down the valley. I accordingly shouted to them to close to the left, saying to the man at my side, "We will keep back towards General Wood's camp, not returning the same way we came, and then come back with some dragoons to get the bodies." We reached camp about 6.30 p.m. I did not see the Prince after I saw him mounting, but he was mounted on a swift horse, and I thought he was close to me.'

Why have I said so? he wondered. But he was near the end now and just wanted this to be over.

'Besides the Prince,' he concluded, 'we lost two troopers, as well as the friendly Zulu. Two troopers have been found between the donga and the kraal, covered with assegai wounds. They must have fallen in the retreat and been assegaied at once, as I saw no fighting when I looked round.'

Carey tidied the papers, caught the bitter scent of ink still fresh upon them.

'Finished, Lieutenant?' said Glyn.

'I have, sir.'

'Cross-examination, Captain Brander?'

'If I may, Colonel,' said Brander. 'Lieutenant Carey has explained that he crossed the donga and then rode... let me see, yes, "a few hundred yards" before he stopped. Is that correct, Lieutenant?'

'Yes, sir.'

'A few hundred yards – far up the hillside, in fact?'

'Yes, sir.'

Carey was trembling inside.

'Could you explain, Lieutenant,' said Brander, 'why you did not halt *nearer*? Before your men became so scattered?'

'I acted on the spot,' Carey mumbled. 'For the best. And, as I thought, for the safety of the party. But they were not exactly *my* men, sir.'

'You still claim that you were not *de facto* in command of the escort?'

'I do, sir.'

'Yet the purpose of the escort was to protect the Prince Imperial, was it not?'

'Yes.'

'And you were part of that escort?'

Brander seemed to be floundering, unsure of the direction he should take. But Colonel Pleydell-Bouverie came to his rescue, raising his hand.

'Might I ask a question?' he said, and Glyn gave his presidential consent. 'Then I should say that I was most impressed by the evidence of Trooper Le Tocq. You recall his words, Lieutenant, I hope? He told this court that the Prince "should have expected help." He said that he would have expected help himself if he had been in similar straits. So tell me, Lieutenant, would you also have expected such help? In the Prince's shoes?'

'Perhaps, sir,' Carey replied. Conflicting emotions stormed within him. 'Yet I think I should have recognised the impossibility of my position also, would not have expected needless sacrifice when I could not have been saved. Trooper Cochrane and Corporal Grubb were both convinced that no useful help could have been rendered to him.'

'Sergeant Willis had a different view, however, did he not, Lieutenant?' said Pleydell-Bouverie. 'He thought that a rally could easily have been organised and that everybody could then have made good their escape.'

'Colonel,' said Carey, 'I hardly know how to answer you. Except to say that I deeply regretted the loss of the young Prince. I regret it still and I shall continue regretting it every moment for however long the Almighty may spare me. If it had been in my power I would have changed places with him – died so that he might live. But I do not believe that any effort of mine could have saved him.'

There, thought Carey, *it is all said and done. I am in God's hands now.*

He returned to the defence table while Colonel Glyn was inviting Crookenden to make his closing remarks. He had none.

'Then Captain Brander?' said Glyn.

'Thank you, sir. Simply a short *résumé*, if I may? Lieutenant Carey is charged with misbehaviour before the enemy in so much as, on Sunday the first of June, when in command of an escort in attendance on the French Prince Imperial, who was himself conducting a reconnaissance, and coming under attack, the Lieutenant galloped away without making any attempt to rally said escort, nor to otherwise defend said Prince in any manner. No word of any witness goes to show that the slightest attempt was made to rally, or to defend the Prince, whereas all agreed that they galloped away. As Lieutenant-Colonel Harrison has said, Lieutenant Carey was the senior combatant officer on the patrol. In fact, he was the only combatant officer on the patrol. The responsibility could not have lain with anybody else.'

Carey expected an adjournment while the Court considered its findings, but their heads were all down, whispering between themselves. He looked at Crookenden. The Captain shrugged.

'Very well,' said Colonel Glyn at last. 'We are unanimously agreed. The Court will adjourn for today and then reconvene to take notice of the prisoner's army service. You will not be required for that session, gentlemen. You are dismissed.'

Carey was shocked. Crookenden muttered something about irregularity.

And who will they go to for my service records? he wondered, though it was a rhetorical question. He knew exactly. They would go to Bellairs. But that was almost a minor consideration now. For he knew, as Crookenden knew, that the Court's decision not to trouble itself with further deliberation could mean only one thing.

They believed Carey to be guilty as charged.

Chapter Fifteen

Wednesday 25th June 1879

'You have been gone a long time, KaMtigwe,' said Ntshingwayo. 'Did you expect that your absence would go unnoticed? Your delay unpunished? Did you think that the Great King would simply sit here upon the *iNkatha* and await your return?'

Unpunished? wondered McTeague, and something cold gripped his stomach.

'We were in the hands of the white iNkosi, lord,' he replied. 'I could not return without an answer for the Great King, yet the Fat Queen's generals also had to deal with those involved in the death of the iFulentshi Prince?'

'All of them?'

'No, only the one they thought had damaged their honour.'

'Ah, like Hlabanatunga kaWandile. Did they impale him?'

'The English do not practise *ukujoja*,' McTeague replied. *Or at least*, he thought, *not literally. Though I suppose that their judgement on Carey bears some remarkable resemblance.*

'Then they are a weak people,' said Ntshingwayo. He occupied one of the huts in that upper section of the homestead close to the private royal quarters of Queen Langazana and reserved for the lesser princes, senior commanders and counsellors. Despite the early hour, it was dark in here, a pall of hearth smoke hanging in the thatch and reflected in the polished floor that, in the manner of the Zulu, had once been coated with dung and then rubbed for countless hours until it shone mirror-bright. So it was a strange trick of the light that presented itself to McTeague at this moment. Ntshingwayo seated before him with a shield-bearer at his shoulder, holding up an *isihlangu* of white hide spotted with small rust-red markings along one edge. Around the commander were his *izinduna*, some of his kin, his personal bodyguard – fearsome men who spread out in two circular wings that met and closed just at McTeague's back. And an *isangoma*, an old man with sightless eyes, his left nostril cut away to reveal the cavity beyond, his ear lobes pierced and each filled by the over-sized molar of some large creature, and his hair grown to the length of his waist, pulled into matted plaits, every one of which was woven with pieces of rotting animal flesh or organ. The stench was unbearable, but the strangeness of the image was created by the reflection of this threatening assembly in the polished floor, so that McTeague felt himself enclosed in a bubble of aggression.

'I have been on the road some time, lord,' he said. 'Might I see my womenfolk?'

The sense of dread still clawed at him.

'You said that you could not return without an answer,' said Ntshingwayo. 'So speak, Three-Eyes'

I would not risk this fellow's wrath for all the tea in China, thought McTeague. *But all the same...*

'Mighty lord,' he said, 'victor of eSandlwana, honoured son of Mahole the Khoza, how might this unworthy servant meet your command yet also obey the Great King's instruction that the white iNkosi's words should be conveyed to none but himself?'

McTeague was careful to avoid direct eye contact with the Zulu but he could feel Ntshingwayo's own gaze upon him. The old fellow was turned seventy now, they said, his face broad, covered by a beard almost as luxurious as that of the British officers, the long forehead topped by a precarious head ring. McTeague's own line of sight was dominated by the chieftain's enormous gut that vibrated when Ntshingwayo spoke.

'The command may be met by recognising that the ears of Ntshingwayo kaMahole belong to nobody but Cetshwayo kaMpande. That my ears are therefore his ears. To convey the Fat Queen's words to me is the same as carrying them to our Great King in person. And also by understanding that, unless I hear those words very soon, I shall have my men take a skinning knife to your hide, peeling it in one piece from your living flesh, and beginning with your ugly white man's face.'

One of the warriors prodded McTeague's stomach with the point of his stabbing spear.

What have they done with Maria Mestiza? he wondered. *And my beautiful Amahle?*

'I am at your mercy, lord,' said McTeague. 'But where to start? Well, first, the white iNkosi has accepted the gift of the elephant tusks and oxen. And with the promise that the *mbayimbayi* are on their way back to him, he has promised that he will not cross the River of the White Patient Ox until the evening of the twenty-eighth day of their present month.'

The *isangoma* whispered in his lord's ear.

'Three more days?' said Ntshingwayo.

'Correct, iNkosi.'

'And he will not raid any more homesteads in the meantime?'

'He did not go so far as that, I'm afraid.'

'And after the third day?'

'He says that the terms of the ultimatum remain as they have always been. At least...'

'At least?'

'At least, lord, for the Great King himself. For the nation's other generals, its princes, its senior *izinduna*, the terms are more favourable.'

Ntshingwayo's bodyguard shifted uneasily and one of them shoved McTeague with his war shield.

'Let him speak,' said their commander. 'We would see the honey that Gingile has brought back to us. To tempt our betrayal. Will it be so bitter a disappointment as the guns you once sold us, Three-Eyes?'

'They were good guns, iNkosi, yet none of us could have known they would be required to match those of the red soldiers.'

'None of us, trader? Did you truly never suspect the intentions of your own people?'

'Had I done so, lord, and had I been the trickster you think me to be, would I still have chosen my brotherhood among the People of Heaven?'

'Your arrival among us was timely though, was it not? Long enough to worm your way into the Great King's affections. Long enough to act as a useful spy for your red soldier friends.'

The chilly fingers bunching around McTeague's innards now became ice-tight. Cetshwayo, he believed, would never have allowed any of his commanders to accuse him so openly. Unless, of course, the commander in question had no intention of permitting the accusations to reach the King's ears.

'I would not dare to question the judgement of the Great King, iNkosi. He honours me with his trust and I should no more betray him than you would. But it is true that he needs somebody as his emissary who is still sufficiently known to the English that they might confide in him the private words that their iNkosi would relay to King Cetshwayo alone.'

'You play a dangerous game with your own life, Three-Eyes. By the time my men had pulled the skin of your head down around your neck you would have screamed those words a thousand times.'

'Yet I cannot speak them, lord, for they are written. And in the tongue of the Great King's Dutchman.'

He pulled from his pocket a sealed envelope. It was a reasonable gamble that, as usual, as one of his totems, Cetshwayo would have kept Cornelius Vijn close to him and therefore no longer in EsiKlebheni.

'The Witch Woman can read this tongue?'

'I think not, lord. But if I might speak with her...'

'In good time. And did you deliver private words also from the Great King to the white iNkosi?'

'I do not understand, lord.'

'He asked you to stay behind for a private audience before sending you on your mission. What was its purpose?'

'Simply to ensure, lord, that I understood his intention to win this war at all costs. To allow me some leeway in the negotiations if I thought it would buy us time to prepare for the battle ahead.'

'Nothing more?'

'What more could there be?' said McTeague.

Apart, he thought, *from Cetshwayo's decision to avoid that battle if he's able, to agree every single term of Chelmsford's ultimatum.* He had not relayed that to either Drummond or Chelmsford, of course. *Something seems to have driven the opportunity for peace clean from my mind. It must have been Carey's Court Martial. Poor fool. What did he think would happen? That Harrison would take the blame for not ensuring there was a proper escort? That Chelmsford might shoulder it for having allowed the Prince to be so close to the enemy in the first place? Did Carey ever once bother to ask whether Lord Chelmsford would have permitted himself to be so far ahead of the column that day? But there must be the devil to pay now. The Bonapartist bloodline lost while in the care of the British army. So a scapegoat needed. And who better than Carey? Yes, Carey's Court Martial.* But he *had* remembered to mention the *iNkatha*. Its importance. The crown jewel of the Zulu nation, that was how he described it. He was relatively certain, anyway, that Chelmsford would not have accepted even Cetshwayo's unconditional surrender. Not now. For he had troubles of his own. Being replaced as Commander-in-Chief by a new fellow. Sir Garnet Wolseley. Chelmsford's mishaps finally catching up with him. So what would he have done? Gone home with the shadow of Isandlwana hanging over him and unavenged? No, Chelmsford would finish it now. In blood. As quickly as possible before Wolseley could arrive and usurp him. And perhaps Lord Chelmsford might then display proper gratitude to the ex-Major of Her Majesty's 4th West India Regiment who had brought such useful intelligence to him.

'I want the words that the red soldiers' general has sent to the Great King, Three-Eyes,' said Ntshingwayo. 'And I want them in our own tongue.'

'It is impossible, lord,' cried McTeague. 'I do not speak IsiBhunu well enough to translate.'

'Why would the English write in that language?'

'Because the Great King always uses his Dutchman to write to *them*. And the mouth of the white iNkosi, a man called Drummond, an *isanusi* of their own, has lived here for many years, speaks that tongue also. Thus he replies in the same words.'

'Yet you must know what they say!'

'I do not, lord.'

'Well, we shall find out very soon whether you are with lies, shall we not?'

And Ntshingwayo's bodyguard dragged him from the hut.

*

Is it any less of a betrayal, thought McTeague, *that the object of a treachery might not know they are betrayed?* The warriors had thrust him into one of the smaller huts already guarded by a pair of evil-looking buggers. And as he burst through the entrance, his eyes at first unable to penetrate the gloom, McTeague heard a scuffling sound to his left, a cough, a small gasp, somebody moving in haste to stand before him. He sniffed the air. It was heavy with musk but something else. A familiar scent. Palm oil hair dressing.

'Simeon, is that yourself?' he said.

'William!' cried Cornscope. 'We feared you lost. How good to see you, old chap.'

McTeague's eyes were adjusting now, Cornscope's bulk more clearly visible, straightening his jacket and shirt collar, his yellow silk waistcoat, tugging at the waistband of his trousers. Behind Cornscope, he could recognise the faces of the other two wives that McTeague had brought here those several weeks before to the *iNkatha* ceremony. And near them, also to the left, knelt Amahle. She looked up, saw that it was him, sprang to her feet.

'They told me you were dead, lord!' she cried.

'My dear,' replied McTeague, 'it is not true, as you can plainly see. But who can have told you such a thing?'

Despite an apparent effort not to do so, her eyes turned towards Cornscope.

'You were gone so long,' said Simeon quickly. 'And after the King left, that Ntshingwayo chap had us locked up.'

'How do you come here?' said McTeague.

'Why, to warn you, old boy. One of Cetshwayo's fellows turned up at Emoyeni with a whole host of his savages. Surrounded the place and began searching, ransacking.'

'In the house?' McTeague imagined all the treasures of his home, the library, the furniture and fine fittings, his clothes, his supply of Encore whisky. It would all be looted. But they were unlikely to search the hilltop, for nobody else but himself knew about that secret cache.

'Yes, the house. The native huts too, of course. I left the good Pastor there to keep an eye on things though I doubt there is much that he can do to protect the property. And why should they turn against us so?'

'I think we may soon discover the reason,' McTeague replied. 'But what happened to Maria Mestiza?'

'She was with us,' Cornscope replied. 'But only for a day. Probably just a few hours. Then they took her away.'

'To where?'

'We have no idea. This young lady tried to enquire, but...'

McTeague turned to Amahle, reverted to IsiZulu.

'Your new sister,' he said, 'my chief wife, did they say where she was being taken? Or why?'

The icy fingers squeezed his bowels one more time.

'They would tell me nothing, lord.'

'When was this, sweet one?'

The title pleased her but the smile she offered was shaped by pity.

'Six sunsets past.'

'They have fed you?'

'They feed us.'

'And my good friend, Cornscope. He has protected you?'

Sweet Lord in Heaven, he thought, *that is a long time to leave three young women in the company of a man with Simeon's appetites.*

'I have guarded this flower as though she were my own,' said Cornscope in English. His grasp of the Zulu tongue was imperfect but sufficient for him to understand the drift of things.

'That's exactly my concern, dear fellow,' said McTeague.

'I am strong, iNkosi,' Amahle told him. 'But these two...'

A glance at the other two women was enough to tell him all he needed to know.

'And when they brought me here,' said McTeague, 'just now, was my good friend Cornscope testing that famous strength of yours, my dear?'

'He said that you were dead, lord. That I would need his friendship.'

'I was simply trying to provide the girl with some comfort, William,' said Cornscope. 'You see that, don't you? These other two creatures needed it so badly, I thought...'

McTeague looked at the other two women and needed no illustrations to fill the details.

'You violated my wives?' he said.

'Hardly that, old man. And wives? Come now, William, let's be realistic about this.'

'They are each of them baptised and lawfully wed in the eyes of God, Simeon.'

Proverbs 6:29, he thought. *"So he that goeth in to his neighbour's wife; whosoever toucheth her shall not be innocent."*

But he had no opportunity to recite the verse, to push the words down Simeon Cornscope's toad-like throat, to choke him with them. There was noise out in the kraal, people approaching, warriors ducking through the opening and filling the space to each side. They were followed by Ntshingwayo with his foul-smelling *isangoma* and, behind the chieftain, by Maria Mestiza.

'Ah,' said Cornscope, 'now here is your *true* wife, William. And how good to see her again.'

McTeague's heart missed several beats when he saw her. He could not be certain about the cause of his fears for her safety, but he was excited to see her.

'My dear,' he said, 'what have they done to you?'

He was even delighted to observe that she seemed no more sober than usual, her eyes downcast and glazed, her gait unsteady. A good sign, surely. Yet his excitement waned significantly when he realised that the next of their visitors was a man that he had never expected to meet again in life. Though this was no ghost, no apparition, but the living manifestation of Theophilus Twinge. And at his heel, a Zulu woman. It took McTeague some time to place her but he finally recognised her as the fourth of the wives – John Dunn's wives – that he had evicted from Emoyeni on the day of his wedding to Amahle. The childless wife. She was dressed exactly as she had been when he last saw her, when he took the riding whip to her face. She still bore the scar, showing beneath the head-band of otter fur that protected her red ochre topknot. She sneered at him. But what was the threat she had issued? *'You may live to regret this day, white man.'* Yes, that was it.

'I have brought some friends to see you, Three-Eyes,' said Ntshingwayo.

'Hello, Major,' Twinge smiled. 'Surprised?'

'Delighted, my old friend,' said McTeague. 'But what happened to you? You disappeared from the wagon without trace. Maria was perfectly distraught. After all her ministrations…'

'I could not let him die,' said Maria Mestiza. 'He was too much a man.'

'Where is the letter?' Ntshingwayo demanded.

'More a man than me, you mean?' said McTeague.

Ntshingwayo ordered one of his warriors to search the white trader, and McTeague was pushed and pulled, his pockets checked until the fellow brandished the sealed envelope in triumph, the Zulu's cow-tails brushing against McTeague's face.

'A woman like Maria needs more than an old boy like you can give her, Major,' Twinge sneered, and took hold of the letter, opened it and laughed. 'The bloody contract,' he said in English. Then, in his weak IsiZulu, 'This. Agreement. New agreement. Between KaMtigwe and red soldier iNkosi. New price, cheap price, to carry red soldier food and guns.'

'Not the words of the white iNkosi to the Great King?'

'No, lord,' said Twinge.

'Then tell me those words, Glass-Eye.'

The Almighty, McTeague had found, would forgive him anything so long as he was honest about his misdeeds. But the Lord seemed to take a dim view of tardiness. Late confessions were always punished by an appropriate riposte. And thus he should have expected that his denunciation of Carey – for which he had failed to seek God's blessing either beforehand or immediately afterwards – might result in a similar action against himself, in this case with Twinge and Maria Mestiza as instruments of Jehovah's justice. Yet he had only viewed his reminder to Bellairs about Carey's past record as a debt repaid. For had not Carey similarly borne witness against McTeague during the Court of Inquiry at Kingston all those years ago? And, yes, it was only a minor *contretemps*, might not have done him any harm, but a debt all the same. Why, he doubted that the worthy members of the Court Martial would even have allowed it any heed when they reconvened.

'I see that I must be honest, iNkosi,' he said.

'Be careful, lord,' said Twinge. 'This is a man who lies to himself and believes every word.'

McTeague looked at Twinge in revulsion. The freightmaster's mule-skinner stink mingled brutally with that of the sightless *isangoma* but, of the two, McTeague knew that he would have preferred the company of the old witch doctor. *Trade will flow*, thought McTeague, then turned slowly to Ntshingwayo.

'Great lord,' he said, 'it is true that I am sometimes careless with my tongue. Yet I see you, iNkosi, and know that you are the most loyal of Cetshwayo kaMpande's generals. My chief wife may have betrayed me, but she told me once that she had seen a vision. And in that vision you remained at the Great King's side. For many years after the Fat Queen's war has ended.'

'Is this true?' Ntshingwayo asked Maria Mestiza.

'It is true, lord,' she replied.

'Cetshwayo's kingdom shall survive after the war?'

'I knew in the vision,' said Maria, 'that it was several years on from now. Cetshwayo still king. But betrayed by many of those around him. A war among the People of Heaven themselves.'

'Tell him the rest,' said McTeague.

Maria Mestiza swayed, her glazed eyes looking up to the roof of the hut.

'You will die as a warrior should die, lord,' she said. 'Fighting to protect the Great King.'

The *isangoma* spoke, a voice that carried the echoes of ages long past.

'I see this thing too, lord,' he said.

'The prospect of making a warrior's end is all that a man might seek,' said the general. 'So, you can tell me the words that the white iNkosi sent to Cetshwayo.'

'If you insist, lord,' McTeague replied. 'But first I must tell you those things that passed between myself and the Great King himself. But they are not for the ears of all.'

'Great lord,' said Twinge, 'this man is with lies. He will poison your mind as he tried to poison me.'

'Yet I will hear him,' said Ntshingwayo. 'Now clear this dwelling. All but the *isangoma*. He will stay, Three-Eyes.'

The hut had emptied, though not without some further protest from Twinge.

The trick here, thought McTeague, *is to tell precisely as much of the truth as the situation may allow but not a single iota more.*

'You must understand, lord,' he said, 'that the Great King gave me leave to use any tricks in my power, first, to buy him more time to prepare for the red soldiers' advance and, second, to gather the main points of their intentions.'

'And did those tricks include – as I have been told they did – an offer to accept each and every term of the Fat Queen's ultimatum?'

Ah, thought McTeague, *so the thing was not strictly just between Cetshwayo and myself as the blighter led me to believe.*

'As a ruse by the Great King, lord. Nothing more. But it was not necessary since it soon became clear to me that the white iNkosi intends to destroy Cetshwayo's capital regardless of whether the People of Heaven want peace – even if they were to surrender.'

'He needs victory,' said Ntshingwayo.

'Yes, lord. And for a very good reason. The Fat Queen has sent another general to replace him. In her army that is a great disgrace. And thus, to avoid returning to his country in shame, he must hurry to battle, while he is still able. One last great battle between two warrior nations.'

'When will this new general arrive, Three-Eyes?'

'In no more than twelve or fourteen days, lord.'

'So the final battle is imminent. And if the vision of your Witch Woman is correct. We must win it. With the *iNkatha* renewed we should be able to draw the red soldiers into a trap. Destroy them all. So there are none left for the Fat Queen to send against us.'

Little chance of that happening, thought McTeague, though it had been a stroke of genius to remember Maria's drunken premonition from a few weeks past. He was about to tell Ntshingwayo, however, that Maria Mestiza seemed no longer to be *his* Witch Woman, but his heart felt as though it were trapped in a cabinet-maker's clamp. His chest was tight, his breathing laboured. Yet there was, in any case, simply no opportunity, for there were cries of alarm outside, distant rifle fire, sounds of chaos throughout the homestead. The *isangoma* ran from the hut and Ntshingwayo told McTeague to follow so that, moments later, they stood with a strong breeze pulling at their faces, in the shade of a wind-stooped tree at a place offering clear views between the beehive dwellings to the Emakhosini Valley below. Other homesteads and military barracks were easily visible from here. And several of them were burning.

There were dark shadows on the land away to McTeague's front.

'Warriors of my own regiment,' said Ntshingwayo. 'They follow instructions to burn those homesteads before the red soldiers have a chance to do so.' He pointed away to the west, to the right, were there was still more movement on the hills. Faster movement. Horsemen.

'As I told you, lord,' said McTeague, 'although the white general has agreed not to cross the White Patient Ox for several days, he made no promise to leave the land this side of the river alone.' The smoke was rolling in thick, black clouds, climbing the side of the valley towards them. 'But why do we burn our own homesteads, lord?'

'To protect us here, at EsiKlebheni,' said Ntshingwayo. 'The red soldiers still fear surprise attack and will not advance to ground that they cannot see clearly. But there is another thing. That it lifts the heart of our warriors to scorch the earth in their path – though, in truth, it denies the Fat Queen's army nothing but their pleasures. And, on the other hand, it breaks our people's hearts whenever it is the horsemen who do the burning.'

'So you think the *iNkatha* safe?'

Ntshingwayo laughed.

'The shades of all our fallen surround it, Glass-Eye. The red soldiers will not venture here. We have six hundred warriors in the valley and, by tonight, there will be two more regiments with us. If the horsemen are still on the land, we will wipe them away.'

'Did you know?' said McTeague, when he had been confined once more to the hut with Cornscope, Amahle and the other two wives. 'About Maria? And Twinge?'

'How could I possibly know such a thing and not tell you, dear friend – though it would have been such a grievous treachery to reveal?' replied Cornscope.

But McTeague did not believe him. Cuckolds are always the last to see the horns placed upon them by a wife's infidelity. It had certainly been so with the man who should have been his father, his whoring mother's husband. Yet he forced himself to remember that Maria Mestiza had never truly considered herself his wife but, rather, mistress of his household, his domain, a bodyguard to him, a partner in crime. One could therefore, he supposed, be cuckolded in a whole glossary of roles.

'Why are we still imprisoned, lord?' said Amahle. 'If you have told iNkosi Ntshingwayo all that passed between yourself and the white general?'

'There still seems to be a question about me in Lord Ntshingwayo's mind, my dear.'

With good reason too, he thought, and wondered how far Maria's betrayal of him might have reached. The sounds of gunfire crept ever closer and from several directions, while the cries and war chants that he could hear appeared more strident, less defiant. Then there was a challenge from the warriors at the entrance, an exchange of words, before Twinge ducked his head through the opening, the scarred face of Dunn's woman following behind.

'The old fellow's coming back for you, Major,' said Twinge. He stayed close to the entrance now, revolver in hand. 'I'm looking forward to watching you die.'

'Now why on earth should Ntshingwayo want me dead? And what could possibly cause you such animosity towards me? I rather imagined *myself* the injured party here, Theophilus. No need for the gun, surely?'

'Animosity? Let me count the ways, Willie boy,' smiled Twinge. 'First, the not inconsiderable fact that you planned to murder me with one of Maria's venomous unguents. Second, the money you owe me and which, with my death, you hoped would be forgotten. Third, the problem of nailing my colours to the mast of one who will soon have neither jot nor tickle with which to repay me.'

'Because I will be gone to meet my Maker?'

'Because deceased or still living, you have lost it all.'

'I have Emoyeni.' *Or whatever is left there*, he thought, *once Cetshwayo's men have stripped it bare.* 'The territory, at least.'

Twinge roared with false laughter.

'You have no idea, Major, do you?' he said. 'Where do you imagine I've been all this time? Since I crawled half-dead from that jawbone? If Maria hadn't spared me out of debt for the satisfaction I'd given her, I would have been dead too.'

The words pressed upon McTeague's shoulders, forced him to his knees. *I am a book that is grown old*, he thought. *Oh, failing manhood. The vulnerability it brings.* He looked down at his good clothes, now so worn by travel and hardship. *I may have the covers replaced, the bindings renewed, but I can do nothing about what lies within. The pages of my life are become thin and thumbed, the print fading with such exposure to the light.* Even with dear Amahle, he had only managed the thing just that once.

'I have no idea where you would have crawled, Theophilus,' he whispered. 'But you really had become too much the liability – even if I did not know the full extent of your worthlessness. So please feel free to enlighten me.'

'Dunn!' cried Simeon Cornscope. 'I'd wager a full finny that he's been with Dunn.'

'Dunn's days are over more surely than even my own,' said McTeague. 'A spent force.'

Twinge sneered.

'All your running back and forth,' he smiled. 'A mark for both Cetshwayo and Chelmsford alike. Have you any idea what His Lordship's promised Dunn? Have you?'

What might Dunn still have to offer? McTeague wondered. *A rag-tag troop of volunteers. But otherwise?*

'Whatever services he might have offered,' Cornscope fawned, 'they cannot come near to those that William has provided.'

'He's given nothing that didn't have his price tag attached,' said Twinge. 'Same as the rest of us. But trade must flow, Willie, as you always say. And John

Dunn's a clever cove. So your precious Emoyeni, Major, is already promised to him. That and every scrap of land around it. Chelmsford has told him the plan. When the war's over, Zululand to be carved up. Taken apart. Twelve separate kingdoms. Rewards for the princes and chieftains who've deserted Cetshwayo. And one of those kingdoms for John Dunn. It's already got a name. Dunnsland. How about that, you old fool?'

The news cut McTeague. Deep and wide. He turned to Amahle.

'Help me up, sweet one,' he murmured to her.

'What is this man saying, lord?' she asked, but he could only shake his head in response.

'I'll put another finny,' said Cornscope, 'on the fact that he's been working with Dunn all along.'

Twinge smiled.

And Maria would have known, thought McTeague. *Known that I could never provide her with the royal domain she so badly sought for herself. But has she told Twinge about...?*

'And Ntshingwayo?' he said, finally back on his feet. 'Why should he want me dead?'

'You broke your own rules, Major,' said Twinge. 'Never to trust another soul. But you trusted *two* people. You had the Dutchman add your little codicil to Cetshwayo's *billy-doo*. And you boasted to Maria about how clever you'd been to tell Chelmsford about the *iNkatha*. Ntshingwayo didn't believe me, of course. Thinks the thing will protect itself in any case. But you hear that, William?' He cocked an ear towards the sounds of distant skirmishing. 'He's waiting to see whether that Flying Column of Chelmsford's shows any sign of a direct attack on this kraal, ignores the easier pickings. If it does, he'll know you're guilty of betraying them. And then he'll be coming for you, Willie McTeague.'

They came for him soon afterwards. A chaos crashing about him too suddenly to register all the details that had gone before. A brief silence when Twinge finally tired of taunting him and left. Some meaningless words with Cornscope. An attempt at explanation to Amahle. Astonishing expressions of concern from the girl, which he did not truly comprehend. Then the angry press and heat of dark bodies, cow-tails, voices roaring in his ears. Rough hands bruised the flesh of his arms, dragged him through the doorway as the heels of McTeague's Maxwell riding boots slipped uselessly on the hut's floor, finding a purchase only when he was hauled outside. He turned his head to seek his companions but saw only enraged native faces, snarling teeth, eyes that sparked yellow on brown, wide with hurried fury.

'Dear God!' he whispered, as the warriors pulled him forward between the beehive dwellings.

He fell, wood smoke in his nostrils; took a blow to his shoulders from a knobkerrie, pain howling down his back and spine, his stomach knotting, heaving up a dribble of bile. *Psalm 27*, he thought, and kept repeating it over and over. *Psalm 27. Psalm 27. "Though an host should encamp against me, my heart shall not fear."* But he did fear. McTeague was on his knees, the thighs pumping to keep him moving forward like a circus midget. He tried to lift one knee or the other, to get back on his feet. Yet his knees were being punctured, again and again. Stony gravel, the twill of his hunting breeches ripped to tatters wherever it dragged across the ground.

'Death! Death!' shouted the warriors. They snatched at his clothing, kicked to keep him moving, his arms forced forward, almost dislocated, over his head so that the sack jacket – the once expensive Harris Tweed – could be stripped from him, swung in triumph by a torn sleeve.

His head screamed. It raged and wept. It implored. He caught a glimpse of Theophilus Twinge near one of the huts, calmly filling his clay pipe, while women and small children ran past, carrying bundles of their possessions. Then McTeague's linen shirt was being slashed, ripped from his torso. His bladder betrayed him as they hauled him through a gap in the thorn trunk palisade surrounding the parade enclosure. Damp heat filled the flannel crotch of his union suit, spread down the legs, up towards his belly.

The fate that awaited him lurched in a series of images, each out of proper focus, as though he were on a ship, the horizon bucking and pitching at crazed angles, his senses dizzied by the irregularity of the motion. But he saw Ntshingwayo towards the centre of the open ground, sometimes watching McTeague's undignified approach, sometimes directing his small groups of warriors towards the continuing sounds of battle. And he saw the knot of men still gathered around the commander, the work in which they were engaged, hacking at the end of a long and slender sapling.

Psalm 27. Psalm 27. "Though war should rise against me, in this I will be confident." Oh, Almighty Father, spare me!

'We will give you the best of views, Three-Eyes,' shouted Ntshingwayo. 'So you can see your red soldier friends when they arrive. You may even be able to greet them. For we will make sure that the spike is still working its way through you, traitor!'

One of the warriors was clawing at McTeague's breeches. He twisted and turned but they held him tight.

'This is a mistake,' he yelled. 'Let me explain.'

But he knew that even if they allowed him any time, he could never now summon the words that would once have come so eloquently. Something hacked at the seat of his trousers. A knife, he thought. There was a rending sound as the seams came apart and the material flapped around his thighs.

His legs had stopped functioning finally and they were dragging him now, the toes of his boots snagging in the dirt, the Zulus laughing when the seat of his union suit was exposed, jeering as they pulled down the flap, his white buttocks forcing their way out as though that part of him at least might escape. Every inch of his flesh felt as though he were beset by a swarm of ants, his skin itching, his insides crawling with the things.

Psalm 27. "The Lord is my light and my salvation; whom shall I fear?" Oh, *Sweet Jesus, but I fear these, Lord. Not this death, Almighty Father. Please not this one.*

'*Ukujoja!*' the warriors chanted. 'The traitors' death!'

McTeague was thrown flat, dust filling his nostrils, his mouth, choking him, pinned down by the warrior's feet upon his arms and legs. *Could I do it?* he wondered. He pressed his face tighter to the earth so that he cut off his own breath, wondering whether his body would allow him to end it quickly.

'Do this thing!' called Ntshingwayo.

He felt them drag his legs further apart. He squirmed and screamed, a jet of red soil pouring from his nostrils. The first tiny sample of the agony to come as the roughly sharpened point of the stake pressed against his anus, his bowels reacting of their own accord, pumping spasms of his bodily waste in a final defence against defilement. The Zulus laughed once more. *Bless me, father...*

There was a shot, much louder than all the background firing. The pressure relaxed on his left arm but there was suddenly a terrible weight upon his back. Something had fallen on him.

A second shot, and the pain in his buttocks fell away. Each of his arms and legs was free now, but still he could not move. There was a warrior slumped across him and McTeague could raise neither the physical nor inner strength to shift him. He had made his peace with the Lord and there could now be no going back, surely? But he thought about Psalm 27 again. *"When the wicked, even mine enemies and my foes, came upon me to eat up my flesh, they stumbled and fell."* Perhaps this was not the day after all. Just a further reminder from the Almighty that late confessions would be appropriately punished.

There seemed to be shooting from several directions now in his immediate vicinity, the warriors yelling and chanting, Ntshingwayo issuing orders about the *iNkatha*.

'And kill him!' cried the general.

A blow to his back, more pain, and he knew he had been stabbed, though he could not calculate how badly the wound might penetrate. He tried to be sick but there was just another trickle of bile. *If the Lord has indeed caused my foes to stumble and fall, perhaps I owe it to Him...*

He dug the palm and fingers of his left hand into the ground, pressed with all the strength remaining to him, straightened the elbow and levered himself sideways. A vicious pain in his back, rending flesh. The most awful burning sensation and he knew that he had knocked away the spear that had stabbed him. He was on his side, a dead Zulu's arms still embracing him and, against his better judgement, he forced himself to complete the movement. Another push and he turned himself completely over, surprised that there was no more hurt, just a numbness and the sense of becoming one with the ground upon which he now lay, as though he was somehow emptying himself into the earth.

He turned his head one way. Ntshingwayo being led away by his bodyguards. Furious, pointing at McTeague but the words lost upon the wind. The other way, to his right, the strangest of vignettes. Maria Mestiza, inside the enclosure, striding towards him, sliding a bullet into the Springfield rifle, murder in her eyes, a curl of smoke still folded around her, at the same time engaged in a frantic and angry exchange with both Theophilus Twinge and Simeon Cornscope while, behind them, the horse-whipped wife fought a deadly struggle with young Amahle.

Above him – it *felt* as though it was above him, for he was forced to tilt his head back to see it – the ground-quaking tattoo and tremor of hooves beyond the kraal, the whinny and snorting chaos of cavalry, military commands, smoke and fire, Zulu families and fighters each caught by surprise, disorganised, uncertain, in the early throes of panic.

Ntshingwayo had gone, disappeared through the palisade. But from the lower slope of the enclosure another group of warriors had appeared. Perhaps forty in total. Fully armed and shields of russet hide. They halted. They stared towards the incongruous party of white folk stranded in the almost empty parade ground. They charged. And the ground drummed to a different beat. McTeague tried to roll back on to his right side but the blood that seeped from his wound somehow held him firmly congealed to the ore-stained soil.

Maria Mestiza raised the .50 calibre weapon, loosed a shot that pierced shield-hide, lifted the warrior that bore it, hurling him bodily among those that followed. At the same time, Twinge took a few steps backward, glanced towards the palisade as though calculating the chances of escape, then shook his head. He drew his revolver, looked quickly at McTeague, returned to Maria's side and knelt, steadying the gun as best he could with shaking hands, and fired. Cocked and fired.

Cornscope, for his part, had gone to Amahle's assistance, grabbed the scar-faced woman by her red topknot and dragged her away from the girl. But his eyes never strayed far from the advancing Zulus. His face was creased by sheer terror. He mouthed something over and over again. Impossible to make out the words though, in this ear-bursting bedlam. Amahle used the respite from Cornscope's action to good effect, picked up a stone that fitted her delicate fist, scrambled after Dunn's abandoned wife – the same that McTeague had evicted with such vigour – and beat her senseless, smacking the rock against the woman's skull.

The Zulus had closed the intervening gap.

'*Ji! Ji!*' they chanted.

A final shot from Maria's rifle. Another from Twinge's pistol. Then the incoming wave caught them up, carried them back, tumbling them over each other as the spears rose and fell. McTeague could not see how Twinge met his end but he watched Maria Mestiza receive blow after blow. Tears trickled across his nose, his lip, down his cheek. She dropped, got to her knees only to drop once more. He heard every sickening puncture of her flesh, the guttural sucking noise as the blades were pulled free again.

'USuthu! USuthu!'

Maria lay lifeless, as still as the succession of honour cuts would allow, each one causing her to twitch and dance, a strange parody of the *Punta* that he had once seen her perform. So, William McTeague – who had cared for little else in his lifetime – found himself moved to racking sobs; to further tears that sprang from some great hollow trough at his core. She had betrayed him to Ntshingwayo, it was true. She had betrayed him with Twinge – yet this was, he supposed, no different than the comfort he himself had sought from his other wives. But, at the end, she had not allowed him to face that awful death that the Zulus had planned for him. It was possible that she intended to kill him herself. Yet at least it would have been clean. Better than this mess in which he now languished. He would miss her, though it was likely that they would be united again soon enough. Reconcile their differences, perhaps. Dispel misunderstandings. For the Zulus did not leave their wounded foes alive for long. They would finish him.

"Thy kingdom is an everlasting kingdom, and Thy dominion endureth throughout all generations."

The girl, he thought. *I hope they spare the girl.* He did not give Cornscope a second thought, however.

"So he that goeth in to his neighbour's wife; whosoever toucheth her shall not be innocent."

He was failing fast, struggled to move his head at all now, but finally located Amahle. Inexplicably, she had positioned herself between the warriors and Cornscope, pointing towards her lord and husband, the scarred woman lying motionless at her feet. *Why, bless her!* he thought. *She's running a bluff.* He coughed, tasted blood on his tongue. *Relying on them not knowing that Ntshingwayo has sentenced me. Playing on the King's good name, perhaps.* Then she was at his side, cradling his head, Cornscope behind her.

'You're a lucky beggar, Simeon,' he croaked. 'You deserved to die, old fellow. Have you seen Ntshingwayo?'

He had not, though Cornscope assumed that the commander had taken his men to the upper sections of the royal homestead, to deal with the threat that had come so suddenly, so directly to that sacred district. Ntshingwayo would survive, of course. He would live to fight another day. Maria Mestiza had foretold it, though she was perhaps fortunate that she had not seen the manner of her own demise. At least, he hoped not. Yet the commander, she had predicted, would die alongside Cetshwayo. And some years hence. Did that mean the war would drag on? Or that the Zulus would win? Had all his conniving at the cause and outcome of this thing been for nothing?

'Have you seen Ntshingwayo, sweet one?' he whispered to Amahle in IsiZulu.

'No, lord,' she sobbed. 'Nor the Great Queen, Langazana.'

Then the world erupted around them. There was a searing wave of heat that rippled across the parade ground.

McTeague craned his neck, despite the pain, and saw a terrible sight. A ball of flame that climbed into the sky. And around the flames, dark shapes that danced and screamed with all the torments from the Nine Circles of Hell. The countless shades of those – the fighters, the kings, the chieftains past – charged by the Sky Lord to protect the *iNkatha yeSiswe yaKwaZulu*. To those spirits had fallen the task of guarding the most valuable possession of the People of Heaven. And they had failed.

Chapter Sixteen

Friday 4th July 1879

Zama was dead. His cattle lost. The *iNkatha* burned. They had arrived too late to save any of it. The whole valley aflame. So many of the royal homesteads destroyed and countless smaller *imizi* besides. People driven from their dwellings and streaming northwards towards Cetshwayo's capital, towards the emaHlabithini plain. The Elder Queen, Langazana, turned out upon the road like a wandering beggar. That greatest of commanders, Ntshingwayo kaMahole, humbled and humiliated. Eight days previously, but Shaba's grief and fury was still unabated, the singing and ceremony sustained all through this long night helping little with his own woes, though he sensed around him the collective healing that numbed the nation's hurt, that cleansed bloodied pride, that restored martial mettle.

And these were the words they sang, gathered in the blackness of oNdini's grand assembly grounds, torches flickering from *bhoma* and watch tower.

"Who are the enemy? Who are the foes?" called the lead voice, the pitch high, the rhythm free and loose.

"Men of the Fat Queen!" replied the deeper tones of the choral singers.

"Scavenger dogs!" sang the oNdini regiments. The pattern repeated. And out in the darkness, around the rim of hills, faint at first, came the sound of a different lead voice, from the next of the Great King's royal homesteads. Perhaps from old KwaNodwengu.

"What have they cost us? What is lost?"

A distant response from that singer's choral section.

"Sacred Coil! Ring of Power!"

The regiments gathered there were joined in harmony with the oNdini men while further still, across the plain at kwaKhandempemvu, a third lead voice.

"Does the loss bend us? Bend our knee?"

The warriors of the three homesteads together.

"Not with your blessing, Lord-of-the-Sky!"

Away to the south, from the new KwaNodwengu settlement, a powerful solo voice.

"Show us the future, Lord-of-the-Sky!"

"We will conquer them! We will win!" the singers echoed around the slopes.

Then all the mighty host of the Great King Cetshwayo kaMpande sang the line together.

"We will conquer them! We will win!"

Before the final collective prayer rose in solemn waves that could have been heard for many miles, even reaching the ears of those who walked in the shadow world with the *iNkatha* itself.

"Walk with us, Sky Lord, give us our Freedom! The People of Heaven shall walk in your Light!"

As Shaba lifted his own voice within the Evil Omen, he knew that the red soldiers would hear them in their encampment on the far side of the White Patient Ox. They would hear them and quake. For there were more men assembled here in their regiments, they had been told, than even before the Battle of the Little House, eSandlwana.

On that occasion they had been gathered down there, nearer the river, at KwaNodwengu, close to the old Shakan capital of KwaBulawayo. But now they were here. At oNdini itself.

It was not circular in form but followed the shape of an ostrich egg. Between the outer and inner palisade fences, they said, stood almost two thousand dwellings, enough sleeping mats to accommodate seven thousand people when its own regiments – the warriors of the Leopard's Lair, the Black Mamba and the Dust Raisers – were on garrison duty. It required two thousand paces to walk the outer boundary. And he knew this, for he had done it in an effort to drive out his memories of the girl.

He had found her where he knew she would be, fallen at the sacred spring of Mthonjaneni, fallen with her sisters and some of the *udibi* boys, fallen with a spear in her hand, fallen in an effort to prevent the red soldiers defiling the water. *What did they think?* he wondered. *What did they say when they knew that even our young women would stand against them?* For he was proud of Zama kaMandla, despite the ache in his heart, and sensed her shade close to him, here in the darkness.

Her grandfather had sought him out also. He may be old, he had said, but the warrior who had once stood at Shaka's side on the Hill of Gqokli was still worth a dozen whites. He would help Shaba, he had promised, to avenge Zama's death, the destruction of his homestead, the theft of their collective herds. So the old one had marched with the Mongrels, the uMxapho regiment in which his son, Mandla kaSibusiso, served as an *induna*. They were here tonight also, mustered at oNdini too, somewhere away to Shaba's right in the heart of this *komkhulu*, Cetshwayo's Great Place, the most modern and grand of the thirteen royal homesteads ringing the plain. It was a marvel of wonders, and most marvellous of all was the square house the King had commissioned in European style at the centre of his inner sanctum, at the highest point, a house complete with windows of glass, English and French furniture – or so it was spoken.

Cetshwayo kaMpande himself was not here, of course. In the ways of his people, the King's role at such time was to focus his spiritual power upon the struggle at hand, his physical form guarded, at some safe location – in this case, the regiment had been told, at emLangongwenya homestead of Cetshwayo's father, Mpande. Of course, there was no *iNkatha* now to help him channel his strength on their behalf, but he would carry with him all the other symbols of his might, his *isigodlo*, his wives; his train of shamans, medicine men and diviners. The preparations were all made, the last mission, seeking an honourable settlement with the white generals, unsuccessful.

And Shaba had been with those emissaries. Two days ago, and the King's most trusted messengers sent to the red soldiers' camp with the words. All previous attempts failed, confusion about the fate of those responsible for the negotiations – Amahle's white trader husband among them. *Perhaps he is dead too*, he thought. *And no loss to any of us.* But Shaba had been chosen specifically by the Great King to accompany the final delegation – so that he and he alone, might carry the sword of the iFulentshi Prince back to the white iNkosi. He had used his brief time at the encampment to look for Klaas the Skirmisher in the hope that he might discover something of his movements, his reason for running to the red soldiers on the day that Shaba had fought the horsemen at eZunganyene. But he had seen no sign of the fellow and simply fulfilled his part with the sword. He had done so on his knees but without any admission that it was he who had killed the Frenchman. The red soldier general had taken the thing from him without a word while Shaba trembled before his enemies despite himself, afraid that the time-counter now hidden again within his civet tails might somehow betray him.

Yet it had remained silent – as silent, implacable, as the general when the emissaries told him that a herd of the King's most prized white cattle was being sent as the ultimate peace offering. Their value incalculable. Flawless beasts. But they had never arrived at their destination, since the young warriors who held the fords refused to let them pass, had turned them back, sending angry words to Cetshwayo kaMpande. Words that Shaba echoed in his heart.

'Do you not trust us, iNkosi,' they had said, 'to drive away the red soldiers? To protect you from them?'

And Cetshwayo had known then that the final bones had been cast.

Now the women sang, different rhythms punctuated by wild ululation, praises for the valour of their men as the regiments themselves filed from the various parade grounds and moved towards the flatter ground near the river for the next stage of their cleansing. The moon was full once more, auspicious, high and bright, the night made lighter still by the burning brands borne by many of the warriors.

'May the shades remain with us when the sun is up,' said Langalabelele at his side as they jogged forward in unison.

'They were not with us yesterday,' replied Shaba.

'The horse soldiers?'

'We should have trapped them.'

'You think they have this Jesucristo with them?'

'No, I think we should have been cleansed before we set the trap, not afterwards. The shades are never content when the rituals are disregarded.'

'How many did you kill with your rifle, Giant Slayer?'

'Whey!' said Shaba, remembering the thing. 'At first light we were on the bluffs. Above the river. The red soldiers were there. Swimming and splashing in the water. Can you believe their conceit? But there are two of them that will swim no more.'

'Their souls remain?'

'Yes. But I know the place. We will stay away from there.'

'We heard the *mbayimbayi* speak. But not until the sun had climbed high.'

'They seemed happy to leave us there. Until the horse soldiers came across. Dung-shirts. And the Basuto riders. They thought they could catch us, my friend. But we had seen them coming. At both drifts so they could cut us off. But by then we were no longer there.'

'They say that it was Zibhebhu that set the trap,' said Langalabelele.

'It was fitting,' Shaba replied. 'He had pulled us all back with his own regiment, with the uMxapho, hidden in the gullies, like a great cattle-run with only one way in and one way out. Here somewhere.' It was hard to tell in the dark. 'So be careful. Watch where you put your feet.'

Zibhebhu's men had carefully prepared the ground, weaving together the brown toughened grasses, plaiting the strands into loops that might snag the horses' hooves, spilling them. Then Zibhebhu had ridden out on his own pony, a white pony that could be seen from far away, risking his own life as a general should do, going forth to challenge the dung-shirt *induna* – that bull of a man again with the enormous beard – to act as bait. And it had worked. For the horse soldiers followed him. Hundreds of them. All the way along the fools' trail he left for them. A few warriors had to be sacrificed in the process, naturally. Some flocks of goats too. But the dung-shirts and Basuto riders followed.

'Yet the trap was not sprung,' said Langalabelele.

'It is the way I told you. The shades were unhappy with us. They caused some of the young men to charge too early. A few paces more and we would have eaten them all.'

At least I killed one more with my rifle, thought Shaba, the blade of his

221

iklwa washed later when he went to open him. But that was later, after they had chased the horsemen back to the river. At one point he had been close enough to keep pace, to touch a hand to the withers of a sweat-streaked beast, foam flecking and streaming from its tongue and flanks, just one of the many panicked by the regiments' attack, the horns almost closing around the fleeing soldiers. There were acts of individual bravery, of course, a few of the whites turning back at the last moment to rescue fallen comrades, although others were left to their inevitable fate. And the killing only stopped when the invaders had been driven back past KwaNodwengu where they rallied, began to fire in volleys, by turns, falling back more slowly until their friends at the drift and the *mbayimbayi* could give them cover. So the enemy had escaped, though it lifted the hearts of the *amabutho* that they had driven away so many so easily.

'They say the shades are unhappy because we allowed the *iNkatha* to be burned,' said Langalabelele. 'And then because we let the red soldiers camp in the Valley of Kings without attacking them. When we could all see that they would have been easy to destroy. When they came straggling across the country for hour after hour.'

'The shades may be unhappy,' said Shaba. 'But that does not mean they are correct. The hearts of the people were too broken after the *iNkatha* was burned to think about fighting. And the Sacred Coil may be lost to us for the moment but it did not fall into the hands of the Fat Queen. A setback. A warning to us all, perhaps. But not the subjugation it might have been.'

Yet despite the ritual which had commenced after the horse soldiers were chased away, there was still the doom-laden thought that perhaps this thing went even further than simple discontent among the shades. For how had the *iNkatha* been so easily discovered and destroyed by their enemies. It was the soul of the People of Heaven, after all. So, they had whispered, might it not be a punishment by the Sky Lord himself? If so, for what heresy on their part?

It had been in all their minds during the evening when they were gathered together for the first purification. Every warrior called forth by the *izinyanga* to drink the potions prepared for them, taking their allotted dose from the clay gourds and then running to the pits where the bitter mixture caused them to vomit the contents of their stomachs into the ground. Shaba could still feel the ache in his belly. He had wanted it to stop, and stop quickly. For he had not eaten properly for many days. Shortage of food, the grief of losing Zama. But it had not stopped for a long time. The retching pain of it. He had been barely conscious when the *izinyanga* brought up bundles of grass, dipped them in the vomit, the warrior essence, and set them aside to be woven later into the beginnings of a new *iNkatha*. The healing process begun.

The stomach cramps had remained with him when the black bull was brought forth, wrestled to the ground by the bare hands of the youngest warriors despite the beast's valiant defence, three of the men gored to death in the process. Then the *izinyanga* had cut slices of living flesh from the animal's shoulder, sliced and roasted its meat, flinging thin strips high above the regiments, the warriors' frenzy building as they vied with each other to catch the smokey scraps, bite chunks from them and hurl the pieces back into the air, the process continually repeated. Shaba had not tried particularly hard to take any of the flesh but at least he had not fainted as many of those around him had done. He had been weak but was now prepared once more for the Blackness, the evil unleashed by the shedding of blood in combat, the bull finally killed only when that process was done.

'All the same,' said Langalabelele to him, 'it seemed to me that the Great King knew we had made mistakes.'

Cetshwayo had addressed them simply. Shaba could see him plainly. No sign of concern in his voice. No challenges encouraged between the regiments. No boastful claims. A reminder of the task ahead. Like bringing in the crops. Like gathering the royal herd from the pasture lands. This time, the service to be rendered just to deflect the threat brought to them by the Fat Queen's invaders. And advice. That when the battle came, they should not advance too fast. Not tire themselves too soon. That they should not attack the red soldiers if they established a fortified position or advanced in strength. Then he had led them in chanting the praise names of the commanders – Ziwedu, Mnyamana, Ntshingwayo, Zibhebhu and Sihayo – who would action his orders, turn the final battle to victory. And, at the last, he had taken his leave of them.

They halted on the near side of the White Patient Ox, unable to make their normal pre-battle mass pilgrimage to the grave sites of the Emakhosini. But they stood here on the very edge of that valley – the Valley of Kings. And if their voices were strong enough, said the *izinyanga*, they would carry clear to the nation's founding fathers who had lain here over the ages.

There was noise too from the white camp on the further bank, noise that gave a counterpoint to the river's water as it whispered over the stones and gravel of the crossing place. Cattle and oxen crooning to each other. The bark of a dog, picked up and echoed by a hyena somewhere out in the lonely bush. The snort of horses tethered to their lines and the metallic chime of chain on peg ring. The occasional shout of a red soldier sentry, an angry response repeated not once but many times as the sleepless complained of the disturbances that they falsely blamed for keeping them awake.

Whey! thought Shaba. *The foolishness that prevents us attacking them now. What chances we waste!* There would have been no survival for their foes had they done so, he knew. But it was impossible. For these hours were dark for good reason. They were those when the world of the shades and the world of men ran perilously close, one to the other. And how easy it was during those hours for the living to stumble by accident into the realms of the dead. Thus a perilous time for fighting. Look what had happened when the regiments had attacked the red soldiers at KwaJimu. But it was at such hours, too, that the Old Kings would walk abroad, striding the valley's byways, already enraged by the destruction they saw there. Easy to reach them, to seek the power of their anger that it might be harnessed in defence of the Land. So the noises from the enemy camp fell to fearful silence, from man and beast alike, as the medicine men — scattered along the army's front — lifted their own voices in a solemn litany to the Lost Lords.

"Great Senzangakhona," they intoned.

And the warriors replied, a slow and mournful chorus that rolled through the still night sky.

"Father of Shaka," went the praise poetry. "Son of Jama. Lord of Reason."

The red soldiers shall know us by these words, thought Shaba, as he felt the power of their ancestors gather to them.

And the litany continued, the victories named, the heroism detailed for each of those others buried in the vale, the genealogy that they knew so well: Senzangakhona's father, Jama; Jama's father, Ndaba; Ndaba's father, Mageba; Mageba's brother, Phunga; Phunga's father, Gumede; and Gumede's father, the mighty Zulu kaNtombela. They sang too of the battles fought here — against their rivals for this land, the Ndwandwe and the Dutchmen. They sang all night until they were satisfied that the Lost Lords were with them. And until, with the first thin warning that the sun was only an hour from making its appearance, the red soldiers' camp was finally stung into action. Four thousand white men, a thousand of their Basuto allies, a dozen *mbayimbayi*, hundreds upon hundreds of horses in tight formation, began their final advance across the drift.

By the time the crimson orb of the sun had lifted just clear of the eastern hills, the army of the AmaZulu had run the width of the plain, gathered itself in another circle back below the thorn-trunk walls of Old KwaNodwengu, below the tomb of Cetshwayo's father, King Mpande.

"Great Mpande," sang the *izinyanga*, exactly as they had done before the battle at eSandlwana.

It filled Shaba's heart when the regiments gave their reply. He felt the throbbing energy build within himself, the lack of sleep fading to hidden memory, the scarlet creature filling his veins, his head. And while they sang, the *izinyanga* came among them, carrying their pots of the *umuthi* Spirit Potions, into which they dipped the tufted tails of the *nkonkoni*, the Revered Champion, the ox-horned antelope. The liquids were flicked and sprayed copiously upon them all, each warrior ensuring that at least a few drops might touch their bodies, protecting them from the red soldiers' bullets. For the medicinal brew contents included the body parts of their enemies, the very essence of their courage, so that the bravery of the whites was stolen from them and gifted, instead, to the People of Heaven.

The nature of the song changed too, the commanders of each regiment, every *induna*, adding his voice to those of the medicine men leading the massed ranks in praise of Cetshwayo kaMpande himself, the Great Elephant, the Unstoppable One.

"*UCetshwayo kaMpande!*" cried the lead voices.

And where shall my home be at the end of this thing? Shaba wondered. *Here, at a victory cleansing if I am wet with the day's blood? Perhaps seeking my father's blessing again when we have overcome the invaders? Or walking the paths of the dead?* He thought briefly about Zama, the possibility that they might be reunited. But it was unlikely, for they would not have fallen at the same time, nor in the same place. More likely that he would be separated from her for all time, alone on the Plain of the Countless Shades, fortunate if he even knew the praise names of those who wandered at his side.

He felt the Spirit Potion splash upon his shoulder. *There*, he thought, elated, sensing the stolen power flow through his flesh, *I am blessed with anger now.* He felt pride too that he had contributed to the magic. The pieces he had taken from the dung-shirts he had helped to kill yesterday. A slice of skin from the member of one. From the white forehead of another. And the third: a fat fellow with skin like milk but covered with a thousand tiny spots and hair the colour of a carrot – rare enough to be considered either a great fortune or a great curse, depending upon one's outlook. He had brought back fistfuls of the stuff. For the medicine that now soaked into his soul.

"*UCetshwayo kaMpande!*"

"*Uklwanaka Ngqengele!*" he sang.

He felt as though he was slipping away from himself, drawn from his own personal story into that of the shared nation, his past, present and future threaded like a string of beads among all those gathered here around him, all those who had stood here so many times in the past, the Spirit Potion reminding them of their common purpose – the defence of their homeland and the total destruction of those who would steal it from them.

They ate at last, thin porridge, when the sun was still low and the regiments had been dispersed to their allotted positions, the smoke from their cooking fires rolling along the hilltops.

Among the gullies on this thorn-strewn eastern rim of the plain, Shaba's Evil Omen lay within the left horn, along with the Fly Catchers, the Bender of Kings, the Leopard's Lair, the Dust Raisers, the White Tails, the Savages and the Mongrels – and the horn itself commanded by Zibhebhu. On the northern hills were the chest and loins: the Umgeni River Source, the Men from uDududu, the Frost, the Skirmishers and the Black Mambas. Somewhere on the far side, the unmarried men of the Sharp Points formed the right horn, although Shaba could see no sign of them from here, for the beast was almost four thousand paces from tip to tip. And down on the plain, away to the south, emerging from the open pass to the river, was the strangest of sights: the Fat Queen's army floating on a sea of low-lying mist.

Could it be that their Jesucristo has conjured the thing? Shaba wondered. *In the way that a great shaman of our own may do?* Yet it seemed as though the mist was slowing them, their advance almost imperceptible the formation tightly controlled. Red soldier regiments in solid blocks, creeping forward but forming the four sides of a hollow square, wagons, oxen and other units in the square's centre. As though their very encampment had become a living, crawling thing. There was music playing, flags flying – those great pieces of coloured cloth that they held so dear. At each corner were the *mbayimbayi*, drawn by teams of horses, and outside the flanks of the square rode the horse soldiers themselves. *There may be five thousand men there*, thought Shaba, *but they are in the open, moving to the killing ground. We are five times their strength. Perhaps six. And even their magic mist may not save them.*

Clusters of the horsemen could be seen breaking away now, heading up the slopes at each side of the pass and within minutes there was smoke rising from the homesteads there, particularly the larger ones at KwaBulawayo and KwaNodwengu. But those places were deserted now, the families, the cattle, the food stores all brought here, to oNdini and the surrounding royal dwellings.

'Bite the root if you have it!' shouted the *induna* of their company. 'It will not be long now.'

The old man lifted his necklace, the precious *iziqu* of willow-wood they had been awarded after the eSandlwana fight, and he began to chew on one of the pieces of *umabope* root strung among the polished beads.

Shaba fingered his own necklace, slung around his body and nestling alongside the cross-belt of black leather that carried his ammunition pouch. He looked around at the men waiting in the gulley below him. A few still vomiting from the effects of last night's ritual. But they seemed fearless enough on the whole, each taking the *induna*'s invitation in his own way, some biting their own *umabope*, others searching for whatever medicines they had privately brought with them.

'You have no snuff left?' asked Langalabelele.

In answer, Shaba shook the small bone-tipped bottle that also hung from his neck. He put an ear to it. Nothing. He smiled. He no longer had a home. Nowhere from which to prepare the ingredients of the *ugwayi*. Before Zama's death, he had thought a great deal about their lives together. Small details exactly like this. The crops they would grow. The pleasures they would share. But the receptacle of those redundant thoughts was now as empty as the bone-tipped bottle.

'But I still have my spoon,' he said. He pulled it from his hair, remembered the way he had given it to the white soldier *induna* to bite upon. To give him some comfort. To make it clear that they would treat him well as a prisoner. Well, it had shown that you could not trust them. And there would be no prisoners this day. Just the red rage of battle and killing.

'Then we can each share the other's bounty,' said Langalabelele. It was something that Umdeni might have said – if the red soldiers had not beaten out his brains.

Shaba lifted his eye-patch, rubbed at his left eye. It offered him some hazy vision now but it was a distraction and his sight was clearer, though restricted, with the leather patch in place. *Perhaps if the Witch Woman had given me just one more dose.* Langalabelele put both hands to his extended ear lobe, pushed out the round wooden pot that he normally carried there and shook it in a parody of Shaba's own earlier gesture. It gave a satisfying whisper of response.

'Ah,' he said, 'it seems that we might be in fortune!'

He carefully opened the lid and poured a small amount of the *ugwayi* powder onto the proffered spoon that Shaba sheltered with his other hand from the rising wind.

'You first,' said Shaba.

'I cannot feast before my guest has done so,' replied his companion.

So Shaba snorted the powder up one nostril, then the other. Lips tight, sniffing fast, he felt the effects almost immediately.

'A good blend,' he said.

'The best. The *nsangu* grows well at my *umuzi*. The soil suits it, I think. It is the best. The spores of the blue fungus come from the forest nearby.'

'Demon's Claw too?' said Shaba, savouring the heat that rose within him.

'So that if we should foolishly stand in the path of a red soldier's bullet, we shall feel no pain.'

Shaba pressed his lips together again, breathed deeply for a few moments.

'Then there is no more to be done,' he said, 'and this is a good day on which to die!'

They moved in silence, bent low, shields above their heads, with no more than the wave-wash welcome of the swaying grass and the breezes breaking around their ankles to mark the regiment's passing. Above them, the robin's egg sky was filling with white-backed vultures, the Cleansers, circling, multiplying and moving northward at the same lazy pace as the soldiers below, a reflection from the surface of the man-made lake that was the Fat Queen's army. *Vultures above and vultures below*, thought Shaba, wondering whether these were also a manifestation of the white men's shamans. He had heard that they sometimes summoned such creatures to fight for them. And he knew men who swore that, at eKhambule, the red soldiers had conjured packs of baboons that bit and clawed at the warriors.

The sun had completed half its climb through the morning, and the enemy had now moved almost to the centre of the plain – almost to the point, Shaba realised, that the Bull *induna*'s dung-shirts had reached the previous day. *Whey!* he thought. *We believed they were lucky to escape, the fault of our hotheads that they managed it.* But he realised now that they had run simply because they had found that which they sought – a piece of ground flat enough to accommodate this force that they brought to oNdini.

'We will break them,' whispered Langalabelele.

'Yes,' Shaba replied. 'But there will be a price to pay.'

The cost of the victory at eSandlwana had been high enough. But how many more would die to force their way through these greater numbers? All, the same, Shaba could already see and taste the slaughter they would inflict on the invaders once they had made that first gap in the red soldiers' lines, exactly as he and the uMbonambi had done all those months before.

The Fat Queen's square had swung a little so that its front face angled towards oNdini and halted. The nearest line was perhaps two thousand paces away, the dung-shirt and black-coat horsemen much closer, several men standing in their stirrups, excited, shouting to the main body, pointing towards the northern hills, the lines of warriors forming there, and the AmaZulu army's commanders that counted the Great King's brother, Prince Ziwedu, Chief Mnyamana and Ntshingwayo kaMahole Khoza among their number, as well as all the royal princes.

Shaba's section held the outer flank of their *iviyo*, their company, which was itself the furthest left of those in their Division, the *isigaba*, of the regiment, in the shallow ravine to which they had been deployed. He and the other twenty warriors of the section hugged the forward slope, generally keeping out of sight but occasionally risking a glance over the parapet edge. The grass was still damp here against his skin. He felt a tiny emerald beetle running along the finger that curled around his rifle's trigger, and he could smell the oil of the weapon's black metal. *I must remember to look for more*, he thought, *when we have destroyed them*, for he had only a few remaining drops of the precious liquid.

He peered once again over the top of the bank. The red soldiers were densely packed and roughly in two blocks on this side of their square. And dividing the two blocks was a pair of guns, though not the *mbayimbayi* to which he was accustomed. These were smaller, slender fluted barrels, though difficult to make out at this distance. But they did not seem particularly dangerous. Perhaps like the lightning screamers that had been so useless at eSandlwana. In any case, they were away to his right, pointing at a neighbouring regiment – the Savages or the White Tails perhaps.

There was a cry to his left, where the gulley curved towards the west, and the Bender of Kings was up, over the top, their shields a dark mottled brown, speckled with white spots.

'*Iya!*' they cried. 'We come to trample you!'

They surged forward to catch the rear-most troopers of the dung-shirts and black-coats. *They have a debt to settle,* he recalled, for these were the same horse soldiers that had led them to such destruction at eKhambule. And the horses wheeled and screamed, their riders loosing a ragged volley that only served to sting and enrage the iNgobamakhosi.

'We come to trample you!' they chanted at the run, their feet drumming the ground, shaking it beneath Shaba's belly. 'And where are your lightning sticks now?'

'Let them not take the bait today!' said Langalabelele, seeing the dung-shirts fall back, drawing the Bender of Kings after them. And not that one regiment alone but the Fly Catchers too, the uVe, following them in the attack. It seemed that their fears were well-founded since a gap suddenly opened at the nearest corner of the square. It was only obvious because, all at once, the red soldiers' line appeared to stretch. There were two *mbayimbayi* at that point, like the cannons still held by Cetshwayo and, beyond the guns, the white men were on the move, making space so that the dung-shirts could gallop inside the square's protective perimeter.

'The thing opens like a gate,' said Shaba. 'Like a living gate.' And he could not help being awed by the discipline involved. He looked around, expecting that they would collectively receive the order to advance while the gate remained open. But it did not come.

'Then let us hope,' said Langalabelele, 'that the Bender of Kings may hold it for us.'

Yet the red soldier line was suddenly beginning to shrink again, closing its formation as the horsemen disappeared inside. The Bender of Kings was within fifty paces of them now and the soldiers' weapons came up in a deafening rattle of wood and metal, the gunners crouched over the *mbayimbayi*.

They will be shattered again, thought Shaba, *as they were at* eKhambule.

But as he watched, the red soldiers wavered. There were a few isolated shots yet, in the main, they seemed surprised. For the mottled shields of the iNgobamakhosi, the black and dark brown of the uVe, had dropped back into the terrain's substantial cover as quickly as they had first appeared.

On the Hill of uMcungi, the commanders raised spears, called out in unison, a haunting cry that filled the emaHlabithini plain.

"*Lord-of-the-Sky! Guide us this day!*" they sang.

Their spears swept towards the west, towards the right horn. To the south, towards Zibhebhu's waiting left horn regiments. And straight ahead, towards the square itself.

Shaba caught a quick glimpse of the Bender of Kings and the Fly Catchers over the top of his shield, saw them rise again like a dark cloud, no more than a hundred paces from the enemy and thundering forward at the charge. No war cries now, just the deadly intent of slaughter on their minds. They advanced, Shaba knew, with all the pride that their history had bestowed on them, facing their future and their destiny with the same equanimity that protected them whenever they were forced to watch their mealie crops devoured by locust or swept away by the wind and rain. They were challenged this day to preserve their freedom or to die in its defence. A line drawn. A line crossed. The force of it all filled him. Yet, despite the *ugwayi* and his own battle frenzy, he still experienced a bout of nausea, a tightness and tingling in his groin, the fear of mutilation. Then his own *induna* was behind him.

'Trample them!' he shouted. 'Blow them away!'

And Shaba was up with his section, the death lust upon him, one of those designated to advance just ahead of the regiment, the best marksmen, thinly spread but with their rifles ready, to keep the red soldiers pinned while the main body closed for the kill. But he had not expected the storm. He had felt the breeze earlier, yet this…? It was like walking into the wildest of winds, when you could lean forward at an impossible angle and still not fall. A hurricane here, though, of lead. Lead and sound. Sound so vile, so ugly, that it deafened him. At his side, one man after another was hurled back into the gulley. Some never even managed to climb over the top. To his left, the married men of the Dust Raisers, the uThulwana, were up too, but in a solid body of white shields, red dappled markings. A proud regiment that now incorporated some of the older *amabutho*, the Sulphurs and the iNkonkoni. They stood briefly to howl their war cry against the Fat Queen.

'*Mina!*' they shouted, then immediately beat spear hafts against shield hide. '*Mina! Mina!*'

Then they sprang forward into the storm.

The sound of the rifles was almost as overwhelming as their bullet storm, though Shaba ran through it, Langalabelele still close to him, but less than half his section still standing. *When the regiment comes behind us*, he thought, *we will avenge them.* Them and Zama too. Umdeni. His cattle. All the others things they had lost. He knelt near a thorn bush, fired into the red line ahead of him. Others did the same. And he saw several of the soldiers fall. It was almost impossible to miss them. Yet he needed to keep moving, try to maintain this thin screen for the ranks that would come behind. He wanted to turn, to make sure that they were, indeed, there. For he had never felt so alone in all his life, could not imagine how this hailstone downpour of metal had not already touched him.

Shaba experienced that strange sensation when all the colours of the day were suddenly muted, leaked into the soil to leave nothing but images in tones of grey and, even then, only those images upon which a warrior sensed the need to focus for his survival, seen through a narrowing tunnel of vision. But he could feel the battle fury slipping from him already. *So early*, he thought, though it flared again as he heard the familiar cries at his back.

'We are the Evil Omen! We are the boys from eSandlwana!'

The drumming on shields then the shaking ground that caused all the scents of the earth, of their land, to rise and fill him. He ran on; saw more of his section fall, many of the Dust Raisers too. He was firing as he moved now, no need to stop, no cause to aim. The ground erupted not far away. A shell from the *mbayimbayi*. An explosion of dirt and stone. A cloud of dust hurled into the air. And floating through the cloud, slow and lazy, the heads and legs and arms of warriors. The men from the uThulwana began to fall in heaps, as though they had been tipped there like firewood, or hung as garlands, ripened fruit, on the branches of low thorn-trees. The earth itself had become crazed, torn by steel and iron, heaving and bucking, wreathed in sour smoke, crops of dead springing up wherever the shell seeds were scattered. Yet he ran on towards the square, able to see now that the line facing them was four men deep, the front two lines kneeling, the second two standing behind. Shaba dived into a hole in the ground, perhaps five paces across, scooped out by an earlier shell while the gunners were finding their range. Several others fell on top of him, converging in the tiny sanctuary. Langalabelele gripped his arm, his eyes wide, nostrils flaring.

'This is not like the others,' he said.

Shaba pulled his arm free.

'What did you expect?' he snarled, and fumbled for his pouch, drew out one of the round-headed bullets in its brass casing, pushed forward the breech lever, slid home the round. He pulled the lever home again, sighted quickly and fired. The butt jarred into his bare shoulder, the gun's report catching him by surprise as it always did. The cordite smell acrid, stinging in his eye.

He grabbed Langalabelele by his cross-belts, dragged him upright and behind him as he left the crater. A rapid glance behind showed the rest of the regiment at their heels. Some of the regiment anyhow. He wondered briefly whether the rest might still be in the gulley. But then he saw the numbers that were down. The failed and faceless dead. The mouthless ones. Those that war had turned to dung, their summers all spent, their fruits all harvested at once. The shells of the *mbayimbayi* were coming more often, shrieking and ripping through their lines and dripping with their blood. The warriors tripped and fell, one upon the other, their insides spilling, storage gourds, tipped and smashed, mealies trickling out upon the ground. Yet those still living were overtaking him in their haste to settle accounts.

Shaba fired and fired again, pushing his way through the heat, the smoke, the solid barrier of sound and fury that dizzied him.

The company's *induna* ran until his lifeless legs could carry him no more, empty fingers reaching towards his necklace until the knees buckled and he crashed forward onto his shield.

"*Bite the root if you have it!*" Shaba remembered him saying.

The old man had been a true lion, a leader of lions. And Shaba spared a fleeting thought for that other ancient, Zama's grandfather, wondered if he yet lived. There was a chance perhaps if, like his own company and regiment, the uMxapho had also managed to reach this zone that suddenly seemed so safe. The wall of noise from the enemy rifles, the vile storm of lead that poured from them, had not lessened. Yet there was a relative stillness, and he realised they had passed beyond the ground that the *mbayimbayi* could pound from their positions at the corner of the red soldiers' square. Hope and anger filled him in equal measure. He fired; saw a soldier fall at the point where he had aimed.

'*USuthu!*' he yelled, leaping forward.

The enemy line seemed suddenly to shudder and tremble. He could almost smell their fear and uncertainty. A line of heads appeared above the rest. Horse soldiers mounting, he realised, as one of their beasts reared and snorted, plainly visible. There were white *izinduna*, also mounted, shouting, screaming at the wavering ranks of their men. Shaba was perhaps forty paces from them, maybe even less, and he knew now that he and his section would soon be among them. Their own fire was intensifying, though it was still ragged. *Why can we not fire volleys like the whites?* he wondered. But ragged or not, they still caused damage in those tightly packed ranks. More red soldiers falling. And he knew they must break the square. Now or never. The bullets from the Fat Queen's army were lessening, men beginning to press back among their fellows, those wicked steel bayonets wavering, the unsteady looking around for reassurance or instruction, their officers still yelling at them.

'We are the boys from eSandlwana!' yelled Langalabelele.

The chant was taken up by those behind, and all along the line, though it was punctuated by a new sound, a strange sound that ranged alongside the musketry. *Clack, clack, clack.* It was so rhythmic that Shaba initially assumed it must emanate from the AmaZulu army itself. *Clack, clack, clack.* But his eye was drawn to the right, along the front of their advance where warriors were now being tossed aside with mechanical precision, ripened crops ready for the reaping and falling with a harvester's efficiency. *Clack, clack, clack.* They crumbled, swept sideways, as the machine passed its blade further along the line, and Shaba's eye was drawn to the source, the centre of the red soldiers' formation, the point where the two blocks joined, the guns that he had seen earlier. Those harmless things, smaller than the *mbayimbayi*. It seemed to take a whole team of blue-jackets to tend them, handles to be cranked, revolving fluted barrels to be swung, raised or depressed; great sticks to be fed into their bellies. But the appetite for AmaZulu souls was unquenchable. *Clack, clack, clack.* The machines fed voraciously, their victims squirming and crawling upon the earth, grubbing in the dirt, gasping for air, fighting the demons come to possess them, finally drowning in their own liquids. The force of the guns' firepower blasted and battered breast and eye, and wherever it failed to find flesh, it deluged them with clods of grass and earth. Shaba found that he was no longer moving in a straight line but, rather, running in a series of zigzags, a hunted creature. There were terrible visions around him, one warrior with both his arms shorn off at the elbows and, next to that one, a man similarly dispossessed of each leg. The raucous chorus of the heaped and groaning wounded.

Something slapped hard against his own shoulder, an impact that stung and burned, and then went numb. He could feel nothing, dropped his rifle, wondered casually whether his own arm had been severed. But he refused the urge to survey it, kept his head raised, knew that the instant he looked down, he was dead. *Keep moving*, he told himself. *Keep moving.* But he was running out of breath now. And he had no idea what he would do in the event that he even reached the enemy line. He stopped, as those around him had stopped also. For as far as he could see. They had all stopped. As though each of those that remained had simultaneously realised the futility, the inevitability. They seemed to stand for a long time, the bullets continuing to eat them – though still defiant, spears beating against shields, or being shaken in the air.

Then Langalabelele spun against him, knocking Shaba down. His friend was clutching at his stomach, a neat hole was pumping blood through his writhing fingers. His back arched from the dirt, the pain tearing at him, a wild beast within, trying to rip its way out, another man's brains splashed across his face.

'I am thirsty,' Langalabelele cried. Shaba could neither help nor comfort him. He looked at his own arm finally, though he feared doing so, saw that it was still there, a simple gash in his shoulder, though bleeding profusely. He forced his fingers to move, clumsily cradled Langalabelele's head in the crook of his elbow, squeezed the face against his chest. 'And I am cold,' hissed the warrior, muffled and through clenched teeth.

'All will be well,' said Shaba at last. He set his shield and spears aside, reached to the lobe of Langalabelele's ear, pulled free the small wooden box that should have contained his *ugwayi*. *Perhaps it will ease his pain*, he thought, though when he shook it, the thing was empty.

'You are with lies, my friend,' said the other. 'A warrior should not die with a lie in his ears.'

'And that is the truth,' Shaba replied, as Langalabelele's light went out.

He set his friend down, looked around. It was over. Everywhere, the regiments were in retreat, whatever was left of them.

233

Shaba stood. The firing had stopped and the red soldiers were cheering, wild with elation. But he knew the thing that would come next, for he remembered the aftermath of eKhambule. He was exhausted, empty and ashamed, though he knew he must run. Find strength from somewhere. He forced his legs to move, abandoning his weapons, even the royal shield. And as he ran, he looked behind him, saw the enemy line stretch again, the Long Spear horsemen surging from the square, gathering speed, racing towards KwaNodwengu, away to the south, and gaining on the regiments, fugitives now in their own homeland.

Shaba fled eastward, unable to recognise even one of the many others around him climbing the ridge. And the *mbayimbayi* had started firing again. The rest was no more than a game of chance. Below him, and at points along the slope, there were clusters of horse soldiers. Dung-jackets, Basuto riders and black-coats. They rode in strange patterns, laughing and shouting like excited children, weaving and turning at the heels of whichever group of warriors they were pursuing, light gleaming on sword blades as they rose and fell. He looked up, saw that the sun itself had barely moved, the morning still only half gone. Had it frozen in the sky? Or had so much destruction and death been wrought in so small a space of time? Closer to him there were still clouds of filth thrown up noisily here and there, shells from the big guns laying down a creeping barrage further and further ahead of the horsemen. It was difficult, however, to make out anything either to the north or west, the smoke and distance making it hard to be precise, though it seemed that the Great King's army was in full retreat everywhere. Yet the Hill of Umcijo, at least, was visible enough, empty, the commanders no longer there.

Only to the south could he see clearly, where a well-rehearsed dance was taking place, the regiments from the left horn-tip climbing uphill in three extended lines while the Long Spears followed behind in a line of their own, one that would surge forward now and again, catch the rear-most of the fugitives, pause, thrust, withdraw. Then the gap would re-open until the beat of the dance called them forward once more, the steps and the slaughter repeated.

Shaba was thankful to be beyond their reach, though he felt like a coward, barely injured and here among so many walking wounded, struggling up through the long grasses and gullies. A man with sightless eyes stretched out to him, slipping and sliding on a pool of blood, reaching with his toes, no longer able to see the path he should take. Some clutched at gut wounds as they fled, each of them emitting the same rhythmic groan and calling for water. Those with broken arms or shattered shoulders adopted a careful gait of their own. And men with injuries to their buttocks crawled universally on all fours, one of them with the sharp white edge of a rump bone protruding from his arse. Most of them could not survive, he knew, and would soon join the ranks of those already departed here – the grinning dead, or those with terror now fixed forever on their faces – or those for whom the journey was almost complete, though not quite, the whiteness in their quarter-open eyes a measure of their distance along the path toward the Land of Shades. And even those with diminishing sight could not avert their partial gaze from the vultures that had now come so much closer, a few already landed, but hopping in circles, pinions spread wide, seeking those who were truly dead and far from the company of the still living. *What has this valley done to you, Lord-of-the-Sky*, Shaba wondered, *that you require such payment?*

Shaba grabbed a handful of grass and hauled himself up, over the lip of a gulley, heard the welcome sound of a stream somewhere near, fell upon its bank and doused water on the dirt and rifle powder that grimed his face, drank greedily to quench his thirst. He believed for a moment that he might be the only one to have survived the slaughter, then realised that all survivors must always imagine themselves unique, alone. And he was far from alone. Clusters of the wandering wounded were here ahead of him and, a few paces away, one young warrior tried to push himself free of two others who had collapsed on top of him, died there.

'Water!' the boy moaned, unable to extricate himself or reach the spring.

Shaba cupped his hands, gathered some of the cool liquid and carried it carefully to the wounded warrior, held it to his lips. The man lapped greedily at his palms, then laid his head upon the grass. Shaba lifted first one corpse from him, then the other, but the warrior was badly shot through the ribs and beyond further help. Yet several others had taken up the same plea, the torment of their thirst made even more intolerable by the stream's proximity and the impossibility of reaching it.

He looked around for something in which to carry the water and eventually found a blackened goatskin bottle on the body of an *udibi* boy. He filled it and began the slow process of moving from group to group. At first he moved cautiously, watching for any sign of the red soldiers' approach. He could hear them, though not see them from within the *udonga*; feel the explosions from the *mbayimbayi* too, a shell occasionally screaming through the sky above this ridge, exploding in the air to rain chunks of iron and steel among the already stricken. And sometimes a stray bullet would whine overhead as though it had a life of its own. *What does their song mean?* he wondered. *Why will this battle not rest now?* But the thing still twitched and writhed and moaned as much as its victims. So Shaba passed among them, dispensing a few drops of pity here, a few more there. But it was a futile task, for the women of all these would be left behind to warble their grief, to clutch and grasp at their children.

*

The barking alerted him. He had been tending a warrior of the Dust Raisers who slipped in and out of consciousness. A spread-winged vulture balanced close at hand, studying the wounded man with all the intensity of an *inyanga* trying to divine the root of a patient's illness. It shook its ugly, naked head from time to time, flapped backwards whenever the warrior opened his eyes or Shaba shook his fist, tossed a stone. But the creature refused to abandon its carrion.

'Vultures above and vultures below,' Shaba whispered, then froze when he heard the yapping. He curled closer to the dying man, peering over his heaving chest and saw that, barely a spear's cast away, six horsemen had crested the ridge behind him. He should not have stayed so long. He cursed himself. They were Basuto riders, those dung-shirts of the abeSuthu that fought for the red soldiers, broad-brimmed hats with red bands around the crown. They were commanded, it seemed, by a white *induna*, a man with a pale blue jacket who directed his slave-boys to a couple of beaten veterans. Shaba had given them water earlier and they were more exhausted by age than by their wounds. But the dog jumped around them, a white thing like that which had tried to defend the French Prince – the foolish animal that Langalabelele had speared. *Foolish*, thought Shaba, *yet it was the only living beast that tried to save the iFulentshi that day!* But this one was simply a sniffer for the Basuto riders. They were pressing the old men with questions now, their IsiZulu good, for though their own tongue was very different, it was still a language of the Bantu, the People, those who inhabited these southern lands.

'Is your king still at oNdini?' they asked.

Or, 'Where are your reserve regiments?'

Or, 'What has happened to your commanders?'

And the men were happy to answer the questions honestly. For it was a polite conversation, the Basuto riders showing proper respect to the AmaZulu captives who were, after all, due every deference that old age conferred.

'Have you told us everything, Baba?' said one of the riders, finally.

'Yes,' said each of the veterans at the same time.

Then the dung-shirt looked to his white *induna* master, who nodded in response. The Basuto took his revolver and shot the first old man in the head, then the second. The dog barked again, scampered in widening circles, came near to Shaba, growled at him, but then became distracted by the vulture. The bird almost fell over its own legs as it tried to retreat, the white dog chasing after it, yapping and panting.

Shaba breathed a sigh of relief when the Basuto riders mounted again, shouting at each other in their own idiom, laughing at the dog's antics. They were about to ride off when the dog gave up its chase, turned back, stood still for a moment, tail wagging, then retraced its steps, nose to the ground, tongue lolling from its mouth. It looked at Shaba again, sniffed at him, began barking afresh.

He lay still, tried to ignore the thing, to hold his breath, pressing his cheek to the grass alongside the now dead Dust Raiser. He heard the horses approach, the easy creak and chime of their harness, the snorting babble of their breathing. He could smell the friendly warmth of their hides, the strange scent of the white *induna*. There was a command that he did not understand, then the unmistakeable sound of a gun being cocked. Shaba opened his eye, looked up into the gleaming teeth of a dung-shirt who leaned down from the saddle, revolver pointing – and death peered back at him.

Yet it was a strange thing that happened next. First, it occurred to Shaba, that something or somebody rose at his side, a shape that was both tall and lithe. The Basuto rider must have seen it too, for he lifted the revolver, using it to shield his eyes. And, at the same moment, just beyond the white *induna*, two unscathed warriors broke from the cover in which they had been hiding, leaping over tussocks and rocks to put distance between themselves and the horsemen. The white man cried out, whooping loudly, and set heels to his mount, putting his beast to the pursuit, his Basutos galloping behind.

And even the dung-shirt who had pointed his revolver at Shaba seemed to have forgotten him, for he was now trying to catch the rest, the yapping dog scampering alongside.

Chapter Seventeen

Sunday 13th July 1879

In the palm-shaded and dusty square of Durban's loop-holed colonial courthouse, the band of Her Majesty's Royal Marines struck up *The Death of Nelson*.

'I shall miss your company, Carey,' said Surgeon-Major O'Reilly, as they climbed the steps to the building's verandah and entrance.

'And you, sir,' Carey replied, 'have been the most sympathetic of gaolers, if you don't mind me saying so.'

'You should not do so too widely though,' said the Irishman. 'It might be taken the wrong way. And I would like to have said that it's been a pleasure – if you had not been in such straits.'

In practice, Carey had only been in his charge over the past four days, the most recent of those that he had spent under arrest. First, there had been the sullen and disrespectful Lieutenant French-Brewster, the Divisional Deputy-Provost Marshal, for the six-day journey from the Upoko camp to Utrecht, following confirmation by Colonel Bellairs that Carey would be sent for embarkation to England, remaining in custody until Her Majesty had made a decision on the Court Martial's findings – although, perversely, Carey still did not know the exact nature of those findings themselves. Second, he had been placed under the supervision of Surgeon-Major Dudley, Carey having first given his parole, his promise of good conduct. And just as well, since Dudley was hardly in a position to enforce Carey's captivity, the Surgeon-Major himself suffering from some recurring fever that warranted his own return home as an invalid. But Dudley was nominally the senior officer within the column of sick and wounded that Carey joined for the march from Utrecht to Pietermaritzburg. And third, in that latter town, when the column was joined by a further group of casualties from the Officers' Hospital, one of whom warranted special care and the personal attention of Surgeon-Major O'Reilly, who then assumed responsibility for the prisoner.

'I hope, sir, that we shall be able to renew our acquaintance on the *Euphrates*,' said Carey.

'I only pray, Carey, that the trip back to the Cape will be less eventful than your outward journey. You have something of a reputation as a Jonah, sure.'

O'Reilly slapped him on the shoulder. Carey liked him, had followed the instruction that he should not discuss the details of his case, but those details seemed to be common knowledge, and the Surgeon-Major had made no bones of his sympathy for Carey's predicament.

'Do you sail from the Cape too, sir?'

They climbed the marble staircase to the first floor administration offices.

'It's straight back here for me, I fear. Once we get to Cape Town and you transfer to the troopship. It's the *Jumna*, isn't it? If so, she has her own Surgeon-Major. Capital chap. The Colonel will be in good hands. Though I'm sure he'll appreciate some more of your Longfellow.'

The second of O'Reilly's two charges was Major Robert Hackett, who had been shot by a Zulu marksman at Khambula – shot through the head at a range of two hundred yards. The bullet had passed through one side of his skull and out through the other. He was the same fellow Carey had discussed with Colonel Davies all those months ago at Griffin's Farm. By rights, Hackett should be dead, yet he still lived. A miracle. Assisted by O'Reilly's medical team, that was true, but a miracle all the same. He could still barely speak, but he had brightened considerably when, on his first night in O'Reilly's charge, Carey had offered to read *The Song of Hiawatha* at the Major's bedside. And Hackett had brightened still further when he had been permitted to clamp the stem of his ivory tobacco pipe between his teeth.

In the office temporarily assigned to Lieutenant-Colonel Bland-Hunt, commanding officer of the Marines Battalion, O'Reilly and Carey each snapped to attention and saluted. The Irishman then passed over the orders he had received – as he himself had received them from the hands of Surgeon-Major Dudley – written in the neat, standard writing style employed by Colonel Bellairs and all others who were well-educated and held positions of authority.

'Sit, gentlemen, if you please,' said Lieutenant-Colonel Bland-Hunt, hatless and seated behind a leather-topped desk. He was, Carey guessed, in his late-forties, a weathered face with white crow's feet around his eyes; moustache and side-burns neatly trimmed. He smelled strongly of soap and, as he read the single sheet of instruction, he could not help glancing frequently towards the open window through which the medley of military marches continued to stir the soul: *Heart of Oak*, then *Greensleeves*. 'So, Carey,' he said at last, 'what are we to do with you, eh?'

The unspoken point, thought Carey. *Army prisoner handed over to the Navy.*

'If I may, sir,' O'Reilly intervened. 'The Lieutenant has given his parole and observed its terms to the letter. Might it be possible…'

'Thank you, Major,' said Bland-Hunt. 'It was a rhetorical question. We have our own Provost-Marshal. Already spoken with him. Unusual case though, being sent all the way back to England without knowing your fate. Must be some temptation to cut and run, Carey?'

Carey met the Lieutenant-Colonel's grey eyes with as much defiance as the difference in their ranks might allow.

'I do not doubt that Her Majesty's decision will be other than just, sir,' he said. 'She is, after all, anointed in the name of the Almighty. It shall be the Lord that guides her hand in this matter, I think.'

'All the same, a long time to wait for judgement.'

A long time, Jahleel, thought Carey. *God waits!* He was tempted to be clever, but decided against it.

'Yes, sir,' he said. 'A long time.'

'Well,' said Bland-Hunt, 'you seem a decent and God-fearing fellow. Anglican?'

'Indeed, sir.'

'Very good. Parole it is then. Have enough to do here already, Carey. Grand Old Duke of York has nothing on this one. Their Lordships send nine hundred of their finest all the way to the far side of the world, then turn us round without a shot fired and ship us all the way back again. Extraordinary! Well, that's the requirements of the service for you, I suppose.'

Carey knew that the Plymouth, Portsmouth and Chatham Divisions of the Marines had been dispatched early in June and only arrived here in Durban after Chelmsford's victory at Ulundi. Too late to share the glory of their fellow-Marines landed from vessels like the *Active,* or the straw-hat matelots who formed the rest of the Naval Brigade. And now the Battalion was returning to the respective dockyards from whence they had come. Aboard the *Euphrates* and then the *Jumna,* to Suez and England.

'I was sorry to have missed the battle too, sir,' he said.

Bland-Hunt looked at him, folded the orders.

'Yes,' he nodded. 'So you must be. Chance to acquit yourself, eh? Well, you'll be quartered at the Alexandra Hotel with my Provost-Marshal until we sail. Young Heseletine. Under his supervision, Carey. That clear?'

Clear? Yes, thought Carey. *That's the word. I shall return to England and clear my good name.*

'Perfectly, sir,' he replied.

'Then you'd better take these with you, Lieutenant,' said Bland-Hunt. He reached into a desk drawer and placed a bundle of letters on the green leather surface, patting them. 'And give you joy of the good news and comfort I hope they bring.'

Carey stared at the bundle. There had been times when he would have given anything for some succour from home, but he was now confused, unable to calculate whether word of the dishonour heaped upon him could already have reached his family and they, in turn, had time to relay their reproaches. Of course, the French correspondent, Deléage, and the corpse of young Louis, should have arrived in London only days before. And therefore nobody could possibly have written to him so soon. But this logic was lost in the strange compression of time that Carey had been experiencing since the Court Martial. He picked the bundle from the desk, tried to smile.

'I was wondering, sir,' he said, 'whether I might be allowed to attend Church Parade today?'

O'Reilly had escorted him to the Alexandra, a relatively new place, at the southern end of Point Road, near the narrow entrance to Durban's natural harbour, with fine views of the Bluff and Salisbury Island on the far side of the bay. The hotel was single-storey, louvred doors and windows, built around a central terrace, which served mostly as a mess and dining room for those Marine officers currently billeted there.

But the terrace was empty just now, apart from its infestation of mosquitoes, so Carey braved their whine and bite, took tea, picked up a copy of the *Cape and Natal News*, settled in a wicker chair with his letters. It was a damned curious state of affairs, he knew, this business of being under arrest. How long had it been now? Almost a month. And not as he had imagined. His expectation of confinement, perhaps some physical restriction – shackles, for example – had only been even remotely met during the initial week's ride to Utrecht. But then it had seemed that the further he progressed from the Front, and certainly the further he mixed with ranks below those of his former fellow-staff officers, the more sympathy his case began to attract. At least among the military, if not the civilian population.

It had been Sister Janet who had first put the thought of a crusade in his mind. She was one of the few who had treated him with any civility at Utrecht. He had been shunned almost totally by Doctor Fitzmaurice, by Landrost Rudolph, and by the town's resident Englishman, James White. They had been standing among the silent crowd that gathered to see him ride in, sneered at him, White spitting on the ground. He had suffered a strange experience too, when entering the hospital tent so that Deputy-Provost Marshal French-Brewster could deliver him into the fever-ridden hands of Surgeon-Major Dudley. Somebody had been singing.

'We don't want to fight but, by jingo, if we do,
We've got the ships, we've got the men, and got the money too.'

Carey had spun on his heel, almost expecting to see Louis, believing against all hope, just for a moment…

But it was simply one of the orderlies. And then Sister Janet Wells had appeared in her familiar grey ward dress. She was clutching a brass toilet pot, stopped when she saw him. No initial expression. None of the delighted surprise that he thought was his due. But she seemed to sense his pain and set the metal pan aside, greeted him with a reluctant smile, but the first he had seen in a month. Later, she had listened carefully as he poured out his grief, despite the stricture against discussing his case, and urged him to clear his name. Perhaps the newspapers might help. The Church too. Yes, certainly the Church.

Psalms 55:23, he remembered. *"But thou, O God, shalt bring them down into the pit of destruction: bloody and deceitful men shall not live out half their days; but I will trust in thee."*

Her words had strengthened him on the road towards the coast, and he had been further buoyed by the normality with which he was treated by those in whose company he travelled. Only at Griffin's Farm had he suffered a setback, since Griffin himself would not allow him in the house and each member of the family treated him like a leper.

Carey thought about Sister Janet again now, picked up his bundle of letters, shuffling them in his hands. Yet each time the cursive peculiarities of Annie's penmanship came to the top, he could not bring himself to open the thing. *Later*, he thought. *I will save it for later. When my humour is improved.* So he settled with the *Cape and Natal*, studied the trade and shipping report, then the text of a telegram from Wolseley to the Secretary of State for War, confirming the consolidation of his forces in the aftermath of Ulundi, the fact that Cetshwayo was still suing for peace but no longer able to field any meaningful host. Wolseley was apparently at Pietermaritzburg and still not joined up with Chelmsford – though Chelmsford was now clearly demoted to a subordinate role.

There were more details of the battle itself, naturally. The Zulu dead were now numbered as two thousand from an estimated force of twenty thousand, while the British casualties were confirmed as three officers and ten other ranks killed, seventy more wounded. "Isandlwana avenged," claimed the correspondent. Every one of Ulundi's kraals razed to the ground, a sketched image of Cetshwayo's European-style house wreathed in smoke and flame. Four thousand huts burned, they said. A wall of fire that raged around the hills of the EmaHlabithini Plain for a distance of seven miles.

Among the dead, it seemed, was the Honourable William Drummond –Chelmsford's Head Adviser, his Chief of Intelligence. Ironically, to Carey's mind, he had been slain when the battle itself was over, cut off by a party of Zulus while the kraals were being destroyed, his body left naked on the veld apart from his boots and spurs. *Probably drunk again*, thought Carey. As he had been when they last met, on the occasion he had interviewed that rogue of McTeague's. Cornscope, of course. The first nightmare revelation that he might be the *same* McTeague he had known in Honduras. And all the information that McTeague was comfortably ensconced at Emoyeni with a harem of concubines. *Is he still there?* Carey wondered. *Living a life of luxury*

242

while our army counts its dead? Well, one thing was certain – that those deals Cornscope had been attempting to broker on the Major's behalf must all now have perished along with the Honourable William Drummond.

A final article caught Carey's eye. It was the copy of a letter from a Sergeant of the Licensed Native Labourers confirming that six Zulu warriors, men who had fought against the British at Isandlwana, had recently gone willingly to England as part of a theatrical troupe. The letter took the form of a contractual arrangement, that the Zulus in question would be well-treated and brought safely back to the Colony when the terms of their employment expired. Meanwhile they would perform in a show: "The Great Farini," at the Royal Westminster Aquarium. *Table d'hote.* What a peculiar world it seemed.

The letter from Annie, he realised with a shudder, was dated 1st June. And, as he unfolded the pages, it now occurred to him that the Alexandra's all-pervading essence of oak barrel was the same odour he associated with their first meeting, at her father's modest plantation and thriving rum distillery on the outskirts of Falmouth, Jamaica. He imagined her as he had seen her then. Seventeen years old. Not an especially pretty girl, but with a flashing personality so immediately evident from her darting dark eyes. His vision of her was always thus, in the guise of a younger Annie Vine. And he saw her in that form now, seated at the writing desk of their modest home, the infant Pel in his crib at her side and Little Edie playing with her wooden Noah's Ark animals upon the Tianjin rug.

> *My dearest husband,*
> *I trust that my words may reach you speedily and shall find you safe and sound. I know that the Lord will protect you, however, and that you are in His hands. But I prayed fervently during this morning's service that He might reunite us before too much longer.*
> *They say that the American President, Mister Hayes, has recently installed a telephonic apparatus in his office, though the poor man had nobody with whom to share this wonder except the machine's inventor, Mister Graham Bell. I therefore imagined the wildest of fantasies on reading this, of course, dear heart – that I might have access to such a machine and that you, likewise, may have its mate with you in Darkest Africa, so that we could converse with each other over their connecting wire. It was a foolishness, of course, but the thought itself brought me closer to you.*

He scanned the rest of the script, knowing that there could not, in reality, be any mention of his misfortune, yet still needing to reassure himself. There were references to the children – though, disappointingly, no mention of their

243

lost Jahleel Junior on this occasion. No mention either of his promotion – the promotion that he knew now would never be his but word of which, hope against hope, he thought may have reached Annie's ears. It would, he felt, have bolstered her against the shock of his grave news when she finally had to confront it. Almost a consolation prize.

> *I took tea with your Ma and Pa last Thursday, and Reverend Carey was most outraged by the tricks being employed by "General" William Booth in attracting crowds to the evangelical meetings of his "Salvation Army." Your father thinks him the worst of mountebanks.*

Papa, thought Carey. *How in Heaven might I explain all of this to him?* Yet his idea of a crusade against the injustice he had suffered already began to embrace his father – or, at least, his father's pulpit. He was influential within the Church and, so long as Carey could put the matter to him correctly, so long as the newspapers at home were less than venomous towards his case, there was every possibility that Papa might discover an Old Testament zeal for his case.

Leviticus 16:10. "But the goat, on which the lot fell to be the scapegoat, shall be presented alive before the Lord, to make an atonement with him, and to let him go for a scapegoat into the wilderness."

The other letters included a missive from his mother, which paid scant regard to any family news but obtusely criticised his own infrequent letters home by asking whether, by any chance, he had lost the Parkins & Giotto writing slope she had gifted to him. She did, of course, detail in substantial depth her own latest literary success, praised the works of Pfeiffer and condemned those of Bevington. Yet her purest adulation was reserved for *Monsieur* Hugo, his recently published *L'Art d'Être Grand-Père*.

> *…Which reminds me, my dear, that we have been reading all about His Royal Highness, Prince Eugène Louis…*

Carey felt an ice-cold figure tread upon his proverbial grave.

> *"…sailing so bravely to join you in our struggle against the savage foe. I trust that, in the likely event of your encounter, you will wish him bon courage from this most sincere of his admirers."*

And there it was. It may be feasible to enlist some support from Papa in his cause, but the scandal, the woe that his mother must be bearing at this very moment would, in all likelihood, break her heart.

He angrily ripped open the three remaining envelopes, a trio of notes, it transpired, from those creditors who persisted in pursuing him around the globe rather than dealing, as instructed, directly with his bank. An outstanding bill for repairs to some storm-damaged roof tiles. Another from his tailor. The last from Pearl & Company.

What an impertinence! he thought, recalling the boots that had, eventually, disintegrated entirely in this climate.

Heseltine, it transpired, was five years his senior and returned promptly to the Alexandra so that Carey might be escorted to Church Parade.

'It's a most damnable country, don't you think?' he said, as they took the train that ran along the bay, from the Point to the town centre almost three miles away.

Thick green bushes grew on each side of the track, which passed the Addington district's new hospital where O'Reilly was now caring for Major Hackett. Then the waterfront warehouses and barracks where the Bantu and Hindu dock workers were housed.

'Rains in torrents all night,' the Captain continued, 'and blows a gale by day.'

There was a ramshackle tin village behind the barracks too, coolie huts and kraals to house the newest influxes of migrant workers to help deal with the town's expansion.

'A place to be avoided at night?' said Carey.

'At night? Heavens, no. It's the very thing, Carey. Singing and dancing. Decent beer, on the whole. Doxies of every colour. Have to watch yourself, of course. But no different from anywhere else. Lots of Chinese. Cunning buggers. Portugee blacks too. And Malay card-sharps. But the rest are fine chaps.'

'Looks like a fire hazard.'

'Oh, the Inspector of Nuisances is supposed to be investigating that.'

They crossed Cato's Creek to the station then alighting, walked the Embankment until they headed up the track leading back to the Court House. It was a fine morning and, as it happened, Carey thought the current season relatively benign.

'If you think the weather's bad,' he remarked, 'you should have been here in the rainy season.'

Heseltine took it as a jest, slapped him amiably on the back as they turned onto Pine Street and headed for Saint Paul's. There was the heady smell of freshly baked bread, the cry of Hindu hawkers selling peanuts from their shoulder baskets.

'What a rum fellow you are, Carey,' laughed the Captain. 'Rum fellows together, eh?' And he went on to admit that his role as Provost-Marshal seemed something of an irony since he, himself, had only recently suffered the punitive injustice of the civil courts under the terms of the Bankruptcy

Act, 1869. 'Judged me *in absentia*,' he said. 'Confound them all. The merchant classes and the money-lenders alike, wouldn't you say? Happy enough to have the likes of you and me out here, chancing our skins to save them from the Zulus. Different kettle of fish though, when our paltry stipend won't pay for even the modesties.'

Carey doubted that Pearl & Company would view themselves as seriously at risk from a Zulu attack and, therefore, set any form of civic gratitude above their thirst for profit.

'It's a poor show,' he agreed, as they passed a row of the settlement's original wattle and daub cottages before reaching the Market Square and the path to the church itself. As they waited outside among the gathered congregation he ruminated on the Captain's bile, turning it over in his mouth, swallowing it afresh. He was sure that Heseltine must be a profligate fellow to become bankrupt and, while his own financial situation was precarious, he had managed, as a gentleman should, to marginally avoid a similar state of affairs. A promotion, of course, would have made all the difference, his pay increased by almost half.

'No offence, Carey,' said Heseltine, 'but is there a finer sight in all the world?'

He looked with open adoration at the dark blue jackets and trousers of the three Royal Marine Divisions. The bandmaster brought *Abide With Me* to a solemn end, the Roman Catholics were required to fall out, march to their own place of worship, and the remainder filed behind Lieutenant-Colonel Bland-Hunt as he led them inside to fill the pews opposite the local townsfolk. It was fortunate that Saint Paul's had been constructed with future potential capacity in mind. The style was modern, however, and not quite to Carey's taste. Cream-coloured façade and central bell tower, red-tiled roof.

The service was taken by the Marines' Chaplain, Reverend Smith, who took as his theme the virtues of patience. It was plainly aimed at his flock of blue-jackets and presumably to appease their sense of frustration at having, so to speak, missed the boat. But patience was a subject that now grated considerably upon Carey. *If patience is a virtue*, he thought, *the virtuous must first find the tolerance to be patient with themselves.*

'And the Gospels remind us,' the Chaplain was saying, '"*But let patience have her perfect work, that ye may be perfect and entire, wanting nothing.*"'

He thought once again, *God waits! And I am content to await the judgement of Your mercy, Lord.* Nothing was more important than the aspiration of admittance into the Kingdom of Heaven, of having young Jahleel restored to him. *But, Almighty Father, would it not be possible to ease my burden, even just a little, not for my own sake but perhaps for that of my wife and family?* In a few days it would be his thirty-second birthday. Was he not entitled to one single opportunity without having the rug pulled from beneath his feet? But God responded with a crushing vision.

The congregation's constituent parts were lustily singing *My Soul With Patience Waits,* and the sunlight pierced the only stained-glass within Saint Paul's, the beasts of the field depicted here, and including a leopard. But to Carey the face that he saw was that of a jaguar, a wickedly smiling jaguar, which transformed rapidly into the image, first, of Commissioner Rhys and second, of Louis Napoleon.

As they left the church, an orderly passed a note to Heseltine.

'You're required to wait here, Carey,' said the Captain. 'Some word about the findings perhaps?'

'I'm not allowed to discuss the case,' Carey replied.

He found that he had become superstitious about the thing. No fear of the authorities, particularly, but an irrational concern that God would punish him still further if he dared breach the stricture.

'No need for *you* to discuss it, old man,' said Heseltine as they waited near the vacant lot alongside the church. 'But let me tell you that there are many of us who think you've had a raw deal. Let's hope Her Majesty sees things the same way. Perhaps Wolseley has already decided to review the case.'

'It will be the Duke of Cambridge who confirms the findings. Or not, as the case may be. The Duke is a good friend of Lord Chelmsford, they tell me. And I think you need to recall that Her Majesty and the Prince Imperial's mother are also very close.'

He could have bitten his tongue for allowing himself to be drawn in, speculated on the punishment that the Lord would inflict on him for this latest conceit as the Lieutenant-Colonel strode towards them, surrounded by a team of subordinates.

Bland-Hunt returned Carey's salute, pursed his lips, chewed the inside of his cheek. 'Carey,' he said, 'I am truly sorry about this...'

Carey braced himself.

'I had no idea when we met earlier,' the Lieutenant-Colonel continued. 'You will appreciate that when the new Commander-in-Chief left here, he would have taken with him all the relevant dispatches pertaining to those within his command.'

'Of course, sir,' Carey replied, a spark of hope re-kindling within him.

'I can therefore only assume that one of those dispatches...' He stretched a hand to the orderly at his side, took a newspaper from him, held it towards Carey with a thin, apologetic smile.

Carey received it, tried unsuccessfully to prevent his eyes from filling. It was a copy of the *London Gazette,* an edition dated 6th June.

'Am I to assume...?' said Heseltine. And Carey nodded. *Such a strange twist of fate,* he thought.

There it was, among the many other listings:

98th Regiment of Foot. Lieutenant Jahleel Brenton Carey to be Captain, vice O.M. Johnson (resigned on appointment to the Army Pay Department).

And the promotion had been declared effective from the first of April, the very day when he had first arrived in Table Bay.

Chapter Eighteen

Sunday 19th July 1879

The Mhlathuze River ran here in a series of meanders through a flat plain of jaundiced grass, its journey from the Babanango Hills almost complete, its destination nearly reached at the bay where Sir Frederick Richards was close to completion of the temporary harbour that would help the British consolidate their new acquisition still further. The river was not especially wide but it was deep, mottled and fast, and the Drift at this point was the last before it found the sea.

On a rise above the Drift stood the charred remains of a large kraal, its three hundred huts scorched and empty, like so much of Zululand, McTeague realised. It had been torched a couple of weeks or more earlier by soldiers from Henry Hope Crealock's Division, creeping up the coast while Chelmsford's force had been advancing on Ulundi and McTeague himself had been lying helpless in the cave.

'It is not just, Lord,' said Amahle, biting back an angry tear, 'that they should be brought here thus.'

McTeague studied them, the two hundred and fifty major or minor chieftains of the coastal Zulu clans who had come to the slight plateau below the ruined kraal, so they might surrender. *They may be defeated*, he thought, *but they are hardly humbled. Majestic buggers!*

So they were, too, clothed in all the exotic finery – the dressed leopard skins, the multi-coloured feather head-dresses, the cow-tail arm and leg ornamentation – of their ceremonial attire. It was a visual delight so that, beneath the canopy erected for the comfort of observers, correspondents scribbled away, artists sketched or applied simple washes to their notebooks, and a brace of photographers adjusted camera bellows, exposed plate after plate. And mingled among these gentlemen of the press was an assortment of other officers, several fellows in civilian clothing, and native dignitaries, representatives of the various native contingents that had fought for the British. McTeague and his woman had not been on the invitation list, but since Amahle's father had been among the gathered chieftains, he had managed to contrive their attendance.

'They seem quite pleased with themselves,' he said. 'The *izinduna*, I mean.'

'You do not understand, husband,' she replied. Since Maria Mestiza's death, she had simply assumed the role of Chief Wife, despite her youth. 'The Fat Queen's new iNkosi knows precisely what he is doing. To bring them to this place. The very *ikhanda* where the Great Shaka Bull Elephant served as an *induna* for the Mthethwa, learned his trade, created the dream that would one day be the AmaZulu *impi*. And later this homestead and barracks belonged to Cetshwayo kaMpande himself, before he became king. It was here that he gathered his first followers, the *USuthus*. Simply to bring these *izinduna* here, like this, is to spit upon them. My father among them.'

'After the battle, at oNdini, Cetshwayo told the chieftains they must look to themselves, did he not? They only follow his command!'

'I think they are traitors,' she said. 'They betray the Great King. They betray all those of our menfolk who have died. My brother among them.'

'You cannot know that he is dead, my dear.'

'They say that our fallen still lie in great heaps upon the ground, exactly where they died. If Tshabanga is not among them then where is he? Not at Hluhluwe, that is certain.'

'With Cetshwayo perhaps?'

'And what will happen to him there?' she said. 'When there are so many who would sell the Great King to the red soldiers. Yourself included, *umyeni*. Is that not so?'

He regretted his confession now. In the sheer chaos that followed the *iNkatha's* destruction, Amahle and Cornscope had somehow got McTeague on his feet despite the stab wound to his back, dragged him through the smoke and flames. Ignored by British horsemen and Zulu warriors alike, they had found refuge in some thorn scrub. He had lost consciousness, awoken again in the dark, his mind filled with visions of Maria Mestiza's death, her lifeless corpse still twitching from the honour cuts inflicted upon it. He had wept for her again, wept too at the way she had cuckolded him, at the contempt he felt for the man who should have been his father, if he too had not been cuckolded by McTeague's faithless mother. And when he had wept enough, there were plans to be made. Where would they go? And how? He was weakened from loss of blood and in great pain, so they could not travel far. Not yet. And they could not journey either north or east, for risk of running into Ntshingwayo. Or the Great King himself who would, he was sure, now have news about the depth of McTeague's betrayal. Amahle had questioned him, of course, about why Ntshingwayo had sentenced him to death. She still did not understand. But he had feigned weakness, confusion, stalled the thing until another day. So they had gone south, crossed the valley, past all the other ruined kraals, stumbled upon a cave already filled with fleeing survivors. Amahle and Cornscope had cared for him, brought him water, cleaned his wounds, fed him thin gruel, until he was well enough to be pressed once more for an answer. So, yet again,

McTeague had told only as much of the truth as he thought might satisfy her curiosity, his part in the negotiations, but also a confession that he had been in discussions with Chelmsford about the possible capture of Cetshwayo. Neglected to mention the *iNkatha*.

'But only, my dear,' he had said, 'to avoid further grief to the People of Heaven, you understand. To bring this tragedy to an early end.'

She had been appalled, but he had hastened to add that he had later thought better of the thing although, by then, it was too late. Twinge and Maria Mestiza had told Ntshingwayo. The betrayer betrayed. Amahle had remained sullen for many days, until the news of the army's defeat at Ulundi reached them. It had a strange effect on everybody. The other survivors instantly became cheered, abandoned every vestige of hostility. For it was clear that the war must now be over. They were at peace, and everything that had gone before was wiped from the dust. And it was the same with Amahle. Whatever he might have done belonged now in the past.

So they had continued south, to the mission station, fifty miles north-east of here, where they had found Wolseley a few days ago. The General had met Chelmsford there for their first encounter, in the midst of much consternation about the fact that Chelmsford had retired so quickly from Ulundi when it could have been held so easily. The word was that he had been scared of something happening to deflect from his victory. The common opinion that he was not fit to even be a corporal, despite the defeat of the Zulus. But Chelmsford was going back to Britain anyway. And then the following day, Buller and Wood – the hero of Khambula – had also left, though to the adulation due of Aries. 'God speed!' the men had cried, honouring those they thought were truly responsible for their victory, rather than Chelmsford.

After that, Wolseley had proceeded to his own forward camp, here at Emangweni – and McTeague's little band had come with them. But at least he had succeeded in keeping from Amahle any suspicion that responsibility for the *iNkatha*'s destruction was his own.

From the southern side of the river, a party of horsemen rode out from the fortified camp that the British had established there. They were few in number, no more than a dozen uniforms, though their attire hardly deserved that description, for there was barely a common item of clothing among them. Breeches of blue or white, tan or tartan, jackets of red, navy or khaki. Yet the noticeable thing about them, McTeague realised from the moment he had first stumbled upon them in his flight southwards, was that they now shone with confidence. Sun helmets no longer showed signs of the tea-staining, once used to camouflage their bright colour, and were now restored to their original gleaming white, regimental badges back in place. And the badges, like all other metallic fittings, were burnished once more to a dazzling sheen, while leather straps and accoutrements were oiled and polished afresh. There was an ease in their riding style too, for their mounts trotted carelessly across the Drift, splashing and side-stepping as though on some casual bridleway promenade in rural England, while the waiting Zulus stirred happily, pointing and smiling, like the hosts of some country house weekend noting the appearance of their first guests come rolling along the carriage drive.

In the midst of the soldiers, and easily discernible even to a casual observer by the deferential space he was afforded from those around him, rode the new Commander-in-Chief, Sir Garnet Joseph Wolseley. McTeague had still not succeeded in arranging a personal audience but he had seen him around the camp often enough, a more populist leader than Chelmsford, something to do with his easy charm, perhaps. But there was also something of the natural hero about him, wounded seriously both in Burma and the Crimea, where he had lost an eye. He forged ahead of his companions now, with just one civilian at his side – a Dutchman, McTeague imagined – spurred up the slight rise onto flatter ground, dismounted easily and alone just in front of the waiting chieftains, one of whom took a couple of steps forward, raised his right hand.

'*Bayete*, iNkosi!' he cried. Be greeted, Lord.

'*Bayete!*' sang the other chieftains.

Wolseley saluted then removed his helmet, ran his fingers through his unkempt hair, limped forward and shook the *induna*'s hand.

'Greetings to you all,' he said, in English, raising his voice. '*Bayete*,' he repeated. '*Bayete!*' Several of the Zulus smiled appreciatively. There were nodding heads. 'But I bring you the words of our Great Queen, Victoria.' He paused while, in various places among the gathered chieftains, translation took place.

This is a well-staged event, McTeague thought, and he turned, giving Amahle a reassuring wink. She did not truly understand the gesture yet but it amused her, especially when it caused the monocle to fall upon his chest.

'We will hear the words of your Great Queen!' said the leading *induna*.

Well, at least today they did not refer to Her Majesty as the Fat Queen.

'Then you should know,' said Wolseley, 'that it does not amuse Her Majesty to see the Zulu people in such straits.'

'What does he say?' said Amahle.

'That the Fat Queen grows fatter by the day,' McTeague whispered to her, careful that his words should not be caught by any of the other IsiZulu speakers.

'I think you are with lies, husband,' she whispered back.

'Some of you already know me,' Wolseley proceeded. 'From my time here as High Commissioner for Natal.' This took a few moments to be digested, explained by the interpreters. 'There were many times when we had dealings together – myself and the people of Zululand. So it grieves me that your kingdom is now finished. It is gone.'

McTeague expected some response from the *izinduna*, but there was none, even though, at his side, he felt Amahle tense and quiver.

'What does he mean?' she said.

'Hush, my dear, and we will find out.'

'Your king is in hiding,' said Wolseley. 'He is gone from you and his kingdom gone with him. Yet there is good news. For the Great Queen, Victoria, now bids you welcome to her own realm. The largest empire that the world has ever seen. And the Zulu people now a part of it. An important part.' There was more nodding of heads among the chieftains, more smiles. 'For your governance, the former kingdom of Zululand shall now be organised into smaller departments, each with its own ruler, though subject to the laws of Her Majesty.'

Ah, here it comes, thought McTeague, and wondered whether there was still a chance that he, himself...

Amahle strained to hear the translation.

'Who will these rulers be?' she asked. But there was neither time nor tautology with which to respond.

'Tell us,' said the leading *induna*, 'the sacrifice that we must make to appease the Great Queen.'

The Dutchman, still mounted, and some yards behind Wolseley, translated the words.

'Only this,' replied Wolseley, solemnly. He paused, seemingly for effect, before delivering the judgement. 'That you shall surrender all your rifles. Every one. And that you must also surrender all cattle and oxen that have come to you from the former royal herds of the outlaw Cetshwayo – since those royal herds are now the property of Her Majesty, Queen Victoria.'

The words were transmitted among the chieftains. They waited. And Wolseley waited too. The observers waited also. A long silence. Until it grew uncomfortable.

'What more, iNkosi?' said the *induna*, at last.

Wolseley looked puzzled. The Dutchman spoke a few words.

'More?' said Wolseley. 'There is no more, sir.'

This is positively Dickensian, McTeague grinned to himself. He thought again of *The Parish Boy's Progress*, of the lad, Twist.

Among the Zulus, heads were turned, one to the other. Comments were muttered and exchanged. The white general's words repeated, queried, reaffirmed. And, at their head, their spokesman composed himself.

'I fear,' he said, 'that we may have failed to understand the words of the Great Queen.' The Dutchman translated. 'When they were conveyed to us,' the *induna* continued, 'by the iNkosi who preceded you, and before the war began, there were many more demands. To disband all the *amabutho*. To surrender one of the regiments. Great numbers of cattle.'

Wolseley listened patiently.

'I regret that the Great Queen's words have been conveyed badly to you. Though not by my predecessor, I am certain.'

The words hung in the air. And then there was a great clamour among the chieftains, the IsiZulu words carrying clear to those waiting beneath the canopy. If they had only known that this was all that the Fat Queen required of them...

'Does he say that the Great King did not tell us the truth?' said Amahle.

McTeague recalled his conversations as an emissary on Cetshwayo's behalf, the King's private instruction that he would accept any terms, even the surrender of the warriors from his most prized regiment. And he recalled the way in which Chelmsford had used the conciliatory approaches to string out the negotiations, to buy himself time, to edge forward, knowing always that there was not one single concession which would save the Zulus from the revenge which he intended to inflict upon them. *Ah, Signore Machiavelli*, he thought, *how the British would have warmed your heart! Just look at them. Lost their land, their entire way of life. Yet grateful because they had been gulled into believing that it might have been even worse.*

'Well there! You see, my dear,' McTeague smiled, 'was your husband not right to try and surrender Cetshwayo to the British? To try and bring this dreadful war to an earlier conclusion? To prevent all this destruction? The unnecessary death? Perhaps even to have saved your brother's life?'

'It's an extraordinary claim, Mister McTeague,' said Wolseley, just a little later. The General had graciously allowed him to be seated on a campaign chair in deference to his injuries, though no refreshments had been offered.

'Yet a just one, General,' McTeague replied, focusing on the noble bridge of Wolseley's nose rather than allowing himself to stare at the fellow's glass eye. It was damnably disconcerting, and he had left his own monocle dangling for fear that it might somehow give offence.

'You say that Buller's attack on EsiKlebheni was directed deliberately at the destruction of the *iNkatha*? Personally, I always thought it was kept at Ulundi. What about you, Crealock?'

'I'm not certain that His Lordship ever discussed the thing, sir,' Crealock replied.

'Chelmsford?' said Wolseley, tapping the map beneath his hand. 'Well, that doesn't surprise me. Never came across anybody who understood the Zulu less than Frederic.' It was spoken almost as an aside, but Wolseley looked to Crealock for a comment. There was none. 'But Buller would have understood its significance, I think,' Wolseley continued, 'if he had known its whereabouts.'

'I am certain that Mister Drummond would have told him, sir,' said McTeague. 'I was very careful to give him the precise details.'

'Drummond?' said Wolseley.

'Advisor to Lord Chelmsford, sir,' Crealock replied. 'Served as His Lordship's Intelligence Officer.' Crealock emphasised his comment with a playful twist of the eccentric loop at the extremity of his moustache.

At least Wolseley has forced him to wear the Queen's uniform, thought McTeague, for Crealock had an inclination towards more Bohemian attire, including his customary Mexican *sombrero* adorned with peacock feathers.

'Really?' said the General, and McTeague found it a wondrous thing that a single word, just one inflection, could imply so much. Widespread doubts about the quality of intelligence either sought or heeded by His Lordship, questions about the part played by Crealock's younger brother, Chelmsford's Military Secretary, in the division of forces that had led to the Isandlwana disaster. 'And is he still with us?' Wolseley went on, when there was again no reply from Crealock himself. 'This Mister Drummond?'

'Died at Ulundi, sir,' said Crealock. 'He was ambushed, it seems, when the fight was almost done.'

'Ah!' said Wolseley. 'A case of *physician, heal thyself*, eh? So, difficult to confirm whether he did, indeed, pass on your words, Mister McTeague. And Buller's left us, too. Damn'd shame. I need some good fellows around me just now.'

His glance in Crealock's direction was dismissive.

'With respect, General,' said McTeague, 'I think the facts speak for themselves. Buller's men came from the south-west, into the valley, and the Zulus had relied on trapping him there when he stopped to burn the lower kraals. But most of his column swung around so they could attack EsiKlebheni directly – and the northern section, sir, precisely the area in which the *iNkatha* was housed. They could only have known to do so, based on the intelligence I provided.'

'All the same, Mister McTeague,' said Crealock, 'I doubt we shall ever know the truth now, and...'

'Just a moment, Crealock,' said Wolseley. 'I'd like to know why Mister McTeague thinks this is so vital. Why all this palaver about granting him an audience?'

McTeague had worked the ground well beneath the canopy. A word here, a whisper there; claiming the occasional credit, hinting at confidences still to be shared. And it had taken no more than a couple of hours before the invitation to the Commander-in-Chief's tent had been swept back to him on the turning tide of innuendo. By that time, the chieftains had happily accepted Wolseley's terms and were still wondering what all the fuss had been about, when the General summoned his Chaplain and enjoined them collectively as amazed participants in today's Church Parade.

'I had clear understandings with Mister Drummond, General,' said McTeague. 'And may the Good Lord have mercy on his soul.'

'Well, Amen to that, sir,' Wolseley replied. 'But you cannot expect such things to be honoured in the current circumstances. Why, I understand that you claim he even promised you one of the new Departments, Mister McTeague.'

'Upon my word as a gentleman, sir. And an officer too. You may not be aware but I was previously a major in Her Majesty's forces.'

'Yes,' said Wolseley. 'West India Regiment, though, I understand. Is that so, Crealock?'

Crealock raised an amused eyebrow.

'My main concern is for Emoyeni, General,' McTeague pressed forward in skirmishing order, fast and loose. 'My home, sir, this past six months. Possessions and so on.'

Possessions, he thought, *and a buried treasure trove*. He had heard nothing from Jago Jupe since the Zulus sacked the place, but he was certain that the good Pastor would still be keeping watch for him.'

'It previously belonged to Mister Dunn, I think? Emoyeni, Mister McTeague. He is the rightful owner, is he not?'

'Well, he could have stayed there, General. Provided the same espionage service that I, myself, developed on behalf of Her Majesty.'

'And he had another property here, I believe, at Emangweni?'

'So I understand, General. The bounty that flowed to him from the Zulus was generous in the extreme.'

'You try to emulate him, Mister McTeague?'

'I think John Dunn is a man with divided loyalties, sir. Divided between his ambition and his greed. Unlike myself, General. I live only for God and the Queen.'

'Well, it seems that Lord Chelmsford had no doubts about Dunn's loyalty. None whatsoever. His plan to bestow one of the new Zululand Departments on Mister Dunn seems eminently sensible to me.'

'And he now has responsibility for Drummond's little network of Zulu spies, sir,' said Crealock.

Not all of them, however, thought McTeague, and smiled to himself.

'Does he?' said Wolseley. 'Makes the point then, eh? He has all the attributes of an honest Crown servant, and he had considerable previous experience of large-scale administration.' McTeague felt his heart sink. 'There is this matter of Zulu women, of course. Four dozen of them, I'm told. It must fly in the face of the Lord's Commandments. Surely.'

'Not one of them baptised either, General,' said McTeague, 'while my own brides are each sanctified by the blessed sacrament of marriage.'

'You had a European wife too, they tell me. Spanish, perhaps. And killed by the blackies at EsiKlebheni?' *Spanish?* thought McTeague. *How she would have berated his ignorance.* But he had neither the patience nor composure to correct the error.

'She died saving my life, General,' he said.

'Then I am sorry for your loss, sir. But the kaffir women. You think that baptism makes a difference in their case. You think the Almighty might be so easily gulled? Why, it is a disgrace. To dilute the blood of our people in this vile way!' The argument sounded horribly familiar. 'I tell you, sir, that the breeding of Dane and Norseman flows in my own veins. Unsullied, sir. How might we preserve our warrior instincts unless we sire strong sons of our own race, eh? We excel as warriors, Mister McTeague. As man-shooters. Is that not the finest of all sports, sir?'

'As you say, General,' McTeague replied, trying to control himself, suppress the conclusion that Wolseley was as mad as a hatter. 'Yet there were other things, sir. Other points to my agreement with Mister Drummond. And through him with Lord Chelmsford.'

'You say so? What, then?'

In truth, McTeague no longer cared about Emoyeni apart from the drive to recover his treasure. But he knew, with total certainty, that moving back there would literally be the death of him. It would be only a matter of time before Ntshingwayo sent some of his killers to cut out McTeague's tripes. So he talked about the freight charges, the possibility of trade expansion. Yet Wolseley dismissed the thing as a commercial matter, hardly worthy of the Commander's attention.

'Then there is this, General,' said McTeague. 'That Lord Chelmsford promised an appropriate reward on the basis that I should be able to help with Cetshwayo's capture.'

'Oh!' Wolseley smiled. 'My dear fellow, we already have that particular matter well in hand.'

Most of the chieftains had taken their leave and left as soon as they felt able. There was momentous news to carry home, for *umuzi* and *ikhanda* alike. But several remained and among them was Ndabuko kaMahanana, the Iron-Shaper. These final few had established themselves along the northern edge of the British encampment and cooking fires were now lit there, close to the sacred *umphapha* thorn tree under which McTeague, Amahle, Cornscope and the Zulu, Klaas, sheltered from the sun.

'There is gain in this for us all, iNkosi,' McTeague told Ndabuko. 'And a simple enough plan. But how many sheep can you muster at Hluhluwe?'

Amahle's father consulted with the *izinduna* around him, checked the figure they gave him over again.

'Within seven suns,' he replied, 'we can gather a thousand beasts.'

McTeague smiled at Cornscope.

'What d'you think, Simeon?'

'A neat enough racket, William. It has all the genius of simplicity.'

'Well,' said McTeague in English, 'the Commissariat jumped easily enough at the chance to purchase the livestock from us. And a thousand head should satisfy them. Perhaps you could draft the necessary documents?'

'Of course, old fellow. An intriguing piece of rascality. One can just imagine the fuss that it will cause too. The back and forth between junior officers and their superiors. Queries to the Commissariat. From the Transport section. The Colonels confused. What japes!'

'They deserve no less for reneging on agreements, dear friend,' said McTeague. 'But the enterprise should turn a pretty penny too.' He turned again to his father-in-law, addressed him in IsiZulu. 'It seems that we are now trading partners, Lord.' They shook hands once. Again, though with their forearms clasped together. Then a third, conventional, handshake.

'Time to build again,' said Ndabuko. 'To sow new crops. To breed new herds.'

'Indeed,' McTeague smiled. And what better way to begin than this? A bogus bill of purchase to Ndabuko and the other chieftains within our modest syndicate. For a thousand sheep. A bill of sale to the Commissariat with a guaranteed delivery date set, for example, at the end of the month. Some trustworthy fellows to set the flocks upon the road, taking care to halt conspicuously at various of the British camps where they are sure to be properly noticed. And then...

'You want us to turn them off the road near Mthonjaneni?' said Klaas. He had arrived in the camp just before the coastal *izinduna*.

'Yes,' said McTeague. 'Leave the shepherds alive to tell the tale of the theft, then drive the sheep north, past oNdini. Hide them well. We must be able to claim that the sheep were carried off by hostiles. And from one of the roads that the army has declared safe, of course. That way we claim compensation from Her Majesty. Then sell the sheep afresh,' he repeated for the benefit of Ndabuko and the other minor chieftains. 'And use the profit to purchase many fine cattle!' They smiled.

'It is just possible,' said Cornscope, 'that this little trick might be repeatable.'

'So long as we sell the sheep for the second time to a different Division,' said McTeague, 'the same flocks should be good for several transactions.' Ndabuko slapped him on the back. 'Trade will flow,' McTeague said to him. 'But I know that my Supreme Wife, your daughter, would give it all in exchange for her brother's return home.'

'He is lost to us,' said Ndabuko. 'He will not come back.'

'I spent some time with him. Our escort to the white iNkosi.'

'He should not have shamed us.'

'You return to Hluhluwe, Lord?'

'As soon as we have eaten. Shall you travel with us? Bring my daughter home?'

'I wish it might be possible. But I am no longer in favour with the Great King or his chief advisors. I fear it would put your daughter's life at risk.'

'Great King?' said Ndabuko. 'The war is over now, KaMtigwe. Without the war, my foolish son could not have wagered away my daughter to this man.' He pointed at Klaas. 'I do not blame him. And my heart was not hurt when he decided to sell away his right to her. I was not unhappy that she took you for her husband. I believe you will help to make my clan strong. But without the war, we may have been strong in a different way. And the war was brought about by Cetshwayo kaMpande. He should not have been so quick to defend Sihayo when his sons went raiding across the border and provoked the Fat Queen's army.'

Amahle clicked her tongue. 'They would have come even without any cause, Baba,' she said.

'You blame him for starting the war, iNkosi?' said McTeague.

'I blame him for losing it!' replied Ndabuko. 'And many others share that view. When Cetshwayo is caught, and those who still support him, then you must bring my daughter home, KaMtigwe. Help to make our clan strong again. Meanwhile, we have sheep to trade, do we not?'

They shook hands again, but before his party returned to the camp McTeague took Klaas privately to one side.

'There is something else that I would ask from you, Klaas my boy,' he said.

'Do you not already owe me enough, KaMtigwe?' smiled the Zulu, running a hand through his wisp of beard.

'Well, this may allow us to settle our accounts, dear friend. Though I hope that I may rely on your integrity?' Klaas smiled. McTeague hated doing this. His trust had already been broken too many times. His own foolishness. But he could think of no other way to recover his fortune. So he shared with Klaas the precise location of his buried treasure, planned with him the means of its recovery.

Even the most base of God's creatures may learn from its mistakes, thought McTeague as the horsemen stampeded through the camp, *but only humankind is cursed with the propensity for repeating the same mistake so many times.*

Dunn's *commando* was a cosmopolitan assortment of mainly Zulu riders, with a few local farmers and soldiers of fortune. A hard bunch, dressed in the Dutch fashion, civilian clothes, broad-brimmed felt hats, cross-belts and bandoliers. But they were universally mounted on the tough little ponies known as the Cape *boerperd*. McTeague could just hold the tent flap aside from the narrow camp cot on which he was taking some afternoon rest, easing his aching back, while Cornscope instructed Amahle in the arcane arts of tea-making upon a borrowed portable kerosene stove.

'The beggar!' said McTeague. 'The infernal beggar!'

'William,' cried Cornscope, waving the muggin teapot, 'how can you expect me to instruct this admirable young lady in the fine arts when you persist in causing such a commotion.'

'I do believe that benighted savage has betrayed me!' He could see Klaas fawning upon Dunn, who was now dismounting. The Zulu pointed towards the tent and McTeague let the flap fall slightly, an inquisitive neighbour caught spying from the parlour window.

'Which particular savage do you mean, sir?' said Cornscope, though McTeague ignored him. Dunn stared towards the tent for a moment but was approached by an orderly from the direction of Wolseley's headquarters. They exchanged a few words then Dunn shouted to his men to off-saddle and tend the horses. He patted Klaas on the shoulder and summoned five or six others to follow him.

'Help me up, dammit,' said McTeague, struggling to lift himself from the cot. 'The cove is coming this way.'

Cornscope banged down the pot, gave an exasperated sigh and came to the tent flap, throwing it wide despite McTeague's belated attempt to stop him.

'Oh...' he said.

'Cornscope!' Dunn exclaimed. 'He hasn't tried to kill you off like poor Twinge, then?'

Dunn was not a tall man, but he was powerfully built, in his mid-forties, grey eyes and a beard to match – a beard that concealed the whole lower half of his face so effectively that it was difficult to see his mouth even when he opened it to speak. He lifted his own wide-awake hat from his head and took a large kerchief from his trouser pocket, dabbed at the square forehead.

'Theophilus was killed by the Zulus,' said Cornscope, finally turning to help McTeague stand.

'Only after Willie's efforts failed, I think. And they almost finished you too, I understand?' he said to McTeague. His accent was a rare mix of Scottish burr and IsiZulu inflection. 'A shame they didn't impale you, sure. Fitting end for a thief.'

'A subject on which you would be well-versed, John,' said McTeague. 'I see you have even corrupted my young friend, Klaas.'

'Klaas?' Dunn replied, with a glance towards the Zulu. 'His own man, I think. And you can hardly blame him for seeking some recompense at last. He tells me you have defaulted on your debts to him. But never mind that. You have now kindly provided the means by which he may, at last, be rewarded.'

He waited for a reaction.

'Is it not enough,' said McTeague, at last, 'that you will take back Emoyeni itself? But my possessions...'

'*Your* possessions, Willie?' Dunn laughed. 'The furniture? The clothes? The books? The carriages?' McTeague thought about that wonderful zebra cart, the day of his wedding to Amahle. 'Is there any of it left?' Dunn continued, his laughter now sunk to angry embers.

'I meant my *own* possessions, John,' McTeague replied.

'What? Your buried treasure beneath the hilltop, with Jago Jupe to guard it? Oh, that pained expression, Willie. Did you imagine Klaas would keep your secret? How very naive. But it will help to compensate me for any damage at Emoyeni, I expect. And then, when we bring in Cetshwayo...'

'You?' McTeague stammered.

'Myself and Klaas,' said Dunn. 'Agreed with Chelmsford two months ago. I shall regret it, of course.'

'Hypocrite!' said Cornscope, supporting McTeague's weight as he sagged a little.

'Let me tell you about the first time I ever came here,' Dunn said. 'To Emangweni. More than twenty years ago. Just a wee shaver then. Old Mpande was still on the throne but his sons were at war with each other – Mbuyazi and Cetshwayo. I ended up on the wrong side, lucky not to be butchered like all those thousands of Mbuyazi's folk. But Cetshwayo had taken all my livestock too. I had no choice except to come here and confront him.'

'Oh, he must have been impressed by your valour,' said McTeague.

'Well,' said Dunn, 'you know him almost as closely as myself. He's a magnanimous bugger, don't you think? Made me his chief advisor. Of course, I shall regret his capture.'

'I think I never saw a man more hurt by a betrayal,' said McTeague, 'than Cetshwayo by your own.'

'Oh, the irony that spills from your lips, Willie. Why, it was Cetshwayo himself who told me to stand aside should push come to shove. Could you say as much, man?'

'Does this qualify then?' McTeague gestured towards Dunn's followers, the men he had led in battle against the Zulus. 'As standing aside?'

For the first time, Dunn seemed genuinely troubled.

'There was no choice in the end,' he said. 'Not unless I'd decided to give up everything I've fought all my life to build. You have to protect your possessions, Willie. Something at which you singularly do not excel, I think. How many wives is it now? That you've lost. All of them? Including the dago woman?'

It cut McTeague, of course, flooded him with memories, some fond, some less so. But, oddly, the memory that surfaced most strongly was his recollection of being herded into the hut at EsiKlebheni by Ntshingwayo's warriors, to find Cornscope there, in the act of molesting the two other wives who had accompanied Amahle to the *iNkatha* ceremony. He had never seen the women again, and he wondered what would have happened to the girl had he not arrived at that moment. He understood Simeon's weaknesses, but he had never again left him alone in Amahle's company – though she, dear thing, seemed to have no fear of him.

'Not all of his wives, iNkosi,' said Klaas, pushing Cornscope aside and holding the tent flap wide so that Dunn could see Amahle, hidden in the shadows.

'Gracious,' said Dunn. 'How exquisite!' He spoke to her in IsiZulu. 'Come here, child.'

'I am not yours to command, Jantoni,' Amahle replied, and McTeague could taste the tension, feel the fear grow within himself, the clenching of his bowels.

The men at Dunn's back were an ugly bunch, and the ugliest of them all was a fellow whose full face had more craters than that of the moon – or so said the astronomers – with cold eyes and a dirty grey walrus moustache. He was well-built and distinguished from the rest of the mob by his lack of rifle and bandoliers, wearing only a service-pattern holster around the outside of his two-buttoned sack jacket and matching waistcoat. He sported a bowler hat, a wing-collar shirt without a neck-tie, and his square-toed boots looked lethal. A personal hired thug, McTeague imagined.

'All the same,' shouted Dunn, 'you will come. Else my men will come and get you. They can be rough.'

'You have your property back,' said McTeague, standing unaided now. 'The promise of your own little kingdom too. And my personal nest egg in the bargain, it seems. You don't need to trouble the girl, John.'

'No trouble, Willie,' Dunn smiled. 'And you forgot to mention the sheep. Nice plan. I need to make one or two adjustments, of course. But you tried to emulate me, old man. Tried and failed. You can't expect to lose the game and still keep any of the spoils. No, the girl, I'm afraid, comes with us.'

'She is my wife, John. Married in the sight of the Almighty. Neither He nor I shall let you take her.'

He took a step forward, blocking the entrance entirely.

Fifteen years older than him, McTeague thought, *and not in the best of shape. But I think I could still give the fellow a thrashing.*

'I fear you have little choice,' said Dunn. 'She was, after all, acquired legitimately by my friend Klaas here. It was only with Cetshwayo's agreement that she then became available for marriage to you. And what has happened, William? You never paid Klaas the gold you promised him and Cetshwayo's word is no longer law. A shame! Yet I fear she must now be added to your list of losses. Young Klaas wants her back and I'm certain that Sir Garnet would see such an arrangement as more closely resembling the natural order of things.'

All a matter of accountancy, McTeague recalled, this issue of how the tally of one's wives might be reconciled. But this was one asset he would not transfer from his balance sheet. He turned briefly to admire Amahle then, too late, caught the serpentine blur of movement from the corner of his eye. Dunn's fist slammed into his back, connected with the wound in a splintering spasm of flame that swept through lungs and heart. McTeague fell heavily to his knees, another bout of pain that raced up through his thighs and ignited the tortured torso afresh.

'Now come, girl!' shouted Dunn, and she stood, though seizing a small knife from the table, near the teapot.

McTeague saw her move forward, sweat glistening on her breasts and belly, while Dunn retreated a step. She rested her left hand on McTeague's shoulder and held the short blade before her, waving it gently from Dunn to Klaas, then back again. *She stands once more between me and my enemies*, he thought, *as she did at EsiKlebheni*. But he doubted she could prevail here.

'How sweet!' said Dunn. Then in IsiZulu, 'But why do you defend him, girl? Do you know what he's done, this KaMtigwe?'

McTeague clasped her wrist.

'My dear,' he said, though the effort racked him again, 'this man is with lies. Do not heed him.'

'Oh, I think she will, my friend,' said Dunn, in English once more, 'when we tell her how you betrayed the *iNkatha*, the soul of her people, to His Lordship. But that can wait – for now!' Dunn turned to his henchmen. 'Bring her,' he said, and McTeague saw the ugly fellow with the bowler hat step forward.

The man, considerably younger than Dunn, swung him easily around by his lapel, hit him with a short right jab that set him on his buttocks in the dirt and, in the same movement, drew the pistol from its holster.

'Mister Behrens!' said Dunn, mumbling through the fingers with which he cradled the bearded jaw.

'I don't work for you, Mister Dunn,' drawled the fellow. *An American,* McTeague concluded, surprise and hope in equal measure overlaying the agony in his chest. 'And it looks to me like we're imposing on the hospitality of these folk.'

'The woman is mine,' cried Klaas, grabbing the American's arm. The man swung around, prodded the barrel of his pistol in the Zulu's stomach.

'Seems to me the young lady's happy where she is, son,' said Behrens. 'Now I suggest, Mister Dunn, that you take your boys here and get about that enterprise of yours.'

'I take it,' said Dunn, climbing to his feet and brushing the red dirt from his trousers, 'that our partnership is now dissolved?'

'I think I can safely find my commodities elsewhere, sir,' Behrens replied.

'I have a claim on that woman,' Klaas protested again.

'That's for another day now, Klaas,' said Dunn. 'And you may find, Mister Behrens, that this is a more dangerous country than you'd imagined.' Then he nodded to his men, picked up the hat and headed off towards Wolseley's tent. But he turned back, briefly. 'Oh, by the way, Willie,' he shouted, 'I forgot to thank you for one thing. Yourself and the dago woman – in one respect, at least, you've been more helpful to me than you can imagine!'

'Partnership, Mister Behrens?' winced McTeague, taking the blade carefully from Amahle's fingers, while Cornscope helped him to his feet. The pain was fearsome.

'I heard of you, Mister McTeague,' said Behrens. 'But our paths don't seem to have crossed before.'

'You've been here for a while, sir?' said Cornscope.

'Since May. I already sent one shipment. Just need one more group and I can get back to London.'

'Who is this man, husband?' said Amahle. 'And what did Jantoni mean, about the things he says you have done?'

McTeague was more concerned with that parting shot. What had he meant? But he quickly set it aside.

'I think he was speaking like a fool,' McTeague replied, then turned to the American. 'My wife wants to know who you are, Mister Behrens.'

'You speak the Zulu language very well, sir,' said Behrens.

'I seem to have a flair for languages,' said McTeague.

Behrens set the revolver back in its holster, removed the bowler hat.

'Then if it's not too much of an impertinence, Mister McTeague, perhaps you might tell your wife that I'm delighted to make her acquaintance. Perfectly delighted. She is, sir, the most enchanting creature.'

'I think she will expect me to have an answer to her question, Mister Behrens.'

At least, thought McTeague, *she may have an answer to half of it.*

'My apologies, sir. My name is Nathaniel Behrens.'

'And your business, Mister Behrens?'

'I expect,' the American replied, 'you might call me a circus man, Mister McTeague. And I guess you could say I'm in the business of mutual benefits.'

Chapter Nineteen

Thursday 7th – Friday 29th August 1879

'They simply moved on?' said Mandla kaSibusiso, *induna* of the uMxapho, the Mongrels, the Shower of Shot, kinsman to Zibhebhu – and the father of his beloved Zama. Shaba imagined her shade, wandering the slopes of Mthonjaneni, the way she must have ventured across the river to search for him among the carrion of oNdini, found him in his hour of need.

'I could not bear to die there,' he said, 'for I sensed that I should never find the shade of your daughter so far from the Sacred Spring, iNkosi. But now I think she was there, after all, protecting me. That it was she who rose beside me, she who dazzled the sight of the Basuto rider. For I watched him cover his eyes, as though from a bright light. And when he looked again, it seemed he could no longer see me. Or perhaps he simply thought to come back and kill me after they had caught the ones who ran away.'

'The horse soldiers had much more to make them smile that day,' said Mandla. 'We were lucky not to be with the Bender of Kings, nor the Sharp Points. Cut down like dogs.'

'The fate of the defeated,' said Shaba. He remembered the way they had pursued the fugitive red soldiers, the *mbayimbayi* riders, the flag carriers, after eSandlwana.

'Of course,' Mandla replied. 'But it is a heavy thing, all the same.'

'Less heavy,' said Shaba, 'than the sight of so many women and young ones clogging the roads north.'

'And the crippled.' Mandla shook his head. 'I never thought that a man whose legs have been shattered could crawl so far. We found some later, a full day's march from the field.'

'Your father?'

'No, he died from the bullets of those fire-spitters that the red soldiers brought with them.' Shaba recalled the *clack, clack, clack* of their turning handles, the revolving barrels.

'Zama would have been proud of him.'

'She would have preferred,' said Mandla, 'to still be sitting at his feet, listening to tall tales, his stories of the Old Kings. And I would give my own life, Shaba of the uMbonambi, to see them there once more, together by the fire, with my daughter dreaming of the young man to whom she might one day be married.'

Shaba felt moisture forming behind his eye-patch, lifted it, though his vision seemed especially misted at that moment. So he wiped away the sadness.

'I had dreams too,' he said. 'Of Zama. And cattle. Honour. The craft of my clan.'

'Those are many dreams for one man,' said Mandla. 'Did you never learn not to be too greedy?'

From Mama, thought Shaba, *and from Gingile.*

'We can still revenge them,' he said. 'When the Great King's messengers tell us they have come back empty-handed again, as surely they must, he will gather the *impi,* draw the Fat Queen's soldiers north again, trap them in the mountains perhaps.'

For Shaba had trodden those perilous paths himself, climbing the sharp shoulders of the Ntabankulu Mountains, the only way to reach this bushland beyond, to the hidden valleys of the isiKhwebezi, to the Ekushumayeleni fastness of Mnyamana kaNgqengelele Buthelezi, the Great King's First Minister.

Yes, he thought, *here we might trap them, destroy them as we should have done during their approach to oNdini.*

'They will not be drawn north,' Mandla smiled. 'There is no need for them to pursue us any further. For they know, as surely as we do, that the Lord-of-the-Sky has forsaken Cetshwayo kaMpande.'

'It was the rituals,' said Shaba. 'Too many of them shortened or forsaken.'

Mandla shook his head.

'No manner of ritual will atone for a brother murdered,' he said.

Shaba tensed. This thing was unmentionable. And who, in truth, could tell the fate that had befallen Cetshwayo's rival, his brother, Mbuyazi? After the war between them, after his supporters had been systematically destroyed in their thousands, Mbuyazi had simply disappeared without trace, vanished – so it was whispered – by the magic of Cetshwayo's own *inyanga,* Manembe. Shaba shivered, for when such an *inyanga* killed somebody, they stole their entire life-chain, used their body parts to create evil medicine; prevented them from entering the Land of the Shades. But Manembe himself was now long dead also.

'On the road,' said Shaba, 'I heard many of the old women say that when Sihayo angered the Fat Queen by raiding across her borders, the Great King should have fed him to the hyenas, appeased the AmaNgisi.'

'And your opinions are always shaped by our old women, Shaba kaNdabuko?'

'We have each seen the red soldiers at work, iNkosi. I think that, if Cetshwayo had surrendered Sihayo, there would have been another demand. And another beyond that.'

'But if we had been less timid?' said Mandla, regret layered like salt upon his tongue. 'At the Hill of the Little House, when we had eaten their camp, if we had waited for the other half of their *impi* to come back, caught them at night, we could have finished this. Or when they were slithering like slugs towards oNdini.'

'We could have taken the war to them,' said Shaba, 'as we did in the beginning.'

'Well, it is too late now. The spirit is broken and the Sky Lord is not with us. And you, Shaba of the uMbonambi, you would do better to go find your family.'

Find them? thought Shaba. *And then what?*

He had harboured a vision, many times, even during the cleansing before the final battle, a vision of his return to Hluhluwe, with so much honour heaped upon him that it would have wiped the offence he had caused his father at Amahle's wedding. He would return and hand back the kaross that Baba had given him. But the kaross, which he had hoped would provide the chance of reconciliation, was now lost in the ravaged ruin of oNdini – the chance lost with it.

'Did you tell them,' said Cetshwayo, 'that we are still gathering cattle as payment to the Fat Queen?'

To Shaba's ears, the question was the whimpering of a whipped hound. And though the dwelling reserved here for the royal presence was large enough by normal standards, it did not match the scale of the houses of oNdini so that, while it made the Great King appear even larger than usual, the woven wicker walls also seemed to constrain and imprison him, the sweetened smoke of its murmuring hearth wrapping tendrils around those crowded within the confines.

'They say,' replied one of the emissaries, 'that they now have all the cattle they could ever need.'

'Did you tell them that before they started this war, I never killed a single white man who entered my country? Not even one.'

'The white iNkosi said that your life would be spared, Lord.'

'Did you tell them I was sorry this war was ever made?'

'He did not seem interested, Lord.'

'Did you tell them that I only seek an *umuzi* of my own here in our country, and to live as a private individual?'

'They say only that you will be well treated. Spared and well treated.'

Shaba wished that he might be elsewhere, for Cetshwayo's desperation dismayed him. He had been in close proximity to the Great King for many days, though largely ignored as befitted his new station, since Mandla kaSibusiso had proposed him as one of the royal body servants, of whom Cetshwayo had retained only a few to support and protect himself, the small entourage of women too, his *isigodlo*. The King had wanted to avoid unwanted attention, he said, though the ruler of the AmaZulu was quite unmistakeable, instantly recognised by any of his people. Apart from his size, his bearing, whenever he was upon the road his drinking water gourds must always be carried above the heads of the maidens tasked with portering them – rather than *upon* their heads in the normal fashion. All the same, Cetshwayo had turned away many sections of the royal regiments that had caught up with his party, wanting to offer their protection. At one level he seemed perfectly relaxed, entirely careless of his safety, a prince secure within his own borders, his own skin; his destiny. At another, there was this ceaseless pursuit of peace terms that smacked of abject surrender.

Yet Shaba, now equipped afresh with new shield and spears, had come to understand more about his master over those intervening days – at least, so far as one of humble birth may be permitted to do so. For, despite the king's efforts to remain beyond the enquiring gaze, there was still an endless stream of supplicants rippling unerringly over the roads and mountain passes to find regal judgement. Each case handled with kind words, with equanimity, with intelligence. And if there was any conflict in Shaba's mind between this form of justice and that afforded to his former *induna*, Mnukwa kaBhekithemba – slain for failing to prevent the opening of the iFulentshi Prince – it was only a fleeting thing.

'I fear that I am misunderstood,' said Cetshwayo. 'We will write once more. Send for my Dutchman.'

Mandla, today in command of the body servants, left the hut to fulfil the king's request, but when he returned with the Dutchman, they were not alone. There was a warrior with them. Tall and thin with a wisp of beard and a crooked smile, wearing the shirt of a dung-jacket and, around his neck, a string of beads and coloured glass – the sort that the white traders carried in the foolish belief that the natives might find them attractive. Klaas of the uNokhenke. Klaas the Skirmisher. Klaas Izimu the Trickster. He entered the dwelling under Mandla's guard and prostrated himself before the Great King, while hatred for the creature seethed through Shaba's soul.

'I crave admittance to your royal presence, iNkosi,' he said, keeping his gaze on Cetshwayo's feet.

Shaba took a step forward, fury seething through each of his veins. But Cetshwayo lifted a hand to bring stillness and silence.

'Where do you come from?' said Cetshwayo.

'From the camp of the white general,' said Klaas. 'He is now at oNdini, where I myself was captured, and where the trader, Jantoni, found me, bade me act as their messenger, their mouth.'

Shaba was unable to contain his anger.

'This man is stuffed with lies,' he spat, 'for I saw him almost two moons ago, already running free in the red soldiers' camp near the eZunganyene ridges.'

He would have slain the man, if it were not for the sure and certain knowledge that he risked instant death himself for killing without authority in the Great King's presence.

'You bring word from Jantoni?' Cetshwayo said to Klaas. 'From the man who was once my most trusted friend? I gave him my trust even when he had fought against me. I gave him shelter, wrapped my own blanket around his shoulders when he was cold, when he was alone. And now it is myself who sits alone. But does he send a blanket for my shoulders? I think that he does not. So what is the message he would have you deliver?'

'Jantoni says that for the sake of the friendship which endured between you for such a long time – a friendship that, he believes, can still be restored – you should surrender yourself, Great Lord, to the mercy of the White Queen. He says that if you surrender, he will do all in his power to ensure that you might have land of your own. He says too that you should send back the clothes and other things belonging to the iFulentshi Prince.'

'These are the words of Jantoni?'

'Yes, Lord.'

'But not the words of the white general?'

'No, iNkosi. They are the words of Jantoni alone.'

Cetshwayo turned to the Dutchman, gestured politely towards him.

'Then you,' he said, 'will write once more to the white general. You will tell him the words that Jantoni sends. And you will say that if he, the white general, will honour the words of Jantoni, if they pledge that I shall have a private homestead, my own *umuzi* within the lands of the AmaZulu, then I will indeed surrender. We will continue to gather cattle and, when he signals his agreement, I will follow behind those cattle to his camp. Do you understand, Dutchman?'

The Dutchman confirmed that he did, indeed, understand – confirmed it in the high-pitched, mangled form of IsiZulu that he employed.

'And there is more,' Cetshwayo continued. 'For when the letter is written, I will send one of my most senior commanders – Ntshingwayo kaMahole Khoza perhaps – to deliver the thing, to speak on my behalf. And to deliver the clothes of the iFulentshi Prince, for they already have his sword.' He turned and whispered to one of his attendants, sent him to fetch the things. 'As a token of our good faith. But first you will leave us, while we see how the shades of our ancestors might spread the bones, offer their vision to guide us.'

The Dutchman was dismissed, Klaas too – much to Shaba's relief, for he did not think himself capable of restraint much longer. He had watched the Trickster's arrogance all the time the Great King had been speaking. And

Shaba knew, with absolute certainty, that there was not a grain of truth in the message Klaas had brought.

'Lord,' he said, while the King's *isanusi* completed the lengthy preparation for the divination, 'forgive me, but that man is not to be trusted.'

'You have a personal interest in him, Tshabanga Giant Slayer?' said Cetshwayo. 'How do you know him?'

'He came to you once, iNkosi, to claim my sister.'

Cetshwayo thought for a moment, and then his handsome face was illuminated, the huge royal thigh was slapped.

'I remember him,' he smiled. 'The *giya* before eSandlwana. He claimed your sister because you wagered her away.' Shaba was suitably shamed. 'And then he gifted her to KaMtigwe. Another white man who has betrayed me. Are they all the same then? All faithless?'

'I know not, Lord. But I know this Klaas. He was raised by them, schooled in their lying ways.'

'Is he a *kholwa*? A follower of their God-on-a-Tree?'

'I cannot say, iNkosi.'

'Well, we shall see,' said Cetshwayo, as his attendant returned with the French Prince's bundle, a thick jacket of dark blue, a faded striped shirt, the leather belts and hand-gun, while Shaba felt the presence of the time-counter once more, within his kilt. 'Good,' said the Great King. 'Propitious.' And he signalled for the *isanusi* to commence. This was the same ancient who had sniffed Shaba out, found him mercifully free of evil after the iFulentshi prince was killed. But as he threw the knuckle bones now, the creature began to cast frightened glances towards the Great King, moving in mewling circles that took him progressively further from Cetshwayo's presence.

'Tell me!' said the king when the bones had been cast several times, their form irregular. 'What do the shades tell us?'

'These are but pointers, Lord,' hissed the diviner. 'As you know. The voices of the dead are indistinct, distant from this place.'

'Tell me!' Cetshwayo demanded.

'There is good fortune here,' the *isanusi* began, his voice quaking as he pointed to the pattern's left side. 'For the shades are certain that you will rule again, and soon, iNkosi, over the People of Heaven.'

'Will I have peace with the Fat Queen?'

'Not only peace, Lord. You will meet her. As one ruler to another.'

Cetshwayo grinned, contentment brimming in his lively eyes.

'And the rest?' he said.

The *isanusi* waved his hand above the bones, though it seemed that he was simply delaying the inevitable. His nostrils flared.

'While you sit once more in oNdini,' the diviner said slowly, 'the white man's venom will flood your house, divide it upon itself. The *Mfecane* will come once more. Brother will slay brother.'

'And the end?' said Cetshwayo.

There was silence in the dwelling, a long and aching silence.

'At the end, Lord,' said the *isanusi*, 'the venom will take your own life too.'
Shaba heard the words and shuddered.

'When?' Cetshwayo said, his voice level, almost dispassionate.

'I cannot see, iNkosi.'

But the *isanusi* was staring at the floor between his feet and Shaba doubted
that anybody believed him. He doubted that the Great King believed him
either, but Cetshwayo did not press the point. Instead, he turned to Mnyamana,
his Chief Minister and iNkosi of this homestead.

'In case these things do not come to pass as the shades have foreseen,' said
Cetshwayo, 'you will care for the Prince Dinizulu. You will remember that
he is my son and heir. Take him deep into the Ngome Forest where none may
find him until the time comes for him to claim the throne. But if the shades
are correct then it is a time to rejoice. We will rule at oNdini once more. So let
us send the Dutchman's letter. Let us send back the Frenchman's clothes. We
will send back this mouth of Jantoni also, with smooth words for the traitor.
And then we will wait for peace to come – as come it must.' He paused for
a moment, the smile fading from his lips as he faced the *isanusi* once more.
'Now,' he continued, 'you will tell us the end of this Spirit-Tale. The house of
the AmaZulu divided. My life taken. Then speak, seer. How long before my
own shade may unite our people once more? Before the People of Heaven are
free again to follow their destiny?'

The diviner delayed until it was impossible to remain silent any longer.

'Not until a hundred winters have passed, Lord,' he said.

An ox turned slowly upon the spit, dripping meat-fat, bloodied spark and
guttering flame, crackling fire-pit and dry-wood snapping, the smoke caressing
faces, greasing them with the sweetness of roasting flesh.

Cetshwayo had sworn those present at the divination to silence about the
isanusi's vision, then recalled the Dutchman and Klaas of the uNokhenke,
telling them only that the omens were sufficiently propitious for them each
to convey their respective messages to the English camp. But then a runner
had arrived, whispered his words to the Great King, so that all but his closest
advisors had been sent from his presence while the feast was prepared. For,
despite the diviner's final words, Cetshwayo was in a mood to celebrate.

'So,' said Klaas, coming up behind Shaba as he stood in the line guarding
the hut's entrance, waiting for the Great King to reappear, 'what did the shades
truly tell him?'

'They spoke only of your death, Trickster,' Shaba whispered, without
turning his head.

Klaas laughed, an ugly and broken noise.

'The day of the evil omen has passed, brother,' he said, stinging Shaba with the play upon those words. For his regiment, the uMbonambi, the Evil Omen, was scattered now upon the winds. 'And you should think about your family. You could return with me when I carry Cetshwayo's words to Jantoni. See your sister again. Marry a woman of your own.'

Shaba tensed, sorrow at the memory of Zama kaMandla cutting him, planting the suspicion that Klaas knew about Zama also, was taunting him.

'What?' he said, over his shoulder. 'And begin to wear the white man's shirt, like you? Or carry his ornaments around my neck in place of the *iziqu*?'

He felt the warmth of the prized necklace of willow-wood beads awarded to the uMbonambi after eSandlwana, but he also saw that the glass baubles adorning the Trickster's own neck were not all beads, some of them more closely resembling small teeth of thin glass or pottery. Then Cetshwayo emerged from his hut, standing tall, left hand resting on the royal belly, Mnyamana and Ntshingwayo following him.

'We have news,' announced the Great King, as a body servant raised the huge white shield above his head to shade him. 'Grave news, my people. For the *izinduna* of the east, those from the length of the Ocean Coast, have all surrendered to the Fat Queen's general.'

No words were spoken among the assembly though heads were lowered. There was inevitability in this, news to be greeted with calmness and patience. But, for Shaba, the words had a special bite since his own father was numbered within the coastal *izinduna*. And though he wished it might be otherwise, he knew that Ndabuko kaMahanana was too pragmatic to stand alone in defiance of his fellow-household heads.

Mnyamana the Chief Minister, standing also partially in the shield's shadow, raised his hand.

'Yet there are words of happiness too,' he cried. 'For the stones have been thrown, the pointers considered. And the shades that direct them tell us this. That the Great King, Cetshwayo kaMpande, will very soon rule all this land afresh. From oNdini. The red soldiers gone back to their own place.' Heads and spirits lifted once more. Chanting broke out among those present. 'So let us feast and rejoice,' Mnyamana shouted, competing with the singing voices in the crowd. 'Tomorrow, the messengers will return to the white general and to Jantoni, carrying with them the Great King's response and the promise of peace.'

A group of women began to call out Cetshwayo's Praise Names, the poetry that told the story of his life, and Mnyamana looked about the crowd until he saw first the Dutchman and then Klaas of the uNokhenke, signalling for them both to come forward.

'You see, Giant Slayer?' said Klaas as he thrust past Shaba's shoulder.

272

'There will be peace again. But you? Where will you go, brother? Shall you follow Cetshwayo into captivity?'

'And the promise of Jantoni?' said Shaba. 'To ensure the King has land of his own?'

Klaas grinned.

'He promises to do all in his power,' he said, and crossed the space to join the royal party.

Yes, thought Shaba, *such are the hyena words of Tricksters.*

The ox-meat had been sliced, the people of the ekuShumayeleni stronghold fed, the *utshwala* beer shared and served.

'Did I not tell you,' murmured Zama's father, 'that the Sky Lord has forsaken him?'

They were formed up still in two oblique lines, shields raised and spears held at their sides, the lines joining just behind Cetshwayo's ministers, his immediate bodyguards and guests.

'He is still the King,' said Shaba, 'and will remain so if the shades speak truth to the diviners.'

'I no longer believe,' said Mandla, 'that the shades may see so clearly. There are too many things to cloud their vision.'

'How many more will surrender?' Shaba said. 'Like my father?' And he wondered how the honour of his family might now be restored.

'There are many who will never do so. Mnyamana. Ntshingwayo. My kinsman, Zibhebhu.'

'Never?'

'Never. These are men who would welcome death before dishonour.'

Shaba was less certain now, but he watched as the Great King summoned the Dutchman and Klaas the Skirmisher to his side. They drank *utshwala* beer together and Cetshwayo regaled them with good-humoured anecdotes before giving the signal which permitted a dozen chosen warriors to begin performance of a *giya*. But Shaba noticed the way that the Trickster's fingers would sometimes stray to his necklace, the beads and bottles of coloured glass. *I have seen such things before*, he thought, *in the house of KaMtigwe's Witch Woman.* He remembered her, KaMtigwe's Supreme Wife, monkey-faced and carrying the stink of stale beer. He recalled the beans of the *umkhoka*, the distillation she had prepared for his eye. It had helped, though he still kept the eye sheltered behind its leather patch. Yes, it had helped.

'Yet there are those among us,' Shaba whispered, 'who know nothing of honour.'

'Jantoni's messenger?'

'The same,' Shaba replied.

He caught the glint of light on glass in the Trickster's hand as he squatted close to the Great King. Too close. Closer still to Cetshwayo's cup-carrier.

What is he doing? Shaba thought, suspicions burning like a fever within him.

He recalled Amahle's words. *'Their juice is poison,'* she had said.

Shaba took a step forward from his given station.

'Where are you going?' hissed Mandla.

The warriors performing the *giya* for Cetshwayo raised dirt as they stamped and spun, spear hafts hammering on shield hide, but Shaba tried to keep his vision firmly upon the Trickster, ignoring the dust and thrashing limbs, the sweat-smeared muscle, catching flickering glimpses of Klaas as he engaged in animated exchange with the King and his Dutchman. But always, Shaba noted, those fingers probed towards the necklace.

He edged further from the line, an unforgivable act, but he could not help himself. And then, as the dancers side-stepped, as heads followed the movement, turned to their left, Shaba thought he saw a sharp movement of the Trickster's hand, something dragged from the necklace, the fellow edging closer to Cetshwayo's cup-bearer. And he distinctly saw Klaas lift his hand cautiously to the cup.

Shaba sprang forward. But his path was not clear. He tried to dodge between the dancers but succeeded only in colliding with two of them, instantly snatching attention from the warriors to himself. All eyes were suddenly upon him, the King's advisors closing around their master and one of them stepping forward to block Shaba's way, though he too was knocked aside.

Shaba stumbled on until there was clear ground between himself and the Trickster. Klaas had turned to face him, surprise wide in his eyes as Shaba dropped his thrusting spear and seized the man's wrist, the fist that was now clenched tight. At the same time, Mandla was behind him, an arresting hand on Shaba's shoulder.

'What is this?' cried Mnyamana, as a dozen spear points were levelled at Shaba's chest, the *giya* brought to a sudden halt.

'This Trickster plans some evil towards the Great King, Lord,' Shaba yelled.

'Evil, how?' said Mnyamana.

'With poison, iNkosi. The white man's venom.'

'Show me!' demanded Cetshwayo, and Shaba willingly let his shield fall, his spears too, switched his grip so that he now took the Trickster's wrist in his left hand, using the other to begin prising open those treacherous fingers. The muscles in Klaas's face clenched, the bunched fingers also.

'You are a fool, little bird,' Klaas snarled. 'This is work for a true warrior.'

But Shaba took the man's fingers, pressed them tight, summoned all his strength to open the fist, to show the thing hidden within. There was nothing.

Klaas laughed.

'You see, Great King?' he shouted. 'This man dishonours me without justification. And not for the first time. I claim the right to settle this in blood.'

'Tell me why you should not both die?' said Cetshwayo. 'For disturbing this celebration.'

Ntshingwayo stepped closer.

'INkosi,' he said. 'I remember these men. Are they not the same who were chosen to *giya* before our victory at eSandlwana?'

'The same,' said Cetshwayo. 'The Giant Slayer of eKhambule. Destroyer of the iFulentshi Prince also. See? He wears the brass arm ring. And it was Giant Slayer's sister who was claimed by this Mouth of Jantoni who, in his turn, gifted the girl to KaMtigwe. And this, I think, is the source of their feud. Is that not true, warrior?'

Shaba did not reply. He was still foolishly holding the Trickster's wrist, the hand above stretched open, empty for all the world to see.

'I request the right once more, Lord,' said Klaas, to settle this with blood.'

Cetshwayo considered briefly then smiled.

'Very well,' he said. 'It pleases me that it should be so settled.'

It was the stick fight lived again, time frozen, as surely as the pointers had long since stopped on the time-counter still hidden among his kilt furs. He understood the thing's working well enough, but whenever he opened the case, turned the small metal stud at its gilded rim, the piece would only speak, its fingers turn, for a short while. Then it would count the time no more. Time frozen. Now, in the familiar crouching stance of the warrior. Though on this occasion there was no *ugwayi* to prepare them, and each man was equipped with shield and *iklwa*, a pair of throwing spears too. Yet these had already been flung, none causing any damage, so that the moment was right to close with each other, stabbing blades prodding, probing. And even without the *ugwayi* stimulant, there was frenzy in them. Shaba could smell it, the scent that began as a small creature, the sour sweat of fear that must be passed beyond. For those that stayed within that fear were dead before the fight had even begun. It must be devoured, cast upon the first ember of hatred and fury, the sourness turning sweet. Burnt honey. Yet even as the fury twisted to flame, this also needed control, to be mastered, only the metal taste of simple weapon reflex remaining. So they circled, first one way, then the other, spear points flickering like serpent tongues until Klaas made his first move, scuttled forward and swept the spear around, a reaping blade, back-handed, letting the shaft run through his fingers to extend its reach, in the stroke that could easily hamstring man or beast.

Those watching the spectacle howled in appreciation, though Shaba had already sprung back, but not too far, so that as the Trickster's arm continued its arc and showed an opening, he jumped into that welcoming embrace, thrusting the *iklwa* towards his enemy's exposed right breast. The blade was easily deflected by Klaas's shield, but it still pierced the fellow's spear arm, sliced a sliver of flesh just below the shoulder. Yet the wound was minor, did nothing to prevent the arm closing around Shaba's back, locking them together. Their faces were pressed together, the Trickster's dung breath in Shaba's nostrils.

'Blood,' Shaba panted. 'You see the blood, Izimu?'

'Still that same thing, little bird?' Klaas replied. And Shaba knew that each of them was equally pleased with the respite.

Klaas used his shield to push Shaba away and, in doing so, the upper edge of the toughened hide caught his face, knocked the eye-patch askew so that white sunshine dazzled him briefly. Shaba closed the eye quickly, shut out the light as Klaas charged forward again, aiming a savage blow that would have felled a bull, passed through belly sinew and spine alike if he had not parried, used his own haft to knock the spear aside. But it still found Shaba's flesh, cut him just above his left hip. The watchers roared again, chanted, while Shaba flinched, not with the injury to his side but with the jarring pain in his arm from the clash of the two wooden shafts.

'Second blood, my brother,' said Klaas as they separated, catching his breath, settling back into the crouch as he planned his next move. He moved cautiously, step by step, around to Shaba's left.

How will this end? Shaba wondered. *If I die here, it will be without honour. And if I kill him, it will prove nothing to the Great King. I am likely to be killed in any case. And my father will think even less of me.* Klaas feinted to Shaba's right. *Yet do I not see myself as Hlakanyana? He who uses the medicine of life itself to defeat the evil ones.* And then the Trickster played his part.

'Do you see the bull, little bird?' he said, his spear arm caked with blood. 'How is your wound?'

Shaba was crouched so low that he could feel the earth's caress against his buttocks, a light breeze stirring against his legs, against the trickle of his own gore that ran there. He looked down quickly at his side – remembered the fatality of such a temptation. And in the space that he had been afforded, Klaas stepped quickly to Shaba's left, his blind side again. Though not so blind now as it had been at the stick fight. Shaba opened his clouded eye as the Trickster closed fast, stabbing spear held low and shield high. Falling back before Klaas, Shaba thrust his own shield forward and down so that the force of his foe's blade embedded itself in the cow-hide.

At the same time, Shaba let his own *iklwa* drop, gripped the edge of Klaas's shield, pulling it towards him, allowing himself to fall backwards, raising his foot as he rolled, planting it in the Trickster's belly, lifting him high so that he turned over completely, slamming onto his back, winded and groaning. And while the crowd yelled his name, Shaba jumped to his feet, snatched his spear, kicked away his defeated enemy's weapon, planted a victorious foot on the Trickster's chest and raised his blade. But the time-counter called to him from its hiding place. He thought for a moment, cast aside the shield, put the point of the *iklwa* to Klaas's throat, shifted to his side, pushed his other hand into the thin leather strip that held the fur tails of Izimu's own kilt.

'Should have killed me, brother,' whispered Klaas. 'You are too weak.'

Shaba glanced up to see the Great King. Those around him were still chanting, some leaping in the air, though Cetshwayo was sitting impassively, a hand on each of his knees. He raised one of them, held it wide, a gesture that Shaba knew was a permission to dispatch his vanquished enemy. But the victor had other plans. He continued to run his hand along the waist-band until he found the thing he sought. It was a small vial of green glass, the twine that had fastened it to the necklace still tied around the top. He held it between finger and thumb, lifted it so that the Great King might see. Then he set his foot back on the Trickster's chest, held up the bottle, tapped the edge of his *iklwa* blade against its upper section, breaking it away. He bent over, took hold of the other man's face, stared into his eyes.

'Do you see the bull, Izimu?' said Shaba, and squeezing the fellow's cheeks hard, until his lips parted, poured the liquid down this traitor's throat.

It was not a clean death. There seemed to be no pain, but after a few minutes it was plain that Klaas had lost control of his body. His arms and legs were affected first, the Trickster unable to move them and, though he tried to speak several times, his face no longer functioned, nothing but the desperate eyes that cast about, seeking a salvation that would never come. Then he lost control of his bowels, the shite splashing along his stricken thighs.

Cetshwayo beckoned Shaba to his side, where the Dutchman was being held. He was gibbering in his own language, a wet stain spreading down the leg of his leggings.

'I should have listened to you, Giant Slayer. I should not have doubted you.'

'I doubted myself, iNkosi.'

The *isanusi* was circling the Dutchman, smelling him, sniffing for evil. But he found none, and Cetshwayo ordered the release of the white man – who ran off to vomit. Shaba glanced over his shoulder at Klaas. The Trickster was moving again, but only convulsions of his stomach, the chest heaving until he moved no more, the heart finally stopped.

Cetshwayo smiled.

'That creature had best be released,' he said, pointing with disrespect at the corpse.

Shaba crossed the ground once more, picked up the *iklwa* and slid it easily into the Trickster's lifeless abdomen, allowing the innards to spill with all the grey and purple beauty of a new calf falling from the womb. He cast down the spear, returned to the King while the other warriors took turns to bury their own blades in the body, sharing the moment, sharing the honour.

'It is done, Lord,' said Shaba.

'And how should we reward you now, warrior?' said Cetshwayo. 'You already bear the *iziqu*. You have received cattle. You wear the brass ring. What more do you want?'

'The cattle were lost, Lord. And my only desire now is to restore my family's honour. My father, iNkosi, is one of the same coastal headmen who have surrendered to the Fat Queen's general.'

Cetshwayo dismissed the matter with a flick of his wrist.

'I do not believe that to be your greatest problem, Giant Slayer, Killer of Snakes,' the King said, seemingly with reluctance.

Shaba looked for an explanation, and Ntshingwayo kaMahole Khoza came forward. He was an awesome presence, this victor of eSandlwana.

'I have been explaining that I was present when the *iNkatha* was burned, Warrior of the uMbonambi. It is a tale that touches you also. Far beyond the theft of your cattle. Beyond the loss of Mandla kaSibusiso's daughter.'

'I do not understand, Lord,' said Shaba.

'Then listen well, Giant Slayer,' Ntshingwayo leaned towards him. 'For the man who betrayed the *iNkatha* to the red soldiers was our old friend, the trader KaMtigwe.'

'Lord,' Shaba stammered, 'that cannot be!'

He might despise the white man, yet it seemed incredible that he could sink to such a depth.

'He was about to be executed for this crime when the horsemen arrived. He was helped to escape us.' Shaba was filled with dread, wished to close his ears. 'By your sister. She was with him. And because of this, their lives remain forfeit.'

Shaba fell to his knees before the King, stared at the ground.

'Great One,' he said. 'The shades have brought many fates together this day. And you remember my sister's story, Lord. She was claimed by that poisonous snake, who now lies dead in his turn before you. And through him, this KaMtigwe sought her as his wife. The fault is not her own, iNkosi. And she would have been no willing party to the burning of the nation's soul.'

'You seem to forget, warrior,' said Cetshwayo, 'that I granted KaMtigwe the right to marry your sister. Do you query my judgement?'

'No, Lord.'

'Well, that is wise,' said the King.

'Then allow me to be the nation's executioner, iNkosi. To slay the white traitor, KaMtigwe.'

'And in return, you will ask me to spare the life of your sister?'

'That, Lord, and to extend your forgiveness to my father for his surrender.'

There was a shout from the watch tower that flanked the outer gate of the

278

stronghold. Strangers craving admittance to the King's presence. And one of them a white man.

'Does the entire world know my whereabouts?' said Cetshwayo, then shouted, 'Bid them enter!' He turned again to Shaba. 'So, Giant Slayer, Killer of Snakes, you have made a wise request. Kill KaMtigwe and your sister shall be pardoned. And when I sit again at oNdini, as the *isanusi* has foretold, your father shall be suitably honoured.'

Then the King looked past Shaba's side, to the procession of bearers who were climbing the slope towards this upper part of the homestead. At their head was a mounted white man who wore a strange hat, domed, the shape of half an ostrich egg. They passed the place where the Dutchman was wiping his face, words were exchanged. The visitors remained on the track, while the Dutchman returned alone.

'Who is this fellow?' said the King.

The Dutchman was more pale than normal, his skin tinged with green. 'He is an American, Great King,' he said. 'He brings greeting to you, iNkosi. And he says he has a message.' He turned to Shaba. 'From this warrior's sister, Lord.'

The American had left many days ago and, in truth, he had brought more than one message. The first was, indeed, from Amahle: news that she and her husband, the traitor KaMtigwe, may soon be setting out on the long journey, by sea, to the Land of the Fat Queen. It had been suggested that they might travel with this same American and a party of Zulus that he had gathered for no better purpose than to entertain the AmaNgisi with dancing and similar foolishness. He insisted that there was great honour in this, and the possibility of some wealth also. But the bait that Amahle principally held out to her brother was the possibility, should Shaba agree to join them in their travels, of reconciliation with their father.

'The Lord-in-the-Sky has sent you this gift,' Cetshwayo had said to him when they were later alone, 'so that you might fulfil your promise to me. Go to them, Tshabanga kaNdabuko, and slay KaMtigwe. Slay the traitor and save the life of your sister.'

It seemed never to occur to the Great King that in the Land of the Fat Queen, both KaMtigwe and Amahle would be beyond his reach, but in any case, Shaba took his duty seriously and so it was arranged that, before the American's party left for the coast, two days after the next full moon, Shaba would join them at Hluhluwe.

The second message concerned Cetshwayo himself since, in his travels north, the American had encountered several patrols of the horse soldiers that were charged with searching all the *imizi* in which the Great King might be hiding, using information provided by local spies and informers. And while the Great King at first refused to believe that any of his people would betray him thus, the American explained that he had, himself, discovered Cetshwayo's whereabouts by just such a method. Indeed, it hardly seemed even a betrayal since the people appeared joyfully proud to know the location of their iNkosi and offered the information with a degree of self-satisfaction. So when the American headed south again, the Great King took counsel and agreed that the Dutchman would be sent back to the camp of the white general, with still more messages of appeasement, while the Great King himself would travel to another of Mnyamana's strongholds, though the First Minister begged leave to remain at ekuShumayeleni.

'Will he hold the red soldiers here, if they come?' said Shaba, as he followed Zama's father and the other body servants of Cetshwayo's entourage out of the isiKhwebezi Valley.

'I think,' said Mandla, 'that Mnyamana kaNgqengelele Buthelezi is heartily pleased to see our backs. And it troubles me that we are heading for yet another of his homesteads.'

It was a propitious remark, for they were no more than two days at their next resting place before word arrived that horse soldiers were approaching. Yet they escaped by secret places, moving steadily north until, at last, they came to the Ngome Forest and the kwaDwasa *umuzi* of Mkhosana, one of the First Minister's own chieftains. It was another natural fortress, a sloping bowl, open to approach only from one side, but otherwise entirely surrounded by steep rocks that rose up to hide and protect it, yet with secret tracks that climbed those cliffs in places to provide escape routes. Safe a place as it was, even here Mkhosana pleaded with Cetshwayo to move still deeper into the forest, to those lands that even his own people did not fully know. And his pleading became ever more strident as, day by day, runners arrived to bring the chieftain details of yet more surrenders.

'Whey!' said Cetshwayo when he received one more bitter piece of news. 'It seems that the last of my brothers has now given himself into the white general's custody. Most of my chieftains too. Even Mnyamana has disappeared from my sight.'

'Then, Great Lord,' said Mkhosana, 'let me lead you to places that the red soldiers cannot find.'

But strangely, Shaba noticed, Cetshwayo did not seem greatly daunted by his situation.

'This is a good place, my friend,' said the Great King. 'I am content here. For all those about me now are my most loyal people. But we can talk about it on the morrow.'

That night, Shaba stood guard alongside several of Mkhosana's men and his gate-keepers. They had no great fear of attack during the darkness since the horse soldiers made such a commotion in their travels that they could be heard from a considerable distance. And here, with the forest's undergrowth and the surrounding cliffs to further protect them, there was even more security. So it was with numbing disbelief that they first heard them, not stumbling among the vines and creepers to their front but behind them, spreading around the outer palisade of the homestead, lighting torches as they ran that soon filled the night with flame and shadow, rifle fire and shouting.

How have they come here? Shaba wondered. Yet the answer was obvious. They had done so by the very secret paths that were supposed to provide the means of escape for the Great King. And that could mean only one thing. That they were betrayed yet again. But there was no time to ponder this treachery, for the red soldiers were now breaking through the forest also, the whole *umuzi* completely surrounded.

Shaba saw one of the gate-keepers with a rifle, a modern gun from eSandlwana, but the fellow was fumbling with its mechanism, untrained in its use. So he snatched the thing away, turned the warrior around so that he could find bullets in one of his leather pouches. Loading quickly, he fired. Then again. Yet it was almost impossible to find a target while, beside him, two of his companions already lay dead or wounded.

He backed away, through the entrance to the inner palisade, loading a final round as he went, retreating with a dozen others across the cattle enclosure to the upper gate and the dwellings in which Cetshwayo and his wives were housed. *Is this it?* thought Shaba. *The place where I die? If so, I am glad of it. For the chance of finding Zama's shade may be slight, but better than no chance at all.* In any case, he calculated, there could surely be no finer way to meet his end than a final battle against the whites, here at bay, with Cetshwayo himself to lead them. Yet there was still no sign of the Great King. Mandla was at Shaba's side and the chieftain Mkhosana too. But not Cetshwayo. Indeed, his absence seemed to have signalled some manner of truce for each side, since the red soldiers, though having formed a firing line across the open ground, had not fired any further, and in their centre, some white officers were in discussion, finally sending forward a tall warrior, one of the People of Heaven, alone towards the huts. As he came closer, Shaba could see that he wore a wooden cross around his neck, a sign of the Jesucristo. The warrior stopped just in front of Mkhosana.

'I see you, *kholwa*,' said the chieftain. 'What do you want here?'

'I bring word from the white iNkosi,' said the Jesucristo follower.

And from the huts to Shaba's rear came the unmistakeable voice of the Great King himself.

'Is that you, Voice of the White Queen?' called Cetshwayo.

'I am that Voice,' said the *kholwa*.

'And what is the word that you bring here?'

'That you must surrender to these red soldiers, Great King. Otherwise, they promise to burn this place down about your royal ears.'

There was silence, broken only by the crackling of the blazing brands carried by the whites, as though to punctuate the warrior's words. The *kholwa* turned back towards the red soldiers, shrugged as though to ask what he should do next. But at that moment, Shaba, hearing some hushed words from Cetshwayo's dwelling, looked over his shoulder to see the Great King duck through the hut's low entrance, then straighten himself to his full imposing height before advancing towards his enemy, his gleaming white teeth fixed in a smile of welcome.

So the morning broke with Shaba having enjoyed no sleep. Nor any other among Cetshwayo's followers. They had spent the short time between the attack and the day's first thin light under guard, with the Great King repeating the same thing over and over again.

'I am astonished,' he would say. 'How strange!'

But the red soldiers had not been inactive, for no sooner had Cetshwayo emerged from his dwelling to greet them, as though they were guests in his home, than they had sent horsemen off at great speed. And the sun was barely risen among the trees when another group of white men also arrived, bringing wagons with them – making the point yet again, for Shaba, that they must have been guided here, to have a camp and wagons so close.

They left the wagons near the outer gate to the *umuzi*, allowing the Great King to cross the cattle enclosure in some ceremony, carefully attired in his finest leopard skins and tails, the royal necklace of lions' teeth around his neck, his eight wives behind him. The first carried his drinking cup, the second and third bore gourds of Sorghum beer, wrapped in basket-weave to keep the *utshwala* cool and held above their heads, and the fourth held the crafted clay jug of the King's Royal Milk. The rest balanced bundles of Cetshwayo's other personal possessions, while Shaba, Mandla and the body servants trailed behind, dressed in as much finery as they could assemble. But the red soldiers took little notice of anybody except the Great King himself. They were formed in two lines, between which Cetshwayo must pass and, as he did so, their *induna* barked an order. The soldiers' rifles came up to their sides as one, and Shaba flinched. But then they swung the weapons in a second movement, held them upright before them, in a clear and crashing salute to the Great King. And, despite all that these enemies had done to him, and done to his people, a tear rolled down Cetshwayo's cheek.

'The AmaNgisi,' he murmured to Shaba, 'I cannot help but love them.' And, as Cetshwayo was handed up into the first of the wagons, he turned to Shaba once more, looked about him to check that he would not be overheard by his enemies. 'Tshabanga Giant-Slayer,' he said quietly, 'I think that here our paths must part. Perhaps for the final time. For I think you have a duty to perform elsewhere.'

Chapter Twenty

Saturday 30th August 1879

The Carey household had all the appearance of a military headquarters on campaign.

The room was littered with paper, one scattered pile of letters already opened and awaiting replies, a second cluster of envelopes yet sealed, a third of part-drafted responses. Then the spread pages of *The Times*, the *Daily News*, the *London Standard*, and the *Portsmouth Evening News*. There was the recently delivered copy of the *Illustrated London News* too. It included the sketch of Chelmsford being handed that damn'd sword by some lieutenant, Lysons. Pure fabrication, of course, an entire mythology of its own now developed around the blade. *'The sword carried by Napoleon at Austerlitz'*, one fool had written. Or another fable, that Louis had died fighting with the sword in one hand and the hair of a Zulu in the other.

Outrageous nonsense, thought Carey, as he threw aside a map of the Cape Colony. Yes, there were even maps, though these were mercifully folded just now so that the apparently endless stream of visitors might at least have somewhere to sit, even though it may only be on one of the precarious spider-legged chairs. It had been this way since his return to Portsmouth eight days earlier. Visitors in droves and some strange ones among them. But it all served to stoke the fire of his endeavours. For the initially sweet word – that the decision of the Court Martial had not been confirmed – quickly turned sour. He might have been released from arrest, yet he was far from exonerated. There was, he knew, a question mark clearly visible above his head in the minds of the public and the army alike, and he must expunge it at all costs. So he had sought leave and made a tactical retreat to Campbell Road from which location his campaign would be orchestrated.

The house was not old and must initially have maintained its own ambitions and pretension, having been named "The Lodge", rather than simply "Number Four". In truth, there was little to distinguish the dwelling from its neighbours. A dark porch and several steps rose to the front door, ornamented above by a panel of stained glass though, sadly, in such a position that no sunlight ever penetrated the barely discernible blues and greens to the vestibule and hallway beyond. At the farthest extremity of the entrance hall lay the kitchen and scullery and, at the very heart of the accommodation, the large parlour, which also served as a dining room, with a window that gave onto a cobbled yard and neglected pots of flowers. Upstairs there was a large front bedroom; a nursery – shared by young Edi and baby Pel; and a guest bedroom at the rear. There was a privy. There was running water. And the whole property had been secured at a rental of three shillings and fourpence per week, with the lease renewable on a three-monthly basis. It was a decent arrangement, though the house, like Carey himself, seemed incapable of meeting the ambitions it had set itself. Still, they had been pleased to find the lodgings, back in January, when – with his studies at the Camberley Staff College completed – they had moved Annie here from Farnham. It had been easy enough to find, since, these days, the entire population of Britain seemed in a constant state of flux. *Will it always be like this now?* Carey often wondered.

'I may take the children later and see how the pier is coming along,' said Annie. She was sitting on the floor, her skirts covering at least some of the mess. 'Edi will be back in school next week and I shall miss our days out.'

They had all withdrawn here to the front parlour simply to make the clutter even worse, it seemed. But at least the scattered paper was lent some animation by their daughter's favourite books: a vivid edition of *Through the Looking Glass*; the lurid illustrations of *The Water Babies*.

'And then may we go to the beach, Mama?' said the seven-year old. 'I don't like the new stories very much.'

Annie closed her mother-in-law's *Naval Stories for Children*.

'Well,' she said, 'we have done our duty, I think. We can at least tell *Grandmaman* that we have finally read the book. I shall tell her that I think these stories more appropriate for young boys, so we shall save them until your brother is older.'

The little one at her side squealed in frustration, having succeeded in standing but still unable to take the steps he so desired, with the inevitable result of yet another fall.

'Should he not be walking by now?' said Carey. 'I'm certain that Edi was getting about long before this?'

'You were barely at home when we were in Gibraltar,' his wife replied. 'All that time you spent seeking a new regiment.'

He had never been happy in the 81st. Only ever seen it as a temporary step.

'We couldn't have lived on half-pay for much longer, my dear,' he said. 'Not with the baby an' all.'

They had married in 1870. In Jamaica, of course. A new beginning after the Honduras affair. But, very quickly, the Almighty had intervened.

"Mortify therefore your members which are upon the earth; fornication, uncleanness, inordinate affection, evil concupiscence, and covetousness, which is idolatry."

He had coveted happiness, of course. An idolatry. And within weeks punished by the news that the 3rd West India Regiment would be disbanded. So they had sailed to England. An opportunity, in any case, for Annie to meet his Ma and Pa. She had stayed with them when Carey had seen another chance to establish himself. For the English Ambulance Service was seeking volunteers. France. Five months helping the wounded on both sides in the war between the French and Prussians. And there he had at least made the contacts that secured him a posting to the 81st.

'I hated it there,' said Annie. 'In Gibraltar. The wives looked down their noses at me. And they thought you quite eccentric. One thing to risk your life for Queen and Country, they would say. Quite another to put oneself out for Frenchies and the like. And when I told them about your bravery, my dear, they would often laugh at me. As though I was lying...'

She paused – a self-conscious pause – helped little Pel to his feet once more.

'What is it, my dear?' said Carey.

'Nothing at all,' she replied. Though it was a hasty response.

Does everybody doubt my word these days? he thought. *About everything. Even my wife?* He was tempted to find his commendation, then realised the stupidity. It was always difficult, coming home again. Studying each other afresh. The discomfort of long-lost strangers. And he imagined how it must have been for her. *My letter to her after Louis was slain. His body coming home at more or less the same time. The nation's grief. The funeral. They say that forty thousand mourners lined the route. But how did she feel? How did she deal with the neighbours, the other mothers in the park, when word arrived of her dear husband's involvement?* And then, of course, word of the victory must have arrived. Ulundi. It should have been such a joyous occasion, surely. Yet Carey knew that it had been overshadowed by the Prince Imperial's death. A national shame. Carey to blame.

'This time, dear heart,' he said, 'it will truly be a new beginning.'

'You really think the regiment is bound for India?'

'According to Uncle Peter,' Carey replied. There was no point having an uncle as Bailiff of Guernsey if he could not be relied upon to provide some worthwhile intelligence here and there.

'But shall I be able to come too?' said Annie. 'And what about the children.' She pulled Pelham Adolphus close to her, squeezed his fat little fingers. 'Will they be safe? I could not bear it if...'

He glanced quickly at the photograph of their lost child upon the white marble fireplace.

'I have no explanation, dearest,' he said. It was the fever in Jamaica that had taken baby Jahleel, yet he knew, logically, that the infant would have been equally at risk here. 'I read last week that one in every three babies fail to see their first birthday. Here, in England.'

'How heartening,' she snapped, 'to be so representative. Just the average family. Is that what you mean?'

'I intended only to say that the children will be no more at risk in India than here. It is all a matter of God's will.'

'And truly a new start? The Good Lord knows that we need one. We must be the most notorious family in the country.'

'Not for much longer, Annie.' He picked up one of the letters. 'Once my name is cleared, we can return to a normal life.'

'Do you not fear that all this simply draws still more unwelcome attention?'

Carey looked around the room. He would be glad to see the back of it. The mantle shelf with its photographs and Bristol glass candlesticks, reflected in the ubiquitous wall mirror above; the blackleaded iron of the fire surround; the heavy curtains trimmed with thick fringes; the oppressive smell of oriental carpet. The littered round table, piled with books, its central vase and fern, the uncomfortable, curved sofa. The empty bird cage and the oil lamps – it would all be left behind. The withdrawing room from which, he hoped, they would soon withdraw.

'I need to set the record straight,' he replied. 'And that task would have been easier, my dearest, if I still had the letter.'

Annie stood, suddenly, lifting Pel into her arms.

'Edi,' she said, her voice brusque, 'come. We will go look at the new pier.' She turned to Carey. 'It seems that Papa blames me for our difficulties yet again.'

'I said no such thing,' Carey protested.

'No, but you thought it, husband, did you not? Thought that I should not have taken the letter to your parents; nor allowed them to share it with that strange woman they call a friend. But perhaps, my dear, the error was more in the writing.'

She walked into the hallway, carrying Pelham and holding Edith's hand, stopped only long enough to slam the door behind her. He knew that she was correct, of course. It had been almost the first thing he had done when he returned from that dreadful patrol. He had sat at the writing slope, emotional, full of fear and self-loathing, blamed himself entirely. The letter brimming with his confusion. By the time of the Court Martial, naturally, he had seen things differently. The disaster not his own fault at all. Nobody's fault, in truth. And yet, during the long voyage home, still uncertain about the hearing's decision, he had begun to go even further, seen the blame resting far more with Louis himself. He had said so since his return. He had said so publicly.

But the letter still vexed him. It was missing. Annie had received it, been disturbed by the contents, and travelled almost immediately to Brixham to visit Ma and Pa. His father, she had said, was sympathetic, his mother less so.

The situation had not been helped by the presence of Ma's friend, Miss Octavia Scotchburn of Totnes, who was staying with the family at the Vicarage for a couple of weeks. Miss Scotchburn was a Francophile also – desperately disturbed, Annie had said, by the death of poor Louis. And though his wife had not directly shared the letter with Miss Scotchburn, she had foolishly left it behind when she returned to Southsea.

It was quiet after Annie had gone out. Too quiet. And he fretted about the conflict that was building between them. But a knock at the front door annoyed him still further. *Is there no end to the visitors?* he thought, as he padded down the hall, opened the door to find a short and stocky fellow, roughly the same age as Carey himself. He had a full beard, wore no hat and his high-buttoned suit jacket was shabby.

'Captain Carey, I presume?' he said.

Carey thought at first that the man was being ironic, for there was nothing in his own attire that would betray the military. He had thrown on a loose linen shirt over his breeches early in the morning, and the smoking cap and slippers gave him, he considered, an entirely Bohemian appearance. But the gentleman showed no hint of humour.

'I am, sir,' Carey replied. 'And you are?'

The man sniffed. 'Biddlecombe, sir. Detective Constable.'

'A policeman?' Carey was puzzled then remembered, 'Ah,' he continued, 'the letters. You took your time, Constable, didn't you?'

'Detective Constable, sir. And we give each case the priority it merits.'

Carey apologised, invited the policeman to enter, ushered him into the front parlour and cleared some newspapers from one of the spider-legged chairs. Biddlecombe sat on it warily, wriggled his backside, testing the chair's steadiness.

'So, Detective Constable,' said Carey, 'the threat to a man's life sits precisely where, among the priorities of the Portsmouth City police?'

'Poison pen-letters are rarely a true threat, Captain. Not in my experience. May I see them?'

'If I can find them,' Carey replied. He rose from the uncomfortable sofa, crossed to the elaborately decorated brass coal-box on the hearth. The letters were underneath.

'How many, sir?' said Biddlecombe.

Carey held them in one hand, fanned them with the other.

'Three.' He passed them over.

'And you've received how many letters in total, sir? About this... this affair, Captain.'

'The affair?' Carey hesitated. 'Well, as you can see,' he gestured around the room. 'I must confess that I haven't counted the rest. Two hundred, perhaps.'

'And the nature of the others, Captain? Condemnatory for the most part, I imagine?'

'Why should you imagine that, Detective Constable?'

'Well, sir,' Biddlecombe nodded towards the newspapers, 'the papers have been full of it. The official report published. The Duke of Cambridge quoted like that, speaking on behalf of the army, he says. That you acted in a manner much to be regretted. Weren't those his words? Attempts should have been made to rescue the Prince? Or am I misquoting, sir?'

'I was tried by Court Martial, Detective Constable. It is the same as standing in the dock at the Old Bailey. And at the end of the process, I was released. How would it be if I was acquitted from the Bailey and then somebody – the Law Lords, for example – began publishing letters saying that they disagreed with the verdict?'

'I can't answer for that, Captain. I'm simply making the point that with all this news coverage – and most of it hardly favourable to you, sir, if you don't mind me saying – it would hardly be surprising if most folk hadn't taken against you.'

Carey desperately wished now that he had indexed the things. He rummaged among one of the piles.

'Well, here's an interesting one,' he said, handing a letter to Biddlecombe. 'It's from a fellow who served with the 90th in the Amatola mountains last year. Against the kaffirs. You see, Detective Constable? He talks about the number of times they were ambushed. How it feels to be in that position. The importance of getting as many men as possible out alive. He congratulates me on saving the rest of the patrol. There are quite a few like that. Others that talk about me being a scapegoat. Then all the political stuff, a few rabid republicans pleased to note that one more symbol of imperialism is dead. Some from France, too. This one even praises me for having caused the Prince Imperial's demise. Down with the Bonapartists, he says. Ah no, that was a woman, of course. And this was a woman too.' He handed across another envelope. 'Sent from La Rochelle. Accuses me of being part of a conspiracy by Her Majesty's Government to prevent the resurgence of the French monarchy. Old enmities and so on. But you're right, I suppose. There are plenty of armchair soldiers among that lot, happy to just brand me a coward.'

'And aren't these so-called death threats just more cranks with nothing better to do? You don't take them seriously, sir? This one, for example,' he turned the script towards Carey. It contained simply the words, *"Die! Die! Die!"*

'The others are slightly more graphic,' said Carey. He took one of the letters back. 'This one promises to follow me until he has the chance to strike me dead. He's from Birmingham, do you see?' He pointed at the third. 'That one claims to come from the leader of a society formed specifically for the purpose of taking my life. And do I take them seriously? Yes, I suppose I do. You see, death has been considerably on my mind lately, Detective Constable. Here's an amusing story for you. I sailed back from the Cape on board the *Jumna*. When we arrived in Plymouth, stopped there on the way here, I was still under arrest, of course. There were enormous crowds waiting. My notoriety had preceded me, d'you see? I was not allowed to disembark, and neither would they let my father come aboard to visit me. But they allowed the journalists. They organised a meeting with them, some sort of collective interview where those gentlemen fired questions at me. And one of them – a fellow from the *Graphic*, I think – asked me the question outright. Whether I thought the sentence of the Court Martial might be death. And, d'you know, Detective Constable, until that moment I had never even considered the possibility.'

'It's a common enough verdict, is it not? For cowardice in the face of the enemy, that kind of thing.'

'It had not entered my head, nor the heads of any around me, that I was facing anything other than the possibility that I might be cashiered. Dishonourably discharged. A terrible fate in itself. But I swear to you, Detective Constable, that those few days that followed, until the *Jumna* dropped me finally, here in Portsmouth, were the longest and most terrifying of my life. In my mind I had gone from the most relaxed house arrest to the condemned cell. Just with that one question.'

'It must have been a great relief then. The acquittal.'

'Is that what you call it?' said Carey, the fear returning. 'The judgement conveyed to me was that the decision of the Court Martial had not been confirmed.'

'And the Court Martial's initial decision had been?'

'Ah, that I have still not been told. They don't, you see. Only that it was not, in the end, confirmed. Oh, and the helpful addendum. That the decision had been received – and I quote verbatim here – with a recommendation to mercy. Can you believe, Detective Constable, that a recommendation for clemency would have been necessary if their decision had been simply to cashier me?'

Some time later, Biddlecombe left him in peace, having determined that the letters, emanating self-evidently from various parts of the country, should more properly be investigated by Scotland Yard. Carey had agreed to take them with him when he caught the train to Waterloo later that evening – though he was certain that the hate mail would continue and he doubted the police would discover anything.

'They were all anonymous, of course?' said Heseltine, when they met later, sharing beer at The Admiral's Head, pale ale for Heseltine, ginger pop for Carey.

'That's the strange thing,' Carey replied. 'One of the three was signed by a fellow from Birmingham. Told me precisely how he intended my punishment and was even kind enough to include a return address.'

'Then he'll be arrested, surely?'

'I hardly think they'll bother.'

'A good thrashing then? We could arrange to have him horse-whipped.'

'I have a better brush to bag,' said Carey.

'Then if you deny me that privilege,' Heseltine smiled, 'I demand a first-hand account of your adventures.'

They had exchanged the briefest of farewells when the escort had come aboard the *Jumna*, relieved Heseltine of his charge, escorted Carey ashore.

'You must forgive me, Heseltine,' Carey said, still somewhat unaccustomed to the equality of their ranks, 'but I seem to have recounted it so many times.'

'But you met the Prince?'

'Yes, Prince Edward of Saxe-Weimar, General Officer Commanding the army's Southern District. He read me the letter in person. From Horse Guards; from the Duke – I'd thought it would simply be an aide, but it was Prince Edward in person.'

'He released you from arrest?'

'Returned my sword.'

'Literally?'

Carey laughed. 'Nobody had even thought to relieve me of it in the first place, You certainly didn't, old chap. No, it was still safely stowed in my dunnage.'

'Oh, we'll make a matelot of you yet, Carey.'

'It's in the blood already. Remember?'

'Ah, the venerated Grandpapa. The old Admiral!' Heseltine looked up at the taproom's beams, 'Of course, how appropriate.'

'I could sense him looking over Prince Edward's shoulder as he read the memorandum. There were some procedural points, it seemed. Witnesses not sworn in, that sort of thing. Made me feel a fool. Hadn't even noticed that, at the time. Then the evidence. They did not bear out the charges, they said. And therefore, to use their very words, I was relieved from all consequences of the trial.'

'All except the Commander-in-Chief's musings on his own account, that is,' Heseltine murmured. 'And it's a bit rum, isn't it, trying to blame Harrison too?'

'It seems that the Colonel failed to give me orders that were sufficiently explicit, or didn't impress upon Louis the duty to defer to myself. So the poor Colonel doubly damned. But it makes my very point, Heseltine, don't you think? Recognition that the fellow wouldn't take orders.'

Yet the thing that really grated with Carey was the Duke of Cambridge's conclusion, his claim to speak with the voice of the entire army when he said

290

that Carey and the other survivors had withdrawn without being sure that the Prince's fate was sealed.

'But it won't do you much good to say so, will it, old boy? Can only help to aggravate matters, don't you think?'

Carey ignored the advice. 'Tell me about Hackett,' he said. 'Have you heard how he is?'

'Well, he doesn't seem to have suffered any repeat of the fit.'

'I thought we were going to lose him,' said Carey, recalling the crisis in the Major's condition as they passed through Suez.

'Yes, me too. But he's safe in Netley now. With Longmore.'

'Longmore?'

'Professor,' said Heseltine. 'World's leading expert on gunshot wounds. Apparently says he's never seen anything like it. Bullet passed right through Hackett's head but didn't kill him. They say he'll make a full recovery.'

'That's good,' said Carey. 'And how are you getting on? Yourself, I mean.'

'Financially? What is this, Carey? Ah, I see. Trying to change the subject. Very clever. But you won't get away with it. I shall keep on nagging you until you give in. You need to let it drop. Get on with your life. For your own sake. Your wife and children too.'

'You think so? You think it's reasonable that I should be relieved from all consequences of the trial yet still be subjected to the Duke of Cambridge's continued allegations that I'm a coward? How can that be fair? Due process followed, an acquittal, but still facing the opprobrium of the authorities. I tell you, it will not do! I shall clear my name or be damned in the process.'

'It doesn't seem like justice, I'll give you that.'

'Justice?' said Carey. 'They fail to find enough evidence to make the charges stick. But then Cambridge, our beloved Commander-in-Chief, issues an invitation in the newspapers that I should be held up to public damnation. But I'm glad you've landed back on your own feet, Heseltine. It's made the world of difference to Annie and myself – a Captain's pay, I mean.'

'Then don't do anything stupid to jeopardise it. That's all I'm saying.'

'As it happens,' Carey replied, 'I've found that I can usually rely on the Almighty to bring me back down to earth. I get the step and then I'm landed with all this on my plate.'

'And what is the Word of the Lord on this, Carey? "*He that troubleth his own house shall inherit the wind: and the fool shall be servant to the wise of heart.*" Isn't that it?'

'Proverbs 11:29,' said Carey. 'I know it well.'

'Let sleeping dogs lie then.'

'That's precisely the advice that Knollys gave me last week.'

'Knollys of the 83rd?'

'The same. He stayed with us last week. Acquaintance of my Uncle Peter.'

'I'm impressed,' said Heseltine. 'And you should heed him. Now, will you have another ginger beer?'

'I don't think so,' said Carey. 'But thanks all the same. I'm heading off to London later. Then Brixham. To see Papa. Try to speak with my mother. Make her understand. I've written a letter to *The Christian*. Asked them to insert a request for praise in their next number. Explained that from the first, I have taken the whole matter to our Heavenly Father. And in doing so, Heseltine, He has brought me to this haven. Do you not think it would be wrong if I deprived our fellow-believers of this example of God's love? I hate publicity, Heseltine, but I think *The Christian* should publish my story. And in the same vein, the public at large deserves to hear the truth.'

'Then may God preserve you in your crusade, Carey. But, for pity's sake, do not allow it to destroy you.'

Carey's third visitor that day, in the middle of the afternoon, was his own commanding officer, Attilio Sceberras. Annie had taken Edi out into the yard, so she might play in the shade, and Pel was enjoying an afternoon nap. She had been curt upon his return from The Admiral's Head, but would never have dreamed of washing their private linen before a guest.

'Might I offer you tea, Colonel?' she suggested.

Sceberras looked somewhat uncomfortable in the parlour's clutter. Carey had thought of taking him through to the back room, but feared that Edi's exuberance, her frequent comings and goings, might disrupt their discussion or simply inflame the Colonel's grief.

'I thank you, dear lady,' the Colonel replied, standing from the sofa and bowing to her. He was a particularly dashing example of the Maltese aristocracy and had assumed command of the 98th in the previous September. Yet he seemed to share the same fate as Carey himself, having suffered the loss of an infant son. 'And the household all well, I trust?' Sceberras continued.

'They are, Colonel,' said Annie, her eyes downcast, apologetic. 'And our condolences on your own loss.'

'It is still so difficult,' Sceberras replied. 'Does it become easier? With time?'

'It's six years since we lost our own,' Annie replied. 'He was barely a week old. Poor little mite. It's hard to imagine the bonds that form in such a short time, Colonel. Yet there is never a moment passes without me thinking of him. I cannot imagine what it must be like to have lost a child after eleven months.'

'Matilda cannot bear even to speak of it,' said the Colonel.

"For this child I prayed," thought Carey. *"And the Lord hath given me my petition which I asked of him. Therefore also I have lent him to the Lord; as long as he liveth he shall be lent to the Lord."*

'We may only find comfort and understanding in the scriptures, do you not think?' he said.

'The Lord moves in mysterious ways, it is true,' said Sceberras. 'One minute we had the news of my promotion, the next poor Charlie fell ill. So sudden, Carey. So immediate.'

He sat again, heavily, upon the sofa. *Yes*, thought Carey, *the rug pulled from beneath one's feet. I know the feeling well.*

'I shall fetch that tea,' said Annie. She shut the door very quietly on this occasion.

'Your wife is still in Malta, sir?' Carey enquired.

'With her family,' said the Colonel. 'And she did not relish the journey to Guernsey.'

Carey had been several times to the regimental depot on Guernsey, and each occasion had provided the chance to visit his own extensive family there. 'New drafts there, I suppose?' he said.

Sceberras nodded. 'There's talk of India, Carey. Things not going well out there again, they say. I'll not be going myself, of course.'

'You still intend to retire, Colonel?'

Sceberras smiled, though it was sad, wistful. 'In March, if all goes to plan. It's time. Stracey will take over, though he hasn't long to go himself, I think.'

'I wish you all the luck in the world, Colonel. But after Stracey?'

'Who can say?' said Sceberras. 'But at least you will be in an infinitely better position as a captain to take advantage of any further opportunities. You deserved the step, Carey. I've rarely seen an officer who deserved it more. There's talk of amalgamation too. But tell me about Chelmsford. He's asked to meet you, hasn't he?'

Chelmsford had arrived back in Plymouth on the previous Tuesday, to great acclaim, and made his way to Bath, before proceeding to London.

'He sent me a note, sir. Congratulated me on my acquittal and invited me to meet him at Horse Guards. I doubt that I shall be so amicably received by the other senior officers though. All the same, I'm due to catch the evening train tonight.'

'Acquittal? Was that the word he used?'

'He did, sir. Although the outcome seems to have been something else.'

'I read the reports, of course,' said the Colonel. 'Bad show, trying to put Harrison in the frame too. I've wondered several times, Carey, whether Lord Chelmsford would have agreed the Prince Imperial's participation in the patrol if Harrison had specifically put the question to him, as they now suggest he should.'

'I don't think you understand, sir. Louis was a man born to command. Not one who could easily be denied. Not even by somebody in Lord Chelmsford's position. If Louis had decided he wanted to go on the patrol, no force on earth, short of shackling him to the bedpost, could have prevented him. Can you imagine if you were asked to accompany a patrol of which

Prince Edward was a member, even an unofficial member?'

'That may be a fair point for the debating chamber, Carey, but it's less than prudent to spread it abroad in the newspapers. The *Daily News* would have been bad enough. But the French papers, Carey? The *Gaulois*. What were you thinking?'

'He was among the correspondents they sent aboard the *Jumna*.'

'And since then? There seems to be hardly a day goes by without your name cropping up. Blaming the Prince for choosing the ground to off-saddle at that damn'd kraal. You think that wise?'

'It's the point I've been trying to make, sir. That whenever Louis made up his mind about something, the men would automatically take it as a command. It's a point that I think even the Adjutant General may have overlooked. So I wondered, Colonel, whether I could trouble you to glance at this draft to him.'

The Parkins & Giotto writing slope had returned with him from Africa, sat now upon the table. Carey opened one of the two front drawers and removed a carefully folded letter.

'It defies all protocol, Captain, for you to write directly to the Adjutant General.'

'Yes, sir, of course. I understand that very well.' Carey was a little offended that Sceberras should have taken him for such a fool as to imagine otherwise. He handed over the letter. 'That's why I wondered if you'd be so good as to send it on my behalf.'

'To the Adjutant General?'

Sceberras stared at him.

'Yes, sir.'

There was an embarrassed silence, broken by Annie's return with a tray of tea. There were few words exchanged while the cups were poured and, realising that the atmosphere would be more difficult to cut than the sponge cake she had brought, she quickly withdrew.

'I cannot believe, Captain,' said Sceberras, setting down his plate and saucer, 'that I'm even considering this. If I was not due to retire, I think I might take a different stance. As it is, well, let me think about the content.' He held up the draft. 'Some of this wording is inflammatory, to say the least.'

'I'm happy to accept any changes, sir.'

Sceberras sighed.

'Very well,' he said, 'a few changes and I will send it on your behalf to the Adjutant General. I'll deal with it as soon as I get back to Malta. As it happens, I agree with your broad point. That it cannot be correct for Horse Guards to continue vilifying you. They need to confirm that you are vindicated.'

Carey was elated. 'Thank you, sir,' he said. 'I could not be happier. But I wonder whether I might impose upon your good nature just a little further?'

'In what way, Captain?'

'I wondered whether, when you're with the regiment again – in Malta, sir – you might read the letter to the officers' mess?'

'Is that a serious request, Carey?'

'A formal one, sir.'

Sceberras coughed. 'Do you not think that might explode in your face, Captain?'

'I simply want to ensure, Colonel, that when I rejoin the regiment myself, there is no doubt in the other fellows' minds about my innocence.'

'Very well, Carey. I'll do it. But I think you're making a big mistake, young fellow. Excessive protestations of innocence can often invite an opposite and equal assumption of guilt, don't you find? And the mess has its own particular brand of politics. You should be enjoying the rest of your leave. Put this thing behind you. And, besides, we need to talk about getting you back on active service. What shall we say? That you'll make arrangements to be in Valletta by the end of November?'

'Of course, sir. But I shouldn't worry about the mess. They are all sterling fellows. And India?'

'That may not be the posting. Why do you ask?'

'Because, sir, if it's possible, I should like to make early application for my wife and family to accompany me.'

'Did you not think to consult me first?' said Annie, as Carey finished packing his carpet bag.

'It's nothing more than an application.'

'You're a captain now,' she replied. 'It's a mere formality, surely?'

'But you've been with me on every posting.'

'Except when you went off to France. And Zululand, of course.'

'Those were active service postings, my sweet one. India will be different. A new beginning. A genuinely new beginning.'

Carey threw the third volume of *The Moonstone* into the bag. He would finish it on the train, though goodness, it had filled him with such visions, such images of India. But Annie remained tense. *This is unlike her, Carey thought. I've never known her stay so cantankerous, so peevish, for so long.*

'Genuinely?' she said. 'A new beginning? Another one, Jahleel?'

There was a hint of sarcasm. But something else, as though his wife was fearful. The death threats? he wondered. Carey wished that Detective Constable Biddlecombe might have been as circumspect as Wilkie Collins's Sergeant Cuff, but perhaps he might find a similarly dedicated officer when he reached Scotland Yard.

'India will be different, my dear. I shall be a few days in London. Then to Brixham. Though the Vicarage is likely to be bursting at the seams. The girls all there. Frances and her children. But I must at least try to get that letter back.'

Annie put her head down, clenched fists at her side. 'I wish you'd never written the thing,' she pouted. 'But you'll not find it in Brixham, my dear.'

'What d'you mean?' said Carey.

'I received a note today,' his wife replied, her voice shaking. 'From Miss Scotchburn. It seems that your Mama gave her permission to borrow the thing. I've no idea why she should have done so. But Miss Scotchburn, the foolish creature, tells me – simply as a courtesy to myself, she says – that she has felt it her duty to forward your letter to the Empress. To the Prince's mother… to the Empress Eugénie.'

Chapter Twenty-One

Sunday 31st August 1879

'You were there when they captured him?' said McTeague.

'Three days ago,' Amahle's brother replied. 'At the *umuzi* of Mkhosana. At kwaDwasa. You must be pleased, Three-Eyes.'

The homestead had been awoken, following the night of the full moon, with the news that there was a warrior with no name seeking admission at the gate and McTeague, already washed and shaved, had been among the first of the curious now clustered near Hluhluwe's watch tower.

'Ntshingwayo called me that once,' McTeague recalled. 'And why would I be pleased at the Great King's capture?'

'Did you not betray him already, KaMtigwe? Betray all of us, by telling the red soldiers about the *iNkatha*. Helping them burn the heart of the AmaZulu.'

'Ntshingwayo told you that?'

'He did.'

'The same Ntshingwayo who promised to die before surrendering to the red soldiers?' Shaba remained silent, and McTeague saw the doubt in his eyes. 'You know already, of course? That Ntshingwayo surrendered half a moon ago?'

The Dutchman, Cornelius Vijn, pushed through the gathering.

'Is it true?' he said. 'That Cetshwayo is taken?'

'I was there, Dutchman,' said Shaba. 'Why were *you* not with him? He trusted you. Like he trusted this one,' he lifted a finger towards McTeague, a sign of great disrespect. 'And Jantoni too!'

'He trusted many,' McTeague told him. 'Like Mnyamana. Like Zibhebhu.' McTeague saw the warrior's finger fall, further doubt creeping into his eyes. There was that difference about him. No eye-patch – and the eye that Maria Mestiza had treated; less milky perhaps. 'It is the truth,' he continued. 'They have both surrendered.'

'My father too, they say,' said Shaba.

And I thank the Almighty for that! thought McTeague. It had been welcome news that Wolseley was now established back at Ulundi and its surrounding territory. And with these coastal chieftains already surrendered, Hluhluwe had at least provided a potential haven, the threat of Ntshingwayo's revenge somewhat diminished. A temporary haven, it had to be admitted, given the

Dutchman's most recent news. But a haven. *Time to consider the future afresh. A time for new beginnings.* And Ndabuko had so far been a considerate host, pleased to have his daughter back within his homestead, proud to demonstrate Hluhluwe's fame as a centre of excellence for iron-working.

'Ndabuko kaMahanana is an excellent fellow,' said McTeague. 'He is a true father to his people. And I think you judge the Dutchman badly also. I think you should hear his story before you accuse him of treachery.'

'After they were sent the clothes of the French Prince, the English offered me much gold,' Cornelius Vijn explained, 'to lead the horse soldiers, to help them find the Great King. But I tried to persuade the white general that Cetshwayo should remain as king. I could not believe what he said to me. Impossible, he said. The Queen would not allow it. And they were already passing a new law so that Cetshwayo could be imprisoned. On the Island of Seals.'

'But it was not you, I think, Dutchman,' said Shaba, 'who showed the red soldiers the place where the Great King lay.'

'I led them by false trails,' said Cornelius Vijn. 'The white general was unhappy. But then Mnyamana surrendered. And the English told him about their plans to break up the nation. To create thirteen smaller kingdoms. Though there would be no land for Mnyamana, they said, unless he worked with them, helped them. So he told them what they wanted to know. He told them where they might find Cetshwayo.'

'Whey!' said Shaba. 'And they found him. They waited until the darkness hid them. Then they climbed down the steep rocks that surrounded the *umuzi*. We thought those rocks would protect us. But they only served to trap us. He was betrayed then. It seemed that he must have been. By Mnyamana himself. Betrayed us all.'

Betrayed? McTeague thought. *Yes, young fellow. I imagine you would feel so. Betrayed by your father. Betrayed by your leaders. Betrayed by me too, I imagine. And do you harbour ideas of revenge, I wonder?* In truth, Amahle's brother troubled him, frightened him. *And in reality we are both betrayed by that scoundrel, Klaas. Although I could not be more pleased that he tricked your sister from you. But where is the fellow? Showing John Dunn where to find my treasure trove, I imagine.* Yet Klaas had not come for the sheep. When McTeague and his party had finally felt sufficiently secure to make the journey north to Hluhluwe, the sheep that Ndabuko and his fellow-chieftains had gathered were still there. Thus, they had proceeded with the plan, found some other trustworthy warriors to act as both shepherd and fox, to drive the flock towards Utrecht, making sure the beasts were regularly noted by a succession of British officers until, sadly, they had disappeared without a trace. Renegade Zulus to blame, naturally. And under the noses of the very authorities that now claimed to have made the byways of Zululand safe once more. A decent period would be allowed to elapse, of course, before the inevitable claims for compensation were tabled. And by then, hopefully, the dear woolly little creatures would have returned, wagging their tails behind them.

'Where did they take the Great King?' said Cornelius Vijn.

'They took him south. But a man never looked less like a prisoner. He went proudly, as though still at the head of our *impi*. Eight wives with him. His body servants too. I should have been one of them. But he released me from his service so I might fulfil my promise to the American, to go to the Land of the Fat Queen. And I slipped away then. Escaped again across the same ridges on which Basuto riders almost killed me after the battle.'

'Then you came here,' said McTeague. 'It was the right thing to do.' *It seems we are all drawn here by the Will of God*, he mused.

He had come here himself, with Amahle, with Simeon Cornscope, and with Nathaniel Behrens – who had outlined more of his plans for their mutual benefit. McTeague was still not convinced that the American might not have more readily satisfied his business needs by remaining in partnership with Dunn, yet it was clear that Behrens despised the man. And when McTeague had arrived with him at Hluhluwe, McTeague had found Pastor Jago Jupe here before him, along with his remaining seven wives and the dozen infants they had borne him. A dozen girls, of course. No sons. *How strange!* he thought, as he had done so often before. All the same, there were considerations to be made.

'The right thing?' said Vijn. 'For how long? The white general is bewitched.' He turned to McTeague, spoke to him now in English. 'It is Dunn, *Mijnheer*, who now advises General Wolseley on which chief should be trusted with each of the new lands.' He reverted to IsiZulu again, 'Thirteen lands and thirteen chieftains.'

'Those that surrendered,' said Amahle's brother. 'Like Ntshingwayo.'

'And Zibhebhu.'

'No,' said the Zulu. 'It cannot be. It is a lie. Zibhebhu kaMapitha is kinsman to...'

But he did not finish. Instead, he looked McTeague directly in the eye, and McTeague saw there a vision of such hatred that he physically flinched.

'And this place?' said McTeague. 'Is it true? About Jantoni?'

'It is true,' Vijn replied, 'that the largest kingdom will go to John Dunn himself. And Hluhluwe will be part of it.'

The crowd clamouring at the gate had been growing steadily and continued to do so now, with the arrival of the shaman, Mutwa. The Spirit-Speaker had become a familiar sight around the homestead to McTeague and the others, followed always by a half-tame and moth-eaten baboon. McTeague had made fun of the scampering beast – the baboon, in this case, rather than the shaman – in Amahle's presence, but she had scolded him, fear showing in her eyes. The creature was Mutwa's familiar, she had explained, capable of carrying him for many miles at unnatural speeds when the medicine man needed to move from place to place, or between this land and that of the shades. And no amount of reminders that, as a child of Christ now, she should set such idolatry aside could dissuade the sweet girl from her belief.

'Why are you here?' Mutwa cackled, withered and disdainful fingers extended towards Shaba. 'There is nothing for you here. You may not enter. The dark night of war is over, Warrior of the Evil Omen,' he said. 'And now, when we awake with the dawn, our enclosures have survived intact, still full of cattle. But where are *your* beasts, warrior? You fell asleep, it seems.'

'It is my father who lives the waking dream, Spirit-Speaker,' said Shaba. 'A dream of Mutwa's making, I think.'

Well, there's no denying that, thought McTeague, who had seen for himself the change that came over old Ndabuko whenever Mutwa was in his company. He wiped his brow, for it was uncomfortably hot today, and McTeague had been dizzy with it since daylight.

'If the war is truly over,' McTeague said, raising his voice above the general tumult, 'then let there be an end to all conflict. Peace within the homestead too. *"A time to love, and a time to hate; a time of war, and a time of peace,"'* he quoted. 'It might be wise, Spirit-Speaker, to send word for the headman himself that his son is here.'

'INkosi Ndabuko kaMahanana has no son,' hissed the shaman. 'And who are you to interfere in this?'

'And I spit on your words also, KaMtigwe,' said Shaba. 'There is nobody who has brought more evil to this family than you, white devil.'

His words washed around the inside of McTeague's head in a manner that was less than comfortable. They swilled behind his eyes like water in a swaying bucket. They rattled around the empty room between his ears. They tightened a tourniquet below his armpits and around his chest.

'It was Klaas who claimed your sister, I think,' McTeague replied. 'He wished for something more decisive to say. Something that would bring this confrontation to an end, allow him to withdraw, to sit in the shade.

'Well,' said Shaba, 'there, at least, is a tale that has an ending.'

What does that mean? McTeague wondered, though it was not the time to pursue his question.

'But it was yourself, your boastful pride,' said Mutwa, 'that wagered her away. How many times have you shamed your father? His cattle neglected while you played boys' games. His crops untended while you looked to your own ambitions. His craft unfollowed while you chose other paths. His daughter's marriage cursed with ill-omen by your self-seeking challenge.'

'And are those the words that you whispered to my father?' Shaba said. 'The words that turned to poison against me in his mind?'

The crowd had swollen still more, Cornscope and Behrens clearing a path for themselves. Amahle too. McTeague could not see her plainly though, for her image seemed distorted. He raised the monocle to his eye, though it fell free again almost at once. *Ah*, he thought, *here she comes. To stand between myself and evil once again perhaps.*

'I need whisper no words to the iNkosi,' snarled the shaman. 'Not as you have whispered words to him against my counsel so many times in the past. And this white man that you despise so much is your sister's husband, their marriage blessed by your father. Would you deny his authority in this also?'

He has a point, thought McTeague, though he quickly found that he could not quite recall its substance. And he felt the band around his chest take a turn for the worse. The world swam and McTeague staggered forward. He stretched out his arms, the crowd's roar resounding in his ears, knowing that he was going to fall. And his hands fastened on the genet-fur wrapping that topped the centre-stick of Shaba's shield. McTeague wanted to ask for help, but no words would come. And besides, his brother-in-law seemed equally dumbstruck, surprise registering on his face, the wicked point of the stabbing spear raised, about to strike.

There were devils that ran hither and thither to the rhythm of a distant drum.

'"*But the fearful, and unbelieving,*"' somebody was saying to him, '"*and the abominable, and murderers, and whoremongers, and sorcerers, and idolaters, and all liars, shall have their part in the lake which burneth with fire and brimstone: which is the second death.*"'

The Book of Revelation? he wondered. Yes, that was it. But whoremonger and sorcerer? That seemed unfair. A surfeit of Encore whisky perhaps, but other than that he had always been forthright with the Almighty about his own deficiencies.

The world flowed back upon him in an exact reverse of its ebb, raging outwards to leave him cold but sweat-ridden, and causing him to vomit copiously onto his own sleeve. He was still dizzy but he looked up to see Cornscope pushing people aside.

'Give him air,' Simeon was shouting, although none but the couple of English-speakers could understand him.

More immediately, Shaba still held the spear above his head. He was shaking the thing, back and forth, but he no longer seemed to pose a true threat, simply confused. Yet behind the warrior, Mutwa crouched, a knife now in his hand. McTeague tried to lift his own arm, but it fell back, weak and useless, onto the dirt. He saw the Spirit-Speaker rise, the knife poised to strike at Shaba's back, while the baboon cowered at his heel.

'Behrens,' McTeague croaked. The American took a step forward began to bend, doffing his bowler. *He thinks I want to speak with him*, thought McTeague. 'Knife!' he managed to say, and allowed Behrens to follow the direction of his gaze.

Behrens turned at the moment when Mutwa sprang at Shaba. The American rose between them with a speed that belied his size, caught the shaman by the throat in mid-air, swung him sideways and slammed the old man against the gate post. Mutwa's head jerked back, cracked like an egg against the timber, and lolled to one side. *Not quite what I intended*, thought McTeague. *But...*

He vomited once more.

There was a howl from the crowd. Outrage. Spears, sticks, hunting clubs and stones raised against Behrens. The baboon screeched, leapt onto his shoulder, clawed at the circus man, bit into his flesh. The American bellowed, dropped the shaman, turned and jarred the ape against the gate post also, unfastening the holster at his side and taking out his revolver so that, as the baboon loosed its grip, jumped to where Mutwa's body lay, he was able to put one bullet into the thing, then another, until it lay as dead as its former master. Another howl and the crowd surged forward, appalled, menacing, to seize Behrens and to seize Shaba also.

As the mob dragged the warrior away, he looked down at McTeague.

'Izimu the Trickster,' McTeague thought he said.

Then there was only chaos. More noise than McTeague could manage, the others pushed, pulled, harangued by the people of the homestead until, finally, Ndabuko kaMahanana was among them.

'Stop,' he shouted. 'You will stop!'

They released Behrens. Ndabuko's body servants ran to form a cordon around his guests, a cordon beyond which only Shaba remained isolated, still held captive.

'I see you, Father,' said the warrior, struggling to free himself from those who held him, 'and I see the shame of our clan, that we have surrendered so easily to the Fat Queen's general.' He spat upon the ground.

'And I see the shame of one who dishonours his sister's wedding, dishonours his father.' They glared at each other for a long time while McTeague struggled to sit, Amahle running to his side.

'Has there not been enough?' she said. 'Does one shame not cancel the other? In the name of the Sky Lord, let it pass!'

Ndabuko looked down at the dead shaman.

'Who did this?' he demanded.

'He tried to kill my brother,' said Amahle. 'Though I think he was only trying to protect my husband in your name, Baba. The American killed him instead. What would you rather have? A Spirit-Speaker or a son?'

'Mutwa served our clan and this *umuzi* for more years than any of us have lived,' said Ndabuko. 'And his counsel was good, even though it was often more heady than the strongest *utshwala*. Perhaps he spent too much time in that place between the worlds. But I will miss him.'

'That creature enslaved this place,' said Shaba. 'This entire clan.'

'Have you no respect for the shades, boy?' replied his father. 'For the burden that Mutwa carried to commune with them on our behalf?'

Amahle tried to help McTeague get to his feet, though he could not manage it, sat down heavily again, vomited for a third time.

'We need help, Baba,' she said.

Ndabuko summoned several of his warriors.

'Carry KaMtigwe to his sleeping mat,' he cried. 'And send for Kwanele the *inyanga*. Care for him.'

'And my brother?' said Amahle. 'Who will care for him?'

Ndabuko nodded.

'I see you, my son,' he said. 'I thought you lost to us. And it seems that you now owe this American your life.'

Shaba looked resentfully towards Behrens.

'I think you will find, Baba,' said Amahle, 'that while the American prevented my brother's death, it was my husband who alerted him. Without his warning, your son would now be with the shades.'

Assisted by Ndabuko's warriors, McTeague finally managed to stand, took an uneasy step forward, gripped Shaba's arm to steady himself.

'It seems, my boy,' he said, weakly, 'that you may now be somewhat in my debt.'

'My brother tells me,' said Amahle, lifting his head from the sleeping mat in their hut and feeding him a few sips of water, 'that you have done a terrible thing, husband. That you betrayed the *iNkatha*. Is that what Jantoni meant? At Emangweni? He asked if I knew what you had done and later you would only answer that he is a man filled with lies. Is it true? About the *iNkatha*?'

He felt as weak as a new-born babe and did not, in truth, want to have this conversation. But he knew he must be honest with her now.

'My dear,' he said, 'I am a man who sins often. But I speak with God about those sins. The True God, mind. To explain myself. A man may sometimes do things badly, but with good intent in his heart. And when he confesses those things to the Lord – who is mightier than all others – his deeds are understood, forgiven.'

'And what did the Lord God say, husband, when you confessed your part in the *iNkatha*'s destruction?'

'That it was necessary for the good of the many.'

'Not simply to gain personal favour from the white general?'

'My dear, those were precisely the words that the Almighty used. Go forth, He said to me, and gain favour with the Fat Queen, that this wicked war might be ended the sooner, that the suffering by the People of Heaven might end.'

'Our God told you to burn the *iNkatha*?'

'Not that I should personally burn it, no. But He moves in mysterious ways, sweet one. As a child of God yourself now, you will come to understand.'

'I may do so, husband, but my brother will not. He had you under the blade of his *iklwa*, he says, and promises that one day he will have you there again.'

'But you see, dear heart, how God stayed your brother's hand? Is that not proof that He has blessed my actions? And how can your brother harm me, when he owes me his own life?'

'The warrior who would not show blind regard for Mutwa the Spirit-Speaker is unlikely to feel himself bound by any notion of blood-debt, husband.'

Yes, that was a worry, McTeague had to admit. *Yet here come many more troubles,* he thought. One after another, his other seven wives came bobbing through the entrance, visiting, their dozen children scattered among them. *How old is the biggest now?* he tried to recall. *Six, I suppose. All strong though.*

The wives chattered respectfully with Amahle, asked for news of their husband's condition, bade each of the children in turn to touch him, to place their gifts, so that he was soon covered in bunches of herbs, clusters of wild flowers, some hand-polished stones and, miracle of miracles, a bottle of Encore, rescued they said from the ruin of eMoyeni. Yet the thing they carried with the most reverence was a book. They had saved his copy of *Nickleby*, and his heart was uplifted at the familiar touch of its green Morocco. *But what am I to do with them, Almighty God?* he mused, when the visit was done and Amahle eventually chased them all from the hut.

Amahle busied herself at the hearth, a pot of broth simmering there, a concoction that the *inyanga* had prepared. As it happened, McTeague felt perfectly fine again. Somewhat debilitated perhaps, but that would be the vomiting, he thought. Yes, something that he had eaten. And at his age, what else might one expect?

What would Dickens have made of it all? he wondered, though he knew the answer, of course. He had read the pamphlets. For there had been Zulus a-plenty in London while the master was writing the final chapters of another tale. *Bleak House*, was it not? McTeague had not seen the shows himself, but he recalled the newspaper reports that rebounded around the world, sensationalising the staged depictions of King Shaka's terrible and despotic rule, of war dances, of Zulu singing. But Dickens had deemed the performances as showing the great gulf that, he said, existed between civilised Europe and barbaric Africa. He did so with typical humour, of course. Satirical too, reminding his readers that some of the show's scenes resembled nothing so much as an Irish election.

Well, thought McTeague, *even the most astute of authors might misjudge if they base their views simply on a theatrical show.* There was nothing of the noble savage in the character of the Zulu, of course, and they could be wild in the face of a sometimes harsh environment, but it seemed to McTeague that their savagery did not come close to the butchery of the Napoleonic Wars, nor the punishment inflicted by the English on its Indian mutineers, nor the careless spread of European disease that had decimated entire races. In contrast, he had come to admire the Zulus' clear governance structures, their independence; the reliability of their grain and cattle economies. And if he followed Nat Behrens, went to England with him, he would miss this place.

But if only, he thought, *the Zulus were touched by God!*

'I saw him for the first time in '61,' said the American. 'I was thirteen years old. It was June and the first battle of the war with the Rebs had just taken place. But that all seemed a long ways distant for those of us that lived around Niagara. Billy Hunt had crossed the Falls for the first time just a year before. And now he was back. I tell you, Major, it was a real slapjack. I was never going to be anything but a circus man after that!'

'They say he was better than Blondin in his day,' said McTeague. He had persuaded Amahle to let him sit in the sun.

'Blondin? Shoot, he was just an amateur compared to Bill Hunt. Wherever Blondin stretched his rope, Billy would come back and rig his own, closer to the Falls. If Blondin walked the rope with a man on his back, Billy would go the following month and carry somebody a stone heavier.'

As it happened, McTeague felt as though he were walking a tightrope too.

'And does your proposition still hold, Mister Behrens?' he said.

'That it does, Major. But d'you think she'll buy it?' Then he whispered, 'Your good lady wife, I mean.'

'Do you doubt my authority, sir? In my own household?'

'Wives can be a tricky business, Major. Had one myself, once. Back in the day. I had a four-car show, all of my own. No big shakes, you know. But that wife of mine, she didn't take to it. Said I had to choose. Settle down back east or lose her.'

'You lost her, I gather?'

'Sometimes there are just things in a man's life that need losing. Hey, don't get me wrong, I still miss her, Major. But like I say, I was never going to be anything but a circus man. The shame of it all? I lost the show too.'

'You hit the bottle?'

'Hell, no! She set fire to the cars. Burned me out. But I came across Barnum the next year. He'd just gone into the circus too.'

'I saw some of his shows,' said McTeague. 'Jenny Lind. Tom Thumb. Magical.'

'Oh, he was a great promoter, Major. But the circus, that's where he's got real talent. The best wagon shows in the world. Back in '74 he had two running at the same time. Can you imagine what that takes?'

McTeague admitted that he could not. 'But this proposition comes from Mister Leonard?'

'Billy prefers to be called Farini these days,' Behrens replied. 'But yes. He came to see one of Barnum's shows, persuaded me to work for him instead. He's had me on the road ever since, looking for novelties. Why, Major, it was me who collected the White Elephant for him – though it didn't make him the profit he thought it would.'

'And now you're collecting Zulus.'

Behrens ran the palm of his hand down the oversized walrus moustache.

'Not just *any* Zulus, Major. We already contracted with one group. And they're doing just fine, I'm told. But I had to take pretty much what I could get, back then. This second consignment's going to be something else. Yessir! Honest to goodness warriors who fought at Isandlwana and Khambula. Ulundi even. Scenes from the royal kraals too. We'd have bought Cetshwayo outright from Wolseley if we'd been able. The old fellow would have come too, I reckon. He's a great man, don't you think?'

'I do, Mister Behrens,' McTeague replied. 'Such a pity that he could not have been left free of the white man's machinations.' He caught the twinkle of amusement in the American's eye, remembered foolishly divulging his own part in setting some of the kindling for the fire. 'But if you can't have Cetshwayo?' he went on, hastily.

'Then Billy Leonard will invent a royal family of his own. And, if she's willing, that beautiful wife of yours – forgive the impertinence, Major – will be front and centre. There may have been Zulu shows before, but there's never going to be one to beat the Great Farini's!'

'They tell me, my son, that you killed the Skirmisher, Klaas?' said Ndabuko.

'I killed him because he tried to poison the Great King,' said Shaba.

There was a considerable gathering around Ndabuko's hearth and, though McTeague had already heard the tale, it still fascinated him. *On whose behalf was Klaas acting?* he asked himself, and not for the first time. *Dunn's? Wolseley's? One of the many Zulu factions now opposed to Cetshwayo? His royal brother, Hamu, for example.* Or was it some independent deed? Something that Klaas had believed would bring its own rewards?

'Not because you were driven by this feud between you?' Shaba's father pressed his son. 'The hatred about your sister's marriage?'

'He wove a web that linked Amahle and KaMtigwe,' said Shaba. 'And whether we like it, or like it not, that link has caused her life to be forfeit. His too!'

Shaba waved his hand towards McTeague, who recalled the way Amahle's brother had so quickly raised his spear against him when he had taken ill. And a new surge of fear rose in McTeague's gullet.

'Our lives forfeit?' said McTeague. 'Who claims this?'

'The Great King,' Shaba replied. 'And the iNkosi, Ntshingwayo kaMahole Khoza.'

'But those are yesterday's men,' said Ndabuko.

'Their arm is still long,' Shaba replied.

'Hluhluwe will soon be ruled by Jantoni,' said Ndabuko, 'as the new king. And though I do not like it, he has no quarrel with this clan.'

'Yet he has one with you, KaMtigwe, does he not?' said Shaba.

Behrens asked for an explanation and McTeague offered a hasty translation, while the others gathered in the dwelling waited on his response.

'Well,' he said, at length, 'whether Jantoni has a quarrel with me, or whether my life is forfeit elsewhere among the People of Heaven, my own path is clear. I cannot stay longer in KwaZulu. So what are my choices? To cross over into Natal? To go live with the Dutch? Or the Portugee? None of these would give your sister the future she deserves. But there is another way. One that the American offers us. To go to the village of the Fat Queen. To grow fat there ourselves from the gold that the American promises.'

'But as what?' shouted Shaba. 'To parade like slaves for the red soldiers' children? Trophies of war?'

'My husband has spoken with me about this thing,' said Amahle. 'And, through him, I have spoken to the American too. To dance the *giya* or *mayile* in that place is not to act the slave, brother.'

'I'm all for it, in any case,' said Cornscope in English, though Pastor Jago Jupe seemed less enthusiastic.

McTeague begged a moment from his host, that he might explain himself to his associates.

'Old friend,' McTeague set a hand on Simeon's shoulder, like a blessing, 'I fear the Almighty has other plans for you.'

There was a flash of fear in Cornscope's eyes. He withdrew from McTeague's grip.

'The freight business,' said Jago. 'What happens to that?'

'The Lord has spoken to me,' said McTeague. 'And these are his words. That Simeon is called forth to oversee the development of our business. With perhaps the occasional extra-vocational enterprise to help trade flow more fully.'

'Me?' said Cornscope, as though a death sentence had recently been commuted to something entirely more benign.

'Simeon, old boy,' cried McTeague, 'who else would I trust with such a thing?' *Who else indeed?* he thought. *All my decent options are dead and gone.* 'It will all be legal. Above board. That petty-fogger, Trounce, in Durban, will see to the details.'

'And you will take your wives with you?' said Cornscope. 'All of them?'

'Only Amahle,' replied McTeague, noting the gleam in Simeon's eyes, the slobbering expectation on his lip. 'The good Pastor will use my own share of the profits to build a mission station, here at Hluhluwe. To bring the word of God more effectively to our friends. And thus my remaining wives, my children too, will have both the protection of the Lord, as well as my stipend, to keep them in the comfort they deserve.'

Disappointment dripped from the end of Cornscope's nose, while Shaba's face worked angrily, waiting for this flow of foreign words to end.

'And who will protect my sister?' he said. 'When you are in the land of the Fat Queen. You, KaMtigwe?'

'To speak truly,' McTeague replied, 'I thought that *you* might be her protection, my boy.'

Shaba laughed, though it was mirthless.

'Whey,' he said, 'I rid my life of one trickster and another enters. You think I would play the white man's fool? Why should I do that? Klaas is dead now, not from my own anger but from his betrayal of the Great King. I am reconciled with my father. And Mutwa is gone also. I would not have harmed him, out of respect for my father's faith in him. But he is gone and I am not sorry. Yet he did not die at my hand and he spoke some true words before his death. That I need to work for our clan now, to learn my father's craft.'

Behrens sought yet another progress report, so McTeague updated him, while Amahle's mother spoke.

'Those things are important, my son,' she said. 'But this war has delayed many things. And perhaps the matters of which you speak can also wait a while longer. If my daughter's heart is set on this foolish journey across the oceans, I think your duty to us may lie in staying by her side, as KaMtigwe has suggested. He is not a bad man, I think, and it may benefit you to spend time in his company.'

McTeague saw the warrior grin. *Ah*, he thought, *he is taken with the idea of forging brotherly bonds between us.* But then he changed his mind, for Shaba's smile reminded him of another he had seen in the past, in Honduras – on the face of a predatory jaguar.

'I must give him this, at least,' said Shaba, 'that if it had not been for the doctoring by his other wife, the Witch Woman, the juice of the *umkhoka*, I would not have the use of this eye once more. And I might now be wandering with the shades, fallen under the *iklwa* of Klaas Izimu.'

McTeague thought often about Maria Mestiza too. Honduras again.

'Then come with us to the Fat Queen's place,' said McTeague, though he had begun to develop a sense of dread that it might not be quite the thing.

'And what of the war?' said Shaba. 'If there are still those who would resist the Fat Queen, there may still be honour and rank to win.'

McTeague interpreted his words.

'Then tell him this, why don't you?' said Behrens, then turned to Shaba. 'Because, son, there's nobody left who *wants* to fight. This war's over. And I can't promise you the honour or rank, but I sure can guarantee you enough gold to buy those steers. And hell, boy, if you like London, you could always come with us when the show moves on to America. All the land you need to go with them. All the land in the world.'

Chapter Twenty-Two

Monday 22nd – Tuesday 30th September 1879

If all the iron-shapers of the world, those among his clan, all who belonged to the amaChube, all the shades that, when they had existed in the lands of the living, had once been iron-shapers themselves – if all those could have conjured a single magnificent dream, they could not have created this one. There was polished timber too, of course, in places but, for the most part, this was a thing of metal, and the metal coated in shining white.

Shaba could begin at the rearmost rail, where the red flag billowed and the sea birds screamed, and he could walk forwards more than a hundred paces until he reached that place beyond which none but those who served the beast could go, at the very point where its sharp beak cut through the crashing waves. It was not a simple path, of course, from one extremity to the other, for there were steps of windswept iron to be negotiated, floors of water-washed iron to be trodden upon, the red-painted iron smoke stack with its blackened tip to be admired, and smaller beasts of salt-sprayed iron to be passed, each hanging by ropes from rust-streaked iron branches. So much iron. And there were, of course, those sections of the ship where he was not allowed to go, since they belonged to the various white amaKhosi and their wives, the rooms and decks restricted on this floating *umuzi* to the highest ranking and their body servants.

Through KaMtigwe, he had learned from the American that the beast weighed as much as ten thousand cattle, and though he knew that this ship was fashioned by the hands of men, he could not help thinking of it as a living, breathing thing. He had felt it from the first moment they had sailed on this, their second journey by sea. They had been nine days travelling overland to the coast, to an *umuzi* of the whites that equalled the grandeur and size of oNdini. There they waited for a smaller and most uncomfortable sea-craft to take them south to another place that made oNdini look small, a sprawling city of the whites, backed by an enormous mountain with an impossibly flat summit. And even this, KaMtigwe had told him, would seem as nothing compared to the Fat Queen's special place at iLondon. Yet in that city, after lengthy negotiations about the price of passage, about the places on a ship that the People of Heaven might be permitted to inhabit, they eventually joined this great vessel, only to retrace their route north again, until they left the coast of his own land far behind to enter the limitless and lonely expanse of the open, turbulent ocean. But back there, in the huge bay from which they had ventured forth, he had first felt the throbbing of the beast's heart through every inch of her iron skin. She vibrated with it, day and night, without rest. Through the harshest storm or the warmest calm. Never ceasing.

He had expressed such enthusiasm for this wonder that he asked whether it was possible to view the living sinews and internal organs of the creature, and he had been rewarded by an invitation to accompany the American and one of the ship-herds down into its very bowels. Though it shocked him, frightened him in truth, for while he had been able to wander apparently without end among the decks and passageways above the level of the sea, he now realised that the creature's greater part was actually below the waterline. Down and down they went on one set of metal steps after another, Shaba's head bursting with questions that he could not express either to the American nor the ship-herd and to which they, in turn, could not have responded anyway. He could sense the ocean all around them, feel its power as they rolled and slapped through its might; hear the iron plates groan against its grip, smell the acrid unguents that smeared every heaving limb, every rattling rod of the colossal machine that created the creature's motion. And he was seared by the heat of the furnaces that fed the machine. There was so much charcoal here. More than could have been gathered by all the tree-burners of the Nkandla Forest in a hundred life-times. But while Shaba had noted some dark skins among the topside ship-herds, he saw that in this place, this deepest hole of the vessel, the furnaces were fed by none but black men, who shovelled and glistened without end.

Is this what has happened to those taken prisoner by the red soldiers? he wondered. *Is this another trap into which I have fallen, and will I end my days here, like these?* He would have spoken with them but could not get close enough. Yet the fears temporarily left him when they eventually climbed back into the sun and he saw two other pieces of further evidence to the living nature of the ship. The first occurred when, to his surprise, great wings of white cloth sprouted and flapped from tree-like poles and cross-branches that rose from the ship's deck, one forward of the red and black smoke-stack, another towards the rear. He had seen smaller sails on the boats that plied the coastal waters near Hluhluwe, but these were vast and seemed to put a different beat to the vessel's motion, supplementing its engines. The second confirmed his view that this was a beast among other beasts, for there was a ripple of excitement through the passengers when the first families of dolphins came leaping through the waves to meet them amidships, then to fall into the churning white waters that streamed away from the vessel's rump, where the creatures would play and spin before eventually dropping behind. Yet each time this occurred, still more dolphin pods would come cruising towards the ship's sides, clearly attracted by her beating vibration like calves towards their mother's pulsing udders.

'Do you not feel the sickness yourself?' Amahle groaned. She lay on the ship's bed from which she had barely shifted these seven days and nights past.

'It is the creature's iron that protects me from it, I think,' he replied. 'For the iron is in my blood, is it not? Just as it is within the blood of our father, and his before him.'

'Then why is it not within my blood also?'

'You are a woman. These things work differently for women. If we had brought an *isangoma*, the healer might have explained it better.'

But there was no such healer on this boat. There was a white man who, according to KaMtigwe, claimed to *be* a healer, but he seemed incapable of curing this illness that afflicted not only his sister but also each of the others within their group – six more warriors – as well as a number of passengers for whom this was also a first voyage across the oceans. It was commonplace, apparently, this sea sickness which, for reasons that Shaba could still not fully understand, occasionally amused KaMtigwe to call *amahle-de-mer*.

'When will it stop?' she implored.

'This beast does not stop, either by day or by night,' whispered Shaba. 'She labours through the water until we reach the Fat Queen's place at iLondon. But your husband tells me that sometimes the sea itself needs rest, that the waves end and the ocean becomes calm. And then there is a place where, he says, we must cross a great desert of sand, on a gentle river that the white men created even though none existed there before.'

'Do you believe that?'

'I believe that a people who could dream this beast on which we sail, and who could turn that dream into this reality, must be capable of many things.'

'Their *izinyanga* must be very powerful,' said Amahle. She retched into the metal bowl at her side, but it was a dry retching, nothing left in her stomach.

'I thought that you would have attributed the thing to your new god, to your Jesucristo.'

'I am finding it hard to have much faith in anything just now,' she smiled. 'I think I am possessed by the Evil One.'

'You need to eat,' said Shaba. 'The white healer did not seem to know very much but I think he was correct in this. He said that you must spurn the sickness by continuing to eat a little and to drink often. Will your husband bring you some? Or will he send a white-coat?'

KaMtigwe had gone off to the eating hall. He had not left Amahle's side since she first fell ill, except when Shaba himself was here to care for her. And this was a great problem. For how would he fulfil his pledge to the Great King

311

if he could not get the white man alone? It was ridiculous. There should have been endless opportunities on this endless ocean to dispose of the fellow but, so far, any such chance had eluded him. Exactly the same as when they had been on the road to the coast. So Shaba had become suspicious. First, that KaMtigwe might, as he claimed, be himself protected by the Jesucristo and, second, that it was Cetshwayo's *isanusi* who had perhaps conjured this illness of his sister – some curse that would not be lifted until he had killed the white man. But, if so, why had the curse also afflicted so many others?

'My husband says that we would need to be ranked among the richer amaKhosi before we might merit a white-coat. But he has promised to bring a little porridge with him when he returns, though the porridge is very strange here.'

Everything is very strange here, he thought. They had not been able to prepare their own food since they first entered the ship, which, KaMtigwe had explained during a rare moment for discussion, was named for one of the Fat Queen's strongholds in her northern lands, from where KaMtigwe himself originally hailed. And the ship had a purpose of its own: to carry countless written messages from the lands they had left to those for which they were bound. This happened every seven days. In both directions. Yet, at the same time, other ships sailed from the Great Bay, with its flat-topped mountain, to other places with still more words. Then those other places generated messages of their own, destined for more lands than he could imagine. But not for too much longer, it seemed.

'You remember the singing wires that we saw upon the road?' he said.

'I remember.'

'Well, your husband tells me that there will soon be such a wire all the way from iLondon to the Great Bay. That his people will then be able to send their words along the wire, rather than on paper.'

'He has told me the same tale.'

'You think he is with lies?'

'It is not for a wife to say such things. But it seems to me that, in my husband's head, the tale and the truth sometimes merge into each other. It is the reason he believes so firmly that his betrayal of the *iNkatha* was a good thing. That he has saved the lives of many more who might otherwise have died.'

'His life is still forfeit.'

'And mine too, you said. But I think, my brother, that you have purchased my redemption from that sentence of death. Is that not so? That the Great King would have offered you rewards for saving him from Klaas the Poisoner. Yet you returned to Hluhluwe with nothing in your hands. And what other reward would you have sought than your sister's life?'

'You must not think yourself so special,' said Shaba, 'for if it had been in his power to give, I should rather have requested the life of Zama kaMandla.'

She laughed. 'Forgive me, Shaba,' said Amahle. 'I do not laugh at your loss but at your honesty. And if I am honest in return, there are times with this illness when I think I would let you have your wish gladly and exchange places with her. But I am sorry for your loss.'

'I think about her every day. How her shade came to me after the battle at oNdini and dazzled the eyes of the Basuto rider. Just one more debt that the whites should pay.'

'Yet not with the life of my husband, Shaba. You should forget your promise now, to have him under the blade of your stabbing spear once more.'

The door opened before he could answer, and KaMtigwe entered, stepping carefully over the raised threshold and steadying himself against the ship's motion, a tray in his hands.

'Ah!' said the white man. 'Here we have it. Porridge, my dear. With honey in it. Though I needed no Ngede, no Honeyguide, to find it.' He moved past Shaba, set the tray down on the small bedside chest. 'It came out of a metal tin.'

'Well,' Shaba replied, 'that is another clever thing. That the white men have taught the bees to produce their honey so neatly.' He thought this excessively humorous, expected his sister, at least, to share his jest. But the sea sickness obviously distracted her and, disappointingly, KaMtigwe began a lengthy correction of his brother-in-law's assumed stupidity. 'In any case,' Shaba cut across him, 'I prefer to use the eating hall.'

The American had paid for their passage, of course. But he must have paid a great deal to allow them such luxury. Not so much as those white amaKhosi with the larger, outside rooms, their own private deck, their own eating place – those parts of the vessel that Shaba had been unable to penetrate – but clearly more than those on the lower decks without any rooms at all, where the passengers still cooked their own food, a process that seemed to never end and which also caused much loud argument, the poorer white travellers like dogs competing for a bone.

'The eating hall is a great wonder, is it not?' said KaMtigwe.

'Not so great as the wonder of the beast itself. The wonder of the iron. And I had a dream last night. There was a boy of our family. Not me, but a boy who looked like me. Yet he was not a shaper of iron. He was one who dreamed the shape that the iron must take. One who had learned all the secrets of such dreams. There will be boys in our family, KaMtigwe, who will learn those secrets.'

'Indeed, I am sure you are right. Education, my boy. That's what is needed. Education. We had a great teller of stories in eNgilandi. He was a strong believer in education, as I am myself. He said, *"Never wonder. By means of..."* Ah, I do not know the words in IsiZulu, I find. But his implication was clear. That we should use education to understand everything, to wonder at nothing. Now, if you would only embrace the Lord God, and His son,

Jesucristo, as your dear sister has done...'

Shaba struggled hard to remember that this ugly white man may just have saved him from Mutwa's evil knife.

'KaMtigwe,' he said. 'my people will have this thing you call education. We will understand these new things just as we understand the manner of birth and life, of survival and death. But we shall understand it in our own way. In the way of the People of Heaven.'

He might owe the white man for his own life, but there was still Shaba's pledge to Cetshwayo. And he fervently wished that he had kept some of those small glass vials from the necklace that Klaas had worn.

There was land away to the east, distant and often impossible to see as the clouds lowered and darkened. A large island, KaMtigwe had explained. Very large. Though not so large as eNgilandi, they said. And, as the weather worsened, as the winds screeched around cord and cable, the ship-herds could be seen high upon the cross-poles, grappling with the huge sails, taming them before they might rip themselves to shreds, hauling the canvas upwards despite the pitching of the sailors' precarious position.

A skill that may be acquired by drinking monkey blood, Shaba assumed, as he clung to one of the stanchions, drenched from head to toe. There was a ship-herd in a shining coat and hat trying to explain something to him, bellowing loud against the tempest. It was plainly advice to leave the deck, to seek shelter within, yet it pleased Shaba at times to play the fool, to feign a lack of understanding even in situations that required neither wire, nor word, nor wisdom for their comprehension. So he finally allowed himself to be guided through an outer door and into one of the rooms in which the white men were fond of drinking their weak *utshwala* or their stronger liquors. There were red soldiers here who lifted their glasses towards him while struggling to maintain their balance, laughing at his dripping form. He recognised it as a respectful salute since his presence on the ship, his free roaming of its decks – at least, those to which his intermediate status gave him access – had eventually been accepted. Though it was rather, he thought, in the way that somebody might accept the company of a wild creature once they understood that it was harmless. For he had consistently refused to wear the white man's clothes that the American had offered. There would be plenty of time for that later, when they reached iLondon.

And meanwhile, he thought, *these red soldiers should think themselves lucky that we did not meet beneath the Hill of the Little House.*

The American was here too. And KaMtigwe – a sign that Amahle might be feeling a little better perhaps, despite these wild seas. A sign that there may now be more opportunities to kill the white trader, who was presently swaying crab-wise across the tilting floor to meet him.

'I see you, Shaba Brother,' he said. 'And come. Look at the task upon which our American friend is engaged.'

Shaba still had difficulty seeing KaMtigwe in return, but the American extended one of his huge hands in Shaba's direction, his customary greeting. Shaba was happy to reciprocate, noting that in the other hand the large American held a sheaf of white papers and one of their writing tubes, steadying himself against a chair on which another white passenger was taking his rest. The passenger took the papers from the American, the writing tube too, smiled amiably in Shaba's direction and flourished an extravagant swirl of black ink across the page, causing Shaba to recall the stuff that he and Umdeni had mistaken for *utshwala* after eSandlwana.

'What is this task?' he said.

'It seems,' KaMtigwe replied, 'that when our friend sent back the first group of your people – *our* people – to eNgilandi, four moons ago, there were many who did not believe they were truly of the AmaZulu.'

'Did they too sail on this same vessel?' He did not really care about the beliefs of the people in eNgilandi, but the thought disappointed Shaba that he might, after all, not be the first from the People of Heaven to experience this wonder.

'As it happens,' said KaMtigwe, 'they did. But it was a less than pleasant journey, it seems. For the ship was then also carrying the widows and children of the red soldiers killed at eSandlwana.'

'Whey!' Shaba said. 'Were the women not honoured to share their journey with such warriors?'

'It seems that some of the passengers were inclined to throw those warriors into the sea.'

Shaba glanced at the soldiers here gathered, one of them trying to offer him a glass gourd of their amber beer.

'But things are different now that they have won their war, I think,' said Shaba. He took the glass from the soldier's hand, pulled himself to his full height. 'I thank you for this gift of thin beer, running dog of the Fat Queen,' he said, with considerable ceremony. KaMtigwe coughed, made a grand speech by way of translation, which plainly impressed their audience. 'And this task?' said Shaba, as the American hauled up against the ship's movement at one moment, then tried to stop his headlong rush downwards in the next, to join them, holding out the papers for the soldiers to also make their mark.

'He has written an accurate description of you all,' said KaMtigwe. 'A description of Amahle, of yourself and each of the other six, and he is asking every passenger, every one of the ship's sailors, even their *induna*, to sign, confirming the descriptions. So that, in eNgilandi, none may dispute that you are truly among the People of Heaven.'

'Have any refused to sign?' said Shaba.

'Not one,' KaMtigwe replied.

The red soldiers were taking turns at setting ink upon the pages and one of them, handing the writing tube to another, spoke to Amahle's husband. Shaba caught at least one of the words he spoke.

'He asks whether I fought at eSandlwana?' he said.

'Indeed he did ask that very thing,' said KaMtigwe.

'Then tell him I fought there. And that I fought at eHlobane. Then at eKhambule. At eZunganyene. At the *umuzi* of the old headman Sobhuza, where we killed the iFulentshi Prince. Then at the eZungeni Hill. Ah, and the Battle of the Emahlabathini Plain too, at oNdini.'

'I think I might avoid mentioning the iFulentshi Prince. Just for the moment, you understand. But can I tell them you were present when Cetshwayo was captured?'

'Of course,' said Shaba. 'Then ask them which battles *they* fought.'

There was a long conversation between the whites.

'Ah,' said KaMtigwe at last. 'They say they were not at any of those places. They are builders of things. Bridges and the like. But they say that one of their friends is the most famous warrior of the war, the white *induna* who led the defence of Jim's Place.'

Shaba laughed. 'At KwaJimu?' he said. 'Tell them this was no defence. Tell them that the red soldiers were cornered there like rats. That they were lucky to face only the old women of the Leopard's Lair, the Dust Raisers and the Savages.'

KaMtigwe spoke in their language, so that the red soldiers smiled happily and nodded their agreement. *This is impossible*, thought Shaba. *I give him my words and he plaits them into garlands.*

'What did they say?' Shaba asked.

'They say that it is told how, before each attack at Jim's Place, at the Drift, your regiments would chant their songs of war and that this was more terrifying than even the fighting itself. They ask whether the American's Zulus might sing for them, one day on the ship.'

Shaba saw the large American shake each of the soldiers by the hand, his head nodding vigorously.

'And you may tell the American,' said Shaba, 'that we will perform nothing until he has written his words for us. The words he promised, with all the rewards he swore to give us in exchange for our agreement to come on this journey.'

'Perhaps I should tell him this thing later,' said KaMtigwe. 'In private?'

'You may tell him now.'

KaMtigwe shrugged, spoke in IsiNgisi for a while.

I still have no idea what he is telling him, thought Shaba. *Which is a problem. I would have imagined that my sister should by now have mastered their tongue.*

316

So that we might not need to depend on the old liar. But I suppose she would not admit that thing to me even if she had learned their words. But it seemed that the translation must be a good one, for the American was becoming angry, while the soldiers were laughing, one of them attempting to tell his fellows a protracted tale.'

'What does he say?' Shaba demanded.

'The American?'

'No, the red soldier with the story to tell.'

'Ah, he says that you barter like an iJuda. Is that the word?'

'Those from the land of the amaIsrayeli? I remember them from the stories of the German preacher, Volker. Did they not kill your Jesucristo?'

'Yes, indeed. Anyway, he seems to think that their news sheet was therefore correct.' And the soldier was, in truth, holding just such a thing, pointing at the columns of tiny words by which the whites passed general information across their lands. KaMtigwe took the large paper in his hands, studied the thing. 'Ah,' he continued, 'by coincidence, this records the opinion of another German, but a German iJuda, who claims that the AmaZulu are one of the lost tribes of the amaIsrayeli. He tells of your huge respect for the elders of your people, your care for the land and your cattle; the purchase and number of your wives; your ceremony of the First Fruits and your shared belief that pig meat is impure; your shared laws on purity, and many other traditions. He even mentions the frequency of names like Abram and Moschesch, and the *ukusoka* of your young boys.'

From where do these people receive their ideas? Shaba wondered. *Do they have nothing better to share with each other than this nonsense?* But it gave him pause too. For the minds of the whites, he realised, were complex. And to understand them, he needed to know their words. He would indeed speak with Amahle about this thing but, meanwhile, perhaps he should not be too hasty in seeking an end to KaMtigwe. Not just yet.

'And apart from this foolishness,' he said, 'what word from the American on setting his own promises to the paper?'

As the sun began to set on the eleventh day of their journey, Shaba was met on the deck by KaMtigwe. The white man was in a state of some excitement, seemed in high spirits.

'Come, my boy,' he said, 'you must see this!'

He was taken forward to stand among a crowd that had gathered around the ship's *induna*, an imposing man with a royal stomach and expansive beard. He was shouting through a speaking trumpet to a person unseen, away in the gloom. There was a light too, burning somewhere ahead.

'What is it?' Shaba asked, uncertain about the level of amusement so plainly evident on the faces of those close to him.

317

'Well,' said KaMtigwe, 'we are about to cross the line that separates the southern lands and seas from those of the north. We are halfway around the world here – and also about to enter the Realm of the Ocean God. Do you see? That is the light from his boat. There.' He pointed. Yet it was also plain that the light, while faint, was only located among the furthest forward cables of the ship's rigging.

'Oh yes?' said Shaba. 'And what does he demand of us, this Ocean God?' Such rituals were, after all, common enough in his own culture.

'He says that he will visit the ship tomorrow morning, at which time all those who have not previously crossed the line must subject themselves to his will. Then they shall be deemed as true Shell-backs; true creatures of the sea.'

'Did you ever hear the tale of Manzandaba and Sea Turtle the Creator?' Shaba asked, remembering the homeless little ones to whom he had once told the story near the smoking ruin of KwaMbonambi. *I wonder where they are now, those children*, he thought.

'No,' said KaMtigwe, 'I believe not.'

'It is the story of how the AmaZulu first discovered the art of telling tall tales, Sister Husband.'

And he left him there, at the rail.

But the following morning, he was as curious as everybody else to see the thing played out. At least, once he had resolved the business with the American. And so it was that another ceremony took place; a ceremony of ink and paper, in which the ship's *induna* was called upon to read each promise aloud, each reciprocal commitment on the part of Shaba and the others. KaMtigwe translated and the AmaZulu – gathered here together for the first time in eleven days, weakened but free from the sea sickness at last in a more gentle swell – signalled their collective consent, each making a mark on the paper, beneath the American's own mark on behalf of the man, Farini, that they would meet in iLondon. It was a solemn thing, binding on them all.

Then, with light dancing on the rippling waves, it was everybody to the outer decks where the Ocean God had finally risen from his watery kingdom. He was a sad specimen though, all things considered, and even the most modest *inyanga* would have shamed him. For the hair that hung loose to his waist, the long beard that matched it, were no more than grey animal manes, from a horse perhaps, and dripping with green sea weeds. The god's face was blackened but his cheeks were brightest vermilion. And no real deity would have been seen in such a ragged collection of vestments, a long over-shirt with frills and the shoulder ornaments stolen from a red soldier, a badly fashioned crown and a spear with three points.

The sails had all been fastened tight and only the merest wisps escaped from the red smoke-stack, the throbbing vibrations, the smell of oils, stilled almost to nothing. But another sheet of canvas had been secured between the smaller boats hanging from their iron frames so that, when the ship-herds worked at the pumps, the sheet slowly filled to create a suspended pool of water with a makeshift platform and chair above it – the chair being attached to a series of ropes and pulleys.

The Ocean God, meanwhile, had been escorted by some body servants to his own throne, set upon a circular table – itself hung about with shells and yet more weed – alongside a white man dressed approximately in the clothes of one of their women.

'That is his Queen?' Shaba laughed.

'Yes, exactly,' KaMtigwe replied. 'Now, all those who may be made Shell-backs must go below and await their turn to be called.'

'Only the ship-herds who have not crossed the line before?'

'For them it is compulsory. But any of the passengers who wish it may take part also.'

'Those who have not already crossed the line?'

'Yes,' said KaMtigwe. 'There are a few travelling to eNgilandi who were born in your southern lands. There is no actual line, naturally. Not one you can see, I mean.'

Shaba had not supposed otherwise.

'And what about us?' he asked, some of the other warriors grinning as he spoke.

'All of you?' said KaMtigwe.

And thus the seven men of the AmaZulu, along with Amahle, were sent to await initiation into the white man's strange customs, though Shaba had the sense that they somehow spoiled the process when, having been escorted back into the sunlight, onto the platform, and made to sit on the chair, he was approached by an old fellow in blue uniform who held up a brush dripping with some foul foam. But when the old one said something in IsiNgisi, kept repeating it, Shaba could not understand.

'He is asking your name,' shouted KaMtigwe from somewhere above.

Yet if I open my mouth to tell him, he will doubtless plunge that brush into it, Shaba decided, pressing his lips tight. So the old man simply daubed some of the stuff on Shaba's cheek, scraped it off again quickly with a piece of iron and, with a dismissive wave of his hand, signalled for the ropes and pulleys to be heaved, tipping Shaba back into the water-filled canvas.

'We have been involved in more exciting ceremonies, have we not?' he said later, to his sister.

'Indeed,' Amahle replied. 'But I still need to know your mind, Shaba. You have given up this thing about my husband's life being forfeit, I hope?'

'We need him, I think,' said Shaba. 'Else who will speak the IsiNgisi for us. And the Great King is a long way from here. I had not realised the distance. It is a different world to which we travel now.'

Amahle smiled at him, though she said nothing.

And Shaba had learned that, among the AmaZulu already sent by the American to iLondon, there was one who spoke the white man's tongue perfectly. *I will be educated by that fellow*, he thought. *I will practise using the IsiNgisi myself. And then there will be a day when KaMtigwe will no longer be so necessary.*

It was on their fifteenth day that the ship came to an actual halt. The huge chains were rattled out and down into the depths to hold her steady, and here the engines subsided to no more than a whisper. There was land on almost every side, though still some distance away, and the vessel had taken up position at the back of a line, other ships of various shapes and size, waiting to run together along that man-made river from this Bay of Suez, across the desert and to an entirely different ocean that KaMtigwe called the Middle Sea.

'It has to be this way,' the white man was explaining, 'since there is only space for the ships to pass each other at certain places. Like the Great Bitter Lake. So we'll have to wait until morning now before this group can start. But at least we are half the way to eNgilandi now.'

'Only half way?' said Shaba. 'And how long on the Suez river?'

'We should reach the Middle Sea by the middle of tomorrow night. Just after you sing for the red soldiers and the passengers.'

Shaba nodded. Now that the contract with the American was signed, they would indeed sing.

'It belongs to the Fat Queen, this river?'

'It is owned jointly by the Fat Queen and by the AmaFulentshi. But the Fat Queen certainly now controls its use. A long story, but the thing was built by an iFulentshi. And when it was finished, ten years ago, it was the AmaFulentshi who had the most power here. There was a feast to celebrate its opening and they wanted a person of great importance to perform the ceremonies. Can you guess who that might have been?'

Shaba knew that this thing would follow him forever.

'The iFulentshi Prince who died at the *umuzi* of Sobhuza?' he said.

KaMtigwe seemed disappointed.

'No,' he replied. 'A good guess, yet the Prince would only have been a boy then. But very close. It was his flame-haired mother, the iNkosikazi Eugénie.'

Chapter Twenty-Three

Friday 24th October 1879

The towers of stone that rose from the fast-flowing, stinking river were nothing. Such structures were commonplace in this iLondon which, so far, had fulfilled all Shaba's worst imaginings for its filth and smoke and chimneys. But the ornamented iron that spun in spider webs between the heads of these particular towers, which anchored them to dry land and which carried the multitudes of white folk, their crawling crowds of carriages, carts and coaches from one bank to the other, this was another thing entirely, some demonstration that their Jesucristo may indeed be more mighty than his own uMvelinqangi.

'If we wait a moment,' KaMtigwe said to him, 'we shall see it open.'

'Open?' he said, following the line of KaMtigwe's arm as it stretched towards the masted vessel approaching the bridge, a vessel plainly too tall to permit its passage beneath. 'Whey!' he exclaimed, when an unseen hand halted the bridge's traffic, cleared it entirely, and the wrought-metal segments shifted, groaned, lifted until they were tensed forearms, raised in praise and deference of the ship as it slid between them, graciously, gratefully, smoke pumping from its iron-sister funnel, steam-whistle screaming.

Amahle and the two other Zulu warriors in their party were similarly impressed, and Shaba tried to discuss the iron magic with KaMtigwe as their own carriage rattled along the sunless stone-clad valleys through which the city's roads were cut – badly fashioned roads too, that shook a man's teeth loose in his head. But the other white man, the one they called Farini, who had been there to meet them when they were disgorged from their ship, seemed obsessed with the buildings themselves.

'Farini asks,' said KaMtigwe, as they passed yet another such structure, 'whether you want to see this place of justice?'

It was not a particularly interesting example of English construction methods – two solid square blocks holding up a central edifice with sloping roofs, a high curved wall resembling half a cattle enclosure, a crowd gathered outside the wall's entrance.

'Those people are all waiting for justice from the Fat Queen?'

'Not from the Queen, no. There are court houses like this all over the country. But this is the biggest. Dozens face trial here every day.'

'Do they have an *inyanga* then? To smell out evil?' Shaba found it amusing now to feign foolishness from time to time. To play the ignorant savage. And at first he thought it not only amusing but also educative, for he discovered that there were indeed men who must track down evil-doers, though here they were called *amaphoyisa*. But he paid dearly for his amusement, having to endure a lengthy explanation from KaMtigwe about the forms of crime that apparently beset this civilised nation. A wonderful and fair system, however, in which another manner of medicine man – the English words that KaMtigwe used were confusing, but the most common, to Shaba's ears, sounded like *iphetifokha* – must use his skills to argue the case of those seeking justice. The guilty were then put into dark holes as punishment for debt, theft and dishonesty but without having to make reparation to their victims. Yet at least the many murderers and baby-slayers were executed, their necks broken by a rope, or strangled with it.

He approved, gathered the thick woollen coat closer around him for it was cold here, their new clothing and footwear providing only limited protection. The men had been equipped at the great dwelling, shortly after their arrival, but Amahle had been taken away by KaMtigwe to some other place, returned with boxes and all manner of white woman's attire, most of it red, and most of it being worn today. She needed it to counter a biting wind that rolled through the carriage windows as they passed into a wide and open area of emerald grassland, trees with leaves in rainbow colours that were beginning to fall and blow in swirling patterns among the many riders and walkers, who all seemed to be driven in the same direction. And the wind carried something else: the welcome scents of animal dung, wilderness noises; the distant bark of a lion. Shaba thought he must be dreaming, but the road, smoother here, curved in a great arc, until it ended at yet another cluster of dwellings.

KaMtigwe and Farini, smiling as though the Zulus were idiot infants, invited them to climb down, led them to another framework of iron where money was handed over and each member of the group was duly permitted to push through the barrier, which turned efficiently as soon as any pressure was applied. But on the other side of this barrier, they stopped, struck dumb by the sight before them.

'Elephant!' said Shaba. It was a stupid thing to say. Though, to be fair, it was the largest any of them had ever seen. It seemed incongruous enough to find the beast here, in the centre of iLondon. But there was something else, for this huge bull elephant, *indlovu*, though it bore no tusks, carried on its back a house of wood, seats for the carriage of passengers, several of them small children. And gathered closely about the animal were clusters of other people, equally unconcerned, it seemed, laughing and pointing.

'Are they witless?' said Amahle. 'Do they have so many young that they can sacrifice them to the Unstoppable One? For they will surely be thrown and trampled.'

322

But the children seemed entirely at ease and, more, the beast allowed itself to be led up and down the path by a soldier in a black uniform.

The elephant, KaMtigwe insisted, had its own honour name. It was called Jambo and they began to follow the giant at a safe distance, until they themselves were spotted and, as had happened so many times before, became an alternative centre of attraction. Another sea of white faces, the loneliness and isolation that they engendered, stared at them. The Zulus had become the living, lost in a land of pale shades. But there was no denying the joy that the AmaZulu presence in the heart of iLondon seemed to evoke. Shaba had feared that, as vanquished enemies, they might suffer at the hands of the Fat Queen's people, though in truth they received such praise that he might almost have imagined themselves the victors. Men appeared, as always, and apparently from nowhere, with the boxes on sticks used to capture images – an invention that Shaba had placed on his list of wonders just below the iron-magic – but which inevitably meant standing motionless for considerable periods and in a variety of locations while the boxes slowly absorbed their light.

Eventually, the box-men tired of them and they were free to go, though not without continuing to be surrounded by admiring crowds that followed them as they passed dirty lakes packed with unhappy waterfowl, and a tiny patch of hard ground from which a pair of disconsolate zebras peered curiously through some bars at their neighbour – that brown variety of the zebra clan, apparently known in all tongues by the noise it makes. *Quagga.* Then they turned right and came across a fearful thing.

'What have they done?' said one of the Zulus. 'Are these the holes that they spoke of? The holes into which wrong-doers are thrown?'

But it was difficult to understand how *ingonyama*, the Master of All Flesh, could have infringed the laws of this place. And he was not alone, for behind the neighbouring bars were several females that might have been the lion's mates.

'And this one?' said Amahle. 'How is this possible?'

Another lion, yet this one stained with stripes of black and white.

'Sorcery,' said Shaba, and his belief was confirmed when, a little later, they discovered a wolf, this one brown, but striped also.

They strolled the grounds for a long time, saw rhinoceros, a white bear, antelope of every variety, pelican, giraffe – and a thing that somewhat resembled the giraffe, but with two huge humps in the middle of its back. There was a house of glass too, in which a forest flourished. Another filled with serpents. A third with the overpowering stink of monkey.

'We should free them,' Amahle said, beating her hands together, for she had been growing increasingly angered by this strange prison.

'There is all the space outside in which they could run,' Shaba replied. 'But they would never be free. And is it not better that these beasts should give the white folk of iLondon at least a small glimpse of the wonders with which the

Sky Lord blesses us each day in our own place? I think I begin to understand now why the AmaNgisi must always be stealing the land of others. For they have no such wonders of their own. I have been envious of their iron-power. Yet I would not trade even that great skill for any single speck of KwaZulu.'

He tried to explain this also, to KaMtigwe and Farini, both of them disappointed that the group had not been more impressed by the visit, but they seemed incapable of comprehension. Yet the two white men rallied somewhat as the party left the grounds to find their carriage.

'Ah,' KaMtigwe exclaimed. 'There. You see it?' A large piece of paper was stuck on the wall, bright colours, painted words, and an image in the centre, a depiction of Zulu warriors. 'Our very company.'

*

'It is an act of unimaginable folly!' said Annie. 'And she might not even attend.'

If we had not come up to town for my new kit, thought Carey, *I would never have been given this chance.*

'I had it on the best authority that she would be there,' he said. *Incognita*, of course. But if the Empress doesn't attend, we will at worst have wasted the price of entrance and, at best, you may be treated to a fine display of the dangers we faced from the Zulus.'

'And what of the embarrassment, Jahleel? The ignominy of seeking an audience and being refused?'

'Worse than this?' he shouted, waving the note at her.

'Please!' Annie implored, glancing towards the door of their room.

He was tempted to say, *To hell with the family!* But he bit his tongue. Carey did not especially like the Kingston cousins, but they were good enough to provide lodging whenever Annie was in town. And it was her opportunity also, with the children safely in the care of Carey's sisters at Brixham, to shop against the eventuality of their possible overseas posting. So he owed them that much, at least – these cousins of Annie, all the way from Kingston, Jamaica, to Kingston-upon-Thames. Yet they had the infuriating habit of treating everything in life as though it were an inane jest – including his own present circumstances.

'I apologise,' he said, softening his voice. 'But the damn'd impertinence of them, my dear. Well, they will have my answer. We are in correspondence, after all. It is surely the most natural of things if I find myself in the vicinity of the Empress and take the opportunity of speaking with her in person. About the same matter.'

'Except that you are not in correspondence with the Empress,' said Annie, 'only with her Chamberlain. And even he will not yet have received your reply.'

A note from the Duc de Bassano had arrived the previous week. It was polite in the extreme, as only the recently raised aristocracy could be. His father, the first Duke, had been Bonaparte's war minister, elevated accordingly, and the present incumbent to the title had served the French Imperial Family, either in power or in exile, for the past sixty years.

Her Imperial Highness, the note explained, was in receipt of a letter purporting to be written by Captain Carey, on the very date upon which the tragic death of her son had occurred. Her Imperial Highness, Bassano hastened to add, had neither solicited a copy of the letter, nor wished to retain it, and would thus happily restore the letter to its author. However, the Chamberlain begged leave to point out, the Empress Eugénie had been saddened to read the newspaper reports, predominantly in the *Daily News* and the *Gaulois*, also purporting to quote Captain Carey. Plainly, there were discrepancies between the words in Captain Carey's private letter and those in the newspaper – the latter expressing certain criticisms and condemnation of the Prince Imperial, alleging that the choice of the fatal camping ground was his alone. The Duc de Bassano was at pains to confirm that Her Imperial Highness set no store by the newspaper reports and was perfectly certain that Captain Carey must have been mis-quoted, that being a common failing of the journalistic profession. Carey was therefore invited to publish a statement refuting the comments attributed to him, since this would serve to eradicate any stain with which the Prince Imperial's good name may have been impugned.

'I posted my reply this morning,' said Carey, and saw his wife shake her head in dismay. '*His* good name, indeed! Well, I have told the fellow, my dear, that I shall refute nothing. And that if they wish to publish private correspondence between myself and my wife, they should feel free to proceed. And damn them all!'

He needed no admonishment this time to remind him of the need for a more subdued tone of voice.

'Was the letter not mine then?' said Annie. 'It was addressed to me, was it not? And if you sent it to me, if the letter was my own, was I not entitled to some discussion about its fate? The contents don't bother me one iota, Jahleel, but the idea that you should agree the publication of our intimacies without consideration of my feelings...'

'But the time is ripe, dear heart,' he interrupted her. 'Do you not feel the tide turning in my favour? Oh, Chelmsford may have been sweet enough to my face, but in the end it was His Lordship who had personal responsibility for Louis. Not Harrison. Not me. But he has fudged it, just as he fudged the blame for Isandlwana. I may have made mistakes, Annie dearest, but they are surely eclipsed by Chelmsford's own folly. The public knows it too. All those music hall parodies. Open hostility in the newspapers. Why, I read a piece yesterday that claimed the invasion of Zululand an act of piracy.'

'That seems a terrible condemnation of all those souls who sacrificed their lives.'

'The whole thing was badly planned, my sweet,' he said. 'If you had only seen how ill-prepared was the army for conditions there.'

'I think I've heard you say as much about each and every campaign,' said Annie. 'And now what? The newspapers say we should never have fought the Zulu after all? Then what was it all for?'

'There was jubilation,' said Carey, 'when I arrived in Durban. Jubilation that, with the Zulus now broken, their economy shattered, the Cape would finally have all the labour it needs for the mines, without having to import yet more Hindus and coolies. Was that what it was all about, after all? But the cost, my sweet. The Boers in Durban were talking quite openly about the weakness of our army. So many defeats. They will be the next to challenge us out there, mark my words. And then what? The Russians again? Germany perhaps?'

'And you blame Chelmsford?'

'Not just me, Annie. It's said that Disraeli will not even entertain a meeting with him. Oh, the Queen and Horse Guards may still protect him. But the people, dearest. Public opinion. The majority, I think, now with me. And that's why, sweet one, I must seize the day. *Carpe Deum*, my dear. You must trust me on this. A meeting with the Empress may be the very thing.'

'You will do as you think fit, I suppose' Annie replied, 'yet I fear that you are destroying yourself, husband.'

*

'And how did your blacks take to such a long sea voyage, Major?' asked one of the journalists. They were fighting each other at the hotel's entrance in their eagerness to press him with foolish questions.

Fortunately, his charges were now safely ensconced with Farini in their quarters at the Westminster Palace, ideally sited for their needs, with the venue – the Royal Aquarium Theatre – literally across the road on the other side of Tothill Street. McTeague, however, holding the journalists at bay on the front steps, could look comfortably over their heads, past the corner of Victoria Street to the façade of the Westminster School and, to his left, the column memorial to the fallen of the Crimea. Beyond the column, the Abbey itself, in all its glory.

'In truth,' he said, 'one might have believed that they were seamen born and bred.'

'No sickness then?'

'None,' said McTeague, though it was a lie. Poor, sweet little Amahle, how ill she had been. At least she had grown accustomed to the motion by the time they reached Suez, yet the sickness returned with a vengeance both in the Mediterranean and then across Biscay. But he had stayed with her throughout the voyage since she had steadfastly refused to entertain any involvement with the ship's doctor. And McTeague had to admit that, apart from a genuine desire to care for her, he had been glad of a reason to maintain a safe distance between himself and her brother. For there had been time without number when, in catching Shaba's eye, he had seen death staring back at him.

'Since you mention seamen, Major McTeague, there is apparently a rumour,' said a fellow from the *Daily News*, 'that these are not truly Zulus at all – that they are simply black seamen enlisted when you returned to England.'

'A scurrilous rumour too, sir,' McTeague retorted. 'My associate, Mister Behrens, had the foresight to compile a statement detailing the names and description for each of our eight Zulus. It was signed, gentlemen, by every single passenger and crew member on board the *Balmoral Castle*.'

'And could you describe, Major,' cried another, 'the mail packet's reception at Southampton?'

'I can only tell you,' said McTeague, 'that one of your colleagues – from the *Portsmouth Evening News*, I believe – estimated the spectators on the quayside at more than twenty thousand.'

'Can you wonder at that, sir?' asked the *Times* correspondent. 'Given that your company has seen fit to transport to our shores the very individuals who, just months ago, were mutilating this nation's young men on the fields of Isandlwana.'

'They were our enemies, that is true,' McTeague replied. 'And their ways may sometimes seem barbaric to European eyes. Yet we are at peace now. And your readers, sir, are asking their own interesting questions about the recent war. Questions of this nature, Mister Clowes: how was it, they wish to know, that the bodies of those brave victims you mention remained neglected and unburied from the twenty-second of January until the twenty-first of May? Four complete months, sir! I saw them myself.'

He thought about Maria Mestiza, wondered whether Jago Jupe had, as agreed, yet managed to send their own search party to EsiKlebheni for the purpose of recovering her remains, giving them a Christian burial. He owed her that much, at least.

'Really, Major,' Clowes began, 'it is very well understood...'

'Next question!' McTeague shouted the fellow down.

'Can you tell us how long the show is expected to run, Major?'

'At the moment, sir, we are billed to perform until the end of March. Three performances, each and every day of the week.'

'And after?'

'America, gentlemen. The Great Farini will tour the United States of America.'

But will the Zulus go with him? he wondered, when he finally rid himself of the journalists and was seated alone in the hotel foyer, sipping at a very fine Laphroaig Old Islay. He was feeling pleased with himself. Apart from that incident at Hluhluwe, he had never felt better. There was a spring in his step that had previously been absent for a long time. His advance from Farini had enabled him to visit Ede & Ravenscroft where he invested in several new outfits, and then to scandalise gentlefolk shopping in the Regent Circus Crystal Palace Bazaar by strolling arm in arm with Amahle among the stalls while she selected suitable clothing, though in truth she was more intrigued, hilariously amused, by that establishment's unique facility – a ladies' lavatory. *Whatever next?* he wondered.

'Ah, Major!' McTeague was startled by the slap of Farini's hand on the beeswax leather of his armchair. 'Oh, my apologies,' the showman continued, 'I startled you.'

'Not at all, sir. I was thinking of Zululand.'

'You must be pleased to be back in civilisation though?' said Farini.

McTeague glanced around the ornate Renaissance French décor for which the Westminster Palace Hotel was so famed.

'A single sunset at Emoyeni would cancel all this in a moment, sir,' he replied. 'Is that not so, Mister Behrens?'

'I can think of nowhere better, Major,' Behrens replied. 'And you'd never get to savour a sunset in London for the fog, I reckon.' Apart from the bandoliers and holster that he had reluctantly now abandoned, his attire was precisely the same as when they had first met, whereas Farini, at his side, was every inch the English gentleman: tweed frock coat, grey plaid trousers – and only the merest hint of accent to betray his American origins.

'Well,' he said, smoothing his generous forked beard. 'I shall take your word for it. I suppose I may be judging the country by the ingratitude of its Zulu natives. The journalists asked no questions on the subject, I gather?'

'Not at all,' McTeague replied. 'And how was your confrontation with the Zulus?'

'The devils still insist that they've been offered a better contract by somebody else. But they won't say who. Just keep telling me they're not being paid enough. It's plainly that half-breed. We should never have brought him.' And he glowered at Behrens.

It was simply one of the familiar sources of conflict between the two men, Behrens insisting that, to help recruit their original group of Zulus back in May, he had needed somebody to translate. And this mixed-race fellow he had encountered in Durban seemed, at the time, an excellent choice. The man had been in London with the troupe since late June and still acted as their unofficial spokesman.

'It couldn't come at a worse time,' said Behrens. 'Rehearsals all finished and the first show tonight.'

'Well,' Farini replied, 'they'll soon learn the error of their ways. Just need to show them who's boss.'

'These are Zulus we're talking about, sir,' protested McTeague, suddenly filled with an unexpected surge of family pride. He wondered how things might be going back there. *Is the freight business still thriving? The mission station built?*

'They're no different from the redskins out West, Major,' said Farini. 'Children. You have to treat them like children. Not your good lady wife, naturally. But the others, well, let's hope they learn their lesson.'

'Lesson?' said McTeague.

'Why, yes,' Farini replied. 'That half-breed's out on his ear now. On the street, gentlemen, where he belongs. And for the rest – the men, that is – their outside clothes all confiscated. They've still got their costumes for the show, of course, but let's see how these fellows get on, parading around London naked as babes. And in October too!'

*

'The man said nothing about my husband?' said Amahle.

'Not a word,' Shaba replied. 'The American, Farini, asked him over and over again to tell about these other white men who say they would pay us more gold. But he would tell them nothing and they sent him away. Has your husband paid him, sister? Paid for his silence?'

'I think not. KaMtigwe said only that he should have waited until the offer was confirmed.'

They waited in this place, this room of green walls with green wool upon the floor, in the depths of the great hall where the Americans expected them to dance and perform later. Soon, in fact.

'They will be surprised, will they not?' he said. 'When they find that we shall not bend to their will.'

'It is a shame,' said Amahle. 'These are fine costumes. Just look at you, brother.'

There was a looking-glass in the room that reflected his image – or, rather, the image that should have belonged to the most senior of *izinduna*. He was not entitled to wear these things, of course, neither the cow-tail festoons that hung at his chest, as well as around his arms and legs; nor the *umnyakanya* ball that formed the centre-piece of a magnificent head-dress, a great cluster of feathers from the ostrich and the *isakabuli* finch; nor the ceremonial shield that should more properly have been carried by the uThulwana. But the willow-bead necklace was his own, still worn with pride. The *iklwa*, of course. The loin cloth and kilt also.

'See how well you fashioned the *umutsha*, Amahle. The belt has never broken. The fur tails good as new.' *And the time-counter of the iFulentshi Prince still hidden within*, he thought. 'Yet look at your own regalia. More colourful even than your wedding attire.'

KaMtigwe put his head around the door and spoke to them in English, then remembered himself and repeated in IsiZulu, 'Are you all ready? It will begin very soon.' Then he noticed his wife. His eyes widened, 'Oh, my dear, how beautiful. How very beautiful.'

Shaba stood. 'We will not dance,' he said, with as much gravity as he could muster.

One by one, the rest of their company came to stand alongside Shaba, fourteen of them in total, each expressing agreement.

McTeague stammered. 'Not dance?' he said. 'But you must.'

'You told us, KaMtigwe, that there are others who want us to perform. And for more gold.'

'Yes,' said the white man, 'but there is no agreement on the thing yet, and our true purpose should be to persuade Farini to improve our payments.'

'But if he does not,' said Shaba, 'we will not dance. And if he still does not agree, we will go to that place we passed today. The place where the people go to seek justice.'

'Well, that is possible, of course, but...' The door opened again, and the other American entered, the man who called himself Nat. He seemed distressed, spoke to KaMtigwe. They spoke at length until, finally, KaMtigwe coughed. 'It seems,' he said, 'that we have a visitor. A royal visitor.'

Shaba had spent too much time as Cetshwayo's body servant to be greatly impressed. 'The Fat Queen?' he asked.

KaMtigwe hesitated. 'No,' he said. 'The Queen of the French.'

It took a moment for Shaba to fathom his meaning. 'You mean,' he said, gripping the *iklwa* more tightly, 'the mother of the iFulentshi Prince?'

'Yes, the same.'

'Does she bring warriors, seeking revenge?'

'I think not. No, she is here to see the performance and has asked to meet you all before it begins.'

'She knows?' said Shaba. 'That I am here? That I killed her son?'

'I think not,' said KaMtigwe. 'There is no way she could know.'

There was a loud knocking upon the door and it burst open. Farini. The other American too. They entered, followed by a white woman swathed all in black, a gossamer veil of the same colour covering her face, suspended from a small, round hat that could not quite contain curls of bright amber hair. Behind the woman, an entourage of attendants, all high-headed, their noses pointing towards the ceiling as though there was something evil-smelling on their upper lips, the females as well as the men. An exchange ensued, the iFulentshi Queen speaking carefully, while the Americans, KaMtigwe too, bobbed and bowed before her.

'This woman,' said KaMtigwe at last, 'is the Queen of all the many Lands of the French. She welcomes you to this part of the world on behalf of her people. She is pleased that peace now allows you to be here and that you were unharmed by the war. She says that her own son died there. One of many. She grieves for him. She grieves for him deeply. The pain of a mother. She regrets that so many were killed. So many other mothers whose sons have been taken. She is a friend of the English Queen too. The Great Queen, Victoria. And she knows that she, too, did not want the war.'

'Then why did she start it?' said Shaba. The French Queen smiled at him through the veil, spoke to KaMtigwe. 'You should tell her what I said,' Shaba urged him. 'What did we do but love our land,' he spat, 'and show loyalty to our people and our king? Are those not virtuous things? But the Fat Queen's generals told us these were relics of the past, that we must change or pay the price for our traditions, our way of life. Their gin had not enlightened us. Nor their missionaries. So they sent the red soldiers' army to instruct us. On the weakest of pretexts. Has the Fat Queen ever fought such an unjust war? But sometimes, as they say, the viper has something to learn from the mongoose. Has she learned, this Fat Queen friend of hers?'

KaMtigwe stood silent. The French Queen pressed him for a response. It took the white man a long time to explain. Longer still for him to deliver her reply.

'The French Queen says this,' said KaMtigwe. 'That once there was an ancient land, a land that was the beginning of our culture. And in that land was a place they called the Gates of Fire where another Great King and his Three Hundred made a stand against a powerful enemy. They all died there because they loved the land and because their laws required them to defend it. They all died there, in that place. But their enemy was broken and their land saved.' KaMtigwe paused. The French Queen spoke again. 'Ah,' the white man continued, 'this part is difficult. It is in the form of a praise poem. But, simply, it says: "*Go tell our people, you who pass us by, that here – still following our laws – we lie.*" It is written on a stone. To this day. In the place where they fought.'

Shaba did not need to look at the others. This was language they would all understand. It was the language of warriors.

'Perhaps, one day,' he said, 'there will be such a stone for the People of Heaven.'

'*Ji! Ji!*' chanted the others, a few beating spear shafts on shield hide.

There was translation.

'The French Queen,' said KaMtigwe, 'wants me to tell you that, next year, she will visit the land of the Zulus. She promises to speak of such a stone, though she goes to see the place where her son fell.'

By that time, Shaba thought, *I shall have fulfilled my oath to the Great King and this KaMtigwe will be dead. By that time also, we shall have all the gold we need to buy my cattle.* He was moved by this grieving mother, remembered all the others like her that he had met among the roads and hiding places of his own land, and he was tempted to return the time-counter to her. Yet maybe that could wait. For now.

'Then tell the French Queen,' he said, 'that we thank her. Tell her this also, KaMtigwe, that when she sails to our land – if our land can still be found in those days – she should see the warrior who took her son's life.' Amahle turned quickly to him, placed a hand on his arm. 'For they say,' he said, 'that the Prince was a lion among men, and there is nobody else who should be trusted to guide her there than he that knows the places where her son's shade still wanders.'

KaMtigwe translated the words, with some difficulty. The French Queen sobbed many times, despite her royalty and her efforts to the contrary. She spoke at last.

'The French Queen asks how she might find this one man, in all the lands of the Zulu,' said KaMtigwe.

'Tell her she should not grieve too badly nor too long,' Shaba replied, 'for the shade of her son does not wander alone. It is in the company of other warriors. Many others. And she will not need to search for the man who slew him, for he will know also that she seeks him and he will be waiting for her.'

*

Carey had been made to languish in two different rooms already, the theatre staff polite but discomforted simply by his knowledge that the Empress was even on the premises. A state secret, something of that nature, they had been told, and Carey was convinced that, this time, the approaching footsteps must surely herald a final rejection of his request for an audience. In truth, he would be almost relieved. He had done his best, when all was said and done. And Annie had warned him as much, declining to join him on his venture and having at mid-afternoon left the house of the Kingston cousins to take tea with the Montforts. But at least she would join him before the performance itself.

'Carey?' The footsteps' echo faded to nothing and Carey looked up into a disappointingly familiar face. 'My dear fellow,' McTeague was saying to him, 'I could scarce believe it when they said you were here.'

'Major!' Carey replied, his voice oscillating between query, exclamation and relief. A familiar face, though hardly a friendly one: rotund; ruddy cheeks, oiled hair and moustache. Perhaps he might have assumed that if the Zulus were here, McTeague may not be too far behind, but he had not reckoned on seeing him in London. And not tonight.

'You will tell me, I suppose,' Carey continued when he had composed himself, 'that you are now in the employ of Her Royal Highness?'

'The Empress?' said McTeague. 'No such luck, I fear. Merely a humble messenger. To say that your request is being considered. But that the lady herself is distressed by her recent encounter and may not be able to meet you in person.'

'Encounter?' said Carey.

'Well,' McTeague told him, 'with my brother-in-law.'

'Forgive me if I do not quite follow you, sir.'

'My wife's brother. Did you not know, Carey? It was he that struck the fatal blow against the Prince Imperial. Though she does not know that detail.'

'You never mentioned this at the Upoko Camp,' said Carey, scarcely able to believe his own ears.

332

'When we were both at the Upoko Camp, I had no idea he was involved.'

Carey saw the warrior's face as though it were yesterday. 'He wears an eye-patch?'

'He has been known to do so. Would you care for an introduction, Carey?'

But Jahleel was confused, his emotions in turmoil. He was still confused when a well-dressed young man crossed the foyer and invited Carey to follow him.

'Perhaps later, Major...' Carey called back over his shoulder as they took the main stairs and a corridor to a small, though finely appointed, office. His stomach knotted and a confusion of possible comments, opening gambits scrambled around his brain. But the Empress Eugénie was not there. Only an elderly fellow, clean-shaven, bald except for a tuft of hair around each ear, and dressed in a style that would have been popular in France when Carey was a boy. He bowed courteously, introduced himself as the Empress Eugénie's Chamberlain, Napoléon Joseph Maret, Second Duc de Bassano.

'And I apologise for keeping you waiting, Captain,' he said. His English was perfect, not a trace of accent. 'I fear that Her Imperial Highness is unable to see you, But I am authorised to speak on her behalf, naturally.'

'Well, I thank you for that, in any case, sir. And I'm sorry to hear that the Empress may have been distressed by her visit.'

'It has indeed been a difficult evening,' said Bassano. 'Yet I should not wish to deceive you into thinking that she would have acceded to your request for an audience even had she not been... distressed. Was that the word you used? And even this encounter, Captain, may only proceed on the basis that, while you remain free to use our discussion in any way you see fit, our respective comments are not attributable to either of us by name. I require your oath, before God, sir, to that effect.'

'Before God, sir, you have it.'

'Very well, Captain. Shall we sit?'

Carey accepted the invitation, smoothed his uniform trousers as he took a chair.

'You received my note, Your Grace?'

'Publish and be damn'd! That was the central point, was it not? But I have to tell you that Her Imperial Highness remains concerned at the slur that has been cast upon the good name of her son. That said, the Empress has some sympathy for your position. And she is a great admirer of your mother's writing. In addition, she appreciates that Louis could be... well, headstrong, shall we say?'

Carey nodded. *Headstrong*, he thought. *Yes, that's a good way to describe him.*

'Your Grace,' he said, 'you mention the word slur. Yet it is myself that has been wronged here. I have simply endeavoured to tell the truth.'

'Of course, Captain. But which truth would that be, precisely? The truth contained in the letter to Mrs Carey – the choice of a camping ground your own responsibility? Or the truth given in evidence at your Court Martial – a simple twist of fate? Or the truth that you saw fit to impart within the newspapers – that the responsibility rested with that poor young man? A young man, I need not add, who is tragically no longer here to provide his own testimony.'

'I feel his loss more keenly than most, sir,' said Carey. And so he did. He understood also that, at times, there is more than one truth. No definitive certainty. What was it he had said? *A shame though, that we can't take a closer look at the terrain down there. More of an adventure too, perhaps.* Hardly a decision. Nor an instruction. But had he deliberately tempted Louis with the word *adventure*? He was no longer sure. And the Prince's response? *'Eh bien, Carey. This is such a dull place. And if we need to take a closer look, well, there is a kraal down there.'* Hardly a formal acquiescence either. But it had happened, perhaps with both of them to blame. Perhaps with neither.

'Yes, I am certain that you must,' said the Duke. 'But we are speaking here of your letter, Captain. Publish and be damn'd indeed. Yet you added a codicil, did you not? To the effect that if Her Imperial Highness was satisfied with your response, perhaps she might prefer to let matters rest. Well, sir, I can tell you that the Empress is far from satisfied.' Carey felt his heart drop. 'But she has still come to the same conclusion,' Bassano continued. She sees no useful purpose in exchanging further correspondence with you, and agrees that the issue should now remain mute. A reciprocal arrangement, I trust?'

Carey chewed his lip. What should he do?

'Do I have any choice, Your Grace? I am guilty of nothing, sir. Nothing. I seek only to clear my own good name. And, by Heaven, no Carey has ever resorted to begging for mercy or forgiveness.'

'Forgiveness, Captain?' said Bassano. 'For what? And from whom? Her Imperial Highness can hardly be expected to forgive the death of her son, regardless of its circumstances. But if you mean to ask whether she blames you, I can tell you that she does not.' Relief flooded through Carey. *She does not?* he thought. *And I may use that, so long as I do not attribute the thing? Lord be praised, I think this may be settled at last.* He smiled, and Bassano raised an eyebrow. 'She does not blame you, Captain,' he said. 'She absolves you. But she pities you, for she now knows that you are the sort of fellow who will cripple himself following a false crusade. Do you know Corinthians, sir? *"There hath no temptation taken you but such as is common to man: but God is faithful, who will not suffer you to be tempted above that ye are able; but will with the temptation also make a way to escape, that ye may be able to bear it."* You must learn to be honest with yourself, my young friend – as honest as that warrior we just met.'

Carey took his leave, unable to continue the conversation, unsure whether they had reached a resolution. He was unsure too about the Zulu. Could it in truth be the same man? The one who had raised Louis's sword above his head in such triumph? He should confront the fellow, surely? Or perhaps confront was the wrong word. Commune with him, perhaps. For did they not share that very twist of fate that Bassano had mentioned? It was a dizzying thought. And he was disorientated still further by the crowds pouring towards him through the theatre foyer, the audience arriving for this evening's show – a show that Carey could no longer bring himself to watch. He would come back another time, perhaps. Speak to this Zulu as well. Find out if he was genuinely the same one.

'My dear!' Annie called to him. She had been sheltering from the rain that had begun to fall outside. 'Did you have your audience, then?'

'I did indeed,' he said.

'And it went well?'

'Yes, well enough,' he lied. 'I think we may finally be able to put all that behind us now. But would you mind terribly if we returned to Kingston? It's been a taxing day. And I have some further news. For I've heard from the Colonel. The note arrived just after you left. He's approved my application that you might accompany the regiment to Malta and then, all being well, to India. Is that not remarkable? Imagine, Annie, a cool hill-station for yourself and the children while your poor husband suffers the heat and privations of Karachi. A new beginning for us, dear heart.'

But even as he spoke the words, a shadow clouded his mind. Surely *this* time the Almighty would not pull the rug from beneath him!

*

McTeague had made a terrible rod for his own shoulders. He could hear the crowd filling the auditorium but here, back-stage, the Zulus remained as intransigent as ever.

'Is it true, or not,' Amahle's brother was asking, 'that another of these showmen has offered us a better contract?'

McTeague turned to his wife. 'My dear one,' he said, 'you must assist me. I have already explained this several times. The offer has not yet been confirmed. It is unhelpful to press the thing at this point.'

'Then perhaps your words were better unspoken,' said Shaba. 'But in truth they make little difference. We will not perform for the American tonight unless he writes another of his papers, this time promising more gold. And also to give back the white men's clothes. He will not treat us either like slaves or children.'

'Brother,' said Amahle, 'I think my husband is correct. Better to perform this night and then negotiate.'

'Have we not learned,' Shaba said bitterly, 'that there is no way to trust them? We will see the gold and the clothes first, perform later.'

The stage-hands were busy with their preparations, placing scenery and equipment, though with little enthusiasm, their attention focused more on the Zulus.

'Get on with your work, damn you!' Farini hissed at them, making an enraged entrance, Behrens at his back, up the wing stairs.

'Ah, Bill!' said McTeague. 'I was just explaining that if the chaps perform tonight, we can perhaps discuss their grievances in the morning.'

'They have a contract, Major. They *will* perform. There'll be no grievances. And what's that fellow saying?' Farini pointed at Shaba. He had still not heeded McTeague's many warnings that such a gesture was impolite in the extreme.

'He's suggesting that they should use the legal system to settle the matter. Let one of the Fat Queen's judges decide. Those were his actual words.'

'Decide what?' said Farini. 'This nonsense about better offers again?'

'The question of their pay,' said McTeague. 'They seem to think they're being short-changed.'

'The wages are fair, Major,' Behrens stepped forward. 'And these others who now seem so desperate to have their own Zulu shows. Who are they? Sanger's? The Gaiety? The Oxford maybe? Well, none of them troubled to go out to the Cape themselves, did they? And I explained those contracts fair and square before we ever left Zululand. Then set them in writing on the ship. Remind them of that, Major.'

McTeague did so, though he chose his own placatory words carefully.

'And what is your view, husband?' said Amahle. 'After all, it was you who brought us word of these new offers.'

'Yes,' he replied. 'That is true. And right is clearly on our side here. But I fear that the English courts would not find in our favour.'

The Zulus hummed like a hive of angry hornets.

'Then where is the Fat Queen's justice?' said Shaba.

'What are they saying?' said Farini. 'Dammit, Major, we're paying you good money here to sort out this kind of thing. I had it on the best authority that you were the man for this job.'

'It seems to me that some form of compromise may be necessary, sir,' McTeague replied. 'Just so we can get the show on the road. And it does no harm to excite these fellows a little. Just imagine how fearsome they'll seem, taking the stage in this mood.'

'Compromise, Major? Here's my compromise. If anybody wants to go back to the Cape, I'll pay their passage gladly. If anybody else wants to stay in London but leave the show, that's fine by me too. Not without them signing a new contract though, to the effect that they won't work in any other theatre. For those that stay, there'll be no more pay than I've already offered. But if the show's a success, and we take it on to America, why sir, that's the Land of Plenty and I'll guarantee them a new deal before we go, an extra ten percent.'

McTeague explained to the Zulus.

'And the clothes?' said Shaba.

'He wants to know about the outdoor clothes, Bill,' said McTeague.

Farini nodded, though his mouth was twisted by reluctance and suppressed anger.

'Then we will perform,' said Shaba. 'For the choices are poor. The journey home would be dangerous for any travelling alone. And they say that those left on these streets of iLondon are led only to the house of work that we saw yesterday, where they are left to die, even your women and children. We do not like the promises of more gold tomorrow, KaMtigwe. But my sister says we should trust these men. For now, at least.'

Relief followed McTeague as he took his place in the box reserved for the management team, though he had the thing to himself when the show began, Farini needing to make the necessary appearances on stage, and Behrens preferring to be down there too, in the thick of the action. So he surveyed this impressive hall. The roof of glass and iron. The palm trees and fountains. The thirteen enormous tanks that gave the Aquarium its name, even though they had never actually been filled with the exotic sea creatures for which they were intended. Seating for seven hundred, every seat filled tonight. Every single seat. And Farini played each of them for all it was worth. He employed a questionable Spanish accent – he was now fully in the part of Guillermo Antonio Farini – into which he had even lapsed in the presence of the Empress Eugénie. *Well, why not?* thought McTeague. *The dear lady is Spanish by birth, after all.*

At the climax of the show, Farini promised, he would walk the tightrope above their very heads, from balcony to balcony, carrying a fully-grown-man on each shoulder. But first there was the female human cannonball, the beautiful Zazel. And La Niña Farini – acrobatic miracles performed by Guillermo Farini's own daughter. *How shocked they would be,* mused McTeague, *to discover that this lace-frilled nymph with the shapely legs is really a lad?* He had never quite fathomed the nature of the strange relationship, for the boy was certainly no natural kin to Farini, and Behrens refused to be drawn on the subject. But the audience sat restlessly through it all. For this was not specifically what they had come to see.

McTeague, too, was impatient for the Zulus' performance. He prayed to the Almighty that nothing else might go wrong, that Amahle's brother was behaving himself down there. *Will he ever get over his hatred for me?* he wondered. He liked the fellow, was pleased that he could claim surrogate credit, through Maria Mestiza, for improving Shaba's eyesight. And then the lights went down, the hall falling to silence that spun on until a red sun finally rose in the distance to silhouette a thorn bush, a trio of giraffes that moved ponderously from right to left against the background noise of crickets, a dim drumbeat and, finally, the familiar sound – to McTeague's ears at least – of spear shafts on shield hide, far away, but drawing closer, a locomotive rattling across points, the first strains of native voices in harmonious singing, becoming louder until, finally, the sounds trailed away. There was silence again. Then, suddenly, the Zulus were among them, a group on each flank of the hall.

'*Ji! Ji! Ji!*' they cried, and stamped forward until they were almost among the terrified spectators.

They stopped.

'*USuthu!*' they yelled, all together, raising their stabbing spears in salute towards the now invisible glass ceiling, then towards the stage. And here came Amahle, in a swirl of diaphanous red, of multi-coloured beads, black hide kilt and scarlet top-knot, leaping and spinning while the warriors danced forward along the side aisles to join her on the stage. McTeague was filled with pride. *Well,* he thought, *she has recovered at last from the voyage.* She even seemed to be gaining some weight once more. And no bad thing!

The show was going well, the stage-hands now bringing archery targets from the wings. They had debated using uniformed mannequins but finally decided that this might exceed the boundaries of good taste. But the spear-throwing was impressive enough as it stood, each of the warriors demonstrating his deadly skill until the performance reached its climax. The part McTeague dreaded. For two of the Zulus dragged Amahle forward. The singing stopped and there was a pretence at tying her to the target, her arms spread apart.

There were gasps from the audience as Shaba crossed to the very farthest edge of the stage, across from McTeague's vantage point.

'*Ji!*' shouted the warriors as Shaba's first throwing spear rose, vibrated and hummed, buried itself in the straw.

McTeague could not see from here exactly the margin by which the blade had missed his wife, but he knew from the rehearsals that it would only be a matter of inches. *Probably just as well,* he thought, *that the Empress did not stay to watch after all.* He had wondered whether there might be some profit for him in divulging to her that the warrior she seemed determined to eventually seek in Zululand was, in fact, already here. But he had decided in the end to keep Shaba's secret safe – for the time being, at least.

More gasps, a few screams, from the front stalls.

'*USuthu!*' the warriors yelled.

Shaba's second spear hammered into the narrow gap between Amahle's knees, and McTeague saw her glance over her shoulder, searching for him. He knew she could not see him, but there was fear in her eyes that seemed to exceed that which the drama required. Amahle's brother was backing across the boards, readying the third spear, while the rest of the troupe chanted encouragement. *My memory is failing,* thought McTeague. *Or perhaps it's the heat in here. The curse of old age!* For he could not recall this element from the rehearsals. It was familiar enough, however. A piece of praise poetry to old Cetshwayo.

'*UCetshwayo kaMpande!*' cried Shaba.

'*UMahlangeni Khumalo!*' the others chanted back.

And then this? Their hymn to the *iNkatha*, surely.

'*iNkatha yeSizwe yaKwaZulu!*' they sang in harmony.

McTeague saw Shaba take three quick steps, almost running, towards the orchestra pit, ignoring Amahle entirely. The warrior halted, pointed the narrow blade towards McTeague's box.

Bless the boy! he thought. *He's saluting me.*

'*USuthu!*' Shaba yelled, and drew back his throwing arm.

McTeague half rose from his seat.

Surely not…

There was that damn'd tourniquet around his chest again. He sat down once more, heavily, the vibrant colours of Amahle's costume swimming to a faded grey beyond which his vision failed to focus. But there seemed to be foliage all about him, dripping wet and steaming. Where was he? Honduras, perhaps. Yes, there was no question. For Maria Mestiza was there too. '*Why not Amahle?*' he pleaded to the Almighty. A tear cooled his burning cheek. He did not want to be here without Amahle. It was too empty. He was too alone. Too afraid. But beggars, he knew, could not be choosers. And there, at least, was Maria. On the crest of the steep slope above him. He tried to climb towards her, for there was a patch of clear sky just above her head. But the jungle was too dense. It raged inside his head, like pounding surf. He wanted to give up, surrender to that leafy embrace. "*It is God that girdeth me with strength, and maketh my way perfect.*" He felt the Holy Spirit fill him, and he began to claw his way upwards, kicking against that damp earth. *I shall break free*, he thought.

A voice behind him provided the welcome excuse to rest, for the pain beneath his armpits was almost intolerable now. Yet he knew he could not rest for long. There was something he had to do. *Climb out! Climb out!* McTeague looked back, saw the man far down there, at the bottom of this interminable slope. It took a moment to recognise the cove but, when he did, it was with some relief. *Yes, Honduras. Of course. And here is Commissioner Rhys come to find me.*

As quickly as he had felt the Holy Spirit fill him, so it emptied him again. Some warm gush of his soul down the back of his legs. The surf pounded still louder, and McTeague fell backwards, knowing that this time there would be no coming back. He kept on falling, down into the jungle dark, until the patch of sky above Maria's head grew smaller, smaller yet, then closed. And closed forever.

*

It was worth it, thought Shaba, to see the fear on the white man's face. KaMtigwe had stayed there, fixed, motionless, throughout the final moments of the performance. He could have thrown, of course, skewered the fat fellow. But it was enough to frighten him a little. And he needed time to think, in any case. For the truth was that Amahle's news had shaken him somewhat. There would be a child to consider now, and regardless of his views about KaMtigwe,

339

his commitment to the Great King, to ensure that the white man paid for his betrayal of the *iNkatha* with his life – the price of Amahle's acquittal from blame, of course – it was another matter to leave her babe fatherless. *Even a worthless white father*, he reasoned, *must be better than no father at all.*

So he had sprung backwards, into the leopard leap, cast the spear in mid-turn, so that it quivered into the target just beside Amahle's ear. And the crowd had erupted, shouting and screaming, slapping their hands together until they must surely have bled. *Yes*, he thought, *I enjoyed that. It was a good moment.* The Americans led them from the stage, talking loudly but unintelligibly. They needed KaMtigwe to translate but he had not come down yet, so the man who called himself Nat, the large American, took them out through a side door. Yet even here there were people swarming around them, men with small blocks of paper, the writing pencils too, who shouted all at the same time, shouted at the man, Nat.

'Are you happy, brother?' said Amahle.

'I see you, sister,' he replied. 'And yes, I am happy. I think the Americans can easily be persuaded to pay us more gold after this. We will have great wealth to take back with us.'

'We will not go to America?' she asked.

'It would be difficult, I think,' he replied, 'for you and the baby. And I would wish to be back in our land when the mother of the iFulentshi Prince comes there.'

'But just imagine the gold we could carry if we went,' she said. 'And my husband, I think, will make sure that the baby is protected. After all, this will be his only son.'

He laughed. 'And how do you know this?'

'Oh, I know it!' she answered. 'But where is that husband of mine? And what about the honour you sought, brother? What of that?'

The big American spread his arms, shielding them so they could pass more easily through the strange crowd and Shaba saw the poster once more, his own image printed upon the paper. The picture showed him in the full regalia of a senior *induna*, the eye-patch making him unmistakeable, with warriors at his back and Amahle at his side in the attire of a royal bride. Behind them, cattle roamed. Fine cattle. Many cattle. He remembered what the white man's signs meant upon the poster. Prince Incomo. His beautiful wife, Princess AmaZulu.

I sometimes wonder, he thought, *whether the Sky Lord and Izimu the Trickster may not be one and the same thing.*

The End

Cosi, Cosi, Yaphela

Historical Notes

As I explained in my Preface, I believe it is only fair to explain the main areas in which I have strayed away from the archives. In this case, they are essentially...

First, Tshabanga (Shaba) – or Xabanga/Zabanga, depending on the source – was, in fact, the Zulu who struck the fatal blow that killed French Prince Imperial Louis Napoleon (Bonaparte's great-nephew) on 1st June 1879. Many sources cite that he was killed at Ulundi on 4th July but others – Colonel William James Clarke and Sir Evelyn Wood – seem to indicate that he was still alive in the following year and may have been among the Zulus invited to Robson's Drift to meet the Prince Imperial's grieving mother, the Empress Eugénie, face to face. This was obviously during her visit to Zululand in 1880, of course, rather than in London, as I have described. I therefore determined to have him survive Ulundi although, one way or the other, he then slips from the pages of history in any case, so the rest of Shaba's story is largely supposition. Shaba did not, so far as I know, ever join The Great Farini's Zulu Show, but the troupe hired by Nat Behrens, on behalf of Farini (William Leonard Hunt), performed at the Westminster Aquarium three times each day for over two years until the spring of 1881, when the show travelled to America – and they did, indeed, go on strike towards the end of 1879 for better pay, taking part in an unsuccessful court action against Hunt. Some time later, one of the Zulus died alone in a London workhouse.

Second, McTeague is purely fictional, although he bears some resemblance to the real (and much larger than life) figure of hunter-trader John Robert Dunn, who makes an appearance in the novel. It goes without saying therefore that, since McTeague is fictional, any episodes or conversations in which he participates must also be inventions. Well, almost!

Third, Jahleel Brenton Carey, on the other hand, was very real. He had the misfortune to be leading the patrol of which Louis was a member on the day of his death. As a result, Carey's tale has been told by historians (and the contemporary press) in a variety of ways, and I have tried to portray his background, as well as the events that befell him, as precisely as possible, although he never met Thomas Alderton (who actually died on 5th April 1879) nor Nurse Janet Wells (who did not arrive in Zululand until July). The story of his court martial following the death of the Prince Imperial is well-known, but readers may be less familiar with the court of inquiry that he faced in 1867, while serving with the 3rd West India Regiment (and reported that year in the *Jamaica Gleaner* on 5 March and the *Sydney Morning Herald* on 4th June) following his alleged desertion of a government official in Honduras and the consequential death of that agent at the hands of rebellious *campesino* Indians. This occurred during an expedition led by a certain Major McKay who thus became the inspiration for my McTeague character. I liked Carey very much though he was, from the self-destructive way in which he sought to "clear his name", for example, a conflicted character and I hope that his family, who still keep his memory alive, will forgive my interpretation of him.

There is no mention of the Honduras affair in the accounts of Carey's court martial, twelve years later, but it seemed reasonable to me that it must have played upon Carey's mind. In addition, I noted that Colonel William Bellairs, Lord Chelmsford's Deputy Adjutant-General and the officer responsible for most of the administration relating to Carey's case, had himself served in the 3rd West India Regiment, although ten years earlier. Would he have known about the Honduras affair? Might Carey at least have been fearful that he did? And it only required a modest leap of imagination to pose the question, 'What if the fates of Carey, his former senior officer in Honduras, and the Zulu Tshabanga should all have been thrown together by the death of Louis Napoleon?' And thus the concept for this novel was born.

Like many historical novelists, I have no qualms about invention where no verifiable archive exists – or even where the 'archive' may simply be a bureaucratic or biased record – but there were also occasions when I made a conscious decision to twist or composite some of the recorded facts. So, for example, I have obviously "dramatised" the Court Martial. We can't know what was actually *said* there, since we only have the official records on which to base our knowledge, rather than any independent and verbatim account. Also, the large-scale skirmish on the slopes of the eZungeni Hill in which Captain Frith of the 17th Lancers was killed took place on the 4th-5th June, rather than 9th June, as I place it in the book. Similarly, there were continuous attempts by Cetshwayo to negotiate a settlement throughout the conflict and, to help with the flow of the story, I changed some of the dates when emissaries were sent to Chelmsford, added fictional characters to the various delegations or simply composited some of them. And, naturally, there are elements of the final chapter that are entirely fictitious.

Similarly, nobody actually witnessed the lonely death of the French Prince Imperial at the Ityotyosi River on 1st June 1879 – except the Zulus who overcame him, of course. The position was not visible to Carey and the others even if they had stopped to look. So my description of the scene is merely a novelist's inventive device. We will never truly know why the patrol ventured so far to that particular spot. But I have relied heavily on the comments of Paul Deléage, the *Figaro* correspondent, who had been sharing Carey's tent and reminds us that Carey had previously scouted the ground in question as a possible route for the army, that Chelmsford had "laughed" at his choice, believing it to be impractical, and that this was preying on Carey's mind – thus making it even more likely that, in an effort to prove the route suitable, it was he who primarily chose to take a closer look at the terrain and therefore to visit the fateful kraal.

There is also the vexed question of the Prince Imperial's sword. Many websites and sources claim that this was the weapon Bonaparte had carried at the Battle of Austerlitz, though this is plainly nonsense. On the other hand, the French expert on the subject, M. Jean-Claude Lachnitt wrote, in a paper for the Napoleon Foundation in 1979, that this was the sword carried by the Emperor during the Elchingen campaign (1805), then gifted to Marshal Ney whose grandson, the Duc d'Elchingen, in turn presented the sabre to Louis when the Prince was exiled to England. This chimes with the assertion by Paul Deléage that this was a "historic" sword and I have chosen to use this version in the story.

Inevitably, the tale itself leaves some of the plot issues unresolved simply because the threads of the Anglo-Zulu War continued to unravel beyond 1879 – and, to some extent, still do so. But there are a few of those threads that we can happily divulge.

Cornelius Vijn is a historical figure, known generally as 'Cetshwayo's Dutchman.' Vijn was only 23 years old in 1879. He spent four years in Zululand and the *Private Journal* of his experiences was translated and edited in 1880 by Bishop John William Colenso.

Major Robert Hackett (90th Foot) appears "passively" in the story as the officer shot by Tshabanga at Khambula and again during Carey's return to Durban while being sent back to Britain following the Court Martial. Hackett was factually shot through the head from a range of two hundred yards by a Zulu marksman at the Battle of Khambula. The bullet passed clean through one temple and out of the other. It was incredible to everybody who witnessed the wound that he survived – not only the wound itself but also the lengthy journey home. He was retired in 1880 and then became an Aide-de-Camp to Queen Victoria. He died in 1893 at the age of 54.

Cetshwayo's fate was linked to that of the Zulu Kingdom. After his capture, the British sent him into exile, to Cape Town and Robben Island. The Dutch and IsiZulu names for this place coincided. They each knew it as the Island of Seals. But to the English it was Robben Island and had been a place of incarceration for many years already – both as a leper colony and as a prison. Cetshwayo was kept there for almost four years (Nelson Mandela would later spend 18 of his 27 years' imprisonment on Robben Island). But within three years friction between the various sub-kingdoms into which Britain had divided the nation, the factions that ruled them, had erupted into a vicious civil war. Cetshwayo was released and travelled to London for an audience with Queen Victoria and, in 1883, in a belated attempt to regain stability, the British restored him to the throne. This was contested by the once-loyal Zibhebhu who attacked Cetshwayo's new kraal at Ulundi. The victor of Isandlwana, Ntshingwayo kaMahole Khoza, died fighting at the King's side. Cetshwayo himself was wounded, fled and died in February 1884. The cause of death is still disputed. It is presumed that he died of a heart attack but some argue that he was poisoned. They say, however, that John Dunn wept bitterly on hearing the news of his death.

Cetshwayo's 15-year old son, Dinizulu, was later declared his successor with the help of the Boers in return for a promise of land. This did not please the British who, as we have seen, had ambitions to bring together all the states of southern Africa into a single dominion. Not only the Zulus stood in the way of this ambition but also the Boers. The British had forcibly annexed the independent Boer Republic of the Transvaal in 1877 and, when the Boers rebelled against this in 1880, the first Anglo-Boer War – the Boer War of Independence – broke out and ended a year later with a crushing British defeat at Majuba Hill and the Transvaal regaining its independence. The Boers' acquisition of so much new territory from the Zulus was seen by the British as a serious threat, and they annexed the whole of Zululand in 1887. British ambitions intensified with the discovery of gold and a second Anglo-Boer War took place in 1899-1902, resulting in a British "victory" (owing a great deal to the use of internment camps in which 27,000 Boer women and children died of malnutrition and disease) and the Boers forced to acknowledge British sovereignty. But British attempts to anglicise the region were failing, and the Boer Afrikaners gaining ever more power. At the same time, indigenous races and immigrant Asian labour were becoming increasingly marginalised, although still badly divided into separate factions. In 1906, 4,000 Zulus were killed in the Bambatha Uprising after rebelling against repressive taxes. As a result, the British imprisoned Dinizulu on the island of St Helena – where Napoleon, of course, had died.

In 1909, the Union of South Africa was established, technically still British territory but with home rule for the Afrikaners. Within four years, legislation was being introduced, which would lay the foundations for the eventual system that we now know as apartheid, that endured until the 1990s, bringing almost a century of segregation and humiliation to the Zulu people and other Black South Africans – themselves fatally weakened through the divisions imposed by the British in 1879. The line of Zulu kings continued, although subsequent descendants of Cetshwayo were denied any real power by the South African government. In 1977 a Legislative Assembly of KwaZulu was constituted, yet the actual status of the region continued to be disputed even after the ANC victory and election of Nelson Mandela in 1994. But at that point, KwaZulu was merged with the former Natal and the current region, KwaZulu-Natal, established. It remains a very distinct province within the modern South Africa and with its own legislature. At the time of writing, there is also a reigning Zulu king – King Goodwill Zwelithini kaBhekuzulu – though without any direct political power, yet still exerting considerable influence.

John Robert Dunn was handsomely rewarded by the British, being given the largest piece of Zululand as one of the thirteen sub-kingdoms and the region closest to Durban. King John Dunn – King Jantoni – ruled there until 1883 when, following Cetshwayo's restoration, his lands were given the status of a Reserve Territory and Dunn himself was given the title of regional chief. He died in August 1895 at Emoyeni and, by that time, had 48 wives and 117 children. Twenty-three of his wives and seventy-nine of his children survived him. It was reported in 2004 that his descendants, the extended Dunn family, then numbered 6,000, scattered across every continent. They had just won a court case giving them permanent rights to some of the land granted to Dunn in 1879. One of his great-grandsons, Daniel Dunn, runs an independent tour company in South Africa, and is Chairman of the Dunn Descendants' Association.

Klaas appears in the archive history of the Anglo-Zulu War as a Zulu Christian convert, also known as Barnabas, and used by Cetshwayo as one of his messengers to Lord Chelmsford, the British Commander, during his various attempts to negotiate a peace. He appears again as possibly one of the guards sent by Cetshwayo to oversee the release of the French captive, Ernest Grandier. He is probably also the same man who, according to the *Natal Mercury* and other sources, was employed by the British, after the Battle of Ulundi, to help recover the Prince Imperial's uniform. The character called Klaas in my own story is therefore clearly not intended to be the same person, but he certainly inspired his creation.

Detective Constable Biddlecombe died in 1882 as the result of a broken leg, sustained while chasing a suspect.

Miss Octavia Scotchburn remains something of an enigma. We know from Queen Victoria's private secretary that a copy of Carey's letter, written to his wife, Annie, immediately after the Prince Imperial's death, had been sent to the Empress Eugénie by Miss Octavia Scotchburn who is described as a former friend of the Careys. The census details show only one such person, born in Driffield, Yorkshire, with dates of birth that vary between 1828 and 1838, but latterly living in Totnes, where she was a teacher of languages. She had previously lived in London as a Governess. So how had she acquired a "copy" of Carey's letter? Was it indeed a copy or the original? Was she a former friend of Annie and Jahleel or, in fact, of his parents? And what would have driven her to send the letter to the Empress Eugénie? You must forgive my assumptions in answering these questions, and the only thing I can say for certain is that she died in Totnes in 1885.

Lieutenant-Colonel Attilio Sceberras retired from the 98th in 1880, at the age of 57, and died four years later. He is buried in St. Paul's Anglican Cathedral, Valletta, Malta.

The Empress Eugénie went to Zululand in 1880 to visit the site of her son's death. She met the warrior who had killed Louis, though she never met Carey, of course. She never really took advantage either of the letter that Carey wrote to Annie after the disastrous 1st June patrol, despite its contradictions. She had, indeed, been sent "a copy" through Miss Octavia Scotchburn but, after an unsatisfactory exchange of correspondence between her chamberlain and Carey himself, she simply let the matter drop. She died in Madrid in 1920, having eventually returned to Spain, the country of her birth. The Prince Imperial's distinctive watch, incidentally, was apparently smashed between two rocks after his death, since the Zulus who found it believed it might contain snuff. Parts of it were then recovered in various places over the next ten years or so and they seem to have ended up in Durban's Local History Museum. The Bonapartist line of succession from Napoleon himself ended with the death of Louis – the Prince Imperial, Napoléon Eugène Louis Jean Joseph Bonaparte. Subsequent claimants to the throne of France have been descendants of Napoleon's brother, Jérôme. The current claimant is Jean-Christophe Albéric Napoléon. He lives in New York City and bears an uncanny resemblance to Louis. And Louis himself is buried in the French Imperial Crypt at Saint Michael's Abbey, Farnborough, with his father and mother (whose body was brought back to England after her death in Madrid) while there is a very fine memorial to him at his original resting place, Saint Mary's Church in Chislehurst, with an impressive monument on the town's Common.

Captain Jahleel Brenton Carey rejoined his regiment and shipped out with his family in 1880 to India, where he died three years later, in Karachi, apparently of peritonitis. The cause of the peritonitis, we are told, was a kick in the groin by a horse but, elsewhere, the circumstances of his death are described as "mysterious." By that time, the 98th had apparently been ravaged by illness and disease. He was 35. His wife, Annie Isabella Brenton Carey, returned to England only in 1901, following the death in Karachi that year of their daughter, Edith Isabella. Annie stayed with relatives in London (1901 Census) and then moved to Kingston, Surrey, where she died in 1922 at the age of 69. Carey's son, Pelham, died in New York in 1913, also aged 35. Edith had remained with her mother in Karachi, where she worked for the Church Missionary Service. The Brenton Carey Hostel for Girls (named after her) continues to provide accommodation and schooling for impoverished young women in Karachi. It was in the news recently because the Bishop of Karachi, the Right Reverend Sadiq Daniel, was served with an arrest warrant, charged with alleged physical assault against the Hostel's female administrator.

December 2013
Wrexham, North Wales

Acknowledgements

I owe all the background, of course, to a plethora of resources which predominantly include:

Historynet.com for their account of Khambula; the *Zulu War 1879* Discussion and Reference Group; the Anglo-Zulu War Historical Society; archive copies of the *Jamaica Gleaner*, 5th March 1867, and re-printed in the *Sydney Morning Herald*, 4th June 1867, that Major McKay along with Lieutenants Carey and Ferguson had been summoned to face a Court of Inquiry in Kingston, Jamaica; the website CareyRoots – the *History of the Carey Family of Guernsey*; archive copies of the *Cape and Natal News*; the National Archives, Kew; University of California Digital Library (CDL) for the copy of *Cetshwayo's Dutchman*, the private journal of Cornelius Vijn; the many websites – like the *CanTeach: African Folk Tales* site – dedicated to providing translation of Zulu folklore; *Nursery Tales, Traditions, and Histories of the Zulus: In Their Own Words*, by Henry Callaway and published in 1868; the website of the South African Military History Society; Marié-Helen Coetzee's 2002 paper on Zulu Stick Fighting; *Zulu Thought-Patterns and Symbolism* by Axel Ivar Berglund; *Africans on stage – studies in ethnological show business* edited by Bernth Lindfors, and specifically the chapter, "Africa meets the Great Farini" by Stuart Peacock; Ian Knight's paper *In Every Way His Own King: The Life of Chief John Dunn*; Prof. G. R. Rubin's paper *The Non-Confirmation of Captain Carey's Court Martial, 1879* (University of Kent, Canterbury); the fine collection of extracts compiled by Adrian Greaves for the Anglo-Zulu War Historical Society from *The Graphic*, an illustrated weekly newspaper, January-December 1879; the paper, *La Mort du Prince Impérial*, by M. Jean-Claude Lechnitt for the Napoleon Foundation, Paris, in November 1979; and David Rattray's stunning series of five Audio-CDs, *The Day of the Dead Moon*.

The books upon which I have principally relied are:

Ian Knight's *Companion to the Anglo-Zulu War* and *With His face to the Foe*; Frank Emery's *The Red Soldier*; Saul David's *Zulu: the Heroism and Tragedy of the Zulu War 1879*; Adrian Greaves's *Forgotten Battles of the Zulu War* and *The Tribe that Washed its Spears*; John Laband's *Historical Dictionary of the Zulu Wars*; William L. Slout's *Olympians of the Sawdust Circle*; and Paul Deléage's *End of Dynasty*, translated from French by Fleur Webb.

My eternal thanks to all the various authors, archivists and website writers mentioned above.

In addition, I owe a great deal, as usual, to my wife, Ann, who patiently struggled with each of the first draft chapters. And to my regular editor, the lovely Jo Field. In this case, Jo's considerable efforts were supplemented by the specialist expertise of Dr Adrian Greaves (President, Anglo-Zulu War Historical Society).

I want to thank Responsible Travel and specifically Candice Buchan from Rainbow Tours for their help in arranging our trip to KwaZulu-Natal in November 2013, as well as the many friends we made and met during that journey. These included: Professor Sarah Andrews (University of Chester) and her family; Elisabeth Durham (from the excellent *Chez Nous* hotel in Dundee, KwaZulu-Natal); Alistair Lamont, Mphiwa Ntanzi and the entire loveable team at the Fugitives' Drift Lodge; and, in Durban, Karen Lotter (Alliance of Independent Authors), Mabusi Kgwete and Mbusi Zuma, as well as Caryl and Errol Legassick at Ballito's Lalaria Lodge. I owe a huge debt to Mabusi in particular who so patiently checked all the IsiZulu spellings and pronunciations. This was one of the most memorable journeys of our life, despite the difficult family situation that we left back in the UK so, even more than usual, I reserve the most special thanks to our wonderful family itself for encouraging us to continue with the trip despite those difficulties.

The beautiful cover was, as usual, designed by Cathy Helms (Avalon Graphics, www.avalongraphics.org) and the crew at SilverWood Books performed their normal magic in bringing the book to publication.

David Ebsworth maintains a website (www.davidebsworth.com) and welcomes direct contact from his readers, for whom he writes a monthly e-newsletter. To receive the newsletter, or for further information, he can be contacted by e-mail at davemccall@talktalk.net

Lightning Source UK Ltd.
Milton Keynes UK
UKOW03f0609290414

230768UK00002B/27/P